A WIND
IN THE WEST

*

by

ELIZABETH
COXHEAD

FABER AND FABER LIMITED
24 Russell Square
London

First published in mcmxlix
by Faber and Faber Limited
24 Russell Square London W.C.1
Printed in Great Britain by
Latimer Trend & Co Ltd Plymouth

Chapter One

[I]

He pulled himself up the last few feet on to the ridge, and averting his eyes from the dazzle of light and colour on the other side, that it might break on him the more completely from the summit, swung himself for ten minutes more over the great grey teeth that were all now standing between him and thin air. Then there was a little, derelict cairn, and he had arrived.

Below him lay Scotland, its islands, its mainland, spread out for ever. No flat land showed. It was all hills, conical hills made tiny by the immense distance, clothed in a perfect golden clarity against the pale blue winter sky. On the side where the sun struck them they were sepia, and on the shadowed side lilac, and the highest were tipped with the silver glint of snow. Range beyond range floated off in that still air that seemed hazy, so benign, so gentle was the light. Yet there could be no haze, else how should he see so far? And turning lazily on his side, he perceived the complete outline of the Long Island, beyond it sea, and at the farther edge of the sea three purple dots that might be clouds, except that clouds, even in the serenity of such a day, would ultimately move, and these were constant. They were, they must be, St. Kilda.

No sign of life broke this pale, sunny solitude. No steamer ruffled the shining waters. The minute white houses of Kyle Arkaig across the Sound were so clear that his keen eyes could pick out their doors and windows, yet they were no more than toys, in no way humanizing the lonely, derelict land. And gradually his own sense of personality drifted away. He seemed to become one with the little sepia hills and the immense golden sky. It was an ecstasy, like creation, like death.

Eventually, he was hungry. The warmth of climbing left him, and though the air still did not move, yet there was a chill in it, for this was winter. He felt in his pockets, and of course there was nothing there, for there was no one to remember to get him food except himself, and he had not remembered. He lay and grinned at his own idiocy, his damned inefficiency and unawareness, and almost enjoyed the sharp sensation of hunger which brought him back to life again, and to the realities.

His eye travelled down the foreshortened grey spine of the ridge to the bay, the jetty, the nine little boxes of the crofts. Three thousand feet below and two miles away, they were dwarfed to the insignificance of a child's model map. And they too were lifeless.

An island in search of a population—that was Sunay on this morning in January. An island waiting.

He tried to imagine it. Roofs on the gaunt shells of the cottages, smoke coming out of the chimneys. Women calling, their eyes shaded against the sun. Children running up from the shore, men with cattle and excited, silent dogs. A whole world of animals and people, washing on lines, cornfields, the homely cackle of poultry defeating the cold lone cry of the gulls.

Yes, that was obvious, easy; but what sort of people would they be? It was not within his power to create people. Lying up here, so aloof, so God-damned objective, he could deceive himself. But when he got down again he would, he knew, be utterly dependent for these people upon Fate. The place would not live till they came, yet when they came it would live violently, regardless of his will, and there might be an all-fired mess. Alternatively, there might be harmony.

If so, it must come of itself. There was nothing, nothing he could do to bring it about—though when he got down there he would start planning, and striving, and generally behaving as though he had the say. But he knew in his heart that he had no say. He was utterly unqualified. He had never handled human material, and he had no aptitude. He could put a roof on a cottage, but he could not mould another soul. Yet if these creatures, these unknown, unpredictable creatures were to fail him, there would be nothing left in life.

For a long moment he knew the agony of complete and prophetic despair. And then, as he watched, there was life on Sunay, and not a life of his imagination. A thin blue pencil of smoke went up from the last croft in the crescent. Rory Mor had come in, and was making the driftwood fire.

Confidence came flooding back as suddenly and illogically as it had gone. Smiling to himself, almost drowsy with contentment, he swung off down the ridge, towards his supper and the welcome of a friend. All would yet be well.

[II]

After an unproductive afternoon spent dogging a minor member of the Royal Family round a cage-bird show, Tony Manning of the *Courier* was not pleased to find a cutting on his desk, with a note from the News Editor: "Pse see me."

The cutting was an advertisement, taken from one of the farming papers. It read:

"Hebridean island, 6,000 acres. Owner wishes form co-operative farming community. Simple housing available. Farming or market-gardening experience desirable, some capital an advantage. Apply Box ——"

"Oh—er, yes," said the News Editor, who, like all his kind, never seemed to have his mind wholly on one subject.

9

"Might be a story in it—Fraser tipped me. The chap is Alexander Sarratt."

"Sarratt? Strikes some chord, but blowed if I can remember."

"Atomic research. Youngest member of our team, wasn't he, or near it. I'm pretty sure it was an *Express* story."

"Lord, yes, so it was. I say, you don't think——?"

"I don't think anything, but it might be worth looking into. Chap himself isn't around, Fraser says, but a man called Fletcher, 13a Endsleigh Street, has been doing the interviews."

"Probably just another of these escapist stunts," said Tony, his crossness returning.

"I'll put Fraser on to it if you don't feel it's your cup of tea?"

"Oh, I'll go." He shouldered on his raincoat and splashed off towards Bloomsbury. Fraser was the Agricultural Correspondent of the *Courier*, and it was a matter of principle among the reporters to keep these specialists out.

The door of 13a Endsleigh Street was opened to him by a creamily handsome young woman; fine eyes, luxuriant black hair with an alluring white streak, Hedy Lamarr type, would photograph, summed up Tony at a glance, while he inquired politely if he might have a word with Mr. Fletcher.

"*Doctor* Fletcher", said the young woman markedly, "is too busy to see anyone, and if it's about the advertisement, I'm afraid our party is now complete."

"But I'm press, *Courier*, and all I want is a story."

"Oh—well, I feel sure Dr. Fletcher wouldn't want any publicity," said the young woman, her attitude visibly altering. "He has an absolute horror of it. But come upstairs, won't you. I'm Mrs. Fletcher. I must apologize for everything being in a muddle. You see, we expect to leave ourselves next month." She led the way to a second-floor flat from which Manning undoubtedly did receive an impression of muddle: grimy porridge-coloured upholstery, letters and papers piled on chairs and floor, and in the midst of them a distraught-looking pale man at a typewriter.

"Simon, this gentleman is from the *Courier*. They want a story. I've told him I didn't think . . . ."

"Oh no, most certainly not," said Dr. Fletcher, to whom this request apparently came as the last straw. "I'm sure Alexander won't want stuff in the papers—not yet, anyway. Everything is still so tentative."

"Of course I understand your feeling," said Tony mellifluously, "but the point is, it's going to be in the papers in any case. A well-known man like Mr. Sarratt——"

"Dr. Sarratt."

"Like Dr. Sarratt is bound to attract attention, and the whole set-up—an island—well, it has a certain glamour, you'll appreciate. Wouldn't it be better, from your own point of view, to give me the real facts, rather than let some other paper get hold of a garbled version?"

"There's a lot in what he says, Simon," agreed Mrs. Fletcher, falling for this hoary gambit with even more than the usual speed. "Just a straightforward factual account—I can't think Alexander could object to that."

"Well—a completely factual account, then," said Dr. Fletcher unhappily. "And I'll need to see what you write."

"Oh, quite." The poor mugs always did say that, and one had long ago learned not to take any notice. "Now then, Dr. Sarratt's line—he's a physicist, isn't he? Atomic research? One of our most brilliant minds—that right?"

"You could certainly say so," muttered Dr. Fletcher restlessly.

"My husband is a physicist too," interposed Mrs. Fletcher smiling. "He's far too modest to tell you about himself, but I might add that in his way he is equally brilliant."

"Atomic too?"

"No. There are other branches," said Mrs. Fletcher tolerantly.

"Er—yes, of course. And the island is . . . ?"

"Sunay. Spelt S-U-N-A-Y, but you pronounce it Sooner. Off the west coast of Scotland, about four miles from Kyle Arkaig. Here, I'll show you on the map."

Maps meant nothing to Tony; he noted a triangular brown lump in the middle of a regular archipelago, and passed on:

"Surely this doesn't mean you and Dr. Sarratt are retiring altogether from science? Might you be going to set up some sort of—well—atomic experiment?"

"Good lord, no." A wintry smile lit Dr. Fletcher's sallow face. "You any conception of the sort of equipment needed for atomic research?"

Mrs. Fletcher again interposed. "But my husband is a keen ornithologist. He will be making a lot of observations. We shall probably do a book."

"But nothing atomic?"

"Definitely nothing atomic."

"Then I don't quite see——"

"Well," said Dr. Fletcher, seeming to realize with an effort that all this hedging was getting them nowhere, "you could certainly say that Dr. Sarratt is retiring from science, at any rate for a time. That's to say, he feels that an experiment of this kind has a scientific value of its own. He is greatly interested in land reclamation, and if we make a success of Sunay—it has not been farmed, you know, for fifty years—it was a deer-forest till he bought it—he hopes that our example may perhaps give an impetus to the revival of agriculture on the west coast."

"All the same, it's curious, isn't it, his giving up a career which has been outstanding? Would it be right to suggest that perhaps he was unhappy over the use to which——"

"I have never discussed it with him," said Dr. Fletcher, becoming reluctant again.

"But isn't it a fact that he was one of the scientists who protested when we didn't share——"

"As far as I know, that has nothing to do with his decision."

"Oh, well, as you say. Now as to the financial side of it. He's bought the island—d'you know what he gave?"

"£3,000, I think. Of course, a lot more capital is required. The houses were in ruins, all but one. The Scottish Department of Agriculture is making us a grant towards repairs."

"Ah, yes. And the rest?"

"We are all contributing—that's to say, all who have any capital are putting it in."

"And sharing the profits in proportion?"

"No, we shall share the profits equally. That is part of Dr. Sarratt's idea. Profits are shared on the basis of work done, you see, not of funds contributed. That seems to him fair."

"Quite, yes. But where, in that case, will most of the money come from?"

"My husband and I are putting in all we have," said Mrs. Fletcher defensively.

"I suppose Miss Todhunter's share will be the largest," admitted Dr. Fletcher. "I have a note somewhere—no, I'm afraid I've mislaid it. Anyway, Miss Mary Todhunter, of Preston. Her father is managing director of the big cotton firm. And then Captain and Mrs. Rossiter. Captain Rossiter was through the Burma campaign. Dr. Sarratt was most anxious to include ex-service people. We have two—Leslie Turner is the other. He was a farm labourer before he joined up. Of course he has only his gratuity to put in. But Mrs. Rossiter has considerable capital, I believe."

"Captain Rossiter's wife?"

"No, his mother. It is a part of Dr. Sarratt's idea, that our community should include different age-groups, and different—well—social strata. We aim to create a balanced society from the first."

"Any children?"

"My two," said Mrs. Fletcher. "They're out for a walk now, but they'll be back any moment. I should like you to see them. Gavin is six and Jamie four."

"Lucky kids," said Tony politely. "Well, Dr. Fletcher, can I have details of Dr. Sarratt's career, and the addresses of all the others, please?" He wrote assiduously. "That the lot?"

"We've forgotten Kurt," said Mrs. Fletcher. "That wouldn't please him, would it, Simon? Kurt Schneider— he's an Austrian refugee. Jewish, of course. He had hoped at one time to settle in Palestine, and studied ecology as a preparation. You know what that is?" she added kindly.

"Oh, yes," said Tony resolving to look it up when he got back to the office. "An ecologist. A brilliant ecologist?"

Mrs. Fletcher glanced at him sharply, but his face was bland. "Well, naturally. Everyone who has been picked for the experiment is first-rate in their line. My husband and I had over five hundred applications to choose from. I wouldn't have you think we've primarily considered the money angle. All of them are experienced—Miss Todhunter, for instance, ran her father's farm all through the war."

"I see. Then you and Dr. Fletcher have done all the selecting? Dr. Sarratt hasn't taken any part?"

"He relied on us absolutely," replied Mrs. Fletcher a trifle stiffly. "We are very old friends, and fully understand his ideas. He's had his own hands full getting Sunay into order —he's up there now, with the shepherd who looked after the place during the war—and so he couldn't possibly——"

"There's that Scotch girl, Hermia," put in her husband.

"Lord, so there is. I keep on forgetting her because we haven't seen her yet. We had very few Scotch applicants— Dr. Sarratt was disappointed, because he'd hoped to start a sort of local back-to-the-land. But this girl had a very good record in market-gardening, and Dr. Sarratt saw her himself when he was down in Edinburgh last. Miss M. Moffat. The M is for Margaret, I believe."

"So with your children", computed Tony, "and Mr. Turner's wife, that makes twelve people. And with the shepherd, if he's staying on, thirteen."

"He will be at first, and that's a nasty thought that hadn't occurred to me," admitted Mrs. Fletcher. "I'm not the least bit superstitious, but I'd rather have started with a nice round number. Don't put that in your paper, will you?"

"And except for Dr. Sarratt and yourselves, none of you knew each other previously? It will be interesting to see how you settle down together." And for the first time his imagination really did travel to that brown triangle on the blue sea, and he really did think it might be interesting. That was the worst of journalism. Always in on the beginning or the end of stories, never the part that mattered.

"Oh," said Mrs. Fletcher brightly, "I expect we'll fight like hell. But we're all going into it with our eyes open, and certain—well—ideals. Most of us, you'll have realized, are giving up quite a lot to take it on. There—I believe I hear my ogres now. Helen, darling, bring them in; I want to show them off." The door opened, and a worn-looking young woman, a dachshund and two pixie-hooded small boys poured into the room.

"Mummy, d'you know what John Sebashun——" began the elder child, and perceiving a stranger, fell silent.

"Come here, pet," said his mother. "This is Gavin—he's looking forward terrifically to living on an island. Aren't you, ducky? Tell the gentleman."

Gavin said nothing.

"You are a couple of lucky fellows," exclaimed Tony heartily; he had no experience with children and dreaded them in interviews. "What shall you do with yourselves on the island?" He racked his brains for the sort of thing they might do. "Lobster-fishing? Playing with the seals?"

There was a hopeful pause. Then, continuing to fix his examiner with a baleful stare, Gavin observed in ringing tones:

"Mummy, d'you know what John Sebashun did? He made a mess in ve square. A big mess. Ve policeman said he mustn't ever again."

"It's no good, I'm afraid," murmured Mrs. Fletcher apologetically. "They'll talk about Sunay for hours when there's no one here."

"Oh well, never mind. I say, may I send our photographer round in an hour or so? One of you with the two boys, perhaps looking at the map——"

"I'm sure we'd be honoured." The Fletcher dread of publicity seemed to have been successfully exorcised. "It's been charming of you to take so much interest in our little scheme. Anything else we can do to help——"

"Oh, you've been most terribly kind. Good-bye, Dr. Fletcher, and good luck."

"Er—thank you," muttered Dr. Fletcher, and made a last effort at self-assertion. "You will be careful not to misrepresent us, won't you? I wouldn't like Dr. Sarratt to imagine . . . You will let me see . . ."

"Yes, yes, I'll do my best. Please don't bother, I can find my way out." He escaped back to his office, and put through a call to a friend who acted as his Cambridge spy.

"Look here, Foster, can you give me any personal dope on a man called Sarratt, Alexander Sarratt?"

"You mean the atomic bloke?"

"That's right, but I've got all that. Seems he's giving it up and going off colonizing a Scottish desert island."

"Really? You surprise me. Yes, I know Sarratt moderately well, and I shouldn't have said he was at all the type——"

"Not the born leader of men? His little pals at this end seem no end in awe of him. He's going to build a new heaven and earth in this place—quite the latter-day St. Columba. Not the sort of development you'd expect?"

"No indeed. He did pretty well here, was considered a coming man, and I shouldn't have said he's anything of the crank. Quiet chap, friendly, nothing to pick out in a crowd. What's he look like?—oh, fair, shortish, quite ordinary, nice smile. Plays a good game of squash, that's where I used to meet him mostly, and dotty about music. 'Fraid I can't tell you much else—I'd have said there wasn't much else to tell. Yes, I know he got agitated over the political implications, but so did most of the atomic crowd. Oh well, I suppose he's just got fed up with labs, and someone's left him a bit of money, and he thinks he'll clear out. Don't blame him. I wouldn't mind a nice quiet island, myself."

"H'm, I don't imagine it will be all that quiet. Anyway, thanks. You can't think of anything else that would make him sound a bit less of the perfect English gent? Well, I must make do. I'll call him dynamic."

"I suppose you can't be prevented," said Foster, chuckling at the other end. "Anyway, it would serve a physicist right." He was a chemist himself. "But I say, Tony, go easy on old Sarratt, will you? He really is as nice a chap as they come. Wouldn't hurt a fly."

"That so? He's helped hurt a quarter of a million Jap flies." Pleased with himself, he rang off.

Yet afterwards it occurred to him to wonder whether there wasn't, in this crack, some sort of a clue. He reckoned to be as thick-skinned as the next man, but was it the sort of joke he would like to hear made about himself? It was not.

[III]

On the day when she first saw him, Maggie Moffat had been on her feet since dawn, and she had a bad cold.

She had caught the cold from Jim, her brother-in-law,

who did the accounts and was supposed to help with the waiting in the little dark teashop below the Castle which the three of them ran together. Jim, feeling very ill, retired to bed, and Jeanie took a lot of time off from the kitchen to nurse him. Maggie, who must have felt less ill, carried on single-handed. But she was not pleased.

Not, in fact, since her mother died had she felt really pleased. Her mother had looked after Jeanie, and with that same sunny efficiency would undoubtedly, on Jeanie's marrying Jim, have looked after him too. She would have continued to control the teashop—for it was plain that Jim, what with his war-wounds and his temperament, was never going to strike out into a line of his own—and Maggie would have been free to pursue that down-to-earth existence in Mr. MacDougal's market garden which held such mysterious charms for her. No one for a moment could have conceived of Mrs. Moffat's relaxing her strong, calm hold on the life and the business she had created. No one could have imagined her dying when she did. Maggie was still, nine months later, unable to imagine it. Each time the reality, as doors opened and it was never Mrs. Moffat who walked through them, hit her with a sort of cruel surprise.

Still, there it was. Jeanie, who was a fine cook but had never run anything, immediately assumed that Maggie would stay at home and take charge of their only financial asset, and Maggie, the funeral over, wrote to Mr. MacDougal and put an end to the four happiest years of her life. And because helplessness was an endearing part of Jim's character, it did not for a long time occur to her that his acquisition as a brother-in-law might be the signal for her release.

But now it occurred to her every day, and with increasing force. Jeanie and Jim could manage; they would take on a lassie for the waiting; for the life of her she didn't see why they should not make out. But never, obviously, as long as she was there. There was no returning to Mr. MacDougal, for he had got a soldier, a clumsy lad, he wrote tactfully, but strong, to take her place. So she began to look through the situations-vacant columns in the farming papers, and thus it was that the piece about the Hebridean island caught her eye.

She answered it because it specifically mentioned market-gardening, and also for a sort of private joke. To one with her background, it was impossible that any scheme with a touch of adventure to it, anything in the least degree romantic, should be a scheme a sensible body actually undertook. It was the sort of daft thing the English went in for, and a lot of crack-brained English would answer it, she dared say. If she were offered the chance, she pretty well knew she would refuse. But it was unlikely she would have the offer, because she had no capital—well, none that she would dream of putting into other people's islands. Her share of their mother's money was necessary to the teashop, and tied up there it would remain.

She was ashamed of her letter when she had sent it off, ashamed to have wasted Mr. MacDougal's fine testimonial on such trash; but she did tell Jeanie. It seemed unfair not to, and if she didn't take this opening, she would take another; one day, very soon now, she would be off. Jeanie gasped, protested, panicked. But underneath the panic Maggie could detect, with a stab of pity for them both, the dawnings of an irrepressible relief.

She need not, she reflected grumpily to-night, have bothered. There had been no answer to her application. Life was still made up of carrying trays, while the great coloured world of growing things hung like a painted backcloth, tantalisingly out of reach. It was winter now, and this did not matter so much, but when the spring came and they started to plant out the carpet bedding in Princes Street gardens, it would be more than she could bear. Better prepare against such torment. Better put in an advertisement of her own.

She sat down for a moment on the arm of the old oak settle indispensable to teashops, to blow her nose and think how she would word the advertisement, so that it shouldn't cost too much and yet produce results. But the cold made her head stupid, and no words came. Instead she stared through the window, at the lights coming out along the Canongate, and thought dully how pretty Edinburgh was at this hour of dusk, and how chill the wind whistled round its corners, and how she hated it. They were not an Edinburgh family. They came from the Ayrshire coast. Mrs. Moffat had selected Edinburgh, partly because where fifty teashops flourish a fifty-first may do well, and partly so that Maggie could go to the university. The war came, and she went into market-gardening instead. And here she was at twenty-four, ignorant, limited, fit for nothing but carrying trays.

It was half-past five, and time the last tables finished and went. She ran her eye over them, and thought that she had seen them all a hundred times before. The minister and his wife, the solitary young man, the two giggling girls who kept telling each other they were not hungry in the intervals of making an excellent tea, the bunch of medical students with their hearts in Murrayfields. The minister was making a sign for his bill; she brought it, and stared ostentatiously at the others. Half an hour later she was rid of them all except the solitary young man.

She was not in the mood to stand nonsense. She advanced on him relentlessly. "I'm sorry," she said, "but we don't serve suppers in the winter."

He started, and began to feel in his pockets. "I say, I'm awfully sorry," he murmured. "I've kept you, haven't I?" She noticed then that he had a nice face, lined and curiously sad, and compunction swept her for her bad manners. After all, as long as she was tied to the teashop, it behoved her to behave pleasantly to its guests.

"Och no, dinna hurry," she said easily, her voice sliding into the Lowland lilt she used when she was friendly. "Bide a wee while longer, ye look tired to death. Ye'll have to excuse my speaking to you like that. I've been single-handed, ye see, and all this running round seems silly sometimes." And, shy at having unbent so far, she picked up her tray and prepared to move off.

"I daresay you'd rather be sowing carrots?" he suggested.

Maggie swung round, and their eyes met. He had grey eyes, and their scrutiny was steady. The tray clattered to the floor. He picked it up, and then pulled out the other chair at his table for her to sit down.

"Which island will it be?" demanded Maggie in an almost accusing voice, taking command, with an effort, of the situation and herself.

"Sunay. Perhaps you know——"

"Sunay!"

"Then you do know?"

"Och, well, I've seen it from the Kyle. Nobody's done more than that. They'd no' let you land. It's queer I never thought of Sunay. I thought it might be Rhum, perhaps, or Tiree——" She stared at him with shining eyes.

"It is an island with several possibilities." He was watching her, smiling, no longer looking at all tired or pitiful, and balancing a teacup in his hand.

"But does it not belong to some rich English lady, that preserves it for a deer-forest, and that's why she wouldn't let folks come?"

"It used to. But now", said the young man, and this time his smile spread into real, gleeful laughter, "it belongs to me."

Now just you be careful, said Maggie to herself. You know nothing about him, and all you've seen of Sunay is a craggy blue hill in the middle of the sea, and you can't make a market-garden out of that. He's English, too. Don't lose your head.

"That's a damn silly thing to say," the young man was pursuing. "A place belongs to the people who work it. I believe that if I believe anything, and so do you, I'll swear. That old man's market-garden must have felt like your own before you'd finished. Sunay had no owner till Rory and I came, and we're beginning to own just the little bit we've fenced and drained and put a roof on. What it needs is a real population—it supported eighty people, you know, before the Clearances. I'm not saying it could support eighty at our present standards of life. But I could make some sort of a start with ten."

"I canna say it appeared precisely fertile to me," said Maggie in her new role of caution.

"But you haven't landed?"

"Ay, that's so."

"Then let me assure you, Miss Moffat, that the soil is old volcanic lava. Would that suggest possibilities?"

"Black currants?" hazarded Maggie, who was not, at all events, going to be patronized on her own ground.

"Well, there's the transport difficulty—we've four miles of sea to the Kyle. But the flat land round the harbour is just so much untapped potash—I've had it analysed. Black currants, possibly. Gooseberries, certainly. You know they sell thousands of pounds' worth off Canna? I don't see why we shouldn't do as well off Sunay, now we've got rid of the lady and her stalking."

"Have ye got rid of the deer?"

"Well, virtually. The Department of Agriculture cleared them off six years ago and put on sheep. I can't say they're good sheep, just the usual Blackfaces, but we can improve the flock in time. And there's no acclimatization problem on an island."

"I wouldn't be knowing anything about sheep."

"Anyway, the point is, the vegetable-growing side would be the most important, at any rate for the first few years. I don't see why that shouldn't pay from the start. Look at the markets—did you ever get a fresh lettuce in any of those hotels at the Kyle?"

"The climate", said Maggie, "will be terrible wet."

"And so it is in Ayrshire. You dislike rain?" Maggie grinned. "You'll have learnt there, I daresay, to choose the strains that don't need so much sun. That is why your experience will be just what we need."

I am being talked round by this laddie, reflected Maggie, and then it struck her that he was not a boy, after all. There was something young about his eagerness, but his face, when you studied it carefully, was lined. And he looked shy, but his grey eyes were very shrewd. Suddenly she remembered that she had a cold and a red nose. She was not a pretty girl, being too short and Scots and square, but when she felt well she had a bonny look that was attractive. Violently she longed to have been looking bonny to-night.

"I expect you're wondering how you'd live," he went on. "There are nine crofts, in a nice neat crescent round the head of the bay. From the mainland they don't show—at least, they didn't, but we're whitewashing. The Department repaired the one we're in now, for Rory, and the workmen come over next week to do the others. One is quite a favourite when one starts reclaiming derelict land. I've been astonished at the things I'm able to get done."

"Do you mean", Maggie asked slowly, "that I'd be having a wee house of my own?"

"Ah! That got you?"

"Why, no; no more than reason!" But she was bewitched, and he saw it. "A wee house—that would be fine, now, if what ye say of the soil is true. I'll admit it's an inducement."

"Well," he said, "I've lived over two months now on

23

Sunay, and in a good deal of discomfort. The houses don't leak, and that's about all you can say. Rory and I open tins when the rabbits give out. I hope and think conditions will be very different by the time you arrive. But even as they are now, it's more like heaven than anything I've ever imagined. It's not only that it's so beautiful, but there's that feeling—I don't know if you've ever experienced it?—of land crying out for help. You look round and see rushes and nettles, and in your mind's eye they turn to corn and carrots. You find yourself putting cows on the bits of green grass by the streams. It's land that could produce anything—makes your fingers itch."

"I've broken old meadow in my day," said Maggie off-handedly. "Did ye say nettles? Good big ones? That'll be an excellent sign."

"Then you'll come?"

"Of course I'll come."

But it wasn't of course at all. She had never meant to say it—at any rate, not at this stage, or with so little preamble. She clutched at an excuse.

"That is to say, I'd have liked to come, only you see, I've no capital. You said in yon advertisement that you wanted capital. Well, naturally, it'll be a verra expensive undertaking. But it was good of you to think of me, and I'm sure I'm greatly obliged."

"I want you for the job you'll make of it," he said. "We'll make the money go round."

"Och, dear me," muttered Maggie, immensely pleased and somehow near to tears. "It's no' true about the capital," something impelled her to add. "I own half this place. But it's my sister's livelihood, and her man's, and I could no' be taking my money out."

"Don't worry. Of course you couldn't.'

"I wouldn't want to be doing less than my share. I could provide my own tools. Seeds for the first year too, I dare-

24

say." And that, again, she had never meant to say. Here she was, committing herself all over the place, and it seemed useless trying any more to hold back. She found herself assuring him she would come as soon as the houses were ready—not till mid-March, was it?—then he must get the potatoes ordered and sprouted because an early crop would be worth a lot of cash. He knew, she discovered, nothing about potatoes. It was pitiful, him thinking he could manage a market-garden on the little he knew. She was badly needed. She grew brisk, efficient, instructive, and all the while felt on her the young man's shrewdly smiling grey eyes.

How glad he seemed to be that she was coming. Perhaps there had been few answers to his advertisement. Awkward to ask him—but she had to know. "I'm not sure, exactly," he said. "My friends the Fletchers have been dealing with them in London. You'll like the Fletchers—Hermia is a wonder, the perfect wife, and they've two jolly little boys. You're the only person I've seen myself, they chose the rest. They had about five hundred letters, I believe."

Five hundred letters! To be chosen out of five hundred, with no other recommendation than Mr. MacDougal's testimonial and her own uppish ways! If the island had been Tristan da Cunha she would have gone.

A thought struck her. "I dinna know your name." And this, which would have been disquieting twenty minutes ago, now seemed a huge joke.

"How idiotic of me. My name's Sarratt, Alexander Sarratt. I ought to give you a reference or something, oughtn't I? I might be a confidence trickster for all you know. Well, let's see, there's one or two people at the Department of Agriculture, or if you like to write to my old professor at Cambridge—I had a sort of lectureship there once, but I've been on war work since, of course."

"I believe I'll be taking you on trust," said Maggie

demurely. She put out her hand and he took it; the thing was clinched. It didn't seem to matter so much now that her nose was red.

"Well," he said, getting up, "I've kept you long enough. I can always write to you here, can't I? I'll let you know how the housing goes, and about the spuds, and where to send your things. We're hoping to have all the furniture and big stuff sent up by sea from Oban." He added, as she helped him on with his coat: "You know, I'm tremendously grateful to you for being so understanding, and so sporting over taking the chance. It'll be a hard life, of course. But I honestly believe we can make it a good one. Anything I can do to make you happy——" Perhaps the similarity to a proposal of marriage struck him too, for his face had a little more colour and his voice trailed off.

"My own way in the garden, Mr. Sarratt," Maggie assured him. "That's all I ask."

"Bless you," he said, and smiled at her, and went out into the deserted street.

She knew full well the destination of that smile. It had gone straight to her heart.

[IV]

In the six weeks that passed before she saw him again, Maggie Moffat went through a variety of emotions by which she herself was startled and disgusted. She who had always been so sensible found herself becoming silly; she who had always looked facts in the face took to imagining things that were not. She told herself stories which she knew to be stories, yet the telling was a pleasure she could not seem to do without.

With Jim and Jeanie she was canny, concealing from them how little she had found out about the island, and using agricultural terms that made its possibilities sound impressive. Even so, she was aware that most of their friends thought her daft. The neighbours chaffed her when her furniture was packed up, and told her they would see her back before the summer's end. That was just like the Scots, thought Maggie grumpily. Always limited.

She dreamed of Sunay continuously, and of him. She saw herself by his side, digging, scything, haymaking. Presently she saw children, so apparently they must have married; och dear, whatever now? The other chosen eight did not enter into the picture at all or at best only in the background, getting meals, perhaps. Then she went through every step of their interview, trying to remember what he was like, for already he had begun to fade. He had grown larger than life-size, and tenderer. She knew he had been friendly; now she convinced herself that he had been more than friendly. Had he not picked her out of five hundred, and as good as guaranteed her happiness?

Lost in her golden dream, she waited for him to write, was a little disappointed when he didn't write, and tried to steady herself by a practical correspondence with Mr. Mac-Dougal on vegetable strains for the wet west. Then came Jeanie with a cutting from the *Courier*, given her by a friend, and observed: "That young man o' yours, Maggie, seems to be a likely lad after a'."

The cutting showed a picture of a beautiful young lady with two bairns, and the caption: "Gavin's Off to Catch Seals." The story itself was headed: "Away from the Atom." And from it Maggie learned that the chosen partner of her future life was one of the foremost of Britain's younger physicists, brilliant, dynamic 36-year-old Dr. Alexander Sarratt, who was giving up a career of outstanding promise in order to found a new type of co-operative community in the Western Isles. The scientific methods he intended to apply were expected to revolutionize Highland agriculture. He would be aided by a picked team of experts, equally brilliant

27

in their way. They included Dr. Fletcher, ornithologist, with Mrs. Fletcher and Gavin and Jamie (see picture above); Mr. Kurt Schneider, ecologist; and Miss Mary Todhunter, daughter of Mr. J. A. Todhunter of the noted Lancashire cotton firm, who had won prizes at many shows with her famous herd of Shorthorns. Followed details of the profit-sharing plan and a few words with attractive, brunette Mrs. Fletcher, who said: "We are all giving up a great deal for this idea." There was no mention of Miss Maggie Moffat.

Jeanie was pleased; to see it all in print made it seem more respectable and secure. But Maggie's dear imaginings came crashing down about her ears.

She sat in stunned misery, staring at the paper, and the lovely, moth-like face of Mrs. Fletcher seemed to be giving her an ironic smile. "She's like yon film star," said Jeanie helpfully, and in spirit Maggie groaned.

All her inborn Scottish respect for learning and culture, for fame and achievement, welled up and bore him infinitely far out of her sphere. He was well known, a person of distinction, a Doctor (and she calling him Mister, how mortifying), while she was the daughter of a primary schoolmaster, an ignorant, limited Scots girl who had never got to the university, who had never in her life, except to wait on them, spoken to people like Mrs. Fletcher, his chosen friend. What had he called her?—"the perfect wife". And then came Maggie Moffat thinking herself good enough for him! The nerve, the blethering folly of it! Thinking it on no grounds, either; for now she no longer deceived herself. The only thing that comforted her at all was that she had had to tell him how to sprout the potatoes.

At first, in her utter loss of self-respect, she determined that she would cry off. And then it seemed that that would be yet more shameful. It would be as good as admitting to herself that she had only been willing to go to Sunay in order to get a husband. And that was, after all, not quite

28

true. She had told him that she knew the ecstasy of breaking virgin ground, and so she did. She had something real to contribute to his experiment, though she might not be important enough to get a mention in the *Courier*. He knew nothing about potatoes, be he never so brilliant. Impossible now to let him down. But there was going to be an end of all such nonsense. She would go to Sunay, aware of the possibilities of folly in herself, and they should never get the chance to blossom again. And after all, if she didn't like it, if these Fletchers and this Miss Todhunter proved as la-di-da as she now felt convinced they would—then there was always the teashop, and Jim and Jeanie missing her badly when they had had time to realize how much of the work she did, and she could come home again.

Dr. Sarratt still did not write—well, naturally, a man of his importance—but the piece in the *Courier* earned Maggie an interview to herself in an Edinburgh paper, rather unsatisfactory because she really had nothing to tell that the reporter didn't already know, and she was by this time beginning to doubt the existence of the island and Dr. Sarratt altogether. And soon afterwards came a long, badly typed letter from Hedy Lamarr's husband, beginning "Dear Miss Moffat,—We hear with interest that you are joining our party——" and instructing her to send all furniture and heavy packages to the railway depot at Oban, where it would be picked up on the 25th by the S.S. *Loch Coruisk*, making a special call at Sunay. She would appreciate that the two motor launches belonging to Sunay were only suitable for the ferrying of personal luggage. Repairs were progressing satisfactorily, and he and his family were proposing to settle in early next month, but he suggested she might like to arrive a week later. If she travelled on the 14th she would have the company of Mr. and Mrs. Rossiter, Mr. and Mrs. Turner and Miss Todhunter, and only one launch trip would be needed to fetch them all. He looked forward to making her acquaintance, and was hers sincerely, Simon Fletcher.

This impersonal communication left Maggie feeling still more depressed. At least, she reflected, she had had the say in the teashop, but on Sunay, where she had dreamed of being queen, it seemed she would just be running about doing as she was told. She did not see by what right the Fletchers should get there first, and have the pick of everything, and probably, under pretence of unpacking and being helpful, poke their scornful noses into her poor little bits of furniture. But their right, of course, lay in being his dear friends, and she might consider herself lucky to be allowed to creep in with the rest of the herd. She began to calculate how soon she could leave Sunay without losing too much face, and it was not helpful that her acquaintance was now openly interested, and made her the subject of envious and affectionate speculation every time she put her nose out of doors.

The furniture was crated and went; she slept on a camp-bed in the wee back room, and clung rather pitifully to any signs of regret or misgiving that Jeanie gave. And then at last a postcard came, written in that small, neat, nervous hand which is the script of scholars all over the world.

> "SUNAY, BY KYLE ARKAIG.
> "*Monday*.

"Of all the hellish jobs. We had to make the boxes too. 3 tons D. of York, one ton Arran Banner, as per your instructions. I daresay some are the wrong way up. Thank God you'll be doing it next year. Roofs on, walls whitewashed, all we want now is the touch of a woman's hand. It's still like heaven. Yours ever, A.S."

She was not for a moment, night or day, parted from the card.

Chapter Two

[I]

Maggie was aware of her fellow-islanders the instant she entered the breakfast car. "Oh, Lord," an English female voice of penetrating loudness was observing, "who cares, anyway? What's over is over. I always thought history was the greatest bore at school."

"Then you missed a great deal, dear, if you don't mind my saying so," replied another female voice on a note of reproof. "Perhaps I am more sensitive than most people to atmosphere—but I always feel that tremendous events leave an impression, a sort of aura, behind them. I never closed my eyes the night we spent in Glencoe. I still think it a great pity that we know so little of the story of Sunay. But if any great battle or massacre did happen there—and after all it's very likely, when you remember the stormy history of all the isles —I know that I shall sense it before we've been there long."

"Gosh, Ma," said a man's voice, almost as carrying as the girl's, "what rot you do talk."

Well, thought Maggie, slipping into a seat from which she could watch the owners of the voices, and raising her eyebrows. That was a funny way of speaking to one's mother, even though the remark seemed approximately just. But no doubt it was the way all the English young went on. The elderly lady, a little round person with a firm, drawn-down mouth and slightly protruberant eyes, appeared hardly disconcerted by it. She merely said: "Ronny, need you be such a boor?" and went on deliberately buttering her toast.

The young man beside her was thin and dark, with a long,

bony face which wore a look of profound impatience and boredom. He was not in the least like her, and yet they were unmistakably mother and son. Most of the time he stared out of the window, but without taking any notice when she, who seemed well-informed, pointed out features of the scenery. The young lady with the voice had her back to Maggie, and all that could be seen of her was a neat leg issuing out of perfectly cut riding breeches, and a head of crisp dark-gold curls.

She began now to ask Mr. Rossiter—for undoubtedly these must be Miss Todhunter and the Rossiters—questions about his farming experience, and was no whit dismayed by his unencouraging response. He had done, he said reluctantly, a year at an agricultural college; whereupon she told him in ringing tones that those places were a sheer waste of time, taught you nothing but a lot of rubbishy theory which you jolly well had to unlearn as soon as you got on to a real farm. The young man made no reply, and continued to glare moodily at Rannoch Moor.

Of course, she didn't suppose Sunay would be a real farm —not yet. There was no one there who knew the first thing about farming, was there? All these doctors and their ecologists—what a yell. She felt sorry for him, really, having to start getting his experience with a lot of amateurs. "That's where I've been lucky," she finished complacently. "I've had the run of my Dad's farms ever since I could stick on a horse. After our bailiff was called up I took on his job. I had sixteen men under me, and four land girls—at least, we had Eytyes instead of girls the last year."

"Indeed?" said Mrs. Rossiter politely. "Didn't you find it difficult, managing men?"

"Lord, no," replied Miss Todhunter with a loud guffaw. "The chaps did as they were told. I'm not one to stand any nonsense—I take after my dad. *And* I never got a single telling-off from the War Ag., though I do say it."

"You'll be wasted on Sunay," murmured Ronny with a look of black dislike.

Perhaps a little of it penetrated this time, for the young lady replied in colder tones:

"Oh, I've my reasons for going, of course. I'd like to build up an experimental herd, for one thing. I've a notion to try crossing Shorthorns with Highlanders, and farms with a reputation like ours naturally didn't want to make any change. I shan't stay unless I'm given plenty of scope. I never believe in going on with anything if it turns out boring, do you?"

"I'm afraid that's not quite my attitude," replied Mrs. Rossiter gently. "I feel we have incurred a definite obligation towards Dr. Sarratt, whatever his plans for us may turn out to be."

"I don't feel much obligation towards a man who's had a fat wadge of my money," said Miss Todhunter shortly. "I don't know how much you may have put in, but I may tell you——" Mrs. Rossiter checked her by holding up a hand.

"All we can dispose of, my dear; but I feel we should respect Dr. Sarratt's wish that the exact amounts are not disclosed. You will find that that will be wisest in the end."

"Well, I've nothing to be ashamed of," said Miss Todhunter, and followed this happy comment by getting to her feet. "Will you excuse me? I must go and see how Lady's getting on. The damn fool of a guard made her stay in the van, and she can't bear being out of my sight for a moment."

She made her way down the coach, balancing her body easily against the swaying rhythm of the train, and Maggie had a brief, dazzling vision of Amazonian beauty. She was a big girl, superbly made, with the chiselled features of a Greek shepherd, eyes the bright blue of the summer sky and that aureole of hair. It seemed impossible that any man should take his eyes off her, but apparently her looks were outweighed by her manners, for Ronny was distinctly heard

a

to mutter, as the door slammed behind her: "God in heaven, what a bitch."

Maggie now became aware, through his audible chuckling, that the young man at her own table had been following the conversation with equal interest, and so had the little, damp, frightened girl who must be his wife. "Is your name Turner?" she asked them in a whisper, and on their nodding: "Mine's Moffat." The young man, who had a flop of fair hair which kept falling into his eyes, pushed it out of them and solemnly shook her by the hand. "It's ever so nice to meet somebody," he said, implying, no doubt, somebody human like himself.

"Would ye say she knows as much about it as all that?" proceeded Maggie, still with caution.

"Might do," said Les Turner indifferently. "Reckon she won't be the only one if she does."

"My hubby's been four years on a farm," said the little girl shyly.

"You're the market-gardener, aren't you?" said young Turner. "I did a spell of that once, place near Uxbridge. Interesting but a bit too fiddling, if you ask me. It's all right for a girl, I daresay." They chatted knowledgeably about Brussels sprouts till it was Fort William, and time to change.

Impossible, on the exquisite hour of journeying from Fort William to Kyle Arkaig, to concentrate on the shortcomings of future associates, who had in any case taken their loud voices off to some other section of the train. Impossible, as each twist of the fantastic line revealed a new glimpse of orange-fringed sea-loch, to fight down a sudden, real, joyous anticipation. Round the next corner but three, or perhaps four, would be Sunay, the island so long imagined that it had almost ceased to exist. And meanwhile, here were Eigg and Rhum. She pointed them out to the Turners with proper native pride. Les, his face pressed against the window and his long hair ruffled by the draught, watched with an intent

34

fascination. Once he observed quietly: "This is the sort of scenery you'd pay good dough to see." His little wife said that it was lovely, but she clung tightly to his arm.

Then there appeared a sharp blue peak which might be the mountain of Sunay, or it might not. After the next cutting there was no doubt. An ugly railway station and a strong smell of herring rushed out from the mountain-side to meet them. This was Kyle Arkaig, and only a four-mile stretch of water lay between them and the new life.

[II]

There are many Kyles up and down the west coast of Scotland, but when the people of Rhum, Sunay and all parts south of Skye and north of Ardnamurchan speak of the Kyle, it is Kyle Arkaig that they mean. And, indeed, the place has some claim to particularity. Two railway lines make it their terminus, which is a distinction in a country of sparse communications. Its pier can accommodate steamers as big as are ever likely to thread the Sounds, and it still, in a desultory way, maintains a dwindling herring fleet. The curing-sheds and cottages of the fishermen constitute, as everywhere along this coast, an unplanned seaside slum. But Kyle Arkaig is not without its ambitions, though they would never include any plan for the removal of what is unsightly. Its modernistic white hotel has a certain elegance, and charges proportionately. There are three boarding-houses, and up the hill-side a fir-clad mansion in the Victorian gothic manner, once the seat of the lady who stalked the deer on Sunay, and now Glenalmond, a hostel of the Pilgrim Travellers' Guild.

Above all, the Kyle has a view of the Islands unrivalled along the coast. They hang, a shimmering opalescent curtain, across four miles of silver sea. One merges into another, so that those unacquainted with the map might imagine they

35

were one great island, and it is hard to conceive that these enclosed waters open somewhere to the Atlantic.

To Maggie Moffat, spending a holiday at one of the three boarding-houses, the Islands appeared as a painted back-cloth, as unreal and inaccessible as they were beautiful. Content with innocuous trips up and down the Sound by steamer and inland by charabanc, she had never thought it possible that anyone should stand on the sharp tip of Sunay's blue peak. Nor, as she leaned against the quay wall and stared across the shining water, did it seem possible now. The island was not a place one reached, nor was the bewitching young man a person one ever saw again. And certainly there was no way of getting across, for there was no boat.

"I thought they'd be sending to meet us?" said Les flatly. His wife, in a thin blue plastic raincoat, looked perished with cold.

Ronny Rossiter came up and introduced himself. His sulkiness had disappeared; he looked excited and friendly. "We were looking out for you on the train," he said. "I don't know how we missed you." Maggie and the Turners exchanged guilty glances. "Anyway, we were to tell you the boat couldn't be in till twelve. Come on up to the hotel and have something hot to drink." And he picked up Maggie's suitcase and led the way.

In the hotel lounge Mrs. Rossiter was pouring out coffee, while Miss Todhunter gambolled on the floor with a silky Welsh collie. She looked up with a friendliness which made Maggie feel slightly ashamed. "I say," she began, "isn't this a moment? I'd no idea Sunay would look so super. I'm so excited I can hardly breathe."

"I'm just a wee bit worked up myself," admitted Maggie, smiling over her cup. "Although I've seen it from here before."

"You're Miss Moffat, I take it," said Mrs. Rossiter graciously. "I'm sorry we didn't manage to meet earlier. Dr. Fletcher particularly asked me to look after you, as you were the only one of us quite on your own." Maggie looked grateful, but she was not pleased; it was bad enough having to acknowledge the leadership of the Fletchers, without submitting to this lady as well. The Turners, sitting on the edge of their sofa, maintained an impenetrable working-class reserve.

"Why, of course," exclaimed Miss Todhunter, sitting up suddenly and shaking off the dog, "you're the one this Sarratt picked out for himself. Tell us what he's like."

"Yes, do," urged Ronny. "You've actually seen the Great White Chief. Jove, what an experience. What are we expected to do when we come into the Presence? Give the Nazi salute, I should think, if half that chap Fletcher says about his likes and dislikes is true. Dr. S. this and Dr. S. that—Alexander the Great expects that every man will do his duty. My last brigadier isn't in it."

"Really, Ronny, that is no way to talk," protested Mrs. Rossiter, but merely as a matter of form, since it was evident that her son paid no attention to her.

By this time, the layers of awe and distance, of passion, frustration, disgrace and despair had so overlaid Alexander Sarratt in Maggie's mind that she really had no idea what he was like at all. But she tried, through the mists, to see again the solitary young man in the teashop. "Och, I'd no' say he was anything out of the ordinary," she began. "Not just to meet, I mean. He seemed a douce laddie, and—well—verra kind."

"Ah, that's often the way," commented Mrs. Rossiter. "That modesty, not putting himself forward—a sure sign of a first-rate mind."

"But what's he look like?" demanded Miss Todhunter. "Is he tall?"

"Tall? Och, no, I don't mind he was. Sort of middle-sized. He'd a nice way of looking at you, that made you feel you'd do what he wanted. Of course I didna' know then, about his being a first-rate mind. I'd never heard tell of him. Perhaps I'd have felt different if I'd known he was famous."

"He seems to have got you on his side, at any rate," said Ronny with a grin. Maggie felt her face go hot, but needlessly; he was not really interested in her feelings. "Well, it's after eleven. I'm going out to look for that boat."

But there was still no boat; nor at twelve; nor at half-past. They had got tired of looking, and very cross and bored (except for the Turners, who held hands in an obscure corner), when at last Ronny's reconnaissance announced a launch in sight. They trooped down to the quay again, and stood waiting, an immensely long time as it seemed, before the black dot increased in size to a smart green-and-white motor-boat with a man at the wheel and a woman in the bows. Maggie was conscious of a slight sickness. She was not, and never would be, steeled to meet him again.

But, of course, it wasn't Alexander Sarratt. He would have other things to do than waste his time in boats. It was a tall, swarthy, raffish-looking Hebridean in a fisherman's jersey, and the woman was Hedy Lamarr all right, smiling up at them without the least apology for her lateness, and looking very smug. "Hello the troops!" she called to Ronny, who yelled back: "Don't get out, we've all our stuff here. We'll come on board."

"Oh, I should think there are cosier spots in the Kyle than the *Gannet*," replied Mrs. Fletcher; the Hebridean had now made fast, and she came up the steps, shivering in her green trousers and jaunty sheepskin coat. "Grr, that was a cold trip. I say, you weren't expecting to start right away, were you?"

"Well—we were, rather."

"My poor poppets. How do you do, Mrs. Rossiter?—Mr. Turner?—you'll be Miss—er—Moffat, I take it? I'm afraid I can't possibly be ready till four—oh, better say five, perhaps.

I have a thousand things to do. Soon you'll all understand what it means to live a week away from the shops. Were you hoping to lunch on Sunay?—how pathetic. You'll be lucky if you get any dinner. Do be an angel, Mr. Rossiter, and make sure the hotel is expecting us. Tell them it's for me— I'm a bit of a favourite there—Mrs. McKellar may dig out something special. Now if you'll excuse me for five minutes, I'll collect the mail." And off she went, blithely. The raffish Hebridean had by this time likewise disappeared into a knot of Gaelic-speaking comrades, and the party on the quay were left among their suitcases, snubbed.

At lunch, for which they gathered round the big table in the hotel window with Sunay tantalizingly in view, Mrs. Fletcher plunged, after a brief excuse, into her letters, which were numerous and apparently of a most entertaining kind. "It's almost worth going into exile," she told Mrs. Rossiter, looking up limpidly unaware of the questions they were all longing to ask her, "to be told so nicely how much you're missed." Maggie studied her bent head, noted the few threads of silver in her shining dark hair, and naïvely concluded that she must be middle aged and therefore could not resemble a film star after all.

"You might tell us how things are going," observed Miss Todhunter loudly at last; she was plainly no respecter of the social nuances. Mrs. Fletcher came back to the Hebrides with a start, and reluctantly tucked her correspondence underneath her soup plate.

"Going?—oh, all right, I think. Everything's in a hellish mess, but then you expected that, I imagine. The houses are dry, that's one mercy. We pushed your stuff in anywhere, to get it under cover. You'll have to sort it out for yourselves. Lord, what a treat it is to eat a meal one hasn't cooked. I've never in my life worked so hard as this last week, feeding four men and two kids. I'm looking forward to pushing everything on to you, Mrs. Rossiter, to-morrow. Oh, and

you, Mrs. Turner. You're a famous housekeeper, I daresay."
Little Mrs. Turner looked alarmed.

"Of course, we shall enjoy doing our share," replied Mrs.
Rossiter coldly.

"I devoutly hope there'll be something to eat this evening
when you arrive, but I warn you, tuck in now, because there
mayn't. I left Alexander and my husband explicit instructions, but they're the two vaguest souls. Well, naturally,
they've other things to think about. It's absurd to bother
them with drudgery. I often think that two minds like theirs
on Sunay are comically out of place."

With the double conviction that there would be no dinner,
and that Sunay only awaited their arrival to be equipped with
its quota of second-rate minds for the dirty work, a gloom
descended on the lunch party, and the rest of the meal
passed in silence.

When, after several leisurely cigarettes, Mrs. Fletcher prepared to move, Mrs. Rossiter got up too, and firmly declared
her intention of helping with the marketing. It was plain that
she was not welcome, but she was not to be shaken off. A
feeling of flatness and anti-climax possessed the others, and
Maggie proposed a stroll up the hill-side. They trailed off,
making the desultory conversation of people flung into an
intimacy for which none of them are ready. But once above
the roofs and pines of the hotel, the view was so enchanting
in its silvery winter brightness, and Sunay looked so close,
that something of the first excitement returned. Ronny got
out his field-glasses and was convinced that he could see the
crescent of the houses. "I can make out a sort of gorge running inland from the bay, too," he assured Maggie. "That's
where we're to build the dam."

"Are we so? I'd no' heard of any dam."

"Oh, yes; that's to be the big feature. We'll have to
mechanize, you know, to get any sort of a decent living
standard, and our own power is essential. Frankly, the dam's

the bit I'm looking forward to. I reckon to know something about it. I've a pal in the Sappers."

"Little boys do love mucking about with mud-pies," observed Miss Todhunter roguishly, and he said no more. But he was not, Maggie decided, as rude and bad-tempered as he made himself out. True, he was consistently rude to his mother, and that she could not but deplore. But honesty compelled her to admit that Mrs. Rossiter was the kind of mother one might easily be rude to.

They reached the quay again at half-past three, and found the housekeepers already in the boat, Mrs. Fletcher looking charmingly impatient. "We've been ready for ages," she said. "But you said five——" began Ronny, and giving it up, devoted himself assiduously to helping the Hebridean load, stack and rearrange the suitcases. Maggie found a warm place beside the engine, and sat clasping a large straw dolly of plants in her arms.

At last they were ready. The boatman's friends called him a farewell in Gaelic—by the sound of it, and their chuckles, he seemed in some way to have their sympathy. The *Gannet* headed out across the Sound. The smell of herrings faded on the breeze, the dreary quays dwindled to grey streaks, and the lone whistle of the day's last train seemed to mark the final severance from the life they knew. Kyle Arkaig, and all that lay behind it, resolved into painted blackcloth in their turn. Sunay lay ahead.

But it lay a long way ahead. It was cold in the open boat, and Maggie wrapped herself in her travelling plaid, giving the other half of it to little Mrs. Turner, who had gone nearly as blue as her plastic mackintosh. This for the first time attracted to her the notice of Miss Todhunter. "I say," she shouted—but above the noise of the engine it was now needful to shout—"you don't mind my pointing out that your clothes are jolly unsuitable? I hope you've got something tougher. You'll have that coat in rags in two days.

And Lord, look at your shoes! Sandals! My good woman, you can't go about like that on Sunay. You'll be the laughing-stock of the place."

Under the force of this attack Mrs. Turner appeared nakedly terrified. Her husband put his arm round her and glared past Mary. "Don't worry, Joycie," he muttered. "We'll write home and get them to send you some other shoes." Maggie interposed a shoulder between the little thing's tears and the world, and found herself meeting the Hebridean's merry eyes, which were turquoise blue and crinkled up against the evening sun.

"It iss you iss the young lady gardener?" he asked, noting the straw dolly.

"I must warn you," said Mrs. Fletcher, "Rory has it in for you."

"That iss a treatful chob you have made a poor chap do," said Rory; he was the only one who did not need to shout. "Stacking those plutty sputs. Weeks we was on them. When I was sleeping I still seed sputs. That iss no work for a man."

"Och, I daresay it did ye good," replied Maggie, grinning. "Wasn't Dr. Sarratt on it too?" Just to talk about him to this engaging creature, and exult in her own small influence on his activities, restored her self-importance.

"He has a lot of patience, the Toctor," Rory pronounced. "He iss a learned man, you see, and he hass other thinks to think of. But me, if I start thinking about a ceilidh or my girl, over goes the whole box, and it's all to do again. A Dhia, what a chob!"

"I daresay smuggling's more in your line?" suggested Ronny Rossiter.

"Ach, no indeet."

"Secret still in the bog?"

"Now, Mr. Rossiter, you have been reading stories. We would not know how to make whisky any more. That wass all long ago." His look of bland innocence seemed to pass to Ronny a secret which delighted them both.

In mid-channel the *Gannet* began to roll. Maggie closed her eyes and tried to concentrate on other things, even fanciful things: Alexander, love, despair. In a minute she would be seeing him. In a minute she would be sick. But it was poor little Joyce Turner who was sick—fortunately, not to windward.

Then, suddenly, Sunay seemed to loom over them, huge, and they came into the shelter of the island waters. The mountain was no longer a flat blue cone; great jagged ridges etched themselves against the sky. Formidable dark brown cliffs seemed to repel a landing. A block of them on the right detached itself as a separate island, with a roof of green. "We call it Eilean Beag, the little island," answered Rory. "I don't know hass it ever had a proper name."

"It ought to be called Latay," remarked Ronny, which, after the interval necessary to assimilate a pun in a foreign language, appeared immensely witty to his new friend.

"You will be putting the sheep on soon, I dare say. There iss goot grass on the top, but it iss a climb to get them up. But all you chentlemen will be famous climbers."

Within the lee of the little island the harbour opened up, a deep U-shaped bay, fringed here and there with scrubby clumps of oak. Round its neck stood the crescent of the nine white crofts, perfectly spaced, close enough for company and detached enough for dignity, and behind them the land rose gently, a pale, reedy green, till it met the first brown wall of the moor. The gorge that Ronny had made out through his glasses was now seen as an impressive cleft running back into the mountain, and streaked at its farther end with the milky white of a fall.

They passed, on the left, a ruined and roofless church, and then the boat turned in towards a neat quay of big grey stones. It must have been built to accommodate steamers,

43

for its top was high above them as they edged their way round to the steps on the farther side. A little group leaning on the parapet stared down at them—two men, each with a child in his arms. A third man began to make his way down the steps, easily, leisurely, to be ready to pull in the boat. He looked taller than Maggie remembered, browner and more authoritative, but there was no mistaking the sideways tilt of the head and that diffident, enchanting smile.

He, and the island, and the cold and weariness and complexity of surging emotion, altogether overcame her. For a moment she closed her eyes. It was more than she could bear.

[III]

The boat had been made fast, and he was helping Mrs. Rossiter out. "This is a big moment for us," she heard him saying, "though I'm afraid it's a grim one for you. You must be worn out, and we aren't nearly civilized yet." And Mrs. Rossiter, restored by his charming manners to her proper place as the most important person there, was answering graciously that no, she wasn't in the least worn out, only longing to turn to and give them all a hand, and if anybody had felt the journey it was poor Mrs. Turner who had been dreadfully ill in the boat. Whereupon he was all anxious concern for Mrs. Turner, till he perceived that she shrank close to her husband and was hoping not to be noticed at all.

Mrs. Fletcher was casually greeting her worried-looking pale husband and her two little boys, who stared wide-eyed at so many new faces. The other young man, who was thin, dark and in a fey, foreign way remarkably handsome, had let his eye wander over the occupants of the boat and come to rest on Mary. "This will be your luggage, I think," and he shouldered her suitcases, easily distinguishable from Maggie's by their elegance. "Permit me to show you your future home." His English was beautifully and unnaturally precise.

44

"Lord," muttered Mary, in what she no doubt imagined to be an inaudible whisper—if so, she must have a lively imagination—"did you ever see such a Jew-boy?" She strode off arrogantly along the quay, and the young man beside her gave no sign that he found her manners other than perfect. Maggie followed slowly with Ronny and Rory Mor, staring about her, silent and bemused.

A well-made road, relic of the millionairess and her stalking parties, followed the curve of the harbour for fifty yards from the quay to the houses, which fronted on to a paved causeway, an unexpected luxury, Maggie realized, in the Western Isles. Their windows looked out on to the ragged, weed-strewn beach and the sea, and away to the paling hills of the mainland; in the last light one could just make out the Kyle. A solitary tree, a wind-bent ash which seemed tall by comparison with the oak-scrub, guarded the endmost house, and below it was a great thicket of leafless bushes. "Them's what they call fuchsias," said Rory in answer to her inquiry; evidently here it was never cold. Behind the houses lay the long garden-piece, enclosed by a fine stone wall. Without having time to investigate further, Maggie satisfied herself at a glance that it bore a waist-high, a truly magnificent, crop of nettles.

The party had paused at the second house in the row. "This is where everything happens," Alexander was explaining. "I'm afraid we've just been calling it the kitchen so far. It was the post office in the old days, that's why it's a bit bigger than the others, and I had the two main rooms knocked into one. We've got tea for you. I know it's nearly dinner time, but we thought you'd be pleased. . . ." Poor laddie, it was probably his solution for all troubles. But as a matter of fact they were glad of tea, even though it deferred for ten minutes the pleasure of finding wee houses of their own.

The room inside was unexpectedly large, with two deep,

45

square-cut windows and a huge fireplace entirely filled by an enamelled and very superior cooker. "I've done us pretty well in the way of gadgets," said Alexander, beaming at Mrs. Rossiter's exclamation of surprise. "It heats the water in the little bathroom at the back." A brown pot of tea and thick white cups stood on the long table, round which were grouped an interesting variety of kitchen chairs; Maggie recognized two of her own. A fine Welsh dresser was loaded with saucepans and china that no one had had time to arrange, and the rest of the wall-space was filled with guns, rods, nets, lanterns, and miscellaneous packages still wrapped in sacking. The kitchen still needed a lot of work, but seen in this chrysalis state it already seemed, what it was in fact to prove, a refuge and a home.

"Now I shall show the young ladies their house," announced the handsome foreigner, and to cries of "Trust Kurt!" and "True to form!" put one hand on Mary's shoulder and the other under Maggie's arm and marched them out. The pronoun gave Maggie a jar. Was she not, after all, to have a house of her own? Were there not nine in the row?

There were, but only six of them had been sufficiently repaired for habitation. The end house, Kurt explained, was occupied by himself, Alexander and Rory. Then came the kitchen; this one next to it, No. 3, was the Fletchers', because it was important those nice little boys should not have too far to go for their meals, this one, No. 4, would be occupied by Mrs. Rossiter and her son, and ah, here we were, No. 5. Their neighbours on the other side would be the Turners. The three beyond were in use as tool-house, barn and byre. "Your new home, ladies," said Kurt with a flourish, and stood aside to let them go in.

There was a little porch, and off it two doors, opening, they found with relief, into two separate rooms. The crofts on Sunay were all of this pattern, except that previous own-

46

ers had put outhouses on to several at the back. "We stuck a bed in each room," said Kurt, as he left them, "but you could put them together if a drawing-room is what you want." "Lord, no——" and "Och, I don't think——" began Mary and Maggie simultaneously, and had each the grace to look slightly embarrassed.

But once inside and alone, it was perfect. It really was; quite perfect. The same square, deep window looking on to the sea, the clean white walls, and one's own bits of things, suddenly and deliciously familiar, welcoming in their very shabbiness. The bed with brass knobs and the white chest of drawers, the rug Mrs. Moffat had knotted herself and the old rocking-chair with the bit of red and white crochet on it—yes, this was her place, with her own personality stamped on it, ready and waiting to reassure her. All she need do was to move the chest and put the bed with its head the other way.

"I say, isn't this jolly?" called Miss Todhunter, and Maggie, taking this as an invitation, peered round the other door and found her standing in inconceivable disorder. A huge double divan (now who did she think was going to share it?) filled a quarter of the floor-space, and a costly cherry-wood bedroom suite took up most of the rest. Clothes, riding-whips, fishing-rods and gum-boots were flung about anywhere, and the dog Lady, observing on the divan a pale blue eiderdown, had ensconced herself in its midst. "Don't think I'll bother to unpack to-night," said the room's owner, gazing round complacently. "I'm in too much of a hurry to see the rest, aren't you?"

"I think I'll be getting a wee bit straight first," replied Maggie, partly because she did in fact feel that it was morally wrong not to set one's house in order, and partly to avoid exploring Sunay in Miss Todhunter's company. It would keep; it could be savoured all the better for a little delay. She returned to her own half of the house, and had hardly got her woollen underclothes into the chest of drawers before the invaluable Kurt reappeared to tell her dinner was ready and to pursue her neighbour up to the byre.

Mrs. Rossiter was already presiding at the head of the table, and doling out stew. Beside her sat Alexander, still, it seemed, with eyes only for her, and he was well hemmed in by faithful Fletchers. Maggie felt grateful for the friendliness of Ronny in keeping her a seat at the opposite end. Kurt Schneider, on her other side, was preparing to devote himself to Mary, who, however, showed him her shoulder, and spent most of the meal disparaging the Sunay cows to the Fletchers, and to Alexander when she could shout loud enough to make him hear.

After a while even Kurt's patience was defeated. He turned to Maggie, and ascertained that her views on fertility and the need to return all waste products to the soil coincided exactly with his own. This was a happy link, and lasted them through a meal which proved to be delicious; for the stew, made from rabbits which he himself had shot and spices added according to some central European recipe by Hermia, was followed by two immense treacle puddings, mixed and boiled by Alexander's own hand. "Not bad for a first effort," he conceded with gentle pride. "But I must say the principle seems to be foolproof. A most interesting chemical reaction."

Cigarettes were lit and chairs pushed back, and the ominous silence fell which suggested that someone was going to make a speech. The last light faded off the sea, and night crept up to the still uncurtained windows.

"Go on, Alexander, pet," said Hermia. "Get it over."

"Well——" began Alexander in his light voice, rocking his chair gently on two legs and fixing his eyes on the table, "well, I don't want to sound pompous, but I suppose that as the nominal owner I ought to say how glad I am you're all safely here, and to make it quite clear that my ownership

48

stops being effective from this moment. We've all put what we had into this——" Maggie's thoughts went guiltily to the teashop, and Mary's face wore a satisfied smirk—"we've all come here to get away from doing jobs we thought silly and being pushed into grooves, and we've all got an equal right to have the say."

"Hear, hear," said somebody, and somebody else added: "What if we say different?"

"Ah yes, quite. There has to be a policy, and I don't suppose the parliamentary system can really be improved on. That's how the old people ran their community here, I believe. Mrs. Rossiter is our historian, perhaps she'll look into it? Meanwhile, I suggest that this hour every day, sitting round this table, becomes our time for deciding what we shall do, both at long range and for the next day's jobs. That all right?"

No one seemed to have any comment, and he was, Maggie guessed, disappointed that it should be left to the yes-man Fletcher to observe:

"For the moment, Alexander, you're the only one who knows the ropes. So hadn't you better dole us out our work?"

"For the moment, perhaps," agreed Alexander reluctantly. "I've a rough policy in my mind, if you approve, but I'm not an expert in any branch. A lot will be left to those who are— the cropping plans and land improvement to Kurt, the stock to Miss Todhunter and Leslie, the vegetables to Miss Moffat, the sheep to Rory and so on. I daresay, when you get around to-morrow, you'll wonder what Rory and I have been doing all these months. Well, we've fenced and we've opened up old drains, and that's about all. We repaired the drystone walls where we could, and put up hundreds of yards of wire fencing. We now have an enclosure big enough to bring at any rate most of the flock down off the mountain for the lambing, like they do in Wales. Rory reckoned last year that he lost nearly half his lambs. We'll hope to do a bit better when the lambing starts at the end of next month. Oh, and, of course, we've sprouted the famous potatoes."

"Them plutty sputs," burst out Rory vindictively.

"Never mind, Rory, it's proud you'll be when they bring in our first money. My notion was, you see, to concentrate this year heavily on the market-gardening side. In this mild climate we can take quick cash crops, early spuds, carrots, lettuces. I've had a talk with McKellar at the Kyle Hotel, and I think he'll take as much as we're likely to produce—anyway, markets won't be the difficulty, the boarding-houses are chronically short of fresh greenstuff. With that and the sheep we'll have our hands full for the next six months. We'll sow a one-year ley for the cows, and go in for silage—not hay, that's a hopeless job with the certainty of a wet autumn. The rest of the crops will be roots, and we can sell any we don't use. Corn looks pretty, I know, but I fail to see any point in trying to grow it up here."

Again no one seemed to have views, and he looked round ruefully, as though afraid he had been boring them; then Ronny asked:

"What about that dam?"

"Oh, the dam." A faint smile crossed Alexander's face. "We've had the sluice-gates and pipes delivered by the *Loch Coruish*—I expect you noticed them stacked down by the jetty. There's a new concrete-mixer with a paraffin engine in the tool-house. McAllister of Glasgow are to send us up a surveyor who will make the plans. But there's no point in his coming till we're free to do the work, and I don't see any of us having time on our hands before August at the earliest."

"Why ever not?"

"Well, you know, crops and stock come first. You can't—er—hold up the spring."

Ronny looked like a small boy deprived of his hop-

50

scotch, and muttered something under his breath about surveyors be damned and his friend in the Sappers.

Mary said in her loud way:

"Talking of stock, are you really satisfied with those two mangy-looking beasties?"

There was a protest from Simon Fletcher. "The two best milkers for sale in Fort William."

"Oh no, hardly satisfied," said Alexander, "but they'll do for a start. They've got into visibly better condition since they were on our grass. Most Highlanders are half-starved."

"Anyway, I'd like to build up a presentable herd."

"So would I, ultimately, but as we can't sell milk off the island, it's not much use going in for cows in a big way till we can process the milk—butter or perhaps cheese. And we can't add dairying to our housekeeper's jobs till we have electric power on tap."

Surely, thought Maggie, she can see that? But apparently she couldn't, for she looked as glum as Ronny; they were only a couple of spoilt bairns. Hermia Fletcher was saying:

"Housekeepers, Mr. Speaker—could we get that settled? I imagine", and she smiled sweetly at Mrs. Rossiter, "we should find it more satisfactory to establish a routine."

"All right, Hermia. The floor is yours."

"Well, my notion is, only two cooked meals a day. That's all you'd get on most farms. There'd be soup at midday, and bread and cheese; beer for those that bring their own bottles from the Kyle."

"Why not fetch a barrel of beer from the Kyle?" suggested Ronny, and to this the beer-drinkers unanimously agreed.

"Then, two women in one kitchen never answer; I'm sure Mrs. Rossiter and Mrs. Turner agree with me. I propose we take the evening meal in turns. Cleaning we'll pool, everyone makes their beds, washing-up by rota. Of course, I've Gavin's lessons to give in the mornings, but I'll fit in my cooking shifts with the other two."

Mrs. Rossiter might have considered that Hermia had brought Gavin on herself, but she made no demur; Mrs. Turner, however, who still seemed unable to raise her voice to conversation pitch, went into a long whispered colloquy with her husband.

"Joyce says——" began Les, turning pink, "—well, Joyce and I haven't been married long, and she's not sure as she could manage on her own. You see, she was a typist, and she's never done much cooking."

"Of course, my dear, we quite understand," said Mrs. Rossiter benevolently. "Mrs. Fletcher and I were brides in our day. We'll take it turn and turn about and you shall help us. I daresay you'll pick up a great deal from watching how we do." Little Joyce did not look as though this were quite the solution she wanted, but she had no courage for further protest.

It occurred to Maggie to wonder what the native thought of all this talk—he who had been the population of Sunay for years on end. She stole a look at him. He still wore the fisherman's cap, which was apparently glued to his dark curls; he was blowing cigarette rings and seemed half asleep. Suddenly his eyes met hers in a turquoise gleam, and one of them winked. This impudence surprised a grin out of Maggie before she could stop herself, rather to her dismay. He need not imagine that because they two were the sole Scots, she, a decent Ayrshire lass, was going to put up with Highland cheek.

"What's the programme for to-morrow?" Simon Fletcher asked.

"Well, I expect you'd all like to muck about on your first day, and spy out the land."

"Surely, Doctor," said Kurt slyly, "you can combine that with some useful task?"

"Kurt, your aim is unerring. I had been thinking that if it's calm, it might be a notion to take the *Carrie* round to the

Camas Ban. It's a fine shell-sand beach on the far side of Torval, and Kurt's hankering after more of it for liming the leys. And you'd get an excellent impression of the island's whole extent. Perhaps you'll take over the milking in the morning, Miss Todhunter? Rory has been doing it, but it's hurt his feelings dreadfully. In the Hebrides it's not considered a job for a man."

"Oh, I've no fancy feelings," replied Mary amiably. "And I don't suppose for a moment he's been milking the poor beasts dry."

"Has anybody else any points they'd like to raise?"

Apparently no one had.

"Well, then," exclaimed Mrs. Rossiter, all brightness, "where are the volunteers for this washing-up? Of *course* not you, Dr. Sarratt; you who have toiled so nobly over this wonderful meal. Ronny will be delighted, I know—Miss Moffat?—and you, Mrs. Turner?—that's right, dear, come along."

"Stow it, Ma," said Ronny sulkily. "Bags I wash."

[IV]

At night it was still cold in the little houses, and when she had finished her unpacking Maggie could not very well sit in her rocking-chair, yet she found herself curiously unwilling to return to the circle round the kitchen fire. She really liked none of them, and then he seemed to like them all so much, and to have no vestige of special feeling for the one who had been his own choice. Besides, that lassie's voice—she couldn't help it, perhaps, poor dear, but a body was glad to get occasionally out of earshot. If only she were not in the next room! Perhaps it could be altered; that was the sort of thing this parliament should be for. Maggie put on her coat, took her torch and let herself out on to the causeway.

53

An immensity of stars assailed her, a great spaciousness of night, the thud of the sea, and somewhere a queer, raucous cry—a shearwater, very likely, didn't they come out at night? A shadowy creature padded up and made her start; but, of course, it was only a dog; not the pampered Lady, but a lean Scottish collie who seemed friendly and kind. He followed her, past the Turners' darkened house, past the barn and tool-house, to the byre.

The sweet, familiar smell of cows' breath was in itself a welcome. They were munching quietly in their stalls, and turned their heads to blink at the torch. Maggie knew little about cows, but they looked to her nice beasts, and the curly horns were most becoming. Piles of half-wrapped sacking parcels filled the empty stalls, and poking out of one of them were the handles of her own garden tools.

On an impulse she pulled out the digging fork, and thought how pleasant it was to have it in her hands again, and how shamefully soft those hands had grown. She would be having blisters to-morrow. She left the byre, the dog still padding after her, and made her way into the nettle-deep garden. Propping up the torch on the wall so that it shone on to the ground, she drove in the fork, pulled hard against the nettle-roots and brought up the first sod. It felt like loam, and contained no stones, and the fork did not touch bottom.

Warm lantern-light drowned the cold little light of the torch, and she straightened at the sound of his chuckle.

"You're never digging?"

Maggie blinked up at the lantern like a sheepish child. "I thought", she remarked distantly, "that I was unobserved."

"You'll find this is an anything but private island. Well, how does it seem?"

"It's over-dark to tell, but I like the way yon fork goes in —seems to go down for ever. I'm thinking I'll not be on your boating trip in the morning."

54

"I never expected for a moment that you would be. Look, come this way. I want to show you something. It feels like my turn to get a little praise."

He led her back to the barn, the collie loping ahead of them, and unlocked the door. "I've kept it locked in case anyone barged in and lowered the temperature. You see how I cling to your lightest word." An oil-stove sent out the ruby glow of its kind, and by its light she saw, ranged on roughly constructed shelves, the dozens of chitting-boxes, the potatoes showing their little bald heads, and here and there, already, a fat purple sprout.

"And only the two of ye!" said Maggie, really moved. "It's a job that took three of us lassies a whole week at MacDougal's. Ye've done well indeed."

"I don't know about two," corrected Alexander, swinging himself on to the seat of a seed-drill and stretching his feet to the stove. "Rory helped me with the boxes, he adores mucking about with his precious driftwood, but he only did two evenings' work on the spuds. And only that because I held his wayward interest with my stock lecture on nuclear physics, which for someone with no mathematical training he followed uncommonly well, I must say. But I never got another hand's turn out of him. That's the Hebridean temperament. They're natural gentlemen. They don't mind poverty, but they won't be bored."

"You'll not have much control over him, maybe?" hazarded Maggie.

"I have not, indeed. On the other hand, as you will have guessed, he is at the moment vital to me. He's the only one of us who knows the job."

"That'll no' last. I know my bit of it, and that young Turner——"

"A likely lad, but this isn't a Midland farm. Rory knows the sheep, and the lie of the land, and the Sound—they're queer seas round here, you can't judge from your passage

55

this afternoon. It will take us six months to be independent of him."

"And ye dinna altogether trust him?"

"Well—I don't know what makes him tick. He's probably a bit of a rascal—but an engaging rascal, and the best company in the world. We were two months shut up here together, and never a dull moment. The essential is to hold his interest. I must give him a good share of the tractoring, which is absurd—any fool could sit on his behind on that thing. But it's a new toy to him. Well, now, about you. Are you glad you came?"

"Yes, terrible glad." The glow in her voice made him smile. "It's the bonniest place I ever was in. I wish it was the morning."

"Well, it soon will be. And your wee house—that all right?"

"That's just fine." Now was the moment to complain about Mary. But she couldn't do it, not to him, and he so pleased with his arrangements. Besides, what others could he make? As she hesitated, he murmured ruefully:

"Pity about that girl's voice, isn't it?"

Maggie was at once startled and comforted by this sign of human weakness.

"Maybe we'll get used to it. I'd have thought ye'd no' notice, being English yourself."

"No more I ought to. This is a poor do, criticizing new-found comrades behind their backs. But she might just as well have had a nice Lancashire accent. They will send girls to these awful schools."

"How are ye off for the cash?" Maggie asked; her sequence of thought did not escape him. "Did ye get enough?"

"Oh, I should say we'd adequate working capital. We can't expect to see any real return on it for twelve months. I trust everyone's patience holds out that long." His long fingers rapped nervously on the bar of the seed-drill, and he suddenly looked dispirited and bored.

"But of course it will!" cried Maggie stoutly. "We're all here for life. I knew the moment I set foot on Sunay that I was going to bide, and I'll bet you the others felt the same."

"Maggie, you do me good." It was the first time he had called any of the newcomers by their Christian names, as she was well aware. "Come along now, you ought to be in bed. Don't farmers go to bed at nine? Here, Bob." The collie abandoned the quest of imaginary mice in corners, and followed them out.

"Your dog?"

"Rory's. That's another of his advantages, he's the only one that can work a dog. I'm to have a pup from a man at the Kyle next week, and Bob will help me train it. But I hope that bitch of Miss Todhunter's is as good as she looks. We need half a dozen dogs, really, for gathering an island this size." Candle-light showed as they passed the Turners' cottage. "That's a gladdening sight," he said. "You can't think what a sensation it gives me to see the place inhabited."

"They don't say when they got married," smiled Maggie, pausing at her own door, "but I've a feeling they're on their honeymoon."

"No?—how too idyllic. I do hope they have kids. That would be a valid note of confidence in Sunay. In fact, come to think of it, till that happens we're all strangers here. I'd like to see a whole lot of marrying and begetting."

"You must leave that to Providence," said Maggie, slightly shocked.

"Don't count your lovers before they're matched, h'm? Very wise. I must say I never thought I'd anything in me of the matchmaker, but once one starts interfering with people's lives it's hard to stop. Sure you aren't coming back to the fire? All right, then, good night."

"Good night, Doctor," said Maggie sedately. For the life

of her she couldn't yet call him Alexander, and she owed him one Doctor, anyway. She heard him chuckle and swing off, whistling, into the darkness, the dog at his heels.

For a while she did not light the candle, but sat at the window in her rocking-chair, thinking over what she had heard. That his whole being was in some way bound up with the success of Sunay, she now divined. They all wanted to make a go of it, of course, but his feeling was almost frantic. Well, it was his place and his idea, and folks were naturally keenest on ideas that were their own. If she were to help him—and she badly wanted to help him—she could best do it, not by sentimental longings, but by resolutely liking her fellow-islanders, even if some did seem la-di-da, and others interfering, and yet others loud-voiced. She remembered the frequent admonishment of her mother, that apostle of forbearance and good sense. "Ye're a good lass, Maggie," would say Mrs. Moffat, "but ye're awfu' censorious. That's no' going to bring ye happiness. And though ye may try to keep your opinions to yourself, folks are bound to find them out." That had been—she acknowledged it now in all honesty—the trouble between herself and Jeanie's husband. It should not happen here.

Peace descended on her as she sat gently rocking, and listening to the rhythmic lapping of the waves fifty yards below her in the darkness. Naturally they hadn't started off well, all crowded together, asserting themselves and making a noise. But on Sunay there was space and scope for all; there was beauty all round them, work crying out to be done, and what more could anyone ask? Even within doors there was space, for here she sat in this cosy wee room, all her own to do with as she pleased; what luxury it would have seemed to the teeming crofter families that must have bred and died here! And warm under all her thoughts lay Alexander; not the lover, certainly, that nonsense was ended, but the confidant, the chosen friend.

She had been half an hour in bed, reading *Catriona* by candle-light to make herself feel yet more at home, when Mary Todhunter and Lady came bounding down the causeway, and with a perfunctory bang on the door precipitated themselves into the room.

"Here—I saw your light and I thought you might like this," and she held out a rubber hot-water bottle.

"Well, if that isn't kind!" exclaimed Maggie, whose feet, although encased in pink woollen bedsocks, were in point of fact cold. "Are ye sure ye can spare it?"

"Oh yes, I've got another. I'm a two-bottle woman when it's really freezing."

It was reassuring that Amazons should have cold feet; most likely they had golden hearts as well. "Do stop a minute," invited Maggie, aware that she had many hard feelings to atone for.

"Oh—all right." Miss Todhunter flung herself into the rocking-chair, and gathered up Lady into her arms. "I say," she added, her glowing face close against the dog's silky one, "isn't he marvellous?"

"Who would ye be meaning?" inquired Maggie, assailed by new and unpleasant suspicions.

"Oh, come off it! Or are you really such a prim little Scotchy that you don't see the difference between one chap and another?"

Now she doesn't know that she's offensive, Maggie reminded herself, so just you be pleasant. Aloud she observed: "I've hardly had time to get acquainted yet, but they all seem nice enough lads to me."

"D'you honestly think so? I'm sure I don't. I never met anything wetter than Ma's boy, and the Fletcher chap seems to do as he's told, and as for the Yid—ugh, I can't stand Yids. Never could."

"That's no way to talk," said Maggie indignantly, "and him so obliging, particularly to you."

"Oh, they're all like that. Smarmy. Try to get into bed with you next." Her anti-Semitism, Maggie perceived, was as idle and frivolous as the rest of her, and her thoughts returned instantly to the matter nearest her heart. "But didn't you think he looked a poppet when he was making us that jaw after dinner? So shy, and sort of fed up? If I'd been sitting next to him instead of the old trout, I'd have hugged him on the spot." Maggie could think of no useful comment, but none was needed, for after a little smiling meditation she went on: "Would you say I hurt his feelings over the cows? I know I speak out of turn sometimes, and of course I really did see his point."

"I'm sure your wish to build up a herd must be verra gratifying to him," said Maggie.

"You are a funny little Scotchy, aren't you? Never give anything away. That's the national character, I suppose, ha-ha. Well, come on, old girl, we'd better get some sleep. I say, aren't you tidy? I haven't begun to get straight yet. If you like you can give me a hand to-morrow. Oh well, s'long."

She banged away, and for ten minutes more could be heard thrashing round her room. Then peace again descended on No. 5 Sunay. Maggie pulled the bedclothes over her head.

So Alexander was a universal taste. Shared with Miss Todhunter, her previous feelings seemed more mortifying than ever. What a blethering great girl she was—but all the same, and especially by candle-light, what a lovely face.

Far into the darkness, a sea-bird called. And after that, silence.

Chapter Three

[I]

On her first day at Sunay, Mary Todhunter was up betimes. Woken up at 6.30 by a ferocious alarm which also deprived her house-mate of further sleep, she climbed into her breeches and went off in the dark to the milking. But when she reached the kitchen with her pail, Mrs. Rossiter was already in command, moving in her deliberate way about the preparation of a breakfast which would show the menfolk how much they had been missing a truly motherly woman's care.

Mrs. Rossiter had not, perhaps, expected that Mary would be the first recipient of her early-morning tea, but she was all affability. She had always prided herself on having no favourites.

Maggie, too excited to lie in bed, ran out to survey the ground. By daylight the garden piece looked smaller, but with careful cropping it would grow a lot of stuff. The spit she had turned in the dark was magnificent—like black chocolate cake. Rejoicing, she made her way to the gate in the farther wall, and out into the fields.

They were green, these wire-fenced strips of Alexander's, except where the plough had been at work on the potato-field, but they were pitifully small. Nor, except by comparison with the moorland wall which rose abruptly behind them, were they even flat. Rocks outcropped ominously here and there, and bracken, entrenched among them, made sallies into the better ground. Two streams came noisily down white rocky beds, one the child of the waterfall and presently to be dammed, the other, which had been led into a tank above the cottages, the source of their own simple plumbing. The lower course of both streams was marked by growths of rushes. There was certainly an immense deal of work to be done; but on the other hand the wire fencing, though it lacked the charm of stone walls, already gave the place the look of being a farm and helped one to imagine crops in the little fields. The two cows browsed along the stream-banks and lent an air of well-being to the scene.

"Do you admire my compost pits?" inquired Kurt Schneider, coming up beside her sunnily, and indicating twin square chasms. "There you see the basis of our entire economy. Myself I dug them, though you will understand that digging pits has not till now been my line. Each took a day, and I find myself still stiff in the shoulders."

"They certainly should hold a lot."

"Strategically placed, too, don't you agree? Equally convenient for your garden rubbish and the rest of our waste products." His gesture included the six wooden cabinets which nestled decently beneath the garden wall. "We can't cheat Nature with a dud penny. What we take from her we must return. In politics I am a Socialist, but in farming, a fierce Conservative." He outlined his plans for composting seaweed, rushes, bracken even. Maggie listened politely. She was far from sharing Mary's aversion to his race, but she did consider that they were sometimes a little tedious in their belief that no one else could ever have had the same idea.

Alexander and Rory were last at breakfast, though one had somehow expected them to be up before dawn. Both were unsociable and preoccupied. The Fletcher children, on the other hand, had got over their shyness and were all too much in evidence. Gavin argued, and Jamie threw his porridge about. Their mother looked on with a detached smile, as though their making nuisances of themselves did not concern her, and it was Mrs. Rossiter who finally decreed that unless they ate their breakfasts they should not go in the boat. It was hardly her business to discipline other people's children, but her methods undoubtedly brought results.

There were two boats at Sunay, the elegant *Gannet*, bought and named by Alexander, and the *Carrie*, taken over by him from the Department, which had originally supplied it in a nameless state for Rory's use. It was therefore still referred to as Rory's boat, and in fact used by him whenever the mood took him, though it was no more his property than anything else on the island. He had chosen the name because he liked it; that it furnished Ronny with material for more puns was just a fortunate coincidence. For dirty work, like ferrying sheep or sand, the *Carrie* was always used. She seldom made the trip to the Kyle because of her slow speed.

Maggie, impatient to get to her ground, and also obscurely unwilling to watch the merry boat-party embark, took herself off after breakfast to the nettles. Honing her little scythe, because it was a long time since she had used it and a cut thumb at this stage would never do, she set about her, nervously at first, and then with gathering confidence as the swing of it came back. Down went the spring-green ranks, every now and then making a vicious bite at her bare hands; an hour passed and they were low, and the *Carrie* had chugged away out of the bay without her being aware. She fetched her rake and Alexander's rattling new wheelbarrow, and laid the enemy in careful layers on the compost heap.

Getting up nettle roots is spectacularly easy if there is no grass to protect them, and on the Sunay garden piece they were well-nigh solid. Up came the bright yellow threads with an elastic, silky pull, leaving behind a black loam which generations of nettle-leaves had enriched since the last of the old folk went away. Up, too, came queerly pitiful little relics: the fossilized mutton-bones of dead dinners, bits of blue-and-white china plates, a teaspoon black with rust, a wheel that might have come off a child's toy, and the inevitable tins that told the wreck of prosperous feeding in the Hebrides. The most considerable of these exhibits Maggie laid in a row on the wall, in case they should appeal to the Sunay historian, though it seemed probable that a cairngorm or a dirk would have been more to Mrs. Rossiter's taste.

Overhead a lark sang, equally to her pleasure and surprise, for she had not expected to find the common field birds on an island. She looked about instinctively for the robin, and sure enough, there he was on the wall, head cocked at this provider of unexpected dinners. The sun had the balminess which never seems so exquisitely welcome as in mid-March, when the winter is behind and the upturned soil takes its first breath. The space of dark brown grew steadily in front of her, and she sank into the mindless pleasure of digging, most profoundly satisfying of all human operations, which seems to link the spirit with forces infinitely potent and with ancestors infinitely remote. Each forkful as it went over supplied new wonders. You never knew what you might find.

Finally the strain on her shoulders made her pause. It was daft to go on like that on a first day, though maddening to stop. Anyway, she ought to get the seed-bed ready. She leant on her fork and contemplated the houses, thinking how pleasant they looked even from this back or lean-to aspect, for no one lean-to resembled another in angle or size, so that the symmetry of the crescent seen from the shore was replaced by a patchwork of felted roofs and one-pane windows. The wall of No. 5, she noted, had space enough to take the peach which had been Mr. MacDougal's house-warming present, and which even now, released from the straw dolly, was recovering in a bucket of water on the causeway. From the kitchen chimney came a charming blue thread of smoke, and as she watched, the pretty little figure of Joyce Turner, in a flowered smock and holding up her hand against the sun,

64

emerged from the pantry door to give the scene the animating touch of life.

Forgetting her, Maggie turned to her ground again, and five full minutes must have passed before a flat little London voice remarked: "My, you do work hard."

It was the first time anyone had heard her speak, and Maggie, straightening—she really was absurdly stiff—looked at her with interest. They were of a height, but where Maggie was sturdy, ruddy and smiling, Joyce was slender to vanishing point, with a milky skin that looked as though it would blister at the first touch of the sun, pale hair built up elaborately over her forehead, and on her face, now that fear had left it, an expression which was unexpectedly discontented.

"Have ye never done any gardening?" asked Maggie kindly, for something to say.

"Oh, no. I don't think I'd like it. Makes your hands dirty, doesn't it? I do like to keep my hands nice." And indeed her hands were pretty, with cyclamen-painted nails; she looked at Maggie's grimy ones with frank distaste.

"Och, it's clean dirt," said Maggie cheerfully. "It washes off. Ye didna' go with them in yon boat?"

"No. I was afraid I'd be sick again. And they said—I mean, it's my turn to help with the dinner. We're to have it ready when they get back."

"You and Mrs. Rossiter are cooking something good, I'll be bound."

"I dunno," said Joyce listlessly. "Mrs. Rossiter's doing it. I just scrubbed potatoes and things." She suddenly seemed determined on confidence. "I must say, it isn't quite what I'd expected."

"Is it not? In what way?"

"Well, I thought I'd just be looking after Les. That's what most married women do, isn't it? Look after their hubbies, I mean. I know we've got our own little house, and that's ever so nice; I do like it awfully, I'm not complaining

E   65

about that, don't think I am. But I don't quite see why——"

"Och, well——" Maggie cast about her. "I think the notion is that by living in a community, for a wee while at any rate, and having our meals together, we'll save ourselves time for a lot of other work."

"Oh, I see," said Joyce, obviously not seeing. "It doesn't seem to save me any time," she added unanswerably.

"And was the idea not that ye were to learn from Mrs. Rossiter——?"

"Yes, I daresay. I'm sure she's ever so kind. I know I'm not much of a hand at cooking. But if I had a kitchen in our house I'm sure I could cook well enough just for Les and me."

Maggie was conscious of a certain pity for this unin-structed child. The idea had certainly been that she would learn from Mrs. Rossiter, but whose idea precisely? Not Joyce's, that was plain.

"It does seem a bit hard not to have your own kitchen," she conceded. "Why do ye not ask Dr. Sarratt about it? Maybe he'd put you in a wee oil-stove and a sink." But Joyce did not seem to think it possible that she should speak to Dr. Sarratt. To her the gentle Alexander was even more than Mrs. Rossiter an object of alarm.

"There's other things too that's not what I expected," she was pursuing. "I thought—well——" The colour came flooding under her transparent skin. "I thought we'd have a proper W.C. I mean to say, all that down the garden. It's not very nice, is it? If you see what I mean."

Maggie stared. "Have ye never lived in the country before?"

"Well, I did when I was a vakky. That's how I met Les, you know, when I was a vakky. My home's in Clapham really, but our school was sent to Bedfordshire, and that's how I got to know Les. We were engaged ever so long. When I was living there we used to go down the garden, but

66

it didn't seem to matter so much, not when I was still a kid. But I didn't really like it, not even then."

This complete non-comprehension of what life in the Western Isles was likely to entail fairly staggered Maggie. Les seemed intelligent; why hadn't he explained? Probably he was quite unaware of having left her far behind. He would have told her that there would be a house, and for the betrothed that would be enough. But not, apparently, for the wife.

"Now see," she said gently, "folks everywhere aye have to put up with a bit less than they'd like. Coming here made it possible for you to get married, didn't it? You'd have had to wait a long time, maybe years, before you got a house in Clapham. And you'd not have liked living with in-laws."

"No," said Joyce dimly, but her tone suggested that Mrs. Rossiter was nearly as bad.

"As for those—those places, ye'll soon get used to them. They're all right if they're kept clean. And we lassies don't have to do that. The men are taking it in turns to clear them out every day."

"Will Les have to?"

"Yes, and not mind a bit. If he's a village lad he'll have been doing it all his life." She refrained from adding details of Kurt's fertility-conservation cycle; that might put the poor bairn off her feed altogether. "Come on now, cheer up. Life here will be no' so bad. And my, don't I wish I were in your place, with a handsome laddie to share my croft and maybe a bairn of my own before long!"

Joyce blushed, but she also looked pleased, till the faintly aggravated voice of Mrs. Rossiter, wanting to know if they were not hungry, brought back the badgered expression to her face. "I was really sent to tell you to come in," she murmured, and Maggie, already a confederate, murmured back: "I'll tell her it was my fault keeping you chatting."

The kitchen, with only the three of them in it, looked

67

sunny and spacious, and on the table stood a brown pot of coffee and a cheese soufflé in an earthenware dish.

"But I thought", remonstrated Maggie, "that there was to be no cooking in the mornings?"

"Not in the ordinary way," smiled Mrs. Rossiter, "but this is our first day and calls for a little celebration. Besides, my dear, we have so admired the way you stayed behind to work while the others went off to enjoy themselves. That is the spirit which will make our venture a success. And then, I have a special weakness for land-girls. You know I ran a Land Army hostel in the war?"

"Did ye now?" said Maggie, her mouth full of cheese. "From what I've seen of land girls' appetites ye must have had a tidy lot of work."

"Well, so I did, but it was happy work, very happy and rewarding. We were just one family. Old Mother Riley, the girls used to call me, and they came and told me all their troubles, just as Ronny always has. Young people have always given me their confidence, and I hope——" she smiled encouragingly at them both—"I hope they always will." And it dawned on Maggie, whose day for being astounded this certainly was, that Mrs. Rossiter did indeed believe that her son confided in her, and thought his manners affectionate and right. Well, perhaps he did when they were alone; maybe it was with no one by. Maybe.

But having no immediate troubles, or at any rate none that required confiding, she escaped presently to the seed-bed, leaving Joyce to bear the weight of Mrs. Rossiter's encouragement alone. Under the rake, the clods broke down to a heart-warming tilth. By rights it should have a few days to settle, but here there was not time. Treading, raking, scattering the ashes saved from months of driftwood fires, pressing under boards and raking again, she worked through the afternoon. The seeds spilled out of their green packets, round brassicas that fell trippingly between forefinger and thumb, feckless featherweight lettuce that would never space evenly, gritty parsley and oily black leek. The drills were closed over, labelled, raked again. The *Carrie* chugged back into the bay, and Hermia's little boys pattered up the jetty, their voices fractious with the fatigue of a picnic's end. But with them were only two men. One got out the tractor, a smart new Fordson, and attached it to a sled. On this the sacks of white sand were bumped up the hill and left in heaps on the strip of ploughed land, later to be harrowed in. As the first load came up, Maggie could see that the men were Les and Rory Mor.

"Where's the rest?" she called.

"The Toctor is bringing them home over Torval," Rory explained. "They will be having a very pretty view."

A jealous pang smote Maggie hard. Then she told herself that she could not have spent a more satisfying day, and that she had a very pretty view from where she was. And maybe, one day, Alexander would take her up Torval by herself.

When the tractoring was finished Les reappeared, having got himself a fork from the byre, and without comment set to work. Maggie knew enough about farm labourers to be aware that digging was no treat to them; she was grateful, and said so.

"Well, it's for us all, I reckon," answered Les curtly; she felt snubbed, but recognized the spirit Mrs. Rossiter had been kind enough to commend in herself. They worked side by side in companionable silence, and the shadow of Torval crept towards them over the brown moor and the little emerald fields. Then were heard distant brays of triumphal laughter, and presently Miss Todhunter, her hair a halo and her Grecian nose just caught by the day-long sun, came pounding down the hill.

"You ought to have been with us," she told Maggie, leaning on the wall and looking over the garden without in the least noticing the changes made in it. "You've missed

69

something terrific. I can't tell you what it's like up there. We could see for ever—St. Kilda and all. And a super climb—two gorgeous ridges—must be a thousand feet of clear drop on the north side and the other's airy enough. No, I'm never giddy, and besides, I'd follow Alexander anywhere. He roped us at the tough bits. You've no idea how marvellous he looks climbing. Gosh, I could eat an ox. I hope the old trout has been doing her stuff." And off she went, leaving Maggie with a strangely sore heart.

Next in the procession came Kurt and Ronny, who also commiserated with her in not having shared their unique experience. "Though I'm sure Zandl will be delighted to take you some other time," added Kurt considerately.

"I don't mind admitting I was scared stiff," said Ronny. "It's not difficult really—the worst is a ticklish drop on this side of the ridge—but it looks the devil of a long way if you fell off. Rule Britannia stood it a lot better than I did. That sort has no nerves." He added as an afterthought: "I will say for old Sarratt, in spite of all the ballyhoo, he seems a decent sort of bloke."

Och, deary me, thought Maggie, grinning after him. Apparently no one, positively no one, was proof against the Sarratt charm.

The rear was brought up by Alexander and Simon, travelling at the peaceable pace of experienced mountaineers. They too rested their elbows on the wall. "My good Simon," said Alexander, "cast an eye over that. Look what's happened to our nettles."

"She hasn't done it all by herself?"

"Och, no, Les has helped me," protested Maggie, going pink. "He'll have been here quite half an hour syne."

"She's been sowing, too. Look at the little white labels—doesn't it seem civilized? What seeds would they be?"

"Only the brassicas. It's important to get them in early, ye ken."

"You must think us absurdly frivolous, wasting half our day while you make this transformation?" said Simon Fletcher with a smile.

"Indeed I wish I'd been with you. Mary says ye saw St. Kilda. That must have been fine."

"I wish we'd had the field-glasses," said Alexander, smiling at her in his turn.

"Ye mean, ye're not sure it was St. Kilda?"

"I mean, I think we could have sat on top of Torval and watched you, bringing this garden back to life."

They turned away and went down the hill, and she stood staring after them through the level evening sunshine, while her heart filled with a gratification deep as tears.

[II]

That was the last holiday anyone took on Sunay for a long time.

March, a busy month on any farm, was desperate on this virtually unmade one. Each evening at parliament Alexander outlined the work; each following day they struggled to keep up with it, and when darkness fell withdrew honourably defeated. Shoulder muscles became red-hot and hands first blistered and then hardened, but nobody had time to think, to regret, to speculate, scarcely even time to dislike. Intense physical activity, in a balmy spring and exquisite surroundings of sea and hills, was for the moment sufficiently absorbing. Overhead the larks sang their hearts out, the great black-backed and herring gulls wheeled down from their nesting-places on the islet, and at evening a pair of gannets, whiter and more beautiful than swans, would cross the zenith slowly, sailing on their majestic way back to St. Kilda. But one scarcely had time to listen or to look.

Operation Spud, as Ronny encouraged himself by calling it, was through at the month's end; seaweed dragged up by the ton from the shore and ploughed in, slag scattered on days alleged to be windless—but no day at Sunay was ever really windless, and the grey stuff got chokingly into one's eyes and nose—the clods harrowed to a tilth, the potatoes planted; hours of back-breaking work. Then it was all to do again for the half-acre of carrots, which Maggie undertook to sow by hand; and they needed a dressing of potash, so that little Joyce spent hours kelp-burning on the beach.

Mrs. Rossiter's hens arrived, with their coops battered by the journey and needing evenings of carpentry; and Les, catching the prevailing stock-hunger, began to talk of pigs and to take lessons in dry-stone walling from Rory, so that he could presently build an enclosure. The other new arrivals were the collie pup for Alexander, a starved-looking black object that cringed when one went near it, and a diminutive pony successfully demanded by Mary, who was able to point out that the tractor was being overworked in all sorts of minor jobs simply for the pleasure the men took in driving it. Peigi looked a toy, but she had a brave heart, and could pull the sled or wear the creels as well as any pony in Scotland. She could also give rides to small boys.

It was about this that Mrs. Rossiter felt it her duty to speak to Alexander.

"You see, my dear boy, Mary wouldn't like it thought that she was spoiling the children's pleasure, but Mrs. Fletcher is really inconsiderate. The seaweed must come first, mustn't it? So I thought that a word from you——"

"I agree about the seaweed, Mrs. R., but speaking to people isn't for me to do. That's what parliament is for. How are the chickens settling in?"

Mrs. Rossiter sighed; a gift of leadership was, in her opinion, something to be used, like other gifts. Alexander's was an almost perfect character, but, by reason of its very scrupulousness, not always quite helpful. Nor was it the first time this facet had been revealed, for Ronny, in her hearing, had demanded: "Couldn't you tick Kurt off about the filthy way he always leaves that tractor?" and Alexander, less mellifluous than towards herself, had answered shortly: "I could not."

This parliament idea—this airing of grievances in front of everybody—Mrs. Rossiter asked herself if it was wise. Alexander was brilliant, but he was young, a scientist, a dreamy creature remote from realities. Her experience was at his service, to warn him that a word here, a hint there, could often set things right when public recrimination only made them worse. Determined though she was not to put herself forward, she nevertheless, if he felt diffident about it, was willing to drop such words and hints; from an older person they might be more easily received. So far he had not seen her point of view; but, the dear boy, he would learn.

Meanwhile, it had to be admitted that the nightly sessions usually resolved themselves into Alexander proposing, with charming hesitation, what was to be done, and everyone else being in accord. Except for Mary's pony, nothing of moment had yet been initiated by the rest. And every evening he looked disappointed.

For the rest of the day he merely looked sleepy, and possibly was, for he found it equally hard to get up and to go to bed, his mind reaching its liveliest when the others, exhausted by twelve hours of toil, were drifting irresistibly towards their cottages. He worked harder than anyone—well, as Ronny pointed out, it was his island and he had the advantage of two months' training—but he seemed to be working in a sort of dream. If one spoke to him his answer was perfectly rational, but his mind had to come back from a distance. A strange and most interesting boy, pronounced Mrs. Rossiter, who loved to discuss him and for that subject at any rate could usually find an audience. A gifted creature, and, like so many gifted creatures, living at a high state of

73

tension. Rare indeed would be the privilege of helping such a one to find peace.

[III]

Kurt Schneider had two major interests, land reclamation and sex.

He was thus solidly rooted in the basic realities, and had achieved an integration about which he was anxious not to grow smug. Fortunate in his own temperament, he was always at the disposal of anyone not so comfortably placed.

It was his passion for reclaiming land which had given him the notion of emigrating to Palestine. He was no Zionist, but one dedicated to the adventure of making deserts blossom, and of disproving the common error that Jews cannot farm. Look, he was for ever telling his English friends, look at what our agricultural settlements have already done in Palestine. He had not been there, but he had seen many documentary films, in which apples and oranges swelled to fill the entire screen, and he spoke on the subject with authority.

It was this passion likewise which had brought him to Sunay. When, bitterly baulked of Palestine, he had seen Alexander's advertisement, a whole new scheme of life seemed to open out before his eyes. Here, in these immense tracts of underpopulated and potentially fertile Scottish country, here might be all the scope that Jewish initiative and enterprise needed, with none of the political unrest and boring religious fanaticism which life in Palestine would have entailed. Kurt's father in Vienna had been a practising Jew, but he himself considered it quite the dreariest of all religions.

Overnight, from despair he switched to excited anticipation, and from Hanbury Brown on Irrigation to Stapledon on Grassland Improvement. He had no capital, but the Aryans would provide that; and then, when most of them

74

had got tired and given up, as middle-class intellectual Aryans could be relied on to do, then he would summon this friend and that, with their families or their girls, and in the west there would arise the nucleus of another Promised Land.

Such, in its outline, was Kurt's plan, for the furtherance of which he was prepared to work himself to skin and bone, and do without Ilse, possibly without any woman, for one of the best years of his life.

The smiling patience with which he endured the insults of Mary Todhunter might astonish the others, but Kurt himself thought their astonishment ingenuous. None of them, except perhaps Alexander and Hermia, seemed to have the most rudimentary psychological notions. Upon Hermia, partly because she collected the mail, it did after a time dawn that he must have a girl of his own. The regularity of fat envelopes addressed in a fine German hand, and the expression of lazy contentment on his face as he opened them, at length attracted her notice. "What's she like, Kurt?" she asked him one day when he happened to be the only one meeting the boat; and Kurt, having quite automatically answered: "Beautiful, darling, rather like you, don't give me away, will you?" began to consider the question within himself.

She was not beautiful, that was certain, not in the least like Hermia and not in the same street with the Aryan goddess. She was small, sallow and volatile, and with Englishmen she tended to exaggerate her vivacity wildly because that was what they expected. Sometimes it would set his teeth on edge when she switched on what she called "my famous Fiennese tscharm". Her letters were immense, often amusing, always desolate and passionate. Answering them adequately was sometimes an effort at the end of a long day's sweat. Ilse never knew what it was to be tired, and as she held an easy and intellectually stimulating job as secretary to a professor at the London School of Economics, she had seldom cause to be. In bed she was extremely competent, having grasped the importance of the art and studied it accordingly. Compared with some of the English girls he had fancied, she really was not very well bred. But Kurt forgave her all her faults, because she loved him so completely, and, when he gave the word, would be ready to follow him to the ends of the earth. Like so many Viennese girls, she had a passion for tight and brightly coloured jumpers, and he sometimes caught himself thinking, without disloyalty and purely in a spirit of abstract comment, that it was a pity she had not Mary Todhunter's breasts.

That she deserved him, and that he would marry her as soon as the Sunay project became financially secure and one of the crofts fell vacant, admitted of no question. In the meantime, technical infidelities were neither here nor there. But anyone who imagined he would find continence impossible underestimated him. He reckoned to be an artist, and all art benefits by practice, but he was prepared to let it lie fallow unless its exercise should prove of definite benefit to a fellow-creature. He had made it his business to know himself, and could safely swear that he was animated by none but unselfish motives in laying siege to Mary.

The poor girl wanted a lover. Nobody, he supposed, was going to controvert that. It stuck out a mile. Loud, assertive, insecure, she was unsatisfied to a degree which made her practically a page from a psychologist's case-book. It was for this reason that he did not mind her anti-Semitism, which struck him as merely pathetic and childish; and no one was quicker than he to recognize the real thing. Once in bed with a handsome Jew, she would conveniently forget that he was of the same race as the fat and greasy ones.

Should an eligible lover present himself, Kurt would be the last to stand in her way. He thought her a fine girl, a type to breed from, and was only sorry to see nobody doing it.

He had actually cast his eye round the populace and fixed on someone who might suit. But at present there was no sign of interest in that quarter, as indeed, with her outrageous manners, how should there be? An affair with himself, conducted with discretion and leaving no results—he would see to that, he would take care of everything—might be to her of inestimable advantage. Her body was pure beauty; he would teach her the rest. This was the entertaining scheme he proposed to himself to while away any moment of leisure. So far, no moment of leisure ever seemed to arrive.

At that, hers was not the only problem on Sunay to which his temperament and his studies in the Viennese school of psychology gave him a clue. Planting potatoes was an odd occupation for a person of intelligence—they were at work in a group of three, Ronny dibbling the holes along the drill, Maggie dropping in the seed and himself closing them over with the rake—but it was enlivened when Ronny suddenly and with uncontrollable passion broke out:

"Gosh, didn't my Ma make an ass of herself last night! All that blah to Alexander about how to listen to a fugue. I bet he's forgotten more about fugues than she ever thought there was to know. If only she'd sometimes hold her tongue."

Little Scotch Maggie had turned pink. This was going to have repercussions. Kurt cocked an amused eye.

"Ye ken—that a lot of us like you, Ronny?" she was beginning, while with infinite care she eliminated all the eyes on the current potato. "And that we do see sometimes, maybe, how it is you and your mother don't quite get on?"

"I bet you don't see half," growled Ronny, still absorbed in his own grievance.

"And that being so," pursued little Scotchy—poor child, it was killing her to have to do it—"you won't mind my saying, Ronny, that indeed you should not be talking of your mother in that way? It is no' right. It's no' right to talk that

77

way of any older person—I can't explain, but ye'll know what I mean when ye're old yourself—and of your own mother least of a'. And besides a' that, it's so awkward for the rest of us. We dinna", finished Maggie, now quite chokingly Scots—"we dinna know just where to look."

The appeal in her voice was useless; Ronny's face was like the north-east wind. It was plainly time for Kurt and his clue to intervene.

"Tell me, Ronald," he began, in that detached and friendly tone with which it was impossible for anyone to quarrel, "why did you bring her with you?"

"Why did I bring her?" Ronny rammed in the dibber, threw back his head and laughed. "God, that's rich! Just tell me how I could leave her behind."

"You did not expect, then——"

"No, you ass, of course I didn't. I knew she was hankering to make a cosy little home for me, and that it'd be hard to shake her off if I got an ordinary farm—for don't you see, Pa left her his all, and so I'm dependent on her for capital. That's why I jumped at this. I didn't think she'd seriously consider coming too, and if she did, I made certain that whoever had the choosing would choke her off. How was I to imagine that Alexander would have the cracked idea of—what does he call it?—balancing the community with poor old Ma? When I found what had happened I pretty nearly backed out, I can tell you that. I would have, only it seemed awkward at that stage. Besides, I thought Sunay sounded rather jolly. So it is, come to that. I don't want to give up now. What I'm hoping for is that eventually she'll get fed up and go off of her own accord."

"If ye knew what it means to lose a mother——" said poor little Scotchy with tears in her eyes.

"Look here, Magsy, I'm sorry if I've hurt your feelings. Really I am. I daresay I'd have liked your mother. I'm sure she suited you down to the ground."

78

"'There is certainly", pronounced Kurt, "a lot of false sentiment obtruding into any discussion of blood relationships."

"You're telling me," grunted Ronny; but he started on the row again, looking slighty cheered. "Anyway," he added presently, "this balanced-community idea is screwy. Ma's not a balance, she's only a dead weight. There ought to be a nice elderly bloke to balance her. Though if there was, I expect he'd spend most of his time looking at Mary's legs."

"Perhaps", continued Kurt, "your mother will get tired and leave, as you suggest. Myself, I think that would be a pity. She seems to me to be in many ways admirably suited to the life. She has immense vitality, and there is work enough here to absorb it all. And in any case you cannot rid yourself of her influence merely by pushing her somewhere else. It will be better in the end that you yourself should conquer your dependence."

"But I'm not dependent, unless you mean for the cash. I don't want to be dependent. It's she who sticks like a leech to me."

"I'm sorry, it was not in that sense that I used the word. What I mean is this, perhaps: first, that you should try to develop towards your mother the detachment the rest of us feel, and see her as an efficient elderly lady whose opinions, while sometimes a trifle provoking, can easily be disregarded; and second, which is more important, that you should concentrate your emotional energies on forming an attachment elsewhere."

"Very interesting, I'm sure," said Ronny. "Anyone in view while you're about it?"

"Well, you have here quite a choice. Ah, Alexander——" The others jumped, but Kurt, it seemed, had eyes in the back of his head. "You arrive at the psychological moment. Operation Spud is completed. Maggie inserts the last of his line, and so, thus, he gets honourable burial."

79

"If you are accusing me of timing my entrances, well, of course," replied Alexander equably. "We've been watching you on the last row with breathless interest. There seemed at one time to be quite a hold-up." Alexander might look sleepy, but nothing really escaped his shrewd grey eyes.

"Of course you know it's absurd," grumbled Ronny, "planting spuds by hand. There ought to be a machine for doing it."

"Oh yes, there is. When we've ten times the acreage we'll get one." Ronny groaned. "Anyway, it's a good job done. What about celebrating this afternoon with a bonfire?"

Kurt was pleased; this was his line; but because he had been suggesting it for the past week and pointing out the blue feathers of smoke that day after day rose from the mainland hillsides, he was careful not to look too eager. "It will need to be most carefully planned. Only those sections must be burned which I can lime and slag later. Otherwise we risk replacing heather by bracken in a few years' time."

"Well, you're in control. Rory and I shall be working the dogs. You'd better get everybody out with brooms and rakes to keep it within bounds. And for heaven's sake see that it's well stamped out before you leave. We don't want to set the whole place alight, and it must be tinder-dry."

"You mean, we're going to burn the hillside?" cried Ronny. "I say, what a lark. The spark's among the heather— hoots, Magsy—up the McMoffats—hooray hooray." He caught Maggie round the waist and capered off with her down the hill, a creature without a care in the world.

Nor did his spirits even flag when at midnight they were all called out of their beds by Rory with news of an ominous glow above the waterfall, consequent on a slight neglect of Alexander's last injunction. Having Mrs. Rossiter for a parent might be in some ways disadvantageous, but she had undoubtedly transmitted some of her splendid vitality to her son.

[IV]

The byre at evening was a pleasant place, Bluebell and Daisy munching quietly, the milk making music in the pail, the door standing open and the last sunlight lying on the sea and the mainland hills. But for three nights now it had been for Maggie a scene of infinite exasperation. She was learning to milk.

"Lord, can't you milk?" had exclaimed Mary with a loud guffaw. "Call yourself a land-girl!" Maggie had never called herself anything but a gardener, but she bore the taunt meekly, since the favour was on Mary's side. And when they started work Mary proved a good tutor, unexpectedly patient and encouraging. But the milk would not come.

Her wrists aching, her face scarlet, Maggie squeezed and pummelled away, while Bluebell, or alternatively Daisy, peered round at her in pained surprise, and Mary frequently assured her that they were the two easiest milkers in all her experience. You only had to touch the teat and down it came. Here, like this. But what it was she did and Maggie didn't, Maggie could not for the life of her see.

And then suddenly, on that fourth evening, the knack of it came. Suddenly she found herself a milker. The yellow flood cascaded into the bucket, and satisfaction into her heart. It was queer stuff, the milk of these Highland crosses, butter-thick yellow cream on top and underneath, after it had stood a few hours, pale blue skim. It made the work of churning easy, even though they still had to do it by hand, but was greasy in tea. Mary congratulated her pupil, and admitted handsomely that it had taken her a week to learn.

"Now you can do Bluebell by yourself," she conceded,

and began on Daisy's toilet. Both cows were kept by her meticulously groomed, so that already they presented a noble contrast to the mucky beasts of the average croft.

"Indeed, I'm verra much obliged to you," said Maggie, and discovered that the voice and laugh no longer seemed so trying; was almost ready to believe, indeed, that they no longer were so loud. On this impulse of genuine liking she decided to enlist Mary in a battle she was disposed to fight. "Would ye have noticed that it's always yon Hermia that does the messages?"

"Does the—oh, you mean, goes into the Kyle. I suppose so, now you come to mention it, but what of it? Probably she likes to look at the shops."

"Well, but so would Mrs. Rossiter, and she's just as much the housewife. And it's she does a' the dairying and most of the laundry, while Hermia makes out she's learning the wee laddies their books. I don't just think it's fair."

"Oh, I daresay, but I'd have thought the old trout could stand up for herself."

"Why, I believe that's just what she won't do, though she'd stand up for anyone else that needed it, or even if they didn't. But she's that keen to make a go of it here, and not seem—well, too old for the job, that she'd let yon Hermia get by with anything."

"Poor old nanny-goat. Of course, I knew the minute I set eyes on her that that Hermia was a bloody bitch." Mary was never at a loss for a simile from the animal world. "But I don't see where we come in. Unless you got Alexander to tick her off. The Fletchers are supposed to be his buddies."

"I don't just think that would answer. I believe", said Maggie hesitantly, "that Alexander doesn't hold with anything that makes him seem the boss, or above the rest of us."

"Well, that's rot. He's a million miles above the rest."

"Maybe, but he'll no' thank you for saying so. No, my notion is, we'd propose at parliament that us five women should take it in turns. Then when it comes to your turn or mine, we make out we've too much on hand and Mrs. R. goes instead. There's wee Joyce, too—I daresay she'd like a bit of change when the sea was calm."

"Okay by me," said Mary agreeably. "I suppose you want me to do the speaking? All right, I'm not scared of the sound of my own voice." Maggie acknowledged the dig with a grin. "Hermia will be livid, of course. I wouldn't put it past her to have a boy-friend at the Kyle—or d'you suppose she and Rory do a spot of necking in the boat?" They worked on in the silent contentment induced by the discovery of a mutual aversion, and then Mary in her turn seemed to feel the need of an overture, for she began:

"You know, I really am falling hard for Alexander. When I fall for people, I do it straight off, all-out. That's my way." She saw Maggie stiffen, and added scornfully: "That shocks you, I expect."

"Och, no," said Maggie, taking a hold on herself and hiding her face in the cow's flank. "Folks are welcome to their feelings. I'd just say it's no' verra wise till ye're sure of a return." Well, for all she knew, Mary might be. He had said her voice was trying. But it was a lot less trying now.

"You believe in the shrinking-violet technique, do you? I don't. It may have paid a hundred years ago, but it won't get you anywhere to-day."

And where have you got? thought Maggie tartly. As if in answer to this comment, Mary pursued:

"I was engaged last year."

"Were ye so?"

"Yes, and the chap threw me over."

Maggie's face flamed. What a thing to say! Fancy telling a stranger, out loud! She would have died rather. And yet she felt an unwilling admiration for one so free from false shame.

"Dear, I'm sorry. But were yé not well out of it? I mean, if he wasna' the reliable sort."

"Oh well, I dunno. I can't remember very well now what he was like. Funny how soon you forget people, isn't it? But I know it hurt like hell at the time. I believe we'd have done all right, if Pop had let us marry when I wanted to."

"But how could he prevent it?"

"Why, by not coughing up the brass. He said that if Alan came into the mill he'd start him off at a good screw, but what was the good of that? Alan was a violinist. He played in the Northern Phil. He'd have been a soloist with a bit of backing. All Pop had to do was fork out, and he wouldn't. Of course it was my stepmother's doing, really. There isn't any filthy trick she wouldn't pull on me if she could."

This appeared to Maggie a frank admission that the young man had only wanted her for her money, but it would hardly be comforting to say so. She was seized with pity for this big, beautiful, spoilt creature, and almost ready to promise her Alexander to heal the hurt. But any discussion of him was highly undesirable, so she led Mary on to describe in fuller detail the iniquities of the stepmother, which ran the gamut from the ruin of her life's happiness to an attempt to force her to wear skirts.

"Anyway, I scared them," she ended on a note of satisfaction. "I nearly went off my head when I got Alan's letter, and I can tell you I jolly well put the wind up them both. Pop's been as meek as a lamb ever since. That's how I got the cash out of him to set up here. He's a bit near with his brass, is Pop, unless he can see a safe investment. But when I heard of this I set my heart on it, and by that time he was damn glad to buy me off. Look here, you'll not breathe a word of this, will you? I'd hate that pussy-cat to know, or the Yid, or any of the chaps. But somehow it's done me a bit of good, letting off steam to you."

Maggie followed her down to the dairy, deep in thought.

Here they were, rivals, if rivalry was quite the word to describe the utter failure of both, so far, to attract Alexander's attention. But as long as the rivalry remained known to only one of them, they might still be friends. Otherwise— och no, better not think of that. All she asked of life on Sunay now was that it should remain just as it was.

At Parliament Mary spoke out, with a fine impromptu heartiness which exactly did the trick. "I don't want to seem to be butting in on Hermia," she began breezily, "but us girls are feeling the itch to shop——" Her proposals were received with indulgent jocularity by the men, and by Hermia with outward pleasantness. Anyone, Hermia declared, was welcome to the three moth-eaten general stores and the one grumpy chemist who made up the shopping attractions of the Kyle. No direct reference was made to Mrs. Rossiter, and Maggie was given first turn as Rory's mate.

She was almost tempted when it came to the point. Living next door to Mary, she had glimpsed a standard of equipment altogether new to her. The year's necessities, foreseen and carefully laid in at Edinburgh, now seemed shabby and inadequate. It was unlikely that gaps could be filled from any stock at the Kyle, but still there were shops, and they must have something. But then she went up into the garden, and saw that the brassica seedlings were through. The faint lines of pale blue-green were her first writing on the soil. She arranged with Mrs. Rossiter to take her place.

The next day small footprints showed where no footprints should have been. There was not much damage done, but her heart missed a beat. She had never had much to do with children, and Gavin and Jamie had been, till then, merely ill-disciplined appendages of Hermia. But catching them alone, she marched them to the spot and harangued them with vehemence enough to produce quivering underlips.

"We didn't know vere was seeds sowed," whispered Gavin.

"Well, maybe not, but ye kenned well ye didn't ought to have been in the garden."

"What's sheeds?" asked Jamie, and was answered by his brother: "Silly. Seeds is what childwen come fwom."

Maggie stared at them in dismay. They knew nothing, or worse than nothing; it was just like Hermia to have told them what she would call the facts of life, and nothing about the life that mattered to a child. It was not merely that they were town-bred, dragged up rootlessly in flats. Hermia's indulgence and detachment, it now seemed to her, proved real lack of interest. As long as they looked pretty and didn't cry, Hermia could not care at all what went on inside their wee heads.

"Seeds are what plants come from. Look, it's pea seeds I have here. Would ye no' like to sow some yourselves?"

Gavin inserted six with precision. "Let I twy," said Jamie, and finished the row.

A notion struck her. "How would ye like wee gardens of your own? Ye could have yon sunny bit by the gate. I was for getting it ready for the strawberries, but we could move them along a space. Then ye can grow your own dinners. I'll mark two plots. A wee bit plot for Jamie, a wee bit for you."

"I ought to have a bigger bit van Jamie's, 'cause I'm ve eldest."

"Och, nonsense. He eats as much as you, I'll be bound. Now each rake a piece and I'll get ye some cress seeds. They'll be up quick."

"Can we have pea seeds?"

"Well now, they're a trouble. They'll be needing sticks."

"We know where vere's lots of sticks. In vose bushes by ve jetty. We want all ve kinds of seed you have."

"A'right, but let's see you make a start now. And I tell you

86

what, when ye've sown the seeds, go down to the beach with your buckets and get some of those white shells. Then ye can write your names on your pieces in shell letters." Their names were the only words they could write, as she knew.

She returned to her hoeing, and an hour passed in absorbed and pattering business. There were striking results to show Hermia when she came out at six to find them. "Look, Mummy, aren't we gweat gardeners?" And really they had managed their names very nicely, except that Jamie's E faced north.

"Darling, how wonderful. Isn't that kind of Maggie? But come along now—bed."

"Can't Maggie barf us?" Gavin went up and put an earthy hand in hers. "We want you to barf us, Maggie." Jamie clutched the other one. "Do, do."

"Nonsense, pets." She smiled at Maggie above their heads. "One night you'll have to, all the same."

"A'right, maybe I will one night," agreed Maggie, regretting it at once. Not only did they play old Nick with Mrs. Rossiter on the nights when Hermia cooked the dinner, but she already divined that Hermia would be delighted to push them on to anyone who showed the slightest signs of weakness.

But all the same she watched them indoors with a soft feeling at her heart. They had been so busy and so good, the poor mites, and sticking at it, too, where most bairns would have lost interest. She smiled at the recollection of their flushed faces, their up-ended bottoms, and their wee, ridiculous, earthy shoes.

[V]

In readiness for the lambing, the pens were undergoing repair. All the men were on it, under Rory's instruction, and as none of them had done any dry-stone walling before their

87

progress was exasperatingly slow. It looked so easy when Rory demonstrated, small stuff in the middle, big outside with a downward slope to take off the rain, and every so often a long one through to bind the whole together. But then Rory could select at a glance the right stone from the piles lying about the half-ruined pens. He had been doing this and all other shepherding jobs since childhood, and had the knack which can neither be explained in words nor learnt in weeks. The liming and harrowing of the top fields, where rape and turnips were to be sown, had been reluctantly handed over to Mary and Maggie, rather retarded than assisted, it was to be feared, by the little boys, who now formed a permanent part of their entourage.

Gavin's head and shoulders swayed into sight round the angle of the pens; he had already acquired the hill-man's roll.

"Zander! Maggie says, would you come? Vey can't manage."

"Drat the girls. What's wrong?"

"I fink ve chube is blocked," said Gavin knowledgeably.

"Oh, all right. Here, Kurt, would you go? Squiring the dames is more in your line."

Kurt did not deny it, but departed whistling, and Alexander grinned to find himself so soon adopting the peasant attitude to women. In London he had liked them helpless, as well as the next man, and remembered sulking a whole afternoon because a girl had beaten him at tennis. Yet here, already, he expected them to fend for themselves, and was conscious of nothing but irritation because Maggie and Mary couldn't manage.

And he might just as well have been the one to go, for suddenly he was dead beat. The blood tingled in his sore finger-tips, the stone swam before his eyes, and he leant against the bit of wall he had finished (with some surprise at finding it would bear the strain) and lit a cigarette. He was trying to cure himself of smoking, which was no habit for

88

people hoping to establish a self-sufficient economy. But undoubtedly it doubled the well-being of such moments as
these.

Here behind the wall there was no wind, and the sun
penetrated through his thin jersey and into every bone in his
body, bringing with it the pungency of bog-myrtle and
thyme. The quiet voices of the others, farther down the pens,
and the scrape of stone on stone were as soothing as the
sound of the fall, very near at this height. For a perfect five
minutes he was one with his island, as he had been, for days
on end, in the months when he and Rory shared it between
them. Rory was loquacious enough at night, but by day, on
the monotonous job of sinking posts and stretching wire,
they had often worked for hours on end without exchanging
a word.

Then had come his population, and it was a blur of faces,
voices, personalities, so that for a time he could hardly see
Sunay, and had the sensation of a playwright whose lines
have been mutilated by strange actors. Even now, when in
the middle of some job he stopped to look down at the
crofts, or up at the ant-like scurrying in the fields, he experienced astonishment at seeing them there. Then what, he
asked himself, had he expected? And it seemed that subconsciously he had been picturing them as peasants, men like
Rory and gentle, slow-spoken girls like his Annag, although
he knew perfectly well that no genuine peasants, unless one
included in that category the sophisticated, far-seeing Les,
had taken the smallest interest in his advertisement, and that
Rory probably only stayed because he was too lazy to make a
change.

These were quite new people who had come to Sunay,
brisk and assertive, without any of the wisdom and patience,
the knowledge of the ground and its abysses, of the sea and
its eddies, which he supposed the old people to have had.
But perhaps, in compensation, they had a vitality which was

89

bringing the island to life again, where the old ones, for all their wisdom, had after all let it die. And they brought money, too—in fairness that must be remembered. Money and all that it implied of efficiency, hot baths and tractors. But the old people would have been quicker at mending stone walls.

They were workers—there wasn't a slacker among them. He realized his tremendous good fortune in that. They might not yet be a community, but they had the makings, since such prodigies of work for the common good could be extracted not only from the professionals, Maggie and Les, but from amateurs like Kurt and Ronny, and on market-gardening jobs which plainly held no charm for them. And he hoped— more, he was sure—that they were happy. The frictions of the first days had largely resolved themselves, and looking round, he saw absorbed, self-forgetful faces, intent on the task in hand. He could only guess at what the rest of them had been like before, but his own friend, Simon, looked five years younger and seemed to be taking life about half as seriously, although still twice as seriously as most of it deserved.

A cloud no bigger than a man's hand, a grit which the most sensitive oyster would scarcely trouble to overlay with pearl, formed itself in Alexander's mind. So faint, so small was this element of disquiet that at first he could not identify it, and was forced to pass all their faces in review, at Parliament, at meals, in the fields, before he could fix on what it was. And then he knew. It was little Joyce.

There was happiness on her face when she looked at Les, there was illumination even, but at other times it was a blank. Addressed directly, she achieved a nervous and perfunctory smile. He could scarcely remember to have heard her speak.

Well, there were people, little girls of Joyce's age and class especially, who lived for love. Most earnestly he trusted that, as Les didn't seem to be bored by it, Joyce would prove one of them. But it would be reassuring to know that she had a second string.

It was unfortunate that so much of her day had to be spent cooped up with Mrs. Rossiter and Hermia. He was quite able to believe that Sunay had come as an entire shock to Joyce. Probably she had expected palm trees and oranges. He had made with himself an unbreakable rule against direct interference, but he resolved to try and find other pleasant tasks, successors to the kelp-burning, which should restore her to some position and personality of her own.

And anyway, he reflected, smiling, it might not after all prove necessary. Love, youth, nature, springtime, very likely had on hand a full-time occupation for little Joyce.

Chapter Four

[1]

Mary Todhunter was one who found herself perpetually angry. Black rages would sweep over her, making her feel terrible while they lasted and ashamed after they had gone. And yet they were not, she was convinced, her fault. She was not by nature bad-tempered. They were forced on her by the beastliness of other people, and especially of those who should have held her most dear.

Since coming to Sunay she had not known them, perhaps because she had been very busy and scarcely ever alone. The long cliff walk to the extreme western tip of the island which was her route on the morning of the gathering was almost her first taste of solitude. And so this day, so much looked forward to by herself and Lady as a chance to show what they could do, started badly with a flood of just those recollections she had been hoping never to entertain again.

It was raining, for one thing, a fine misty rain which was the first they had had, and Maggie had annoyed her by welcoming it for her silly seeds, when everyone of sense knew that you needed a fine day for a gathering. Impossible to put it off, however, because Rory's silent young brother Donald had come over specially the night before, bringing, what was even more important, his two dogs. And even so, gathering half-wild sheep from six thousand acres with only five dogs and eight people, five of them raw to the job, was going to be no joke.

Hunching her shoulders, bending her head down into the wet wind, Mary trudged westward, an equally disgruntled

Lady at her heels. She felt her spleen mounting, a vicious force independent of her will, and for some reason concentrating itself on Hermia, who had never done her any harm. Then she discovered that it was because that slick London manner and pussy-cat face reminded her of her stepmother, Marjorie. There might, then, be something in it. Marjorie had queered her pitch with Alan—precisely why or how Mary never knew, but she was convinced of it none the less —and this Hermia, who was supposed to be his bosom friend, might be preparing to do the same by her with Alexander. She had a feeling against the type; it would damage her whenever it got the chance. Sly where she was open, cunning where she was straightforward, patient where she (she knew it, she acknowledged it) rushed loudly and blindly at the object of desire, the Marjories of the world would defeat her wherever their paths crossed. And one more defeat like the one she had suffered over Alan, one more such shattering humiliation, would be the end. I'd kill myself, thought Mary fiercely, her lovely body the epitome of youth, life, splendour, but her spirit wilting like a flower broken off at the root.

Well, that being so, might not the advice given her by Maggie Moffat be worth considering after all? Sensible little Scotchy—she might not get much fun out of life, but she would never land herself in a mess. Oh, shucks, thought Mary, some of the rage transferring itself to Maggie, who wants to live like that? All right for you perhaps, with your round red face, the chaps won't bother you much anyway, but really I was born for something more. I've twice the looks Marjorie or that Hermia ever had, I'm only twenty-five. I'll have a packet one day, and I'd have held my man all right if nobody had interfered. And she dwelt for a moment —although she knew by experience that it would only mean more bitterness afterwards—on the early days of his passion. He had desired her utterly, with such force that she shrank

93

from the impact at first, feeling it not quite decent. There had always seemed to be in it an element of hate, but of that she had been rather proud. Other people loved smugly, cosily. Only she and Alan knew the real thing. They scrapped a lot, but that was a part of it. And then, without her being in anyway to blame, without her altering towards him by one iota, or giving him a moment's jealousy with any of half a dozen other chaps she might have had, then, then, then . . .

Mary clenched her hands in her raincoat pockets, and the tears ran down her cheeks, mingling with the rain. It was over, over a year ago, she was now in love with somebody else. What did he matter? What a damn fool she was. But she knew in the depths of her being that he did matter, because he had taken away her confidence, that most necessary weapon in a woman's armoury, and left her without courage, without attack. Here in what was practically a desert island, with no single rival in sight (for candidly, who was there?), she was still so little sure of herself that at bad moments like this, when it was raining and she was alone, she didn't in her heart believe that she would get Alexander after all.

The ground had been rising steadily, and all at once she found herself by a little, tumbledown cairn. This must be the highest point of the western headland, dignified on the map by the name of Carn Mor. She took a few steps down into the mist, and sure enough, everything heeled over. Lying on her stomach she peered down, seven hundred feet sheer into the sea. A black-backed gull wheeled lazily below her. Razorbills screamed from their niches on the cliff face. "Well, if it comes to the worst," said Mary to herself, "this would be a handy spot to end it all."

An elaborate time-sheet, worked out by him and Rory Mor the previous night, had given them set hours and points to start from, so that they should converge simultaneously upon the *ffridd* above the village. It was not an ideal arrangement, but as, even without this damned mist, there were not enough of them to keep within sight of each other from the first, it was the best that could be devised. Mary's start was from this cairn. She looked at her watch, stared at the sea-birds for another ten minutes of misery, and got to her feet, noting as she did so that the rain had stopped and the mist was rising. A gust of wind rent it suddenly, and there was her pointer, the pyramid of Torval, shining blue in what looked uncommonly like distant sunshine.

Recalling Lady's mind to business, she plunged east. Carn Mor was rockier on this side, but a shallow heathery gully led easily down between high walls. Almost at once there was a sign of life below. Girl and dog stiffened, but the five—six—seven graceful shapes that fled swiftly along the skyline were certainly not sheep. As she watched, a clattering stone behind her made her jump. And there, at the head of the gully, stood the stag. He studied them carefully, summed them up as unarmed, and with superb contempt charged them full in the face. Instinctively Mary ducked, and Lady, terrified, flattened herself against the rock. The stag passed within five feet of them, his slender legs stepping with exquisite precision between the loose boulders of the gully bed. His dappled coat caught the first gleam of the conquering sun. Then he was away, swift as thought, to join his ladies in the valley.

Well, thought Mary, ecstatically pleased. "You idiot," she said to Lady, who looked ashamed and tried to reassert herself by loud and ineffective barking—but how was a dog bred on the homely moors of Lancashire to understand the etiquette of superior Scottish hills?

So there were deer left on Sunay after all. Did he know it? —and did Rory? For a while she contemplated keeping this exquisite secret to herself, though she knew very well that she hadn't the temperament. That was going to be a splendid creature. Not very big, perhaps, though of course deer al-

95

ways looked smaller than one expected from pictures—but he would look something when his antlers were grown. A ten-pointer, perhaps. Come this autumn, one would have some fun.

Still no sheep appeared, and Mary had begun seriously to doubt there being any, when the next fall in the gently undulating moorland revealed a grassy bottom with a ruin in it, probably the remains of an ancient shieling, and a dozen ewes grazing. This was the test, for there was really nothing to prevent their getting away on either side. Advancing with great caution, and motioning to Lady to circle out widely and cut off their retreat, Mary was almost on them before they knew it.

"Whee, whee, whee!" she cried, brandishing her stick; and turning up the valley to escape her, they confronted the collie, a menacing dark streak. There was a tense moment of defiance, a half-hearted attempt at scattering, but Lady, with her prestige to retrieve, was superb. She might have been seven dogs. Finally, panic; the whole bunch rushed up eastward over the skyline, followed triumphantly by Lady and Mary, and in a moment more were joined to their careering sisters in a downhill flight before Rory, Maggie and the canny dog Bob. From the left came more sounds of shouting; Kurt and Les, dogless but undaunted. She detached Lady to help round up their handful. The great gathering was on.

"Whee, whee, whee!" yelled Mary, pounding on into the sunshine. This was glorious. She had always loved gatherings, but on this wild island, still virtually unknown country, it was twice the fun of home. The ewes of course were heavy in lamb, and some of them carried great draperies of fleece which suggested they had not felt the shears for long enough; indeed, how could Rory, with an odd man or two to help him, ever have gathered them effectively? But heavy as they were, they yet were wild and full of spirit and gave fine sport. The dogs had to be in ten places at once, and one scarcely dared send them after a stray.

Home was in sight now; the bay opened out beneath them, the crescent of the cottages; they were emerging on to the great shelf of gently sloping moor which ended in the steep wall just above the fields. A dark fold marked the course of the burn plunging down from Torval towards the fall, and along it two more figures were driving a knot of sheep—Simon and Alexander, who had climbed with the new dog two thousand feet up the flank of the mountain, while Rory swept over the pass below them. They joined forces by the stream, the dogs circling warily to keep the sheep away from the gorge. Then the whole lot went pouring, another, greyer waterfall, over the easy slope to its left, down to the gate in Alexander's fence, invitingly held open by Mrs. Rossiter, Hermia and the two ecstatic small boys, and so into safety. Round the corner by church and jetty and up the hillside towards them came the last reinforcement, driven by Donald, Ronny and the two visiting dogs, who had cleared the eastern side of Torval and the heathery peat-hags between it and the sea.

Now that it was all down, the flock looked vast. Its bleatings were deafening, its excitement and agitation infectious, but Mary knew enough about sheep to guess that it was but a scanty population for the extent of ground it covered. Not a thousand, she calculated. "There will be about eight hundred, yes?" said Rory, quite woken out of his Celtic detachment. "It was eight hundred you paid for, wasn't it, Toctor? You will be about right."

"Ah yes, I daresay," replied Alexander, staring about him with a sort of bemused delight. "But they look like untold wealth to me. For the first time in my life I feel a millionaire."

The evenings at Sunay had, till then, been the least success-
ful part of the day in evoking communal harmony. Generally, they had all been too tired to argue, or to think of anything but sleep. But there had been undercurrents of feeling,
centering chiefly round the wireless.

Segregated as they were, with only a weekly delivery of
papers which, arriving in batches, proved impossible to
read, the wireless had become their one real link with the outside world. Five sets had been brought, but only Alexander's
ran off batteries. The rest were speechless till such time as
Sunay should have current of its own. Alexander brought
his into the kitchen, and used it, like a farmer, for the weather
forecast, and like a runaway worldling, for the news. Backed
by Kurt and the Fletchers, and to a lesser extent by Maggie,
who hankered after an enlargement of her Scots limitations,
he also aimed at concerts, particularly of Bach, Bartok or
Brahms. But his principles and his natural courtesy also
caused him to give weight to the tastes of the other two
elements.

Ronny, Mary and, it was to be feared, the Turners liked
dance bands, the louder and more continuous the better, and
having got them to maximum pitch they then ceased to
listen and addressed each other in shouts. This so exacer-
bated Kurt that the atmosphere became volcanic.

Mrs. Rossiter, an element on her own, liked talks, and
when they were over she liked airing her own views of the
speakers, which she called stimulating discussion amongst
ourselves. This, unfortunately, and in spite of the admirable
example set him by Alexander, infuriated Ronny, and provoked those bouts of rudeness which left the rest of them, as
Maggie lamented, not knowing where to look.

So that in the long run it had become politic to listen only to the weather and the news. Peace was thereby restored, but certain frustrations, especially on the part of the intelligentsia, might be guessed at below.

But on the evening of the gathering, a general sense of satisfaction was combined with even more than the usual fatigue. As Ronny put it, two cows and a lot of bloody spuds didn't make a farm, but when you had a thousand sheep—well, 865 or 891, according to the Kurt or the Rory count—then you had something. The day had to be lived through again, the dogs' performances analysed, and Mary caused fully the sensation she had hoped for with her stag.

Rory, she satisfied herself, hadn't known after all. He wouldn't let on, of course, not he, but he questioned her closely.

"I wish I'd been with you," said Alexander. "Though of course they're nothing but vermin, are they, if one's going in seriously for sheep? We'll have to get rid of them, I suppose."

"Oh, look here! The place is huge—it could take twice the flock and still feed a few deer. Anyway you won't do anything till the autumn, will you, when we can have some sport?"

"Don't worry, Mary. I've far too much else on hand, and I can promise you my share of the sport." He twisted his stockinged feet luxuriously to the fire. When she saw the stockings, and their immense, cobbled, multi-coloured darns, Maggie loved him unspeakably. She wondered if she would ever dare offer to make him new ones. But it was Mrs. Rossiter, fortunately placed woman, who observed:

"My dear boy, what works of art. Really I must set to and knit you some as soon as I've got this out of the way." The garment in her hands was unquestionably a jersey of Gavin's, and Hermia said, rather crossly:

"I begged you not to waste time mending that old thing, Mrs. R. Gavin has several more."

"I know, dear, but he seemed so fond of this one. And if a

99

thing is worth doing at all it's worth doing well, don't you agree?"

For a moment Hermia's famous poise was not in evidence, and it was, perhaps, to make her amends that Alexander picked up her book.

"Kafka—h'm, a curious choice for light reading in the Hebrides. Though I don't know why I'm so dogmatic to-night. It must be the effects of fatigue." He dropped the volume back into her lap.

"I'll own it's just a wee bit melancholy," said Hermia, brightening; she more than anyone had been complaining of the cultural vacuum. "But what else can you suggest that would be better suited to the leisure of the castaway? And don't give me Shakespeare and the Bible. We are no longer in a parlour game."

"Well then, let's see——"

"*Wuthering Heights*," said Simon.

"Oh, nonsense—are you implying that we live here a life of gloom? No, I'd like something elegant, golden, with a feeling for Nature but no descriptions, lots of dialogue and a happy ending. *Persuasion*, of course, but that hardly counts; I'd like *Persuasion* anywhere. Boswell—yes, the *Life* and the *Tour*. They have it all between them."

"Not enough feeling," said Hermia. "I'll take Turgenev. I like to fancy we rather resemble *A Month in the Country*, anyway."

"Here", pronounced Kurt, "one has a unique opportunity for the solid in fiction. I intend to start on Richardson. After that, Balzac, Proust, Romains, Thomas Mann—how grati--fying to have read them instead of merely talking as though one had. Meanwhile this is an engaging romance I have in hand. It is laid in the Hebrides. At the climax a beautiful young girl is taken out in a boat and drowned."

"Splendid," said Ronny, "that's what ought to happen to all girls. Pass it over when you're through."

Dare I mention Stevenson? wondered Maggie wistfully. No, better not. The English just think he wrote for bairns. That's no' just true, though. There's *Weir of Hermiston*, but I doubt they'll have heard of it. Then she heard Alexander saying:

"Has no one a word for the native talent? Maggie—what about R. L. S. ? There, surely, was a major figure—anyway, given a few more years and a wee bit less charm. I've a theory that genius writes its own epitaph; his comes at the end of *Treasure Island*, something about being too much of the born favourite. But he outgrew it. Look at *Weir of Hermiston*. That is already a masterpiece."

There you are, thought Maggie, crimsoning with equal pleasure and frustration. Always so busy over what folks'll think that you can't speak up like a sensible body even when you've something to say. Never mind, he likes *Weir of Hermiston*. Och, yes, we've a lot in common. I'd be brave enough if I had him alone.

Mrs. Rossiter, beginning on Gavin's second sleeve, was remarking in her composed way:

"I daresay you'll think me old fashioned, children, but in my view there's a great deal to be said for Scott. Many of his tales give a wonderful picture of the past. *Tales of a Grandfather*, for instance, or *The Heart of Midlothian*. How would it be if we passed the winter evenings by reading one of them aloud?"

"God, what a bloody bore," cried Ronny instantly. "Anyway, I loathe all this kind of highbrow blah. I daresay it's fun for those that do the talking, but it's pretty dreary to listen to. Come on, Mary, let's see if we can't screw a bit of cheerful sound out of this juke-box." And he pounced on the wireless with a sort of ferocity.

The sheer brutality of the intervention produced a stunned silence, at the end of which it seemed that there might be several protests. But Kurt, his eyes dancing, held up a warning hand. Incredible, he thought, that he should need to; how these Aryans did miss their opportunities! Here they sat discussing the literature of the passions, but let somebody present them with what was practically a case-book page and all they thought fit to do was to take offence.

[III]

By the third week in April, the beauty of Sunay was enough to break an idle heart. The banks of whin along the burns and under the moorland wall were so thickly gold that no green showed, and even down at the village one could still smell their heavy coconut scent. Primroses made pale stars around the roots of the gaunt heather. Each morning the sheep-park was dotted with another dozen lambs, charming, cream-coloured babies with sooty faces. The exquisite weather and the early growth of grass helping their mothers, they were a sturdy crop. But Rory and Alexander, in an unspoken vow to bring the losses down to nothing, seemed to be on the prowl at all hours of the night. At any moment the current housekeeper might be summoned from her sauces to warm and feed a morsel whose mother had no milk for it, or who had been born too weak to suck. And the passionate pageant of the sea-bird matings was for ever calling Simon Fletcher's eyes from his work, though never, owing to his unfortunate conscience, for long enough to take the full glory of it in.

One morning, however, Rory, coming home along the cliffs after a search for stray ewes, put his foot on a seagull's egg. "Them is good eating," he told Mrs. Rossiter at lunch, "not fishy at all. Huntrets I have gathered in the old days when I wass here alone." It was therefore decided that Simon and Ronny, who deserved some compensation for a back-breaking week of earthing up early potatoes, should take the *Gannet* across the bay and visit the little island, to which

Ronny's name of Latay had stuck. The gullery of Latay had already shown itself a menace to the rabbits, the chicken food and even the new-born lambs. Retaliation would do good all round.

Simon, Ronny and Gavin embarked in the afternoon, and were pursued across the bay by Jamie's bitter howling. It had been explained to him that he was too little to make the climb up the cliffs, but Jamie felt the matter with his heart, not his head. The sea was completely calm, for only on such a day could Latay be approached, and Simon took the boat through the narrow channel between it and the mainland, and round to the northern side, where was the only line of weakness in its otherwise vertical cliffs.

Here the rocks were more broken, and the boat's appearance gave a shock to a colony of sun-basking seals, which flopped with loud splashings into the water. Inside the second cave, had said Rory with the faint reluctance of one imparting useful information to a possible enemy, they would find an iron ring, where the old people had tied their boats when they took sheep on to the Little Island. And sure enough, there it was, rusty but looking, somehow, as though it had been used since the old people's day.

Gavin, tongue-tied with excitement, was lifted out and had the rope put with a middleman's noose round his waist. His father set foot on a ledge above the ring, swung round a corner and vanished. Five minutes later it was his turn. Up he came, hand over hand, agile and confident as a baby kitten. Ronny followed with the egg-bucket over his elbow, remarking that it was nothing but a scramble, really, but a nasty drop if you chanced to fall.

The roof of the islet was an almost flat plateau of grass, rich with sea-bird droppings, and as they ran forward a cloud of gulls went wheeling and screaming up into the air. The sound was stunning; one could almost feel that Latay rocked in the sea like a tower on its base when the bells are pealing.

Simon crossed to the farther side, from which they looked back again at the village and the bay, and flung himself face down. "Here, Gav, keep close to me. Don't go near the edge. It's rotten with puffin burrows." At that moment a puffin put its comic black-and-white face out of its hole, examined them with the curiosity natural to puffins, and burst into loud, indignant squawking. Gavin and Ronny exploded with laughter. They did not yet know many birds, but puffins were unmistakable. Sea-parrots, they were called, but Gavin considered they were more like his nursery penguins. Whoever heard of black-and-white parrots?

At an immense height above them the great squadrons were still wheeling, each bird as it turned catching the sunlight and for a moment flashing white. "Like Spitfires," said Ronny.

"Common gulls and black-backs, most of them, but kitties too, and some herrings," diagnosed Simon, focusing his glasses. "Here, Gav, you have a look. These little ones, now, they're terns. See what a lovely flight. Sometimes they're called sea-swallows, but no swallow could float in the air like that. Watch them diving, now—they've got used to us, they're going back to look for their dinners. Isn't that a wonderful drop? Now there's a black-back swooping, like a dive-bomber. Yes, they're bandits, all right. They don't just fish, they go for the smaller birds and smash the puffins' eggs. I daresay it was a black-back took out the eyes of that lamb Alexander was so upset about. That's why it's all right for us to take some of their eggs. Let's have a look along the cliff. More black-and-white—puffins, probably—no, I think they're razorbills. That's a bit of luck. Aren't they smart with their black heads and white shirt-fronts? There might be guillemots, too. This is just the sort of place they like."

"What a lot you know," said Ronny admiringly. "You ought to write a book."

"So my wife tells me," said Simon, recalled rather suddenly to earth.

Ronny turned his head with a quick look. "It's the sort of thing people are always saying. Silly, really. There's enough blah about as it is. Much better to know a lot and not write a book."

An odd creature, reflected Simon. He seemed ordinarily so dense and was sometimes so perceptive. Most of Simon's sore places had healed themselves recently. But this one, thanks to the persistent suggestion of Hermia—never, even in his thoughts, would he have called it nagging—seemed to stay sensitive.

Simon could acquire knowledge, easily, even brilliantly; he could not, in his own view, impart it. As a lecturer he felt that he had failed. Students had cut his lectures because he bored them. The blow to his confidence had been great. Without Hermia—without her wonderful loyalty, her unwavering support—he hardly knew how he could have recovered. And she, herself the daughter of academic brilliance, might have had her pick of chaps who had made the grade. His gratitude to her was tremendous. A lifetime was hardly enough to express it all.

The war rescued him, gave him the life he was best fitted for, the arduous, inconspicuous existence of a backroom boy. When that ended, he saw the ordeal of the university arena looming ahead again. But then came Alexander's blessed project, and he had his second chance of escape. For Hermia it meant, of course, abandoning many ambitions. But she had proved herself gallant and game.

He was aware, nevertheless, that she was not quite reconciled to the prospect of permanent mediocrity. She hoped for certain things from Sunay, and one of them was that he would write a popular bird book that might make them known as no laboratory triumph was ever likely to do.

Ornithology was the rage; a lot of people dabbled; there was a sure market. Her faith in his abilities was still strong and splendid, and he meant, as soon as the farm-work gave him time, to justify it. But he did feel that life would be simpler if she just occasionally considered the possibility that he might fail again.

"What about vose eggs, Daddy?" Gavin was demanding; the concentration of six years old will not endure for an infinity of sea-birds.

"All right," said Simon, getting to his feet. "But nowhere near the edge, mind. You'll find plenty of nests in the long grass." And it was true, for Gavin at once walked backwards on to one. Big, untidy nests littered the island, with clutches of one, two or three eggs, and they took all that they could find. So early in the year as this, the gulls would lay again. "Quite a weight," said Ronny when the bucket was full. "I suppose I'm to have the jolly job of getting it down without a smash."

Simon belayed the rope at the climbing-place, and they watched Ronny down, his long body held out well from the rock, his weight occasionally coming on the rope, and the arm with the bucket swinging out behind him against a dizzy background of swooping gulls and sea. It suddenly struck Gavin that it was going to be a lot more frightening climbing down. Ronny disappeared, and his shout told them he had reached the boat. With the rope round his waist, Gavin felt steadier, and not for the world would he have let his father know how his inside was turning over. But he longed for the sea to stay quite still and the kittiwakes stop making that screeching noise.

Then he was off, on rock warm to his sand-shoes, and, after all, found he did not need to look very far down, only to the next ledge where he was going to put his feet. There was one bad moment, rounding a corner, when Ronny's face came into view as a white blur far below, and it seemed he was going to drop straight into the boat. But he slipped a few inches on the rope to a big knobble, and then it was all right. Presently Ronny's hands were round his waist. "Well done, son," said Ronny with a shrewd look, and Gavin, instantly convinced that he had never been scared at all, bounced away into the stern of the boat and shouted himself hoarse to make the gulls get up.

Down came his father, so steadily that it didn't look fast, and yet he took half the time that they had. And, of course, there was no rope to keep him safe; Ronny just drew it in as he came, and did it up in a neat coil. Gavin's heart swelled with pride at having a father so clever and brave.

"I somehow don't see us getting sheep up there," remarked Ronny as the *Gannet* chugged back through the channel and into the bay, "and God, how I'd hate to get them down. It's a mercy there's enough space on Sunay for all the sheep we're likely to have in the next ten years." Nor was he ever afterwards heard to sneer at the old people, no matter what evidence came to light of their ignorant or improvident ways.

Jamie was waiting on the jetty, his feelings in good repair. "We've got a fousand eggs!" yelled Gavin, and Jamie yelled back: "We've got annuver pet lamb!" That, of course, was more important than eggs, and Gavin left his father and Ronny to tie up the boat, and tore ahead to see.

Simon followed leisurely, the rope over his shoulder, the bucket in his hand and in his heart something like peace. The kitchen door stood open, and the evening sunlight slanted into the pretty old room through the small window at the back. A bowl of primroses stood on the table set for dinner. Hermia, her face intent and tender, was bending over a flaccid morsel in a basket by the fire, and feeding it drop by drop from a fountain-pen filler.

"There." She laid the lamb down, and covered it with an old blanket. "To look, mind, but not to touch. He's very weak still." Over their concerned little backs she smiled at her husband. "Did you get a lot of eggs?"

"Well, we got the bucket full. I should say a couple of hundred."

"Mrs. Rossiter will be pleased." But he knew she was not thinking of Mrs. Rossiter. She raised a finger and beckoned him gently, and he went across and took her in his arms.

[IV]

May came in brilliant. A heat haze hovered now over the mainland peaks in the early mornings, and Maggie's talk of a drought began to be listened to by the others with something like concern. The cuckoo called incessantly from the windswept ash tree, a sound which took the mind oddly to English meadows. "So the Hebrides really do have cuckoos," Alexander commented. "I always suspected Wordsworth of howking them in for the nice rhyme." The lambs cavorted quaintly round the stony hillocks, and those which had been made free of the kitchen were now as sturdy as their brothers and twice as brazen. The first great effort of the island year was triumphantly achieved. Letters from London told of cold spring winds, of hailstorms and sleet. Alexander lost no opportunity of congratulating his fellow-islanders on the contrast. More experienced than they in Hebridean weather, he knew that presently it would begin to rain.

They drilled the mangolds on a day so sweltering that the men worked stripped to the waist, Kurt gradually acquiring a becoming Tyrolean bronze, and Ronny, who had the white English skin, gradually acquiring blisters. Nobody, however, was quite prepared for the effect when Mary appeared behind the cows, wearing a two-piece white bathing suit. She might almost as well have been naked.

"Aha! That hits you, does it?" murmured Kurt, torn between glee at the look he had surprised on Alexander's face and a faint dismay at the force of his own reaction.

"One is not a stick or a stone," admitted Alexander regretfully.

"Oh, pooh," said Ronny. "I grant you she's a nice shape, but she has no sex-appeal." He spoke without malice. He and Mary had overcome their initial animosity, and if not exactly affectionate, were now linked by a sort of general Philistinism and a faculty for hitting on the same wrong moment to guffaw at other people's opinions.

Kurt returned to work with a shrug. These Englishmen, he gave them up. Apparently equipped with all the normal instincts, they yet immured themselves in laboratories and theories for the best years of their lives. This fastidiousness would get nobody anywhere. What did it matter that she wasn't intellectual? She had vitality, which was what one would chiefly wish to transmit to one's children. And really the intelligent ones were often a trifle tedious. He recalled Ilse's last letter, which went on for eight pages and wanted endless answers, had he read this, was he keeping abreast of that, he wouldn't let the island life cramp his horizon, would he, darling? It was a lucky thing for Ilse, commented Kurt within himself rather tartly, that that naked dream walking continued to give him the cold shoulder; and he determined in his reply to leave all the questions unanswered and describe the bathing suit instead.

Down at the village it was creating a parallel sensation, the Scottish element being openly shocked. "That iss not a proper way for a young lady to be tressed," said Rory to Les, the spirit of John Knox glowering for an unexpected second out of his raffish pirate eyes.

"I know from the magazines that London lassies put on that kind of thing to go swimming," confided Maggie to Mrs. Rossiter. "But I canna get used to it—not here, on the farm."

"Well, dear, it wouldn't do for everyone, I agree," replied Mrs. Rossiter, who prided herself on her broad-mindedness. "But Mary is an exceptionally beautiful girl, and with her look of radiant health——"

"Oh, quite," concurred Hermia. "I've always thought she looks just like an advertisement for somebody's laxative." And Maggie acquired a little more unpleasant self-knowledge. She had, she found, been foolishly hoping that no one else noticed how pretty Mary was; Mrs. Rossiter's expressed admiration made her wretched; Hermia's silly spite cheered her up again. She took refuge now in Mr. MacDougal's favourite advice, which was a cure for more than weeds. "Keep yon hoe moving, lass," he used to say, "keep yon hoe moving." Maggie kept it moving assiduously throughout a sweltering afternoon.

However, Mary's figure as a topic of conversation was soon eclipsed by the vanishing of Rory Mor.

That evening at Parliament he remarked, with his usual courtesy:

"Will one of the chentlemen be coming with me in the boat to-morrow? I am for biding a wee while at the Kyle, so I'll not be able to bring her back."

"Staying? What for?" demanded Mary. Her manners no doubt jarred on Rory, who would never have questioned anyone else's decisions, but he replied patiently:

"My brother the Minister iss at home for a holiday, and I shall want to be seeing him."

"Well, of all the inconvenient——"

"That'll be all right," said Alexander, and if an appeal passed from him to Rory, it was not in words. "Like to take it on, Ronald? You're used to handling the *Gannet* by now."

Ronny, when it came to the point, found himself in command both ways, for Rory took the *Carrie* as a matter of course. No one was about to see them start, and Ronny could not somehow find that it was his business to object.

There was, however, considerable indignation about it at Parliament, an indignation which increased as a week went by and Rory did not return.

"We have to remember", said Alexander, who took no part in the outcry but looked every day more worried, "that he was magnificent over the lambing. He's earned a break."

"Well, so were you. He ought to have asked. Just going off like that is bloody cheek."

"Yes, and we need the *Carrie*. We could have made a dozen more liming trips."

"It's inconsiderate, of course, but the *Carrie* was his for six years, and I daresay it's hard for him to remember that she isn't now. And I sometimes wonder", pursued Alexander hesitantly, "if it hasn't been a bit trying for Rory, living cooped up with people who don't even speak his language. I believe I'm going to learn it. Anyway, one of us had better. We'll never be on real terms with any of them till we do."

"He's paid good money," said Mary, "the only one of us that is, and I just don't get the need for all this pampering. Let him stick at his job or let's find someone else. There are plenty of unemployed hanging round the Kyle." And she proceeded to give Alexander the benefit of her father's experiences in handling labour. The aim, it appeared, was to have an even longer memory than the unions and get rid of any chap who had once played you up, no matter how long you had to wait. Nobody was indispensable, and when the next slump came you weeded the undesirables out.

"And does it not worry you," asked Kurt, "that you live on the proceeds of a regime based on victimization and fear?"

"Well, it's their own faults if they get in wrong with my Dad. He may be a hard man, but he's just. Those who do a good day's work will be looked after all right—anyway, as long as times are good. I say, are you one of those half-baked Socialists?"

"I have that honour. In fact, I am now without a country as a result of it."

"Oh, is that why? I thought it was because you were a——"

"You forget, Mary," cut in Alexander, "that here you're a half-baked Communist yourself."

"Oh, well, that's a bit different. Anyway, none of us are paid a sou, and we all work like a lot of blacks. That's what I always tell my Dad when he writes to know when he's going to see a return on his money." Any references by Mary to her share in the island finances always had the effect of dispersing her hearers.

A one-year grass ley was sown, two acres of cabbages planted out, endless rows of carrots and lettuce thinned, hundreds more gulls' eggs collected, several tons of seaweed composted, all without Rory's assistance.

"I must say old Rory chose the right moment for his disappearing act," commented Ronny, who had never missed a night's sleep during the whole of the lambing. Alexander continued to say nothing and looked worried. Only Les and Maggie, perhaps, could fully appreciate his reasons.

And then, ten days after his departure, Rory returned with equal unconcern. The *Carrie* came chugging into the bay with the last light, and there he stood, smiling up at the row of faces above him on the jetty—for already at Sunay they had acquired the true islanders' habit of gathering to watch any boat arrive. Now was the moment for reproaches. But nobody said a word to Rory, and it was he who observed to Alexander, in the tone of one resuming a conversation: "Them lamps looks good. We could be cutting them any day now, and turning the ewes up the mountain."

Mary, perhaps fortunately, was busy at the evening milking and did not see him arrive. When she heard in the dairy how he had been welcomed, she was indignant. She at any rate, she told Mrs. Rossiter, wasn't scared of Rory. He was going to hear exactly what she thought.

"If I were you, dear, I wouldn't," counselled Mrs. Rossiter. "I happen to be very sensitive to atmosphere, and something tells me that Alexander doesn't want Rory upset. I think we can trust Alexander to know the best way to handle him, don't you?" And such was the effect of Mrs. Rossiter's championship that although he was the pivot of her existence, Mary as she left with her pails was distinctly heard to mutter: "Alexander can go to hell."

Rory made his peace with the womenfolk by the easy expedient of grinning round the kitchen door and holding out in either hand a couple of bottles. "I brought you a present," he said.

One bottle was rum, one brandy, and the other two unlabelled. "Them is whisky. I know ladies don't like whisky, that's why I was after bringing the others."

"I'm sure it's most kind of you, Rory," began Mrs. Rossiter, uncertain whether so dubious a peace-offering ought to be accepted, but Hermia pounced on the rum and brandy, murmuring something about her grandmother's recipe for punch.

"I thought perhaps we could be having a *ceilidh*," pursued Rory on a note of wistful appeal.

"What's a cayley?" asked Ronny, coming in for dinner. "Hello, what's in those bottles? Lord, one whiff's enough to knock you backwards. That's Glendhunan or I'm a pussyfoot. See here, Rory old man, just what have you been up to with your prother the Meenister?"

"A *ceilidh*", said Rory politely, "iss singing, tancing, perhaps a little trinking . . ."

"Oh, I see. A party plus. Well, I daresay a drop of this will warm us up to it. Here, Alexander, have a sniff. A present from Rory, and no questions asked."

"I wass after buying them at the hotel," said Rory, still politely, but somehow the subject had grown a little dangerous.

"And have ye really a brother that's a minister, Rory?" Maggie asked.

"Why yes, indeed. We are three brothers in my family, Tonny you know, he iss at the fishing now, and my eldest brother Chames is the minister at a village up beyont Lochalsh. He wass the one wass good at the book-learning. He got a bursary away to Aberdeen. It is a pity us two wassn't like him. Never any book-learning could the teacher get into my thick het." He thumped his black curls. "So for us it was chust crofting over again. In the war Tonny went in the Navy, but they didn't learn him anything new there. He iss chust back at his olt chob now. Those of us that haven't the book-learning don't get far in the Isles."

"Somebody has to alter that," said Alexander, "and who knows, Rory, you might be the one?"

As the last light faded from the mountains across the Sound, chairs were drawn round the fire and the essential ingredient of the *ceilidh* began to circulate. It was the first strong drink to reach Sunay, and the effect was electric. The anonymous whisky warmed the heart and lightened the head; one suddenly knew that everything was coming out right in the end. What a fool I've been, thought Alexander, keeping us all at work like this. No wonder Rory thought us prigs. We ought to break out every so often—do something absurd, magnificent—what's the good of living on the edge of the world, where the king's writ scarcely runs, if all we do is reproduce there the surburban respectabilities? What do I care where this stuff came from? Rory could have got untold gold for it, and instead he makes it a present to us. A rascal, but an engaging rascal. *Slainte mhor*.

"*Slainte mhor*, Rory!" cried Kurt, who knew what was necessary in every language. "Here's a song in honour of your brother the Minister." And he took down the accordion which till then had hung neglected on the wall, and gave them an anticlerical piece from medieval Austria, all about burning the Abbot's corn. "We'll set the red cock on the barn, yo, ho, ho!"

"That's a fine song," said Rory, the agelong rebel in him instantly responding. "There iss an olt Sunay song iss a little like it."

"I want to dance," cried Hermia, jumping up and catching her husband's arm. "Come on, Kurt, that's enough gloom, turn on the Middle-European gaiety. Give us a waltz."

I am drunk, thought Maggie, the spicy amber elixir making her head spin. Yon Hermia said it would be nothing but a sort of hot lemonade, but man, how she lied. I, a respectable teetotal Scots lass, am getting drunk. Somebody will see. And instinctively she looked round for Alexander, but he had gone over to Mrs. Rossiter and was inviting her to dance. Then she herself was seized by Ronny and swung into the maze. Hundreds of dancers there seemed to be, spinning, swirling, on that tide of heady Viennese music, like gnats above the stagnant water, like kittiwake gulls between the blue air and the sea. "I say, Magsy," called Ronny's laughing, impudent voice from a long way above her, "I believe you're tipsy. You look almost human. You've no idea what an improvement it is."

I am not, insisted Maggie, as drunk as all that. I am enjoying myself now, but soon it will be heaven. I shall know what it feels like to be in his arms. He has done his duty by Mrs. Rossiter, now he partners Hermia, sooner or later it will be my turn. Meanwhile, Ronny is a good friend, a fine tall lad and safe to hold on to, and who cares what daft things he says? Look at yon wee Joyce, how her eyes are shining. Now a body can see why it was Les married her. Fancy being as much in love as that! Yet I could be, too, if I had the opening. The satiny rhythm caught her head and her feet. The Vienna woods had come to Sunay, and were going round, and round, and round.

115

"Ach, I am exhausted!" exclaimed Kurt, and the accordion subsided in a wail.

At this there was an outcry. "You can't fold up on us now. We're just getting into the swing. Have another drink." And everybody had another drink, after which Kurt plucked up fresh heart.

Now it's my right to have you, cried Maggie, now, now, now. He had turned to look at her—they exchanged a smile. And then that great blethering Mary must come charging up and grab him, positively grab him, with both her hands. He laughed at her, liking her impudence, and they whirled away together. Maggie could have cried with sheer bafflement, but of course that was silly, for she had only to wait five minutes more. And Rory was now her handsome partner, light and lissom, with the devil in his feet. Rory knew how to handle a girl at a *ceilidh*. All through the music he was singing to her in Gaelic; she couldn't understand a word, and maybe it was just as well. But through the fun and tipsiness she could still see Mary's face, could still tell how Mary felt, lost, bathed, drowned in bliss. . . . Then she caught sight of Kurt's face, too, bent above his instrument, saw him look up and fix his eyes on Mary, and knew that she would never dance with Alexander after all.

"I play no more," said Kurt with finality. "No, no, positively no. What fun is it for me to see you all gyrating like drunken tops? I have, I consider, been very obliging. Yes, of course, I will have a drink. And now, Rory, the Sunay song."

Vienna vanished; its woods melted into Hebridean darkness; great cliffs stood up out of the mist; the green waters tempted galleys to their doom. The claymores clashed in the relentless rain, and on the topmost crag stood a king's daughter, looking for her lover, leaping to her death. As Rory reached his third verse the accordion took up the melody under him; Kurt's quick ear could catch a rhythm so alien to his race, and hold it with exquisite sympathy.

On and on went the haunting tenor, the noble Gaelic words. One could fancy them to mean what one liked. Probably it was all nonsense about the king's daughter. Probably, like most Gaelic songs, they only said: "How sad am I, that the cruel English have taken away my kilt and forced me to wear trousers."

But equally, perhaps, they might mean:

I love you, I love you, though you are separated from me by the deep gorge, the white waterfall and the wide sound. I love you though your eyes are on the stars, and mine on the green seedlings written into the ground. I love you and one day we will be together, though I may not reach you this side of the grave.

Chapter Five

[I]

The evening of the *ceilidh* seemed in the history of Sunay to mark a turning-point. What had been needed, apparently, to weld them into that community so earnestly desired by Alexander was not so much a Parliament, or hard work, or the spirit of disinterested devotion to the common cause, as just a real good binge.

It also ended the evenings. For now each night grew shorter, and the great northern twilight, silvery and serene, kept them from the fireside and from bed. After dinner the boats were out fishing, Kurt and Alexander taking the *Gannet* into the contemplative security of the bay, Rory and Ronny pushing the *Carrie* more adventurously out of sight beyond Latay, to the grounds where they had sunk lobster-pots. Simon and Hermia took glasses and camera and went bird-watching along the great cliffs to the west, and Hermia began to talk of Simon's book, at first as though it were actually started, and soon as though it profoundly mattered. Mary took her rod up to the lochan which lay cradled in the giant lap of Torval; it was so full of trout that none were sizable, and it badly needed dragging, but still she could supply them all with breakfast. Les, when not engaged in walling a strip for his pigs, took Joyce for walks over the saddle to the Camas Ban, and, it might be surmised, made love. And at ten or even eleven at night they would all come trooping back to the kitchen, where the ever-patient Mrs. Rossiter gave them oatcakes and tea.

To Maggie the enchanted days and nights brought a reconciliation with herself, a delicate adjustment of feeling and sense. In this she was helped by her conviction that for the moment, at all events, Alexander was not prepared to love anyone, having other matters on his mind. When he was not there she followed him in her thoughts, with a longing that now was hardly painful, and under the alchemy of love he grew a good two inches and seemed remote and resolute, a king among men. When they were together his natural friendliness dissolved these chilly illusions away. For how could one break one's heart over somebody who entered so thoroughly into one's troubles, who was as concerned as oneself over the drought, the flea-beetle, the risks of rabbits getting into the garden, and the inability of Ronny to distinguish between turnips and weeds? True, Alexander entered equally into everyone else's troubles; perhaps that was what Mrs. Rossiter had meant when she said he lived at a state of high tension; if so, considered Maggie, it was a fine thing to live at and a few more like him would make the world a better place.

Then, too, their close domestic intimacy was more conducive to surface friction than to romantic yearnings. There was never time or chance for tête-à-tête, there was always more work to do than could be got through, one felt so well and was nearly always hungry. Except for Joyce, they all had excellent appetites. Alexander might twist the heart by still looking occasionally like a disembodied Ariel, but it was a certain cure to watch him tucking into Hermia's goulash.

Parliament grew overnight as lively as it had been taciturn. Alexander delivered no more reluctant monologues; it was all he could do to make himself heard. Everybody was for branching out, and chiefly into more stock. Les kept on clamouring for pigs, Mary for an in-calf heifer; Mrs. Rossiter, though she knew nothing about them, put in a courageous claim for bees. Kurt did not mind what stock people kept as long as it produced dung.

"We must have more dung. It is the key to balanced farming. How do you expect me to maintain soil fertility with only two cows, and they hardly ever in the byre?" To hear him talk, you would imagine that that was the main reason why the cows were kept.

"But see here, Kurt," said Alexander, in whom the urge for stock was checked by doubts of their ability to feed it, "it's agreed that we fold the lambs on rape and turnips, and revive the cows' yield on the new ley. There's nothing to beat that for increasing fertility. Stapledon says so."

"And what about Maggie's garden? You won't fold the lambs on her lettuces, I suppose? What about next year's carrots, and this gooseberry plantation we hear of? This year we are cashing in on virgin soil, but next year you will come to me wailing for compost. And how can I make compost if I have no dung?"

"Anyway," declared Mary, "Bluebell's yield isn't going to revive on any ley. She'll be dry by October. Yes, I know what they told you when you bought her, but I happen to know something about cows. Now if I pick an in-calf heifer we'll know just what we're getting. And we need one to calve by September at latest."

"That'd give us plenty of skim," put in Les, seeing his chance. "Nothing like skim for weaners. Mrs. Rossiter says she often has milk over as it is."

"Les, dear, I didn't mean that exactly——"

"And there'll be chat potatoes as soon as we begin to dig. Why, a village of our size at home could feed two pigs on household swill alone. You take it from me, Alexander, pigs is something I understand."

Compounding at length for two pigs and the heifer, Alexander congratulated himself on having at any rate shelved the bees, and was about to suggest an adjournment to the fishing when the first bombshell of her island existence was dropped by little Joyce. Opening her mouth with the sudden shrillness of the timid, she observed:

"One Sunday, if it's quite convenient, I think I'd like to go to church."

No maiden speech could have produced more effect. Les broke the silence by protesting, with a vehemence which proved that this was no fruit of marital consultation:

"But I say, Joycie! Whatever for? You didn't use to go to church at home."

That of course, thought everybody, gave the game away. Joyce was discontented and just wanted to be gadding. She was reminded that it would mean someone's giving up a Sunday's work to take her over and bring her back, and that could hardly be afforded as things stood now. So much she would see for herself, when she came to think it over.

"Oh, all right," said Joyce, pink and close to tears. "I don't mind about it reely. I just thought it would be nice some time, and—you know—like what people do."

Alexander's quiet voice cut into the general relief. "To me it seems right and natural that Joyce should want to go to church."

Silence fell again.

"After all——" He stared at the table, a frown of concentration between his eyes—"I don't want to sound pompous, but that is a side of life which even the most primitive communities thought essential. We've just left it out. We've got used to thinking of the old people as poor and backward by our standards, but hang it all, out of their poverty they built and maintained a church. They may, for all we know, have had a minister. Anyway, they must have been able to persuade a minister to come over and hold services. It seems a poor look-out if we can't do as much."

"No doubt we could, but do we want to?" objected Ronny boldly. "Seems to me we know how to behave ourselves without calling in a lot of out-of-date superstitions. Perhaps that doesn't quite go for the bad hats like me and Rory—but anyway no services are going to do us any good. I don't want to hurt Joyce's feelings, but seeing that Les has told us she doesn't go to church as a general rule——"

"None of us do, I suspect," said Alexander. "But all the same, if we could get to church from Sunay, I daresay Joyce isn't the only one who'd care to go. I'm not an official believer myself, but before we're through with this place we may all have our moments of relying on God. Tell you what, Joyce. When things are easier—perhaps after the harvest— we'll make up a boatload one Sunday, and all go over to kirk at the Kyle. That make you feel better?"

"It's ever so kind of you, reely," said Joyce in the flat and listless little voice that was all he ever got out of her. Maggie, seeing the disappointment on his face, could have put two hands round her milky throat and squeezed hard. Could it really be that she didn't like Alexander? She might have— plainly did have—her legitimate grievance, but not against him. He was never anything but thoughtful for her, often more thoughtful than Les himself. Maggie, a supporter of Joyce as long as she had seemed downtrodden, was now inclined to consider that she was, after all, a gormless little body on whom sensible folks expended more patience than she deserved.

Joyce herself scarcely knew why she had asked to go to church. It wasn't really what she wanted—but if she had asked for what she wanted she wouldn't have got it, so what was the use? She wanted to be left alone with Les, not to take orders from Mrs. Rossiter and Mrs. Fletcher, not to do other people's dirty work. Was that so shocking? Most married women only worked in their own houses, and nobody thought them lazy; on the contrary, everyone knew that a woman's work was never done. She wanted to keep her hands nice, and to buy tasty things in tins, just for Les and herself, and to eat white bread, not this coarse stuff Mrs.

Rossiter baked and everyone else called lovely and nutty. And, most of all, she wanted to go to the pictures.

Of this last and most passionate craving Joyce was, in fact, ashamed. Sunay had been in some ways not at all what she expected, but of course she had known that there wouldn't be any pictures. As a married woman, in love with Les, she had decided that she wouldn't want them. Yet here she was, more than ever in love with Les, and wanting them badly. It was as though, without them, her own love-making did not seem quite real. The lovers on the pictures showed you what to do. That was why Alan Ladd had always been her favourite—because he reminded her of Les.

It was not true, what they thought, that she was all the time unhappy. She loved her home and was immensely proud of it. She could have spent hours in the upkeep and contemplation of her three-piece leatherette suite, her beige and orange folkweave curtains, her cut-glass ornaments with green fluted edges, and the big framed photograph of herself and Les on their wedding day. Her distasteful duties took her into all the other houses, and she knew there was not one that could compare with hers. Mrs. Fletcher's might be considered smarter, but all that white iron furniture and funny pictures of people with eyes above their foreheads gave Joyce the creeps. Mary had nice things, but her place was always in a mess, and Maggie had nothing worth looking at. As for the single boys—how uncomfortably they lived compared to her and Les! Everyone made such a fuss of Dr. Sarratt, yet he was content just to pig it in a room with Kurt, no pictures, no cushions, nothing but a bed and a cane arm-chair each, smelly bottles on a shelf and a few dry old books that weren't even tales.

Joyce loved tales, and her favourites appeared in a magazine called *Romances of Filmland*. This she missed dreadfully, and had asked her best friend, Roma, to be a dear and post it on to her when done with, but Roma had only remembered once. It never occurred to Joyce to send some money to *Romances of Filmland* and have it post itself to her monthly. One bought books off bookstalls, and if there were no bookstalls one did without.

When she thought of her home and Les, Joyce knew she was a lucky girl. When she thought of Sunay she felt lost and frightened; the dogs might bite her, the sheep might run at her—well, the rams, and how was she to know which was a ram?—the cows might turn nasty, or if she went for a walk by herself the mist might come down and she would be lost and very likely walk over a cliff. And when she thought of Mrs. Rossiter and Hermia, she often wished that she were dead.

They treated her, she felt, as a servant—she who had been a switchboard operator and typist, and never done more than the washing-up at Mum's. And in truth that was just how Hermia did treat her, having on the first day decided that she was incapable of learning anything, and might most profitably be set to peeling potatoes and sweeping floors. Mrs. Rossiter, on the other hand, continued to display an indefatigable patience, daily explaining, correcting, deploring, and seasoning her admonishments with encouragement and praise. Yet of the two, sad to say, Joyce hated Mrs. Rossiter by far the most.

"You're not mad at me, are you?" she asked Les that evening as they walked along the cliff-top, their arms round each other's waists. Usually they walked in blissful silence, but to-night Joyce felt a need for explanation. "I mean, for saying that about church?"

"'Course not." He gave her a squeeze. "Though I do think it was a bit of a funny thing to say."

"Oh well, I dunno why I did." She searched within herself. "I daresay it was seeing you so stuck on those pigs."

"Why, what's that to do with it?"

"Well, sometimes I think you care about pigs and things more'n you do about me."

"Go on," said Les, "don't be so soft." But he pulled her round to face him and set his mouth on hers, and for a long, twilight moment the cliffs and the sea-birds, the housework and the drudgery, the loneliness and manifold peril of life on Sunay faded away, and Joyce, like any lady of the screen, was safe and proud in the arms of love.

[II]

In the middle of June the weather broke. The little chill easterly breeze which ever since March had brought the long and golden spring suddenly went round, and became overnight a warm western wind which rolled in wave after wave of mist from the Atlantic, turning as it struck the crags of Torval into fine and penetrating rain.

The change, so long foreseen by Alexander, yet caused general astonishment, and at first, delight. Overnight everything grew and swelled. The apron of flat land which in March had been a pale green, broken here and there into brown by the plough, was now a patchwork of many greens, as the rich loam of Sunay showed what it could produce at the touch of man. The cabbages spread huge blue leaves that touched and hid the earth. The runner beans sown by Maggie in the shelter of the cottages rushed up their poles. And fast as the crops grew, the weeds, on land so long untended, grew yet faster. Nettles, dockens, thistles, spurge—they fell before the hoe and were next day up again. Bracken sallied out from its lairs among the rocks and had to be forked out by hand. Onions, while one's back was turned, disappeared in a forest of wild parsley. Wherever one looked, there was this madness of growing. It was magnificent, and it was also war.

Kurt, remarking that after this he should apply for a quiet job as municipal gravedigger, opened out his first silage pit. He had found an ideal gravelly spot by the burn, and he and

Ronny dragged out the virgin concrete-mixer and spent a happily argumentative morning lining the sides. If they wanted encouragement they had only to look around and watch the grass growing.

When it had rained for ten days without a break, there began to be complaints. Ronny and Hermia in particular were restive. Hermia recollected that mists had always made her feel claustrophobic, and Ronny, the fun of concreting over, began to talk grumpily about grey homes in the west and to spend long hours gossiping with Rory in the barn. But no matter how hard it rained, the two of them still took the *Carrie* out every night, and sometimes, it would seem, all night long. Mrs. Rossiter more than once remarked that she had never heard them come to bed. "Then you must have dropped off, Ma," said Ronny firmly. "We were a bit late, I daresay, but opening out new lobster grounds is a process of trial and error." And certainly there had not been many lobsters yet.

At last it lightened, the transitory lightness, all fitful gusts and brilliant sunshine, that Alexander remembered as characteristic of Hebridean holidays. The boat was fairly blown over to the Kyle. And that was a great day to Maggie, for it was the start of her harvesting.

The actual honour of the first-fruits belonged to Gavin, who had already supplied the village with rather gritty cress for its tea. But this would be the first sale, the first time money had come into Sunay instead of always going out. Maggie's heart was in her mouth as she lifted the first potatoes, but in spite of the drought they were all that had been predicted, shapely and a nice weight, and with that exquisite flavour that only seaweed-fed potatoes possess. The boat took half a dozen hampers, a crate of lettuces, a sack of carrot thinnings neatly done up into bundles, and a creditable cageful of lobsters.

That day also brought the island its first boatload of tourists. The boatman was Rory's silent brother Donald, the one who was at the fishing. Evidently he found it more profitable to be a fisher of men. Having landed his party, he sat down against the jetty wall and lit a cigarette, too polite to make his way to the village unasked. The party came up the track by the burn, and Alexander paused in his work to watch them. They were very young, perhaps a student group, and the leading two were wreathed in ropes. When within shouting distance they hailed him rather diffidently.

"We've come to climb Torval. Is that all right?"

"Of course," said Alexander hospitably. "Go ahead. It's all yours. We make no charge."

The leading two detached themselves and shyly advanced, the girl inquiring:

"You wouldn't by any chance be Dr. Sarratt?"

"I believe I would." He saw with amusement that his work, which was scraping and cleansing a sheep struck by the fly, caused her surprise.

"We were frightfully interested to read in the papers about your—your experiment. Your new methods and everything. It must be a marvellous life."

"Well—it's damned hard work. I'm afraid what you read in the papers was mainly bosh."

"We couldn't stay and help you, could we?" asked the boy. "I mean, we don't a bit mind about Torval, really. We just wanted to see the island. We don't know much about farming, of course, but if there was a job that we could do——"

"That's terribly nice of you, but I think it would be a pity to miss the climb. Torval's a grand viewpoint, good as any in the Isles, and you'll find the ridge sporting just below the top."

Watching their wistful backs as they plodded on uphill, he remembered the many times on holiday that he had stopped to speak to farmers and shepherds, had offered his services, and had been tactfully told to run away and play. Now he knew just how those farmers and shepherds had felt. Yet all day the young things were an undercurrent in his thoughts. He was conscious of their presence on the island, aliens in those wastes that belonged only to his sheep. Already he enjoyed the sensations of an artist giving a glimpse of his creation to the world.

Donald MacLeod was, of course, asked in and given lunch, for which he paid by a shy, grave charm as taking in its way as his brother's pirate impudence. And the young things were asked in and given tea, for which they paid in hard cash. Mrs. Rossiter, slightly perturbed, came up to tell Alexander about it after they had gone.

"They got caught in that shower and were wet through, and they asked so nicely, I hadn't the heart to refuse. And they really seemed upset when I said we didn't charge. So I asked what the usual charge was at the Kyle, and they told me one and six."

"That's all right, I should say, Mrs. R." But he was surprised to find himself also perturbed. "I admit my first impulse would have been to stand them tea, but we are not the deer-stalking lady, and that lairdly attitude is just what we don't like and can't afford. After all, if it doesn't debase us to grow food for the visitors at the Kyle, it shouldn't debase us to sell it to them here. One and six means about a hundred per cent profit, I suppose?"

"If you think it was too much——"

"Ah, no; who are we to undersell the local product? I only trust that Hermia will have had an equally repaying day."

Half an hour later the *Gannet* was home, and news of Hermia's proceedings was brought to him by Maggie, who came flying, ruddy with triumph, up the hill.

"Fifteen pounds! Alexander, that's what she got—fifteen pounds! I had it worked out that a fair price would be about ten. Of course there was the lobsters—I didn't think to ask how much of it was for them. But there's not been a lettuce at the Kyle till now. Maybe one crate from Fort William, and they were yellow. Yon manager at the hotel says he'll take anything we can send. He wants to know when we'll have peas. There's a wee bit o' competition, you see, with the boarding-houses and the stores. That's where Hermia had him. Och, you're right, she is a wonder. And we havena' really begun yet—no dairy stuff or fruit. Think of it— fifteen pounds!"

She discovered that he was laughing.

"Dr. Sarratt, has a body ever tried to box your ears?"

"Mistress Moffat, would ye no' like for to be the first?"

"Och, no. You're too much of a gentleman."

"Don't you believe it, Maggie lass. Go on, hit out—oh well, I'll do it anyway." He turned her face in his hand and put a kiss on one scarlet cheek. Maggie departed in a daze. She knew perfectly well that she had been sauced and ought to feel affronted, but her heart said: he's woken up.

But at Parliament, as well as triumph, there was dispute. In the mail brought by the boat there was a letter for Alexander from the editor of the *Daily Courier*, requesting permission to send a representative to Sunay and report on the progress of the communal experiment.

"I assume", said Alexander, "we're all agreed that I refuse?"

"Now why on earth?" demanded Hermia, her opposition gaining weight from the fact that this was her day quite as much as Maggie's.

"Are you asking me seriously? After that—that monstrous exhibition of journalistic inaccuracy and sensation-mongering ineptitude? Atom island—the very title was a lie —as though we kept a heavy-water factory up the burn. And all that stuff about scientific methods and revolutionizing Scottish agriculture—said of a set of amateurs who can't even shear a sheep—it must have made us the laughing-stock of the Isles. It'll take us years to live it down."

"My good Alexander, you live in a world of your own. I understand the value of publicity if you don't. Old McKellar at the hotel has got that *Courier* cutting on the smoking-room mantelpiece, and he makes a point of telling the guests that he gets his greengrocery from the atom isle. That's how I was able to screw top prices out of him this afternoon. I grant you, Maggie, they were fine lettuces, but the *Courier* had swelled their hearts to twice the size."

"Silliness," said Alexander crossly, "cannot possibly be of permanent benefit. The respect of the folk in these parts will do us more good in the end than lying tales. When we have something to show I'm prepared to show it—though not necessarily to the *Daily Courier*. Well, Hermia and I have made our feelings clear. Anybody else ache to have Fleet Street snooping round?" His angry eye, travelling the table, fell on Simon's stricken face, and his heart smote him. Nothing had previously been said about that interview, but that the guilt of it had been haunting Simon there could now be small doubt.

For once in a way Mary's robustness had its uses. "I must say", she commented, "I think it's a bit previous. Why not put the chappie off, at any rate till we've built up a decent herd?"

"Or", put in Ronny, pursuing his King Charles's head, "till we've built the dam?"

"Ronald, when we've built that dam, we'll invite the Kyle Advertiser and Sound of Arkaig Bulletin in person, if there is one, and you yourself shall break a bottle of Rory's name-less poison over its scandalized head. Meanwhile, is it the will of the majority that I choke the *Courier* off? Hermia, please don't think I minimize your achievement to-day in meeting the flinty Highlander on his own ground. Maggie, from now on McKellar gets as much stuff as you can send.

Call on the help you want for lifting and grading. Kurt, I think we feel brave enough to face the accounts to-night, seeing this is the first time you've something on the credit side. The floor is yours."

But watching his moody face as he sat listening to Kurt's precise and orderly report, Maggie perceived that the exquisite pleasure he had shared at her news was somehow tarnished. Plainly, as far as she was concerned, Dr. Sarratt had gone to sleep again.

[III]

It was not strictly true that none of them could shear a sheep. Les could, and Mary too, though she was rather out of practice. But they and Rory could not between them manage the flock, and the MacLeod help was again to be called in. Not only the silent Donald, but old Mr. MacLeod himself were to come over when shearing on their own and their neighbours' crofts was done.

In the present state of the weather, with one fine day to five wet, it did not seem likely that this would be before the middle of August. And no doubt it was as well. Each day the dogs rounded up one or two ewes for the beginners to practise on. Progress, as in everything else to do with shepherding, was dishearteningly slow. Alexander's first sheep took him forty minutes, and he was little reassured by the reminder that they would be easier later on when the wool had had more time to rise. Ronny, congenitally clumsy, showed no aptitude at all, and the sufferings of an animal under his fingers were pathetic. It was rapidly decided that his muscular body and long arms would be best employed on shearing day in carrying the sheep from the pens.

It looked easy when Rory did it. He began at the back of the head, worked round to the throat and cut back the fleece from the chest, then away from the right foreleg and down the belly to the hind leg and tail. The fleece fell back gently, ivory white and exquisitely soft on the inside. In two minutes more the sheep was clear and naked. At that speed he would nick them occasionally, but the sheep hardly seemed to mind, and a dab of antiseptic was put instantly on the cut.

But Alexander had a horror of nicking them, and therefore, in spite of his sensitive physicist's fingers, continued painstaking and slow. Kurt, more light-hearted, got on famously, which he attributed to the original tailor in his ancestry.

To Rory they all seemed comically butter-fingered. "*A dhuine*," he would remark at intervals throughout the sessions, "but my Tat will laugh."

"Let no one imagine", said Kurt, busily dabbing picric acid, "that we are taking all this trouble for the benefit of our sheep. Our prime and no doubt unattainable object is to escape the scorn of Rory's Dad."

It was now tacitly understood that Rory only worked with the sheep. All the hoeing and lifting and grading, the rejoicings over good boat-loads and prices, were regarded by him as so much childishness. If it gave them pleasure, that was well; but it was not the kind of work he was prepared to do. And certainly no one could say that he was idle. All day, in the mist, he was out with the dogs, ranging the island, looking for ewes in trouble or struck by the fly. When there was time Alexander went too. He loved the sense of eerie, spaceless solitude, the opportunities of getting lost on a really thick day, and as the weeks wore on, the gradually acquired feel of the hills, so that he began to be subconsciously certain of his whereabouts in no visibility at all. In time he gave up carrying a compass, and by sniffing the air, like the dogs, found his way home. Most of all he loved to come out suddenly on the great cliffs to the south and west, imagine the Long Island lying fifteen miles beyond the grey curtain, and feel the soft wind off the Atlantic bringing in the endless rain. Being wet to the skin was something he came to take for granted; what did it matter, when one was always warm?

The flystruck sheep worried him. The spread of this particularly cruel pest was favoured by the muggy weather and the thick growth of heather over so much of the island. He and Rory treated all they could find, and Rory took it unconcernedly, assuring him that the attacks were much less serious than those on the mainland, where one could find sheep still on their legs but eaten alive.

On the rare days when the wind, shifting a point, brought wild riven skies and shafts of glittering sun, the scythes came out, and the mower was taken over such bits of fenced ground as had been saved for meadow. Kurt's pit silo seemed voracious. When the mist hung still at five hundred feet and the sea was glassy, they crossed again to Latay and took a cut of that wonderful grass, which was bundled up in sacking and let down by ropes. This was an operation which gave uncommon pleasure; it combined thrift with the enterprise and adventure generally expected of an island life. The return after that to potato-lifting was undeniably an anticlimax. Perhaps it was no wonder Rory looked bored.

At length, one August morning, when the smell of rain seemed for the moment to have left the wind, old Mr. MacLeod and Donald arrived unheralded. All hands mustered for gathering, and the sheep were down in the park by late afternoon, after which the visitors were taken on a tour of inspection. Alexander was aware of an absurd nervousness. It was the first time that anyone knowledgeable from the outside world had seen the farm.

Mr. MacLeod looked old and small to be the father of two strapping sons (or three, if the minister might be presumed to take after the others). But he was probably not more than fifty, and might have been inches taller in his youth. The harsh life and miserable diet of the Highland crofter had left him bent and gap-toothed, as in due course it would leave his children. Nevertheless he was shrewdly formidable, with uncertain English, and the deprecating smile common to the family did not conceal his real opinions as effectively as it did his sons.'

"What do you think of our sheep now they're down, Mr. MacLeod?" asked Alexander anxiously.

"Ah, not pat, not pat. You will be getting some fresh rams next month?"

"Yes, indeed, and we'll be most grateful for your advice. But ultimately, you know, we aim to switch to Shetlands. I'm told they're not nearly so prone to attack by the fly, and we'd get a much better price for the wool."

A dreadful change came over old Mr. MacLeod, though his smile remained glued to his face. It dawned on Alexander that a brick of appalling dimensions had been dropped.

"And the muttons! Where will you be getting such meat as the Plackfaces? Tell me that now?"

"But the Shetland are equally——"

"You will haf the Goferment price for the wool."

"Yes, but I hate relying on a subsidy, and it would be so much more satisfactory to produce a wool that was good for tweed."

"I am not knowing anything about them Shetlants. I haf nefer hat to do with Shetlants. Plackfaces is goot enough for me and for all the farmers hereapouts. But they tell us you will be hafing many new iteas?"

Alexander apologized and disclaimed, but the harm was done. The breed that was Mr. MacLeod's life and religion had been disparaged. He led the way back to the fields, trusting that in grass and cabbages there might be less occasion for hurt feelings.

Mr. MacLeod approved the ley, and looked at the other crops with an envy which was reassuring, though he seemed determined to assume they had grown of themselves. "There wass always peautiful grass on Sunay," he commented. "It iss goot soil you haf here." He agreed that the folded lambs were fattening nicely, but pointed out that it would be difficult to get them to market; a boat went round the Isles in October, taking off the unfinished sheep, and gave a price that most farmers were contented with. Alexander meekly indicated that those at Sunay hoped to do better. Mr. MacLeod passed over the market garden, which interested him no more than his son, and deplored the shocking weather which, he noticed, had so far prevented them from making any hay.

"Ah, but we've made our first pitful of silage. We can do that in any weather. Come and take a look."

"That is fery interesting. There iss a chap in Ardnamurchan makes it, I heard. But when the petter weather comes, you will haf some goot hay from this grass."

"Why, no, I think not. We plan to turn all our grass into silage. Hay is such a gamble in this climate, and the loss in nutritive value——"

"No hay at all? And that will be all the oats you haf?"

"Just for feeding in the sheaf to the stock."

"You could haf grown a fine crop of oats on this lant."

"Yes, but Mr. MacLeod, we haven't any threshing tackle, and with the difficulties of transport——"

"No hay. No oats. Only this silech. Ach well, you will be hafing new iteas. Round these parts we are fery conservative." He looked about him unhappily, as if seeking something friendly and familiar. "There iss goot peats on Sunay?" he suggested. "I mint helping cut the peats here when I wass a little poy."

Alexander's sense of guilt deepened. "Well—the fact is, we haven't cut any peats this year. We were enormously busy in March, as you can imagine. Indeed, I question whether it will ever pay us to cut peats. Later we hope to have our own current, and meanwhile I believe it's worth importing coal and leaving ourselves free to work on the early vegetables."

"Yess. You will be puying coal. To you the money will not be mattering."

"Let me assure you, Mr. MacLeod——" Suddenly Alexander knew it was no use. They returned to the village in a courteous, smiling, unhappy silence. Only in the byre was any friendliness revived. It was milking time, and Bluebell and Daisy, together with Mary, made a picture to soften even a Covenanter's heart, the weather fortunately ensuring that Mary was covered from open-necked shirt to toe. Mr. MacLeod all but patted her on the head, and told her he had never seen bonnier cows. He liked to see a woman occupied about the cows, where she belonged.

The two days of shearing passed off amicably, and if Mr. MacLeod was laughing he did it inwardly, while his comments, being in Gaelic, were only comprehensible to his sons. As a matter of fact, Alexander considered that he and Kurt did not do too badly; by the second day their time was down to ten minutes. Ronny and Simon, with the hard job of drawing the ewes from the pens and bringing them over to the shearing benches, had the sweat pouring off them, and reached the second afternoon white with fatigue, and there were pauses while the shearers waited. Mr. MacLeod shyly moved his bench next to Mary's and whiled away these minutes in halting gallantry. And Mary responded admirably. Not a damn or a bloody escaped her. She was used to farm men and knew the way to handle them. Kurt, in the intervals of admiring his own performance, alertly noted this display of tact in a girl who to Alexander continued pitiably clumsy and loud. His smile as he honed her shears was knowing. For Kurt's assiduities had so far prevailed with Mary that she would now ungraciously demand his services where before she had ungraciously repulsed them.

The MacLeods departed in their little boat, the *Annabella*, with the twilight, the old gentleman politely wishing Alexander luck and warmly engaging Mary to visit him next time

136

she was at the Kyle. The rain was coming down again, and the others had trooped back to the village to wash off the filth and exhaustion of the day. But Alexander remained with his elbows on the jetty wall, staring out to sea long after the boat was swallowed up in the mist. To himself he suddenly seemed pompous and impertinent, his knowledge a matter of book and hearsay, cockle-shell fragile beside the long seasons of experience that lay in that old man.

A soft voice behind him made him start. "Never you mind, Toctor, what my Tat was after saying."

Alexander bit back a smile. There had never been a sign till now that Rory identified himself with Sunay, and was prepared to back it against the clan. And perhaps, even now, it was just his Highland tact.

"He thinks us an extravagant and scatterbrained lot, I'm afraid—and who's to say he's wrong? After all, his system has worked for a hundred years." He felt in his oilskin pockets and found cigarettes for them both.

Rory muttered something in Gaelic, a tongue of which Alexander now knew enough to recognize the words "bodach garrach" with a certain shamefaced delight. Presently he added: "The olt men round here are never wanting any change. That's why things is never getting any better. Too many olt men there are, in the Highlants. It makes us young ones want to be getting out."

"D'you want to get out, Rory?"

Rory smoked on for a while, deep in reflection. Then he observed with a grin:

"*A Dhia*, he's not seen petter lambs than ours, no, nor petter cows neither. He won't be able to help telling them that, this evening at the Kyle."

Chapter Six

[I]

Mary got her heifer at the end of August. Her conquest of Mr. MacLeod had borne valuable fruit, for autumn-calving cows are not easy to come by in the Isles. But Mr. MacLeod sent word by Donald, who now regularly brought over boatloads of damp tourists, that a neighbour had a nice little Shorthorn which might be what she wanted. Rory and Alexander, experienced in ferrying over the two previous cows, went with her in the *Carrie*, and at the last moment Maggie was forced into the party on someone's remembering that she had never yet revisited the Kyle. "Tut," said Alexander, "these peasant women. One can scarcely get them to stir from the croft."

It was, in fact, a strange sensation to be crossing the water again, to see bustling quays, pleasure-boats putting out, a red-funnelled steamer alongside, a train shunting in the station, and what looked like enormous crowds of people. Summer visitors had overrun the Kyle, eclipsing the native population of loungers which had seemed to Maggie so hostile when she saw them last. Now, on the contrary, these were friends, and it was amusing to feel oneself one of them and a Highlander by right of toil. It was amusing to have Donald hail her as the *Carrie* drew in to the mossy stone slipway, and to hear the English telling each other that that must be the boat from Sunay, and clicking their cameras. At once elated and abashed by all this notice after her months of solitude, Maggie busied herself superintending the unloading of the vegetables, which were piled on to the hotel truck; though really there was nothing for her to do, willing hands apparently considering it an honour to assist.

Mary and Donald went off to look at the cow, and Maggie set to work on the marketing list entrusted to her by Mrs. Rossiter. It was pleasantly short, for nowadays they were importing only a few basic groceries. And this was just as well, for there was certainly nothing much to buy. She was again struck by the anaemic poverty of this central and important Highland township. It had no greengrocer, and the three general stores were alike in the dreariness of their stock. The same shabby packets of cereal filled up the windows, the same over-large boxes of kippers were failing to tempt the English tourist by their cumbersomeness and their smell. Even the picture postcards dated back to the dawn of photography. There was a market here for ten times the food that they could grow.

Wandering about the three streets, one met and re-met the same faces, and presently she ran into Donald, who said shyly that his mother was expecting her for tea. The family croft lay up the hill-side, at the end of a filthy mountain lane along which were scattered other crofts at untidy and un-related angles. Small attempt had been made at any to culti-vate the garden pieces, which by Sunay standards undoubt-edly did look barren and unencouraging. A black cow was tethered at the MacLeods' door, and Mary's loud voice could be heard within.

She lolled in the best chair, her long legs in their tweed breeches stretched out, and gave the delighted Mr. MacLeod a lively description of her haggling with his neighbour. The room was tiny, crowded with cheap pale-brown furniture, and quite comfortless. Place of honour on the mantelpiece was filled by a photograph of an elderly, set-looking man in black; this must be the minister, who in fact was only five years older than Rory. Mrs. MacLeod, who spoke little Eng-lish, stood by meekly, and with her a tall girl whom Rory sheepishly introduced as his young lady.

139

Maggie looked with interest at this Annag, whose pale oval face would have been beautiful if she had not lost two front teeth. Both women had the whiteness of anaemia and a house-bound life. One guessed that they lived on bannocks and tea. These were now produced, together with a shop-bought raspberry jam unnaturally full of seeds, and a tin of prawns which must, Maggie feared, have made sad inroads on the housekeeping resources. And suddenly it struck her that on Sunay they lived like fighting cocks, and that if Rory was ruddy and bouncing where Donald was pallid and shy, it might partly be a question of sheer nourishment. Under cover of Mary's merriment she tried to draw Annag into conversation.

"Were ye not ever on Sunay, whiles?"

Annag shook her head. It appeared she had never been anywhere by boat from the Kyle, except up the Sound to Skye on the steamer.

"Did the lads never take you fishing?"

"Ach no," said Rory, "what would a girl like her be doing in a fishing-boat? Girls iss only in the way."

"And she never visited you on Sunay all those years when you were there alone?"

"Why would she?" Rory winked. "I wass always visiting her."

"Well, I call it a shame. I dinna know why you lassies put up with such treatment. Get him to bring you over for a stay on Sunay. It's a bonny place, ye'd find."

"That iss a goot itea." Apparently it had not before occurred to him. "One of these days I will be bringing her across, when there iss a croft to spare." And he said something in Gaelic to Annag which turned her bright pink, when, in spite of her worn face and her toothlessness, she unmistakably looked a pretty girl.

It was time to get back to the boat and Alexander, who had been in conference with the bank and the hotel. Their appearance on the slipway with a cow, obviously about to be embarked, created an even greater stir than their arrival in the morning, and rows of heads soon lined the steamer pier under which the slipway sheltered.

"Hi, what d'you think of her?" shouted Mary as soon as Alexander came into sight.

"You know I don't understand the first thing about cows. She looks a nice little beast enough, but isn't she a bit thin?"

"That's because you've got used to Bluebell and Daisy. It's six weeks till she calves, and you'll be astonished at the difference our good grass makes. Now then, Polly girl. It's all going to be over soon."

"Why do cows have such dreary names? Couldn't we call her something more picturesque?"

"It wouldn't answer," said Mary seriously. "I mean, she wouldn't. Cows are always called that sort of name." She got into the boat, which had been lined with turves and sacking, and held out to the much-perturbed Polly a handful of oats. The four men simultaneously seized the poor creature and heaved. A cheer went up from the heights above. The cow found herself in a strange world that smelt and wobbled and was full of noise. But kind hands were patting her neck, and bravely she faced the unknown.

The jetty at Sunay, with its steep stairway, was useless for landing cows. But the barnacle-covered rocks below the church, which, it might be guessed, had been used by the islanders before jetties were thought of, answered the purpose very well. It was a matter of some delicacy, even with Kurt and Ronny to help, inducing a mainland cow to step out into nine inches of water and pick her way over slippery seaweed. But at last it was done, and Mary led her off tenderly to the byre.

"We'll have to get a bull," Alexander commented. "We can't go through this performance every time the cows need one. I don't feel so half-hearted about it now I see what fodder Sunay can produce." He and Maggie had drawn abreast of the church, and he suddenly asked her: "Have you ever looked inside?"

"I believe I never thought to."

It was roofless, but not without dignity. The walls had been solidly built and stood firm. They passed under an archway that had once been filled by a door, and found themselves in a little green ruin, carpeted with turf nibbled short by the sheep. The inevitable nettle-clump had established itself in one corner, and brambles climbed in through the eastern window that framed the view of the Sound and the Kyle. The place had been loved and tended once, a centre of comfort in a hard and lonely life, and a sort of compunction swept them both as they stood and looked at its forlornness. Then Maggie perceived that it was tended still. "Look," she said, taking him by the arm, and there, under the window, where the altar should have been, was a bunch of withered flowers, crammed into a jam jar.

Neither Mrs. Rossiter nor Hermia, who did the flowers for the kitchen table, put them into jam jars.

"Poor kid," said Alexander, his voice taking on the tenderness which it always held when he spoke of Joyce. "Nobody remembered that promise. We were all too absorbed in our little games. What a lousy shame."

"We've been verra much occupied. Come to that, we still are."

"I don't care, we'll take the boat over next Sunday. Or no —why shouldn't we hold a service here? It feels to me a better place than that tin tabernacle at the Kyle. D'you think that minister would come for a set of English heathens? I've run into him once or twice, and he seems a nicish sort of chap."

"He'd have his own services to attend to."

"Well then—when Rory's brother is about and can relieve him. Didn't the family say he was expected soon on holiday?

Look, Maggie, you were brought up a daughter of the kirk. You ask him."

"Och, no, I'm a lapsed daughter. He's far more likely to do it for you.'

"Would he feel insulted at being asked to hold a service in a ruin? If he has a drop of the old Covenanting blood he ought to jump at it. What sort of service would he give us? I don't know anything about Presbyterians. Would we have to sing metrical psalms? I'd like to sing the 121st here, but not in some horrid jingle."

"I daresay that could be arranged. A lot of the kirks don't use the metrical version any more."

The suggestion when he made it at Parliament aroused no interest in anyone but Mrs. Rossiter. Joyce looked merely blank. "Don't let me interfere with anyone's idea of fun," said Ronny, "but this church parade isn't compulsory, I suppose?"

"I'm sure Gavin and Jamie would like it," said Hermia, "particularly if they're allowed to sing 'All things bright and beautiful'. They favour me with it every night at bedtime, but they really need a wider audience."

"I was going to say", interposed Mrs. Rossiter, "that there would be some difficulty over the music. We have no instrument except Kurt's accordion, and that hardly seems quite suitable."

"I beg leave to contradict you, Mrs. R.," said Kurt, sitting up suddenly. "In the hands of an artist the accordion could sound perfectly reverent. I shall myself supervise the music for this service, and Ronald, of course you will be present. You have the only bass on the island. Shall it be said that we, a set of cultivated people, at least four of us musically gifted, cannot stage a performance adequate to the requirements of a simple Highland pastor? Arrange with your Mr. Farquharson, Alexander, what items are wanted for the occasion. Then leave the rest to me."

Kurt's notions of worship on Sunay might be slightly theatrical, but his unexpected enthusiasm turned the tide. Mr. Farquharson was approached by Alexander on the next boat-trip to the Kyle. He was a spare, gentle ascetic, whose feeling towards his new parishioners seemed to be mainly nervousness. The request obviously gratified even while it surprised him. He felt sure his brother-minister would be willing to take his place the following Sunday evening. He agreed to a simple form of evensong that should suit all parties. It did not seem to worry him that only Miss Moffat and Roderick MacLeod were members of his church. He had evidently not expected the others to be members of any church at all.

Preparations for the event at Sunay caused a considerable stir. The total muster of books of devotion produced a Bible, prayer and hymn books, the property of Mrs. Rossiter, and a prayer book, bound in white vellum and patently unopened, which had been a wedding present to Joyce. Ronny arranged to move in with Rory for the night, that the minister might sleep in worthy privacy. Kurt held daily choir practices after the midday meal. Alexander scythed the nettles in the church, and suggested to Hermia that Joyce might do the decorations. "She'll make it look like nothing on earth," said Hermia.

"Well, does it matter? I don't suppose Mr. Farquharson has ever heard of Mrs. Spry."

Maggie had for some time past found herself responsible for the religious education of Gavin and Jamie, rather to her disquiet. But with them it was impossible to avoid for long the subject of God, who was a real person, though not always quite distinguishable from one of Rory's *bocains*. "My farver can climb cliffs better'n anyone on Sunay," Gavin would inform the passer-by, "'cept, of course, Jesus." Their perpetual questioning of the divine behaviour—which, when sheep were flystruck or lambs lost their eyes, did sometimes seem illogical—baffled Maggie, and she appealed anxiously to Hermia to know what she should tell them.

"Oh, whatever your common sense suggests to you, my dear," replied Hermia amiably, and her tone added: as long as I'm not bothered.

Maggie's common sense, after some probing, suggested as much as she could remember of her Sunday-school instruction. It might not seem now as incontrovertible as it had then, but at least it saved a lot of argument, and was received by Gavin and Jamie with the liveliest interest and pleasure. They looked forward keenly to the service, which would keep them an extra hour out of bed, and had several searching theological problems saved up for Mr. Farquharson, who, they had been promised, would hear their prayers the night he came to stay.

On the Friday the wind veered again, and there set in the hot, hazy September which is frequent in the Isles. Being warm and dry again, peeling off clammy oilskins and squelching gum-boots, seemed to bring everyone back to life. Rory and Ronny had to be reminded that there must be no Sunday fishing, and Mary that on no account should she affront the minister in the white swimming suit. She was also asked to wear a skirt, but no such garment existed in her wardrobe. Mr. Farquharson would just have to take her best corduroy trousers in his stride.

The *Gannet*, sent over in the afternoon to fetch him, came back through a heat-haze, the colour bleached out of sea and sky, the great sheet of heather which now covered the flanks of Torval turned a rusty red, and the very stones of the jetty warm to the touch as he ascended its steps. Like all other visitors, he was full of decent and shy curiosity. Mrs. Rossiter showed him the village, and Alexander the fields, which were a scene of sabbatarian emptiness. Even the children and the dogs were struck into respectful silence.

"It's a bonny place you have here," said the minister at the end of his tour, "and prosperous, by the look of it. A change indeed since yon good lady's day, when there would be nothing stirring on the island but the deer. This is more the Sunay I mind when I was a boy. It bred a fine race of people then." He looked round at them benignly and seemed about to add something, then checked himself and followed Mrs. Rossiter back past the jetty to the church.

This was Kurt's moment. The accordion crashed into "O God our help in ages past" almost as impressively as though it had, in truth, been an organ; and his handful of voices soared bravely up to the open sky, and mingled with the gulls' crying, the bleat of a distant lamb lost by its mother, the soft plod of the sea ripples on the rocks below, all the many noises that made up the great symphony of sound on Sunay. So, thought Alexander, had voices rung out, strong and confident, in the old days which the minister remembered. Something was being brought to life again—or was it only a play-acting, a pretence?

Simon read a chapter from Isaiah, and then they knelt on the soft turf to pray. And now, above the minister's quiet voice, the island sounds came very plainly. Alexander caught himself wondering where the lamb was. Not all at once could he detach himself from the fields that were his charge and constant care, or from the vast empurpled swelling of the moor, dangerous in its loveliness.

"My text", said Mr. Farquharson, leaning his hands on the little table which had to serve him for a pulpit, "is taken from the twelfth chapter of St. Luke. 'Fear not, little flock; for it is your Father's good pleasure to give you the kingdom.'

"Ye must, I think, have often noticed how the imagery of sheep and shepherding runs all through the Bible. Ye have come here from many different walks of life, but now ye are all shepherds yourselves. . . ."

With the top level of his mind Alexander intelligently followed Mr. Farquharson's sermon, which was simple, rather

courageously adapted to the mentalities of his widely different hearers, and compelling in its effort to make them feel,
here and now on Sunay, in their comings and goings about
the farm and the cliffs and the mountain, the living presence
of God. But underneath his thoughts, like a fugal theme,
there ran, on and on, endlessly, the words of the text. Fear
not, little flock. Fear not. Fear not.

He had always been anxious and afraid. He still was. Fear
had sharpened the excitement of finding the place and its
population. Fear of storms, losses and disasters in a life
brought so close to the elements. Fear for the others, that
they would not be happy, not settle, not work hard enough,
falter and fall by the way. Was this a reassurance? Was it a
promise? Words from such a source—surely they, if anything, could constitute a promise? Fear not, fear not. It is
your Father's good pleasure. But was it?

He looked round for Joyce; her face was happy, but the
cause, it seemed, was some remote day-dream, and secretly
she held Les by the hand. Ronny—he wore his familiar look
of scowling concentration, but most probably it was for his
lobster-pots. Maggie appeared alert and interested—bless the
girl, she was all right, she always was—and Kurt, pleased
with his own part in a creditable performance, was critically
appreciating Mr. Farquharson's. Rory was unnaturally
brushed and bland; perhaps in his youth he had heard too
many sermons to listen to this one as it deserved. Mary's
pagan splendour was curiously dimmed in the shadowy ruin;
she looked lost and restless; now her eyes met his, and this,
as so often, suddenly embarrassed him. On Simon's face he
surprised a look of real desolation; poor lad, why could he
never let up? On Sunay he had at first seemed to be coming
right with himself; would it all be to do again? Hermia—her
eyes were on her children, and she wore that creamy smile—
wonderful creature in spite of a few pretty obvious weak-
nesses. As for Gavin and Jamie, sitting on their little chairs

in the front row, they drank in, open-mouthed, every word the minister said. Their most excited hopes were confirmed by this gentleman who obviously knew. God was on Sunay, and any day now, when they were out on the hills, they might meet Him face to face.

Fear not, little flock. What ecstasy to let go this painful, fragile finger-hold on reason, and fall back into the strong and buoyant sea of faith. What comfort to say and believe those three blessed words: not my responsibility. Fear not— it was a guarantee. All will be well.

He got hurriedly to his feet; the others were already standing, and about to launch into the children's hymn. Kurt had it most elegantly arranged; one verse for the women, one for the men, one for Gavin and Jamie by themselves, everybody in the chorus. "The purple-headed mountain, the river running by. . . ." How very nice and suitable. What a lot of cheerful noise they could make when they let themselves go. Hurrah, hurrah, amen.

They walked back to the village in the last misty sunshine, carrying their chairs. "A very moving experience, Mr. Farquharson," Mrs. Rossiter was saying, and there were positively tears in her prominent little eyes; poor soul, she had her troubles, and for all her tiresomeness she never made a fuss. "Will you forgive my hurrying on? I've a dinner in the oven."

"Bed, infants," said Hermia. "No, you can't ask Mr. Farquharson any questions now. I'm sure he'll very kindly answer them when he comes to hear your prayers." Her place by Mr. Farquharson's side was taken by Mary, who invited him in her confident way to come and see the cows milked. "I don't mind telling you", she could be heard observing as she led him off, "that I'm not much of a one for churches as a rule. But somehow, this evening, it was okay." And Ronny had substituted "All things bright and beautiful" for the dance tunes he usually whistled. Perhaps, even to him, some sort of message had got through.

As a matter of fact, he was to whistle "All things bright and beautiful" for a fortnight on end, till finally it became rather more than anyone could bear.

[II]

They sat in a half-circle on the causeway after dinner, everybody present to do honour to the minister—hardly since the *ceilidh* had such a muster occurred. The shadow of Torval crept up behind them, but still the village caught the long northern sun, and the haze lifted with the coming of evening, to show the mainland mountains opalescent against an almost white sky.

"Doctor," said Mr. Farquharson, "I've a favour to ask." Alexander, who was coming to know this opening, smilingly got ready his lecture on nuclear fission. And sure enough, Mr. Farquharson was not quite clear on the difference between the two forms of uranium, and was, moreover, fully able to follow an explanation in rather more than elementary terms.

"It is a verra wonderful discovery," he remarked at the end. "Infeenite possibilities." He looked at Alexander in his nervous, friendly way. "I'll not disguise from you, Doctor, that there's been a certain amount of speculation as to just why ye gave up your researches, and took to this—well— rather spectacularly different way of life."

"Yes, just why did you, Alexander?" Kurt put in. "We've all been dying to ask you, but no one had the nerve."

"If I have been impertinent——" began Mr. Farquharson in some distress.

"Heavens, no, sir. But I don't see that I've any answer that anybody here couldn't make. Like the rest of us, I got tired of my groove. That was all."

"That's not fair," said Kurt crossly. "The initial impulse came from you. We merely followed. And as Mr. Farquharson was implying, you were not in a groove."

"Well, I'm not going to be the only one to stand and deliver. If this is life-histories, then we all play."

"We know, Alexander—you don't want to sound pompous," said Ronny sympathetically, and in the face of a general laugh, Alexander was obliged to proceed.

"All right—well then, first, as to grooves. Only those can judge of them that are in them. I've been accused, I know, of running away—atom isle as ivory tower—that sort of thing. I categorically deny it. The lab was the ivory tower to me, a nice safe spot to look on from, full of intellectual stimulus and self-important geniuses with panaceas—while other people did the fighting. Subconsciously, I suppose, I was always dissatisfied, and I can tell you I wasn't the only one. Then one day it got to the top layer. I noticed that real life was going on outside. So I thought I'd get out and grab my share of it while I was still young enough."

"But look here," protested Ronny, "you can't just oppose science to life. Why, I've read somewhere that your own line could warm and light the world in ten years' time."

"It's conceivable. But will it be allowed to? There's my answer. Thousands of us working on the means to increase knowledge and power—nobody doing anything effective to ensure that we use them properly. The balance is wrong."

"But there is not", said Mr. Farquharson, "such a thing as the scientific vocation?—a sort of divine curiosity, if I may put it so?"

"Indeed there is, and anyone worth his salt has some of it, but I don't think it need be confined to scientists. I know I've had plenty of occasion to exercise it here on Sunay. And there are certain people—my professor at Cambridge was one—who undoubtedly have it in such a degree that any other course than the pursuit of pure knowledge would be for them unthinkable. But for the rest of us, you know, it was largely a matter of fashion. The clever boys of my generation were pushed into the laboratory as the clever ones of yours, sir, were pushed into the Church. We came in for the backwash of the great Victorian belief in science as the new religion. And—if you'll forgive my putting it like this—just about the same proportion of us discovered, when it was too late, that we really had no vocation at all."

"I've never pictured you in orders," observed Hermia, "but I daresay you might have done."

"I think not. Politics or preaching are the two logical courses, I agree, for anyone who is disquieted at the misuse of knowledge, but I haven't sufficiently positive convictions for either. I do utterly believe, though—saving your presence, sir—that I'll only have this one life, and that anything left undone at the end of it will never be done at all. When I was younger I thought the finest thing one could do with a life was to add to the total of knowledge—no, I don't suppose I thought, I merely assumed, because that was the mental climate of the time. Now I've a suspicion that knowledge will look after itself. The discovery that isn't made in one generation will be made in the next, or even in the next year or so a couple of countries away. I've seen it happen time and again. The remaining secrets of the universe can wait a while longer. They'll all come out in the wash."

He brooded, his eyes on the sea. "But imagination, emotion, happiness—those are irreplaceable, unique. To add in some way to the total of them now seems to me the highest one can aim at. Don't imagine I've any great conceit of my capacities, either. Just to increase the amount of food and shelter in the world, make it possible for a few more kids to be born, help a few other people to get out of grooves that don't suit them—that seemed to me enough for a start. Anyway, those things are basic, and a lot of the rest is frills."

"And so", said Mr. Farquharson gently, "ye set about looking for Tir nan Og?"

"Sunay?—Oh well, that was partly accident. I'd been overdoing things, and went up to Skye for a rest, and the farmer I stay with there is a member of the War Ag. and had an inkling while I was there that this island might be for sale. All I knew was that I wanted to farm, and if possible on land that no one else was using, and it seemed a pointer. I rushed off to the trustees, a set of staid Edinburgh lawyers, and offered them the only price I could afford. I think they were just startled into accepting it by the uncanny way I'd materialized. If they'd been more fly to the ways of Fleet Street, they'd have advertised it, waited a bit while the publicity was whipped up, and then got ten thousand."

"Which, I suppose," said Hermia with sudden interest, "we might still get if we sold out to-day?"

"But as for your Tir nan Og, sir, I believe we'll query that. It still suggests the escapists' paradise. But we claim not to have left science behind. We've a tractor and two motor-boats, we make compost and silage, and one of these days, as Ronald will tell you, we'll build a dam and generate our own power. That's our justification for coming here. We've a lot less agricultural wisdom than Rory, whose brains we pick. But we've technical knowledge and capital, and we may be able to show you Hebrideans what you'd have done for yourselves long ago if you'd been possessed of our advantages."

"Generously said," acknowledged Mr. Farquharson, still fixing Alexander with his gentle smile. "And so those were your motives. Well, every man has his bias, and so you'll forgive me, laddie, for saying that ye've left out the most important. Did ye not come here looking for God?"

Alexander considered this politely. "Partly, perhaps, a question of terminology?" he suggested. "And I think, sir, that from the strictly theological viewpoint we can't assume that God did not exist in the laboratory also. 'All things wise and wonderful——' as we've just been singing. I should be inclined myself to say that I was more specifically looking for man."

"Man!" Ronny let out his cheerful guffaw. "You look for man, and you find us. Talk about a prize draw!"

"Do go on from there," said Mary, her eyes dancing. "Tell Mr. Farquharson what you've found."

"If you want my opinion of each of you severally, I shall be delighted to oblige, but not, I believe, in front of Mr. Farquharson. Anyway, I've done my share of the talking. Somebody else can lay bare a soul. All right, Mary, let's have a motive or two out of you."

"Me?—Oh, I dunno." Mary was suddenly deflated. "I suppose I was just fed up at home."

"That goes for most of us, I daresay," added Ronny moodily, and the challenge had gone out of him also. "We hadn't anything better to do."

"Speak for yourselves," cried Hermia, her mainspring touched. "I happen to know that Simon, for one——" She caught her husband's agonized look, and ended in a sort of exasperation: "Oh, well, what does it matter? Don't you think it's gone cold out here, Mrs. R.? Mr. Farquharson ought to be ready for the kitchen fire and a cup of tea."

Land and sea had turned an even pale grey, and the kitchen in the lamplight was human and comforting. Kurt brought Maggie over her tea. "It begins to appear", he said confidentially, "as though you and I were the only ones whose motives in coming here were pure."

"Pure?" queried Maggie hoping that her stab of guilt was well concealed.

"Yes—we alone were driven by an unmixed urge to increase the food-bearing properties of the soil."

Well, and wasn't it true? Hadn't she craved to be digging and planting again, long before ever she saw Alexander? "Wouldn't you say Les has it quite as much as us?" she suggested.

"Why, Les was at work on the land already. He came here to be his own master—and so that he could make that deplorable marriage." Kurt's view of Joyce had been long since formed. He did not insist on brains in women, but to marry one without vitality was indeed a fiasco. "He should divorce her," he observed judicially. "There are several agreeable girls at the Kyle would make him better wives on the food they would get here. That Joyce, have you noticed, she is the only one of us that has not improved in physique?"

"A good job Les hasn't your farmyard notions of marriage," said Maggie, giggling. "And don't let yon minister hear them, either."

"Nevertheless," said Kurt, "for Les it would be better. You mark what I say."

Les had taken no part in the discussion on the causeway. He seldom did take part in discussions unless they were directly agricultural, having a peasant mistrust of giving himself away. But he followed them intently, and had a habit of raising points with the speakers afterwards. To-night he waylaid Alexander, and into his usual offhand manner there had crept a new and confiding note.

"It was a funny thing, your saying that about making it possible for more kids to be born. What I mean to say is— Joyce has been thinking lately—well, as a matter of fact, she's sure."

[III]

Alexander's delight at this news was such that really, as Ronny remarked to his confederate Mary (who for once let him down by not finding it at all amusing), he might have been the father himself. Had it lain with him, Joyce would have done no stroke of work all winter. Mrs. Rossiter, however, warned him that she ought not to be encouraged to think of herself as an invalid. She was for ever talking about doctors as it was, and needing to be reminded that pregnancy was not an illness. And presently it emerged that

Joyce was determined not to have the baby on the island. Alexander, at first greatly taken aback—for had not Sunay bred its own children for generations?—himself agreed, when he considered, that they dared not risk dependence on the Kyle doctor in so stormy a month as March. A bed was accordingly booked for Joyce in a maternity hospital further south. It could make no difference to the triumphant fact that the Sunay community was on the increase.

Joyce thus, as it seemed to him, solved, there remained one other problem child. Ronny now appeared almost converted to the Hebridean view that work on the land was a degrading bore. He had been magnificent over the shearing, and could still produce the same demonaic energy at any shepherding crisis, but he was not going to lift potatoes, grade carrots or scythe grass for more than a couple of hours on end without discovering that there ought to be a machine for doing it. He and Rory would still vanish in the *Carrie* on calm evenings. The lobster fishing was extremely profitable, for not only did they now bring back reasonable catches, but they were able to dispose of lobsters to the Skye fishermen who came over to their grounds. It seemed to be a regular mid-ocean market. But profitable or otherwise, the conduct of Ronny, as a partner in Sunay, was entirely his own affair, as Alexander pointed out to his mother when she once more suggested that he should intervene.

"But I can't help seeing, of course," said the poor lady anxiously, "that Ronny isn't pulling his weight."

"I assure you, Mrs. R., we none of us——"

"No, dear boy, I know you haven't. But it hurts me to see him so—well—lackadaisical, and I'm not certain that you are handling him in quite the right way. You see, I know Ronny so well. He would do anything in the world for the people he loves. I happen to know he has a tremendous admiration for you, and if you could see your way to give him now and then a word of praise——"

"But Mrs. R., it would be fearful cheek. Who am I to go about praising people? We're all in this equally. We must work because we want to and for no other reason."

Mrs. Rossiter sighed. "Of course that is how it should be ideally, but people aren't all ideal, are they? And I sometimes wonder if we make enough allowance for all that Ronny went through in the war. If it unsettled him a little, can he be blamed?"

"There, I'm afraid, you have me," said Alexander with a rather wry smile. "But doesn't the very fact that I got off lightly, while Ronny had beastly things to do and see, make it all the more unthinkable for me to lay down the law to him now? I'd probably be a damn sight more unsettled in his place. Naturally, as his mother, you're anxious for his happiness. But I feel sure he's past the age where another person can help him out. He'll find his own way back in time."

Mrs. Rossiter departed uncomforted, and it seemed to Alexander that there had been something glib about his assurances. Was it really true that he could do nothing for Ronny, or merely that he was evading a tedious responsibility? He earnestly wanted to see Ronny contented, preferably married to some fine strong girl (a pity he and Mary were evidently unattracted), but of personal interest in Ronny's emotions he knew, rather guiltily, that he had not a trace.

He had frequently the benefit of Kurt's opinions, for Kurt was a great gossiper at bedtime. Kurt diagnosed that Ronny's case, so far, was progressing well. He had almost detached himself from Mother (and, indeed, it was a fact that occasionally his manner to her was scarcely rude). The transference had been at first to the interest of new surroundings and work; transference to a father-substitute was plainly the next stage.

"Have a shot at it yourself, my lad," Alexander suggested.

"Nothing would give me greater pleasure, but that my

temperament unfits me for the role. I am far too hetero-sexual a type."

To this obvious bait Alexander declined to give any other response than a grin. He knew all about Kurt's correspondence course philosophy, his yardstick measurements of the human soul, and did now and then wonder whether some day they might not let him resoundingly down.

Fertility at Sunay now seemed to be in the air. Lady was in an interesting condition, the father being, by surmise, Bob, and much was hoped from a litter with such shepherding heredity. And Polly the new cow calved in the middle of a drowsy afternoon. "It's no joke, a heifer calving," had said Mary ominously, and Alexander was filled with panic, and also with an obscure irritation against her, that he should be so ignorant and so entirely in her hands.

But with Les's help she officiated unconcernedly at what was, in fact, a fairly tricky birth, and presently Alexander found himself watching her rub the queer little long-legged morsel down with a wisp of straw. Her face as she bent over it, intent and self-forgetful, was so lovely that for a moment he caught his breath. If only she could look like that always, and not say a word! Then she looked up at him, and instantly the embarrassment which made any real relation with her impossible came flooding back again.

"Come along the gallery, we've jobs of our own," he observed to Maggie, who had been the other spectator of the lying-in; and added, rather ashamed of himself, as they sauntered back along the causeway: "I'll say this for Mary, she has guts."

"Och, ay, she did a fine job," Maggie earnestly agreed. Not for worlds would she have minimized Mary's achievement. But in her heart she did consider that it was primarily the cow that had had guts.

Now they were a promising heifer calf to the good, and it seemed a propitious moment for the Department of Agriculture to inform them on a flimsy strip of ill-typed paper that it would have pleasure in calling on them shortly in the course of its tour of the islands, and that it was their obedient servant, Alex. Fraser, Inspector.

"Doesn't say precisely when. Probably the essence of the thing is that he catches us in a horrid surprise. Oh well, we've had a wadge of the Department's money, so it's fair enough."

"I call it snooping," said Ronny. "You'd think we could be shut of Whitehall up here—oh well, then, Edinburgh, or wherever it is they hang out. Know anything about this Fraser, Rory?"

"Inteet yess. He hass his office at Lochachtraig. He iss a nice wee chentleman." Pressed, Rory could add nothing more to the description, though he would probably have given a telling word-picture in Gaelic. "I expect he will be coming in Tonny's boat," he added. "Tonny is often after taking him about."

"Doesn't the old Department provide him with a boat?"

"Ach, no. There iss not so many places having no steamer service."

"Rightho then, you tell Annag to light a fire on the headland when Donny leaves. That should give us plenty of warning if it's any kind of a clear day."

"No last-of-the-Mohicans' stuff will be required," said Alexander stoutly. "Mr. Fraser is welcome at any time. I consider we've not much cause for shame." But he had his misgivings, remembering the judgment of old Mr. MacLeod.

As it happened, Ronny was not after all destined to make the Department's acquaintance. He and Rory had set out at dawn for Carn Mor, where it was thought there was a ewe with a broken leg. Soon after eleven the *Annabella* chugged up out of the haze, and Alexander, going down to the jetty to meet her, found that Donald MacLeod's passenger was young, small and dark, with an olive-skinned elfin face, and wore shorts and a tweed jacket liberally covered with leather patches and holes. He was staring inland with an expression of astonished ecstasy, and returned his host's greeting with the simple words: "Good God." They were enough to mark him as a species of native hitherto unmet, the public-school Highlander.

Alexander took them at first for praise of the farm, but following the direction of Mr. Fraser's gaze, found that it had come to rest on a distant view of Mary in the white swimming suit.

"She feels the heat," he hastily explained. But it was not disapproval that lit Mr. Fraser's large dark eyes.

"You know," he murmured, "living up here, it's years since I saw anything like that. Would it be an average specimen?"

"Well—I suppose Mary's our star turn. But the general standard of female looks is high."

"Delightful island," said Mr. Fraser sunnily. "I anticipate a happy day."

"I trust it all shows in your report. Which would you wish to see first, the ladies or the farm?"

"Och, the farm, I suppose." Mary and the cows had now disappeared, and Mr. Fraser turned to him with an unblushing grin. "Pray forgive me, Doctor. I've heard of what you're doing here, and I'm all agog. But you'll just have to allow for this sudden impact of civilization on a poor backward Gael. I was once at Cap d'Antibes myself. Indeed, and I have known better days."

But no one could accuse him of inattention when he actually reached the fields. "Aren't you good, good boys!" he murmured lovingly when shown the silage, the compost heaps, the newly-planted gooseberry field, the garden, the cabbages, Les's pigs. "Aren't you the answer to the agricultural improver's prayer! *A Dhia*, what cabbages! Sulphate of ammonia, I suppose?" He received Kurt's indignant denial with limpid charm, and it struck Alexander that there was nothing he had not known about their methods before he came.

"What's two pigs, anyway?" said Les in his surly way, while his eyes sparkled at Mr. Fraser's praise. "If I had a couple of dozen, I could clear the hill of bracken quicker than Kurt with all his slagging. You can see for yourself, though, the difference these two have made. And they're putting on weight nicely. Mae West'll cut up by Christmas." The pigs were Les's spare-time masterpiece. Himself he had dry-stone walled a piece of the bracken-covered hillside where it rose above the garden, and set up the movable sty. The rooting and manuring of the two pigs were the first stage in getting rid of the bracken; in the spring the strip was to be ploughed, cleaned up with a potato crop, and eventually added to the garden, while Les walled in another stretch. "A first-rate plan," declared Mr. Fraser. "I've been trying to get the crofters to do it for years."

"I bet you haven't got anywhere," said Les. "You should hear our Rory—'them smelly thinks', he calls 'em. Of course, they're not smelly if they're kept properly, which I daresay no crofter's would be. Of all the lazy b's! You'd think they were all the sons of lords."

"Well, so they are," sighed Mr. Fraser. "That's our trouble in the Highlands. We can't forget the blood, and so it gets thinner each generation. You go ahead with your pigs, Mr. Turner, and I'll bring a crofting delegation over next year to look at them."

He beamed upon the lambs, which now bore no resemblance to the pretty creatures of the spring, but were nearly as large as their mothers and a great deal sleeker. "That's our solution—the finished product. We send off far too much half-finished stuff, for which of course we get a rotten price. You've exceptional grass here—still, there are a hundred crofts in my area where they could fatten lambs. You're good boys, that's what you are." He promised to help with transport to market. He suggested that they should grow seed potatoes and a slightly different mixture for next year's ley. By the time they turned back to the village for lunch, he was Sunay's most popular visitor to date.

"I don't mind admitting", said Alexander, "that we shall treasure your kind words. Our last Hebridean farming expert left us fit to cut our throats."

Mr. Fraser chuckled. "Ah, that'd be old MacLeod. A tough nut. Most of the older generation are, as don't I know. The barrier's really emotional. Speak the lingo?"

"Well—like Caliban. We know how to curse."

"You'll never break down their prejudices till you do. But the young ones are different. They adore machinery, and any new toy that doesn't involve real hard work. There's one or two likely lads are pals of mine—a chap at Lochachtraig who goes in for compost and black currants, another on a wee island north of Skye who's experimenting with the Soay sheep. We must arrange a round of visiting."

At lunch, where his urbane manners put Hermia happily in mind of Bloomsbury, Mary had her opportunity to complete the conquest already begun. "I don't mind letting you know", she flung at him across the table, "that I've never had much use for all you inspector johnnies. You think you know a hell of a lot and come snooping round, giving us orders, but it stands to reason the practical farmer must be a far better judge than you."

There she went again! Maggie felt her face grow hot, and observed Alexander's disappearing into his beer mug.

Little Mr. Fraser never flickered an eyelid. He replied pleasantly that in secret he agreed with her, and filled in an awkward pause by inquiring if it was really true that they kept a ten-pointer somewhere on the moors?

"Now how on earth did you hear of that?" inquired Mary excitedly, and quite unaware of having put a foot wrong.

"Och, well, from us departmental snoopers nothing is hid."

"No one's got close enough to him lately to vouch for the ten points," said Alexander, "but there's certainly at least one stag. You were supposed to have cleared them off. And now we'll have to."

"D'you know, I wouldn't put it past us to have winked an eye."

"I've been promised a stalk when we're through with harvesting, haven't I?" demanded Mary. "Tell you what, Inspector. You come over then. I bet you know all the dodges."

"Why, I believe I do. Although stalking deer with the owners' good will would be an unnerving experience."

"You surely never mean that you—well—that you poach?" asked Mrs. Rossiter.

"My dear lady, but of course. Whenever I get the chance. Salmon too, grouse, anything. I see I shock you. But candidly now, how otherwise would you have a landless, dispossessed, deeply resentful and incompletely pacified race get its own back on the conquerors?"

"But you're a civil servant," said Hermia, amused. "Mightn't it be awkward if you were caught?"

"Why, yes, indeed. I'd lose my job. That gives an added zest to the pursuit. But you see, the people whose business it is to catch me are mostly dispossessed and resentful too. They're glad of a haunch, besides. Poached game is never sold, it goes into the pot, and the average Hebridean pot can do with a bit of enrichment, as you know. What a contrast with your epicurean living here, if it's not an impertinence to say so," and he smiled winningly at the housekeepers, who had certainly done him proud.

"It must be borne in mind," said Kurt, "that we are living on capital. That is to say, since mid-July we've sold more stuff than we've paid out for grocery, but there's been no question of interest on our money, and no one has had any personal expenses. Apart from our fat lambs we shan't have much to sell in the winter. The flock ought to be twice the size, and it may be years before we sell off ewes too. To make the place really pay, we have to get electric power, a good dairy herd, and cheese and butter for market all through the year. That's our aim, anyway. Can I show you our accounts?" The accounts, which he kept exquisitely, were treated with perfunctory interest by all the shareholders except Alexander. Mr. Fraser's close attention now made him amends.

"Whatever for did ye want to affront the poor laddie like that?" demanded Maggie of Mary as soon as they were alone; she found herself increasingly unable to endure Mary's gaffes in silence. "As good as telling him to his face that he doesna' know his job! What will he have thought?"

"Well, who cares a damn what he thinks? Everybody knows it's true." But Mary, though she never on principle outwardly repented, was gloomy and depressed all the afternoon. Come to think of it, it was a damn-fool thing to say. Alexander must be livid—and the trouble was, you would never know if he were livid, because he never showed a thing. Shame invariably had the result of making her yet more off-handed, and she did the honours of the byre and displayed the new calf without a jot of the smiling grace she had brought to bear on old Mr. MacLeod.

But Mr. Fraser had, it seemed, no sort of fault to find with his day, except to regret to Mrs. Rossiter that he had not had the chance of meeting her son and renewing acquaintance with his old friend Rory MacLeod. He promised to come back and stalk the Monarch of the Glen, and congratulated everybody all round on having brought so many of his cherished dreams to life.

Alone with Alexander on the jetty for the five minutes it took to get the *Annabella*'s engine started up, he added in a different tone: "As one Alexander to another, and both of us with pretty much the same new world to conquer, there's just one thing I'd like to say."

"Why, by all means."

"What you're doing here could mean a lot to us. I know Rory's father was a washout, but there's a younger generation, and some of them are open to new ideas. Your example may teach more than all my precepts."

"That was what we had the nerve to hope."

"Well then, frankly, man, is it worth jeopardizing a grand piece of constructive work for a spot of fun?"

"I assure you I virtually have no fun at all."

"I'd hate to have you think that we departmental snoopers are all in some unholy league. But naturally I know most of what goes on. The Customs people in Portree are friends of mine. They know all about the Glendhunan leak, and they have a notion how the stuff is getting out. That's all. I just felt I must drop you the hint." Then, seeing the look on Alexander's face, he suddenly added: "Good Lord, have I spoken out of turn?"

"No," said Alexander, pulling himself together. "Of course not—I'm infinitely grateful. You must think me a prize specimen."

"Well, I didn't. I thought you a hard-bitten buccaneer. But I see I was wrong. Maybe you are a specimen, but you seem rather a decent one. Ah well, so long." He chirruped himself away down the steps, and the *Annabella* headed out into the Sound.

Alexander walked back to the village, and found Maggie on the causeway, grading a mountain of carrots. "Isn't someone helping you?"

"Well, it was to be Ronny—but he's maybe kept on the hill."

"All right, I will." He sat down and set to work, but his face had none of the elation Maggie had expected from Mr.

Fraser's visit. She considered his downcast eyes and the set of his long, beautifully modelled mouth, and wondered what way the tension was pulling now.

"Yon laddie seemed to approve?" she ventured after five minutes' total silence.

"Yes, but I wonder if that means a lot? He's the same sort as us—all products of what Rory calls the book-learning. We're his perambulating textbook. Makes me feel a bit suspicious." So Rory's Dad rankled still. The greatest men, thought Maggie indulgently, had yet a childish streak.

Mary bore down upon them with her pails, and stopped to point out the superb quality of the new cow's milk, not all butter-fat and blue skim like that Highland stuff. Kurt led the pony down from the hay-field, and stopped to share in the general discussion of Mr. Fraser's suggestions. Their backs were to the mountain, and Ronny and Rory were upon them unawares.

"Have half the flock got broken legs?" Mary jocosely inquired. "You jolly well took your time——" Her voice trailed off as the burden over Rory's shoulder was slumped to the ground.

"There iss a surprise for you," said Rory with his most engaging smile. "He will eat peautiful when he hass been hanging a week. Ach, he wass a wily one. We wass crawling all the way from Carn Mor to Torval. Ronny hat him in the ent, in that wee corrie up above the beach."

"I say, Mary, you aren't cross, are you?" began Ronny, who appeared vaguely aware that all was not well. "We didn't seriously intend to get him. We were all morning with the sheep. Then the whole herd blew right into our laps, and as I happened to have taken the gun——" Mary continued to stare at the stag, and all the blood drained out of her face. Then she let go.

Never in her life had Maggie heard anyone swear like that, not a man even, let alone a girl. Words she was ashamed of

165

knowing, other words she had never heard before, came pouring in a molten stream out of Mary's lovely mouth, engulfing the red-faced Ronny, the nonchalantly smiling Rory (yes, they shook him, for all his smile), the poor limp carcass at her feet. On and on she went with a dreadful passion, a creature beside herself, possessed by demons. It was the sort of frightening rage that occasionally would shake poor little Gavin, but Mary had words for it where Gavin had only screaming. At last she seemed to wear herself out; she looked at the rest of them as though only now realizing that they were there, her white face flushed again, and she walked off to her own house.

"Magnificent," said Kurt, with genuine admiration.

Maggie, who was sick and trembling, stared at him in astonishment. Then she perceived that none of them, not even the two culprits, were shocked at all. Even Alexander was biting back a smile.

"Inteet she hass a gift," acknowledged Rory.

"All the same," said Ronny sulkily, "it's a bit excessive. I did tell you, if you remember, that she'd cut up rough. But I really don't see that she's the right to carry on as if the deer on the island were her private property."

"Without being able to equal Mary's—er—robustness of expression," said Alexander, "I'm inclined to share her feeling that she's had a dirty deal. All right, Rory, take that bloody thing away," and Maggie knew suddenly that his uppermost feeling was one of pity and disgust, that the exquisite friend of so many chance encounters should be reduced to a piece of butcher's meat.

"Would you be wanting the antlers, for putting up in the kitchen maybe?"

"I would not. That's to say, it's not for me to decide, of course. I'll mention it at Parliament. If you don't object, Ronald, I'd like five minutes of your time."

"Right ho, what is it?" asked Ronny, who had been for following his partner in crime to the kitchen.

166

"Our friend the Inspector called when you were out."

"Did he? Dash it, I'm sorry not to have seen the ogre. What's the verdict? Do we all get a month's notice?"

"Why, no. He seemed delighted with our methods. We're to be the model boys. That was why he thought it his duty to warn me that whisky-running didn't finally pay. When I said I wasn't doing any, he took me for a bloody fool. So", added Alexander pleasantly, "must you."

"Oh—I see." Ronny sat down slowly on the causeway wall. Maggie wondered if she ought to go away. But she was longing to hear the rest; Kurt showed no signs of moving, and if Alexander had wanted to sort Ronny in private he could easily have contrived it. There was a pause while they smiled at each other; then Ronny murmured:

"You know, I made sure you'd a pretty good idea."

"Incredible, isn't it, that I hadn't? I suppose I'd so much else on my mind. And that goes for the rest of us—or am I the only one that's been taken for a ride? Anyway, we'll leave that for the moment, but I'd like to hear the details."

"Well, I don't know how it's worked at the Skye end. I made it my business not to inquire. There's some sort of leakage from the Glendhunan distillery, and they'd been storing the stuff on Skye, but the Customs people got suspicious and it wasn't safe. So one of Rory's cousins who has a fast lobster-boat arranged with him—that was when he went off, you remember—to use the Latay cave instead. We had several meeting-places, all on legitimate fishing-grounds. Honestly, we took every precaution. I'd have sworn that nobody knew."

"As you see, you would be wrong. Well, and is that cave stacked with it now?"

"No, there's almost none, and I'll see that what's left gets taken off pronto. Chap's due to make a trip to-night."

"He collects it, then? You merely store?"

"Mostly." For the first time Ronny looked unhappy.

"Donny took a load or two in the *Annabella*, while his parties were off picnicking. I'm afraid Rory and I took it a few times when we went into the Kyle. The hampers hid it absolutely, you know, and the *Gannet*'s so well known, she'd never be searched."

"First time she had been, the whole damn lot of us would have been implicated. You realize that?"

"I'd have seen to it that you weren't." Ronny's voice was almost pleading. "I say, I know all this makes me sound no end of a louse. But honestly, I only did it for the lark. Rory needs the swag—well, you know, he's hoping to get married. I put my share into the general profits. I'd hate to have you think I was on the make."

"Ah yes—the lobster market in midstream. Gracious me, what a lot I've swallowed. Kurt, you must have known—you aren't that dense." Kurt smiled and murmured that if some people wouldn't help in fixation-transferences, he himself was broader-minded. "Well now, Ronald, my lad. I don't feel qualified to lecture you on the ethics of smuggling. But I must remind you that we are all partners in this concern, and therefore whatever anyone of us does the rest share in—and that applies equally whether the law finds us out or not. Rory is not a partner, and if he likes to smuggle he can, as long as he doesn't do it in our cave and our boats. And I don't want to have to sack Rory. He's not only the king-pin of our farming, he's our one real link with the Isles, our best chance of having any sort of influence. It's part of our job to convince Rory that there are better ways of earning a living than the ways he and his grandfather knew. You've learnt a lot from Rory—doesn't it strike you as unfair that he's getting nothing from you in return? All you've done for Rory is to confirm him in his notion that whisky-running is a lark. Lark!" ended Alexander, suddenly exasperated. "Why can't your job here be a lark? Bringing a dead place back to life is fifty times better fun than humping a lot of alcohol in and out of caves."

"Oh, all right," said Ronny, rising to his feet, his face dark. "I'll guarantee that that's the end of it. You can spare me the rest of the sermon."

Maggie held her breath. If Alexander should condescend to lose his temper with Ronny, she could never, never love him again. The moment passed. Alexander's face relaxed into the familiar ironic grin. "Ronald, you're unique. Graciousness personified. We rely on you to get rid of the stuff before Mr. Fraser's pals are upon us. You might keep a bottle or two for Christmas."

"Well, well," remarked Kurt, when Ronny had gone. "A highly interesting day. You don't deceive yourself, my friend, that that is a solution?" Alexander shrugged. "If you do not care for the children's games, you had better invent for them some of your own."

"How infinitely I prefer adults."

"Come now, Dr. Sarratt," said Maggie boldly, "ye canna go through life expecting everyone to have your principles."

"Come now, Mistress Moffat, what other principles can I expect them to have? To expect anything lower than my own would be the God-damnedest impudence. Here, I don't feel in the mood for carrots. It's not going to freeze to-night. Let's cover them with sacking and leave them till the morning."

Maggie, rather apprehensive, went along to her cottage, and sure enough, the sounds of muffled sobbing could be heard. Mary lay sprawled on her face across her enormous bed. Timidly, for she always felt inadequate in scenes, Maggie bent over and touched her on the shoulder.

"Dinna take on so, lass. It's no' worth it. Maybe there's other stags."

"Oh, damn you. It's not the stag." Mary sat up, and that her face could be so altered by crying was indeed pitiful. "It's him. What must he have thought? I'll never dare look him in the face again."

"I'd no' worry about that if I was you. I dinna believe it's the kind of thing that lads mind at a'."

"Yes, but he's different."

"I'd no' say that." Mary looked up quickly, and was much reassured by finding on her friend's face a grin. "Anyway, he stood up for you after you'd gone, and fair sorted Ronny."

"Sorted? You mean, told him off? Did he now, bless his heart? God, how I adore that man." She got off the bed and sponged her face. "I say, d'you think I look fit to appear at dinner? I feel miles better, and I'm simply ravenous. Of course, it was a filthy trick. I'll never speak to Ronny again."

"Ye know, I'm pretty sure it wasn't Ronny's fault. Rory's the one that needs sorting. And it's no' really his fault either, for that's the way he was brought up, not to think that the lassies count. Did ye know he has never even taken his Annag out fishing?"

"Good lord. I wonder she stands it. Has Alexander been sorting Ronny all this time?"

"Well, there was another wee matter——" The entrancing episode of the whisky completed Mary's recovery. She went in to dinner in high good humour, and was soon telling the unresponsive Hermia exactly how long venison ought to be hung before it was cooked.

Maggie and Alexander got up early next morning to finish the packing of the market stuff. But it had disappeared. The *Gannet* lay at the jetty steps, filled with neatly stacked hampers, and Ronny was fiddling with the engine, his back a picture of elaborate unconcern.

To treat him with anything like decent consistency was, reflected Maggie, quite beyond her powers. For how could one help hating him when he was such a trial to Alexander, such an irresponsible, intolerant, brutal boor? And how could one keep from liking him when every now and then he had it in him to be such a love?

Chapter Seven

[I]

Contrary to the general surmise, Rory did not pack up and leave. Alexander's representations to him were made in private, but it might be guessed that they had a materialistic rather than an ethical appeal. At all events, they seemed to answer. Rory went about his shepherding as cheerfully as ever; nor was his Celtic composure ruffled when even Gavin, from whom little could be hidden nowadays, remarked in his clear little English voice: "Why have you and Ronny been such naughty boys?"

"Ach, well, we're to be goot boys from now on."

"What were you doing, zackly, in ve Latay cave?"

"I've tolt you, the *each uisge* will get little boys what ask too many questions." This was a monster, half horse and half fish, which lived in the lochain under Torval and had been seen by Rory on three separate occasions.

"But is vere somebody inside?"

"Well, between ourselfs, there was a wee bocain in the cave wass a frient of mine, and Ronny and me used to take him over a jug of milk after dark. But he's away to Ardnamurchan now for the winter."

When, a few nights later, Alexander brought up the subject of the dam, it was impossible for Ronny not to feel himself at once forgiven and talked round, and he was in consequence ungracious. But the dam had been the dearest project of his heart ever since he came. Everybody else had got their wishes, and here at last was his. When he was unanimously elected as foreman of works he accepted casually, but his eyes were dancing.

Alexander proposed that a surveyor should be summoned from the Glasgow engineering firm which had already supplied them with materials, to plan the dam, help get the sluice-gates erected and supervise the starting of the work. Ronny instantly demurred.

"We've got all the stuff here; what do we want a surveyor for? Just adding to the expense. There's only one place to site the thing, that's obvious; so why don't we just go and build it? I've been over it all, step by step, with Ken Barnes, my friend in the Sappers, and I don't see where we can go wrong."

"Of course, Alexander doesn't mean any reflection on Kenneth, dear," said Mrs. Rossiter, who still did not know when not to intervene, "but after all he hasn't actually seen the site, and I think we'd do better with expert advice."

"Oh, you do, Ma? Naturally, you're well qualified to speak on the subject."

Heading Ronny off from being rude to his mother had become a favourite Sunay parlour game, in which Alexander, by a quite uncanny deftness, usually won. He now called Ronny's attention to the enormous amount of work which had in any case to be done pending the arrival of the surveyor. The concrete-mixer and tons of gravel and cement would have to be dragged up above the waterfall, and for this a roadway with surface firm enough to take the tractor would have to be engineered up the moorland wall. Ronny, officially freed from other work, and empowered to call on labour as he wanted it, spent a riotous morning heather-burning up the wall, and discovered, under a growth so deep that Gavin and Jamie could get lost in it, the remains of the zigzag track which must have been made by the old people when they took their carts over to the Camas Ban. This lessened what was still a heavy job with pick-axe and shovel, but at the end of the week the tractor was able to make the ascent, a sand-pit had been opened out in the bed of the stream above the fall, and Ronny did his first concreting, a platform at waterfall level where the machine could operate.

Mr. Fraser and the Department lost no time in proving their friendship. They had prevailed on the *Loch Coruisk*, which plied between Oban and the Kyle, to take in Sunay three times during the winter and transport the lambs to market. On this first call, Alexander and Rory were to go down to Oban and see for themselves how Sunay produce held its own in the outside world. The crossing of the Sound, which took the fast *Gannet* three-quarters of an hour, was made by the *Loch Coruisk* in fifteen minutes, and for most of the islanders this was the first time a real steamer had been tied up at their pier. She looked enormous, and Ronny rushed for his camera.

The *Loch Coruisk*, and her sister ship the *Loch Scavaig*, which plied north to Skye, were familiar adjuncts of the scene at the Kyle. In point of fact they were both small and shabby, with fading red funnels and peeling paint, and the general hang-dog air of vessels that know themselves to be merely marine buses. But if not glamorous, they were useful and friendly. They had dining-saloons that smelt of herring, first-class saloons that were always empty because everyone travelled steerage, and in the steerage plenty of deck-space for sheep, cows, dogs, lorries, caravans, motor-bicycles, and any other bric-à-brac that needed to be shipped about the Isles. On both of them a heavy item of invisible cargo was gossip. Captain MacLeod of the *Loch Coruisk* had brought all the furnishings to Sunay in the spring, and the wonder of Hermia's painted iron chairs was passed on by him to the entire west coast. He was charmed by the opportunity to know how things were progressing at Sunay, and although the ship only stayed ten minutes, he formed an accurate idea. Gavin and Jamie were entertained on the bridge, and Gavin was foiled in a spirited attempt to climb into a lifeboat, and frog-marched back on to the pier.

"I wanted to be a towaway, Mummy," he explained.

"I daresay," replied his mother, adding to Maggie: "I wouldn't mind being one myself. The hectic night-life of cosmopolitan Oban would be a marvellous change. Getting all excited over a dirty little tub like this does make one realize how utterly we live out of the world. Wouldn't it be agreeable if she were a Channel steamer, and we could just pop over to France?"

"What would ye be wanting to go to France for?"

"Oh—Paris, good food, good talk, fun. I never feel half so alive anywhere else, do you?"

"I was never out of Scotland in my life," answered Maggie, and wondered crossly why it was that she always seemed to be amusing Hermia, when Hermia was really the one who was a joke.

The ten minutes were up, the lambs safely aboard; Alexander and Rory were seen off with frantic wavings, as though they were departing for a long voyage; the *Loch Coruisk* slowly slid away from the jetty, and a few moments later was a dot on the horizon. Maggie's gaze followed her wistfully, but not because she seemed a link with any continental pleasures. For this was the first time Sunay had been without Alexander, and she was ashamed to find what desolation swept her at having him only two nights away.

What had Kurt said about purity of motives?—clever Kurt, how little he knew. Then she felt Gavin's tug on her arm. "Maggie, are we going to make ye tato-camp?" It was true, she had promised them that they should help her house the maincrop. Half an hour later Alexander was forgotten.

When he and Rory returned they brought with them the surveyor, a Mr. Campbell, red-haired and dour like his clan. He had been talked by them into a relative interest and good humour, which Ronny at once proceeded to dispel by marching him at an exhausting speed up to the fall and holding forth aggressively on the advantages of the site.

"Och, ay," said Mr. Campbell unemotionally, and set to work with staff and level. After a time he observed, addressing his remarks to Alexander, although Ronny had been presented to him as the foreman: "To get the power ye are requiring, ye'll not need to mak' it less than fifteen feet high."

"Here, I dispute that," said Ronny. "We've a drop of three hundred feet to that barn that's to be the power-house. The lie of the land should give us plenty of head."

"Ye'll require," pursued Mr. Campbell, still addressing Alexander, "to double the minimum flow of the stream."

"But look at the volume of water going over the fall at this minute."

"Was it no' raining yesterday?"

"No—well, a shower, perhaps."

"It was raining verra heavily at Oban."

"You must admit, Ronny," said Alexander, "that the fall got a bit lacy-tracery last June after we'd had a three-months' drought."

"Och, a three-months' drought, now—ye'll never get sufficient volume to withstand that on an island this size. Ay. It was an exceptional spring. But if ye have yon gorge filled nearly fu' for its entire length, that should give ye a reservoir capable of withstanding, say, four weeks. I canna promise more."

"This burn drains a mountain of three thousand feet," said Ronny savagely. "There's another loch four hundred feet above. The whole hillside is a natural reservoir. My friend in the Sappers . . ."

"Your friend in the Sappers, Ronald, seems to be a mine of solid misinformation," said Alexander, goaded. "We've got Mr. Campbell here to do the job. I vote we let him get on with it." He was sorry when he had spoken, for though Ronny would bludgeon his way through anybody else's opposition, criticism from himself seemed, for some reason, to have the effect of a whiplash. Ronny turned red now, and relapsed into silence.

But as Mr. Campbell went about his work, sighting, measuring, and marking out with ground-sticks the contours of the lake-to-be, the imaginations of both were gradually gripped by real excitement. Suddenly it was possible to visualize a new sheet of water, reaching back into the mountain-side. They would leave their mark on Sunay, and on the map. Pipes would run down the hill, a dynamo would hum. It was an assertion of man over nature; yes, and it was a harking back to the golden days of childhood, damming streams in the wet sand. Presently every other male on the island found it possible to leave his work and wander up to the gorge to see how Mr. Campbell was getting on. The burn ran merrily along between its rocks and rowan trees, made its delicate eighty-foot plunge down the fall, and danced away through a series of pools to the sea, while they plotted against its life.

At dinner there was a tendency to get out pencil and paper each time anyone mentioned the dam. Mary brought it to a head by admitting that she couldn't see what they would do with the burn while they were damming it. "We divert it to the left, fathead," said Ronny, "and when we've finished the right-hand half, bring it back through the sluice again," and several voices simultaneously gave her a lecture on the working of sluices.

It was the first real cleavage of interest between the sexes. Maggie and Mary, working beside the men in the fields, usually found themselves siding with the men in matters of policy, and were accorded certain male privileges in consequence—a development much resented by Hermia, who would frequently deplore the Fascist trend latent in peasant societies. But in this matter of the dam, Maggie and Mary were perhaps aware that mere muscular force was going to count for much, that their part would be limited to the shovelling and carting of pebbles and sand, and that none of the initiative would be theirs.

The housekeepers, who had most of all to gain from electric power, were completely apathetic. Joyce would never have to clean oil-lamps any more, nor Hermia rub sheets on a board, nor Mrs. Rossiter churn butter by hand. The apparatus which should spare them this tedium lay wrapped in sacking in the barn. Yet they smiled indulgently at each other, and talked of small boys and mud-pies. The truth seemed to be that none of them really believed the dam would work.

Next day all hands were mobilized, the stream diverted by means of a peat-bank, and the bed of the dam cut out with pick-axes. On the two following days, under Mr. Campbell's direction, the concrete seating for the sluice and section of pipe through the dam was cast, and the vertical steel girders to hold the sluice-gate fixed in place. The pipe section was laid, with a valve to control the outflow from the future lake. And Kurt, who had thought himself inured to fatigue, discovered variants of it that caught the thigh-muscles, and made him regard the inanimate matter remaining to be man-handled in the gorge with a sort of sick loathing. In particular he hated the concrete-mixer, that negation of fertility and life. "You ought to be damn grateful you don't have to do it by hand," said Ronny, to whom the concrete-mixer was wife, mother and friend.

By the end of his stay Mr. Campbell was very nearly softened by Ronny's enthusiastic vigour, and prepared to concede that the rest of the job was something he might direct on his own. The two of them endlessly rehearsed it. Concrete would continue to be poured into the foot-deep metal shuttering to a height of fifteen feet. Then the stream would be switched back through the open sluice, and the other side of the dam built to match, except that it was to contain a spillway on the line of the present diversion, as a further precaution against flooding. A trench would be dug and blasted from dam to power-house, and the pipes laid, and Les, who was a competent electrician, would wire the village. After that, Mr. Campbell was to be advised, and would bring up and site the turbine and generator. He calculated it would take them till the spring.

"Spring my foot!" said Ronny. "We'll have it done by Christmas." And on Mr. Campbell's repeating that sceptical "Och, ay?" he added truculently: "We aren't Hebrideans."

Ronny was Rory's particular friend, and might perhaps on that account make such statements in Rory's hearing without giving offence. But Alexander, catching sight of Rory's face at that moment, surprised on it a look of irony, and something else—a look of foresight, as though he knew who would and wouldn't fail. No one had yet credited Rory with the second sight, but damn it all, with these Celts one never could be sure.

[II]

Now the nights rushed up at them quickly; winter was at hand. But as long as the hours of daylight lasted, so did the heavy, slogging job. Hauling loads of pebbles from the beach, digging barrowfuls of sand from the bed of the stream, pouring the concrete, comparing the results with what Ronny referred to as his blueprints, endlessly arguing. Mist and wind made no difference; in any case there was shelter between the steep walls of the gorge. Slowly the white scar crept over its northern half, and Rory proudly reported it visible through glasses from his father's croft at the Kyle. At this news, Ronny's excitement and energy, if it were possible, increased. He who had been the naughty child was now the school prefect, for ever goading his team. "It's a pity we aren't in Russia, Ron," Alexander commented. "They'd give you one of those titles, and a free pass to the Park of Rest and Culture." The tension between them no longer existed. Indeed, nobody minded Ronny's goading. It was a pleasure to see him happy at last.

It had never been expected that Rory would take to navvy-ing in its most brutal form. But the unpredictable creature liked working on the dam. "And why should I be too grant for a chob that is all right for the learned toctors?" he answered sunnily to Mrs. Rossiter's conscientious commendation; a piece of hypocrisy that positively deprived her of speech.

Kurt was the first on whom the essential soullessness of the labour came to pall. He continued to dislike the mechanical and inanimate, while aware that this was a mainly emotional prejudice and should be overcome. He put in as good a day's work as anyone, but at four he would firmly walk out on Ronny, and make his way two hundred yards across the moor to where the first of his Reclamations caught the evening sun.

These were the strips of hill-side off which the heather had been burned in the spring. All told, they were a handkerchief in the vastness of the moor, and had been conceded to him, he well knew, as a plaything, but it was a game which would be serious in the end. For any fool could grow crops in the valley, on that rich pocket of volcanic soil, but to change the brown to green up here was a true enlargement of the human frontiers. The ground was peat, the natural vegetation heather and bents, with moss and bog-myrtle where the ground grew water-logged as it sloped towards the moorland wall. It was a typical stretch of unregenerate Highlands, and any impression made here might well be the starting-point of the new Jerusalem.

That was still the dream which had drawn Kurt back to the hillside on evening after evening all through the summer, so that now the exquisitely lovely view of the mainland from this high shelf, the blue teeth of the Skye Cuillins which showed just over the crest of Latay to the north, and southward the faint feather of smoke from steamers making their way down the Sound, seemed to have woven themselves indissolubly into his inner life. Landless man of a landless race, here he had grown his first shy roots.

They were, he admitted as he slouched about smiling to himself, very little roots. He had opened trenches at intervals down the hillside, to drain off the stagnant water into the lower course of the burn. There was no way of getting the tractor up here, but Peigi and the sledge had dragged tons of shell-sand up to whiten the ashes of the heather. Then what could be spared of the precious slag—nothing at all really, utterly inadequate—had been scratched into the crumbly surface, and in the soft warm rains of July Kurt had scattered the seeds of grass mixtures and clover. That was all there was to show—tufts here and there, a fighting for survival of better stuff beside poorer, and signs that the area was popular with the sheep.

But it was a beginning. The patches were already undeniably green; this time next year they might even be velvety. Then he would move on. Southward, right round the flank of Torval, the green carpet should creep. It was an easy slope, nowhere very rocky. The cows could be brought up, and with them real fertility. There should be a little alp up here, and what had been barren and inimical mountain would become a peopled world.

In his letters to Ilse, this was the side of his work on which he loved to dwell. Ilse knew nothing of farming, nothing of nature except what she could see from a ski-tour or put into a vase. But she was imaginative and intelligent, and had at once perceived the scope and meaning of his dream. She would join him as soon as he gave the word, and was meanwhile recruiting a group of fellow-exiles willing to help create a new world out of nothing. Ilse had never been really enthusiastic over the Palestine idea. She had regarded the place as dangerous, Oriental and vaguely dowdy. A Hebridean island, on the contrary, touched chords in her romantic soul. Nor had her friends any difficulty in believing that insular farming had peculiar virtue. They, who had been driven over so many frontiers, were here to find a spiritual security more precious than any economic wealth. "Not bad," murmured Kurt aloud, looking round on his tufts of wild white clover. "Not at all bad for a poor urban Jew."

A figure stood up on the edge of the moor, against the glittering Sound; small, wavering and aimless. Kurt regarded it indulgently. The most important of all fertilities naturally met with his approval. He liked to see his female friends with child, particularly when they looked neat and had the proper clothes. He appreciated the fine bloom that pregnancy so often brought to skin and hair. But it was obvious, even at this stage and from this distance, that Joyce had not got the proper clothes.

In the ordinary way Kurt took no notice of Joyce, who seemed to him cardinally insignificant. But now her condition, her aimlessness and his own inner satisfaction combined to soften him. He shouted to her to come over. Joyce came, but unwillingly, and he guessed that she felt her body to be shameful. Poor, fatuous little thing.

"Were you going anywhere in particular?" he asked when she was within speaking distance.

"Oh no. Just for a walk." Indeed, where in particular could she go?

"Well, come and look at this." And he showed off his grasses and clover; not that he supposed she would be interested, but because it might please her to be taken notice of. "My plan is", he explained, "to have an alp up here—a grazing hillside, you know, as we have on our mountains in Austria. Wouldn't it be nice, now, to see a big herd of cows on the hillside, perhaps each one wearing a little bell?"

Joyce looked alarmed. "I don't think cows ought to be loose. They're better kept in the fields, if you ask me."

"But they wouldn't hurt you."

"That's what Mary's always saying."

"Why, you know yourself they never have hurt you."

"I don't give them a chance," said Joyce sulkily. "I heard Alexander say he was going to get a bull."

"Well, it wouldn't hurt you either. Come now, you ought to get over all these townee scares. You try handling the animals yourself. You'd soon make friends."

"It makes me feel sick", observed Joyce with sudden violence, "to see the way Mary puts her hand inside that dog's mouth."

Undoubtedly, thought Kurt, there were still rifts, gulfs, chasms between Joyce and her environment. Look at her shoes, now—why didn't Les or Mrs. Rossiter insist that she had one decent pair of boots in her wardrobe? Impossible not to be irritated by her, but, poor creature, that was not the way to be of use. On a real impulse of interest and pity he inquired:

"Do you really hate it here as badly as ever?"

"Hate it?" said Joyce, startled and taking hold of herself. "'Course not—whatever made you think that? I'm ever so happy." Then, utterly unsuitable though it was that she should confide in him, the need to confide in someone seemed to prevail. "It's just that sometimes—well—I get a bit worried."

"For instance?"

"Well—it's funny to be such a long way from a doctor, isn't it? I mean, if anything was to happen?"

"If you mean about your baby——" Joyce winced, but hang it, if there was to be useful confidence she'd have to get over that inhibition—"surely that's all fixed up. You're going off well ahead."

"Yes," said Joyce, "but you never can be exactly sure. And it isn't only me. Les or—or any of us might be taken ill."

"So we might, but we aren't. Living outdoor lives and not going near any germs, we really aren't likely to contract any diseases that Mrs. Rossiter couldn't cure."

"I daresay. She keeps telling me having a baby isn't an illness. Fair gets on your nerves."

"It must be rather aggravating", Kurt conceded, "when you don't feel terribly bright. But as a matter of fact I believe it's true. And she's had a child of her own, so presumably she speaks from experience. Didn't I hear her holding forth about a ten-mile walk the day before Ronny was born?"

Joyce sniffed. "It's such a long time ago I expect she's forgotten what it was like. Hermia only had Jamie four years ago, and she said it was hell."

Did she now? thought Kurt. What a fool, what a bitch, what a self-centred, vanity-consumed child that otherwise intelligent woman can become the moment her ego is seriously touched. Alexander would be livid. I feel pretty cross myself. "She had no business to say that," he burst out.

"She didn't mean me to hear, of course. They all treat me like as if I was a kid."

"The childish person in this case is Hermia. She has her points, but you must have noticed yourself that she always has to be the centre of attraction. I daresay she just got annoyed by Mrs. Rossiter and wanted to show off. Anyway, she has no notion of truth. I shouldn't be surprised if in fact she had Jamie with the minimum of trouble, and was sitting up half an hour later smothered in lipstick and calling everybody darling."

Joyce smiled, but wanly. "There's another thing. The baby might be ill. I don't see how I'm to bring up a baby if I can't send for the doctor."

"But hundreds of babies have been brought up on this island, and in those days they didn't even have motor-boats." But he saw that there was really no diverting her from the obsession. "Talking of boats, do I see the *Gannet*? Ah well, not everyone can have my eyesight, but you take it from me, she's a mile out of the bay. If we start for home now we'll be in nice time for the mail."

Joyce brightened. "Oh, I do hope there's a letter from Roma. That's my best friend. But she hasn't written for ages. People aren't awfully good at writing, are they? I mean, when you're such an awful long way away." Kurt smiled and sympathized, and his thoughts flew to Ilse, whose long, racy, sentimental, exasperating and profoundly *gemütlich* letters never failed.

They left the Reclamations, descended the wall, here only broken outcrops down which even Joyce could scramble, and picked their way through the bog and cranberries at the bottom, which reminded Kurt that he had read somewhere of an American strain of cranberry giving huge yields. A plantation here would provide another item of export, besides exquisite jelly for Mrs. Rossiter's tourist teas. Joyce, who had already had to pick cranberries, knew that they made a terrible stain on your fingers. But she raised no objection, because after all, once she had the baby to look after, she could never be asked to do odd jobs any more.

The return of the *Gannet* from the Kyle, although it happened every week, still kept the almost breathless excitement of a lifeline safely aimed and held. Letters were sorted on the kitchen table, shopping commissions handed over and paid for and the day's marketer damned with faint praise, for those who seldom visited the Kyle were quite unable to remember how sparse was the choice afforded by its shelves. To-night it was Hermia who defended her doings and dispensed the mail.

"Your usual, ducky." She flipped across to Kurt the grey envelope addressed in purple ink which was as integral a part of Ilse's personality as her Viennese accent and her jumpers. He held it without opening it, for he knew what would be in it, and other people's correspondence was an unfailing source of interest to such a student of character as himself.

By now he could recognize most of it from the outside. Alexander and Simon got scientific quarterlies, and letters

184

from learned friends who had small, light handwritings like their own. Hermia had always an immense *courier* from the feminine admirers who were so unaccountably devoted to her. Mrs. Rossiter heard weekly from a circle of sisters. Nobody wrote to Ronny, unless it was an occasional postcard from an Army comrade now settled in one of the remoter colonies. Maggie was on the look-out for the progress of her sister's baby, who looked like beating Joyce's by a short head; her other regular correspondent was the market-gardener who had formerly employed her, a man after Kurt's heart and in whose counsels he was permitted to share. Les and Joyce got from their families letters which had plainly cost an infinity of labour, and little parcels of chocolate which often came undone in the post. Mary had a weekly typed letter from her father, and subscriptions to half a dozen fashion magazines, from which she presumably derived new ideas for trousers. She heard from no lover, as Kurt had made it his business to know. Poor girl—with her looks and temperament, no wonder she was in a sorry way.

"I've had a notion, Alexander," he called across the table. "American cranberries in the bog. I read about them somewhere—you get a huge annual yield from any acid soil, with no labour except the picking."

"Do you so? The idea of going with instead of counter to the natural conditions certainly has appeal. Where would we get the plants?"

"I don't know, but I'll find out." He would ask Ilse; she had the trained secretary's knack of digging out any desired information. Recalled to the fact of her existence, he slit open her letter.

"Gosh," said Mary. "I'm all in to-night. Of all the hellish jobs give me humping pebbles for your damned concrete. I shall tuck up my feet and have a nice snooze with *Vogue*. I say, Kurt. You. You can swill out the dairy for me this evening if you're a good boy. Hey, Kurt!"

"What's that?" said Kurt, looking up slowly from his letter.

"I said, would you like to swill out the dairy?"

"No. No, I wouldn't. Do your own dirty work."

His words brought a sudden silence into the crowded, humming room. It was the first time, in spite of infinite provocation, that anyone had heard Kurt be rude to Mary. She herself stared at him like a child whose indulgent parent has slapped it across the face. "I say," she muttered, "what's up?"

Hermia knew what was up. So did Alexander. The explanation flashed on them as surely as though the spidery words in purple ink lay beneath their eyes. Kurt's girl had left him.

[III]

That night the wonderful weather which had held throughout October broke with dramatic Hebridean violence. A great wind swooped out of the west upon the little houses. It was six weeks before the *Gannet* could put to sea again.

There had always been a breeze on Sunay, often a big, billowy blow, but this was their first experience of a real gale in the Isles. For the first twenty-four hours it exhilarated, and after that it was enormously exhausting. Every movement was an effort in the teeth of noise. To reach the kitchen from any of the other houses was a struggle. The climb against the wind to the dam left one gasping; coming back, one was carried down to the village as by a great warm hand in the small of one's back. The houses themselves seemed now to possess a merely spurious snugness. Draughts whistled down the chimneys, defied all padding of window-frames; any door or shutter left unlatched would bang without mercy; at night the eerie *bocain* screech of the gale gave

186

Rory's ghost-stories an unpleasant flavour of possibility. The incessant waves of sound stopped all outdoor speech. They even deadened thought.

Sunay, its lifeline cut, had to live wholly on its resources. Materially they were ample. Mrs. Rossiter and Hermia knew the satisfaction of having prepared for the emergency. They had flour and groceries to last till Christmas, and rabbits, game, fish, vegetables came as they were wanted to the kitchen door. The beer gave out presently, and then the cigarettes, but no one went hungry.

The hunger was for news, fresh faces, letters, contacts, and after a while it seemed to die away. The long nights of the northern winter shut down on the island like a black hood, emphasizing the lesson of the wind. They were alone at the edge of the world, their sole solace and protection to be found in each other. The island life folded in upon itself and drew them closer together. The sense of community that would not come for any planning came when needs must. There was a moral there, reflected Alexander with a rather grim amusement. Let nature be sufficiently inimical, men became friends.

Work on the dam was not interrupted. On the contrary, it increased in intensity, because there was now little else to be done. The gorge with its high walls gave admirable protection from the wind. In six weeks from the start of operations the left-hand side of the dam was completed, and the stream, swollen and yellow with the incessant rains, sent surging back through its original bed. The right-hand side was begun. The work was abominably heavy, the cement unmanageable, the ground churned into grease under their feet, and nobody except Ronny now found much satisfaction in the job. But his daemonic energy still drove his henchmen on.

It was in the evenings that solitude became most absolute, diversion most necessary, and now the musical element asserted itself. Ronny was no longer asked for his opinion.

Having been obeyed all day, he sank into comparative insignificance by the fire, while Kurt, always now stony-faced and silent, would turn off the dance bands and find something to his taste. When there was nothing he brought out gramophone records, and then sonata and symphony, the voices of culture upraised against chaos, filled the kitchen, while outside howled the wind.

To Maggie these weeks of storm were strangely happy, after the first shock of finding half the gooseberry bushes blown clean out of the ground, and the painful effort of stringing sacking and wattle over the wire fences in place of the dry-stone walling that should have protected them. For the three people she loved on the island suddenly seemed to have come much closer. It was dark now at tea-time, and Hermia seized the chance to point out how busy she was about the cooking and how happy the children would be to have their dear Maggie put them to bed. And the annoyance of finding herself the dupe of Hermia's schemes was heavily outweighed by the charm of her children's company. As well as being fed and helped to wash, they required to be read to, for Gavin, though now rising seven, steadfastly refused to read, having more absorbing occupations for his time. The Bible continued their first favourite, followed by the worn green volume of Celtic fairy tales. "Read us Elijah!" she would be told, and then: "Read us Manachar and Munachar!" The events of both narratives were received into their minds on the same plane of merry improbability.

Dinner and Parliament over—and there was little discussion at Parliament now, the daily round having narrowed to navvying on the dam—she took from Alexander's bookshelf those poets best calculated, because hitherto unknown even as names, to enlarge the Scots limitations. Vaughan and Herbert, Crashaw and Blake, with their mingled passion for beauty and righteousness—these were the influences that had shaped him, and through them she might draw nearer to his ways of thought. Or the room was filled with the waves of sweet sound that were his delight, and she learned to lose herself in them, while her hands moved peacefully over knitting for Jeanie's baby. And although there was no reading aloud of Scott, sometimes he would force her (because, he told her impudently, he adored her glottal stops), to read them Burns, and expect her moreover to know the meaning of the obsolete words, which of course she didn't.

But whatever they were doing, she was always aware of him. She watched him playing chess with Simon, who could beat him—Simon at chess or in scientific argument seemed to come to life, and it was then less difficult to understand why he should be Alexander's chosen friend—or teaching chess to Rory, who shaped well. She heard him jollying along Mrs. Rossiter and Hermia with the particular brands of teasing best suited to each. She knew, and was ashamed of her glee in knowing, that he was never at ease with poor Mary; she knew when he refrained from scoring off Ronny, and how he rejoiced in the gradually increasing communicativeness of Les. She knew him so well now that she might almost cease loving him. Perhaps the time would shortly come.

The Fletchers were not always present, for Hermia had announced that the long evenings were an opportunity to concentrate on the book, and taken to lighting a fire in their own cottage, in spite of the tacit understanding that unnecessary fuel was not to be burned in this first year. The assertive chatter of the typewriter could be heard during lulls in the wind, so that it might be presumed the book progressed at last.

But Simon continued to look unhappy.

"It's a shocking thing to be born without ambition," he murmured one evening, with a smile to Maggie, as he took his seat beside her for a concert. Confidences were so little characteristic of Simon that Maggie was startled, and tried

189

earnestly to find some encouragement which should not seem like direct criticism of his wife.

"Och, I'd say a lot of ambitions were gey and foolish. If ye succeed ye've nothing left to live for, and if ye fail ye break your heart. Haven't the most of us come here to get away from just that waste of time?"

"Yes," said Simon, looking at her fixedly, "yes, you're right. There's a great deal of natural protection to be had on an island. I admit that for one I'm enjoying the storm. I wouldn't mind, would you, if we were cut off for ever?" The opening bars of the music silenced him. Drat the woman, thought Maggie, consciously abandoning the last remnant of her view of Hermia as the perfect wife. Why can't she leave the poor laddie alone?

In the fifth week of their isolation the wind made broadcast news. There was a creditable list of isolated islands: Fair Isle, Foula, Canna, Eigg, Soay and Sunay, "on which, listeners may remember, a group of English settlers is making an experiment in co-operative farming." "Well, I nefer, Maki!" said Rory in his cheeky way. "Inklish—that's a pit thick." But he was delighted to find Sunay famous, and in such smart insular company. So, secretly, was everybody else. Hermia now knew the happiness of worrying over the anxiety of her many friends. "I daresay", she told Alexander, "the B.B.C. will want to send somebody up here when we're open again. Helen's boy-friend is something in it. If you like I'll get her to give him a hint."

"No."

"No-just-like-that?"

"I meant, no I don't like. Nothing to prevent you putting it up to Parliament. Probably everybody else would adore to have the B.B.C."

"You know perfectly well", said Hermia crossly, "that neither Simon nor I would ever want anything you didn't approve." Behind her back Alexander briefly grinned at

190

Simon, and received, as Maggie was quick to notice, no sort of answering smile.

She herself shared Simon's view that there was something cosy about being cut off from the world, and she considered that the way they were enduring it—yes, even Hermia—did them all credit. She doubted if Jeanie would worry much, not with her pregnancy to occupy her attention. And that was fair enough. What worrying, now, did she do for Jeanie? Had she not three people immeasurably more dear? "I couldna' love them better if they were my own," she told herself, and wondered, then, if she had really given up all hope that one of them would be? In that case Mary's assessment was deserved. For, of course, she knew well enough what Mary thought of her: a born old maid.

[IV]

Against this background of elemental turmoil, Kurt Schneider fought out his solitary battle.

At first he had expected an easy encounter with those wayward desires which he, as a psychologist, knew how to assess at their true worth. He had never loved Ilse. Always he had had towards her a strong sense of condescension. She was in every way his inferior. In leaving him—in getting, damn it, the chance to leave him before he left her—she had hurt nothing but his vanity.

In that case, the wayward desires suggested, wounded vanity seemed able to ache quite as agonizingly as wounded love.

Well, but it was a nice smack in the face! To keep him, with all his experience and technique, so completely in the dark that to the last he had taken her affectionate letters at their face value—that was a feat of which a brainless little bitch like Ilse might be proud. She had done the thing thoroughly. The other man was—but of course, of course—her employer, the professor of economics. She had detached him from a perfectly good wife and three fine children. The wife, she wrote, had been wonderfully understanding—Kurt dimly remembered her, a reserved, pale face at a sherry party, pitifully inadequate as a match for Ilse and the Fiennese Tscharm.

"I think you have long guessed my feelings," wrote Ilse—curse her, she knew that he hadn't—"and then I think too, dear Kurt, that it will be better for each of us to marry someone who is English."

She spared him nothing, no, not she. It would have been too easy to have spared him that. She wasn't going to mate with a Jew.

She was half a Jewess, but she thought that in time it would be forgotten. Perhaps she was right. She was marvellously adaptable. Almost he wished on her an English Gestapo, to ferret out her secret after prosperous years.

He looked at his face in the slit of mirror—thin, dark-skinned, black-eyed, sullen. Once he had supposed that he was handsome. Mary, now, considered him untouchable. Damn it, he wasn't going to start thinking that way. That was the sort of lie that was likely to drive a man mad.

In the last ten years of his life, Kurt had known tragedies beside which the passing troubles of these well-fed Aryans seemed merely childish. Of the boys who had gone to school with him in Vienna scarcely one was left alive, and some of them had died in ways it made him sick even to remember. He had himself escaped by a miracle of luck. This background of horror was a dark burden he would always carry, but it was also, in his belief, a privilege. It made him more completely adult than any Englishman could ever be, gave him a braver realization of evil and its fifty-fifty chances of coming out on top. That being so, he would have said that it also armoured him against the sillier sort of suffering; against brooding and bleeding, for example, when he was thrown over by a shallow, worthless girl.

Yes, but Ilse stood for home. She was his one remaining link with childhood, with the world in which he had had roots. She had been his mistress and he could get another, but she had also been his irreplaceable friend. She was to link Vienna with Sunay, and to find the other members of the New Jerusalem. Thinking on that, Kurt ground his teeth in an agony of rage, and then he laughed aloud. Ilse had never meant to come and bury herself on Sunay, any more than she had meant to go and bury herself in Palestine. She had strung him along, he now saw, from the start of their re-acquaintance as refugees in England. She had always meant to catch an English husband if she could. It was he who had been a fool—a fool, a fool and a fool.

A psychologist, if there were one around—but, of course, he didn't need a psychologist, he could do everything for himself—would say that all this had to be gone through, that you must wallow before you recovered. He had wallowed, but he did not recover. Each day the life on Sunay seemed more pointless and unnatural, and the celibacy which he had endured for Ilse's sake more stupid and forced. He could not, like these English, make a virtue of going without. On the contrary, he was proud to possess all the normal desires. He had been bent, and nearly broken, by a woman's futile treachery. How, in the crazy isolation to which he had condemned himself, was he ever to grow straight again?

They were all very kind to him. Loyalty was not, perhaps, a speciality of Hermia's, but it was no part of her principles to give a fellow-adult away, and for the first week, while he still put a good front on the affair, she said nothing and wished him a speedy consolation. But when, overnight, his resistance collapsed, when his smugness changed to a settled gloom, when the change and its reason were speculated on by all, when in fact he so plainly ceased to care whether they knew or not, then she felt herself bound to simplify matters by producing her explanation. Hermia liked Kurt; she had always got on well with Jews; she had many Jewish friends. But it was a characteristic she seemed to have noticed: when in a jam they really had no self-control.

A Kurt sad, shut and silent was a figure so unfamiliar that all of them were disconcerted. His cocksureness, his invulnerable and good-tempered dogmatism had often been annoying, but now they were sorely missed. The sulks of the problem-children were one thing, but Kurt had always been the antithesis of a problem-child. To see him thus thrown off his balance spread a disquieting sense of insecurity.

Mary, naturally the last to learn the truth, was of course taken aback when she did. "What did I tell you?" she commented to Maggie. "Never trust a Yid. Jolly good thing for me that I wasn't taken in by his smarmy ways." But once having expressed her justifiable resentment, she found herself curiously ready to forgive. For the first time she admitted Kurt to be handsome; it suited him she thought, to have that smug smile wiped off his face. And then, too, she thought she knew—perhaps she was the only one who could know—how he felt. She had been through it too. She had long considered herself the only unsatisfied person on Sunay, the only outcast, the only failure, and here was the clever, worldly Kurt landed just as she had been, for all his knowing ways. No doubt it served him right, but that wouldn't prevent it from hurting like hell.

One evening she made towards him her first, gauche gesture of friendship, calling him (for unless approached directly he now never came near her) into the byre at milking-time. Kurt leant against the door, looking at her with sardonic amusement, and when she had finished he made it clear, in a few politely brutal words, that friendship would not meet the case.

Well, there you were. That was all the thanks you got for trying to be nice to a dirty foreigner. They were all alike. Angry and disillusioned, Mary withdrew again into the fortress of her English girlhood. But everybody else, as unobtrusively as they could (for as well as pitying they also slightly feared him), continued to be very kind to Kurt.

Alexander watched and said nothing. Kurt was not a Ronny, to be comforted with petting. He was adult, or nearly so—for in truth, to assume that anybody was completely adult began to seem in itself childish. To see him suffer was painful, and also impressive, for one had not supposed him capable of so much feeling. It struck Alexander, with a sense of shame, that he had wholly underestimated Kurt. He still found himself taking people at their face value, and thinking them superficial merely because they chirruped. Now Kurt's lonely struggle, so totally without means of relief, appeared very nearly heroic. He knew that he had no way of breaking the silence; it was Kurt who broke it eventually, one night towards the end of the storm, by snapping out, as though he had been contradicted:

"Say what you like, there are only two basic human activities: keeping yourself alive and reproducing your kind. Disregard either of those and you're in a mess."

Alexander considered this politely. "What about the instinct to make things more difficult? The instinct that makes one prefer a rock-climb to a saunter, or life on Sunay to life in London? We all have it—some of us have it overmasteringly—and I don't see how it derives from the other two, so it must be basic too."

"That is a typically idealist, English notion."

"What nonsense. Since when have the English monopolized the spirit of adventure?"

Kurt shrugged contemptuously, but at the far end of the stifling tunnel, in which he was condemned to grope for ever, he seemed to see a pinprick of light.

"Do you realize", asked Alexander inconsequentially, "that it is only a month to Christmas?"

"Christmas! What is that to me? I am not a Christian, and I take no part in your sentimental festivals."

"No, but there's the kids to consider, and if this wind ever drops, I believe old Farquharson intends to come over and give us another service. I didn't ask him. He offered to himself."

"Well, let him come."

"We'll have to have some music."

"If I am to have my eardrums insulted by 'Hark the herald angels' and the rest of your English muck——"

"It's hard to see how you can escape it. Unless, that is, you provide an alternative."

"I touch nothing but Bach."

"You could not make a better choice."

"Possibly something from the Christmas Oratorio. Or a couple of chorales. There are no scores but mine—not that that makes any difference, no one but yourself is capable of reading music, for all their talk. I should have to teach the whole thing by ear. It really is too much to ask."

"Right, we fall back on the herald angels."

"No, damn it, we don't. I'll do it if it kills me—and besides, it's time friend Ronald was shoved about for a change. His power-complex is about due for a puncture. Shall I put out the candle?"

"Oh, do. Good night."

In the darkness Kurt observed:

"What marionettes we are."

"Why, that's of course. But to be aware of it indicates, surely, a detachment in some degree godlike. Most people never know."

"Thank you, my good friend," said Kurt. "You have now done your duty and may sleep in peace." But sneer as he might, he could not deny that the pinprick of light had widened.

He lost it again as the night wore on and sleep never came. Between him and his rest were Ilse's breasts in the tight jumper—or perhaps they were Mary's in the white swimming suit—and longings as sterile as death.

Chapter Eight

[I]

Three weeks before Christmas the wind dropped, leaving a sea smooth and dark as pewter. Loaded with cabbage the *Gannet* put out, and was received with something like triumph at the Kyle, for Sunay was the last of the beleaguered islands, the *Loch Coruisk* having two weeks since got round to the rest. Donald MacLeod was waiting at the pier to congratulate them on the dam, now clearly visible to the naked eye. Any more labour that might be required would be glad and proud to offer itself, for the dam had caught the imagination of the Kyle's youth. It was Rory who suggested that Donald, at least, should come back with them. "We can't pay him, you know," said Alexander awkwardly. "It's costing us the hell of a lot as it is."

"*A dhuine*, it's not for the pay," Rory exclaimed. "He does want to say after that he wass working on that tam."

The enormous mail was doled out in the kitchen, a six-weeks' accumulation of love and anxiety, magazines and Christmas catalogues, and exuberant letters from Mr. Fraser of the Department. Only the familiar grey envelope addressed to Kurt in purple ink was missing. He had not expected it, and if it had come he would have put it unopened into the fire. Nevertheless, he turned white when he saw that it was not there.

"Lord, what muck," said Hermia, distastefully turning over the catalogues. "I suggest we cut out presents among grown-ups." This was welcomed; the thought of amassing a hundred and twenty separate gifts on Sunay had been daunting. But Maggie for one was not pleased when she continued: "I've no doubt the offspring will be enraptured with whatever it is you're carpentering in Ronny's bedroom. Poor kids, it's not much of a Christmas for them. No parties or goings-on."

If there were two small boys in the whole of Scotland whose happiness could not be called in question, they were Gavin and Jamie. For some reason it suddenly suited Hermia to make them out ill-used. Maggie bit back her indignant retort. It didn't do, she had discovered, to upset one of Hermia's acts. If one ignored them she would usually tire of them herself in a couple of days. Provoked, she had a faculty for saying just the cruel things that stuck, though she herself had forgotten them half an hour afterwards.

"Just think," said Mrs. Rossiter brightly to Joyce, "this time next Christmas Sunay will have a baby of its very own."

Joyce stared at her for a moment without answering. This baby, which was to be her passport to freedom, which had already got her off most of the housework, and was going to give her and Les the private home-life they ought to have by rights—this baby, it suddenly occurred to her, would be no more exempt from the interference of Mrs. Rossiter and Hermia than anything else within their reach. They would know what was right, they would tell her what to do and make scenes if she didn't. And a notion, bold and terrifying, took hold of her mind. But all she said was:

"What'll I do if we get a storm like this in March?"

"Now, dear, that's not at all likely, and you're leaving a month ahead. You know it's been all worked out. You aren't worrying, are you? Nothing could be worse for baby than worrying. You ought to go out more, get some roses in those cheeks." While not precisely a sensitive woman, she became herself aware that this sort of encouragement didn't really work with Joyce. "I wish", she added on an impulse, "that you had some friend here of your own age."

"Oh well, there's Gavin," said Joyce.

Mrs. Rossiter had not needed this remark to know that Joyce, though usually cowed and listless, could on occasion be pert. She had made it a rule never to lose her temper, nor did she do so now, but she found the effort severe.

With Donald to offset any flagging there might be in enthusiasm for mixing concrete—not that Ronny or Rory ever seemed to tire of it—the dam leapt ahead, and the harsh white wall now bestrode the other side of the gorge. Work was started on the trench to carry down the pipeline, brute navvying work with pick and spade, up a slope of one in three, which sent them in reeling with fatigue at dusk. It was plain that Ronny would make his boast true, and word was sent to Mr. Campbell to bring up the turbine and generator on the *Loch Coruisk*'s next call in the first week of January. Les, whose life as village factotum had included much experience in electrical gadgetry, was to wire the cottages. Hermia caught the mounting excitement, and suddenly began to turn buckram and silk fringe into lampshades.

"Them frames we're to make you," said Les to Maggie, "why don't you let me run a low-voltage wire under 'em? You'd have lettuces in seven weeks."

Maggie was piqued that he should have to think of it. Electrically-heated soil had been a dream of her late employer's. But in Dumfriesshire current cost too much. Here it wouldn't cost anything at all. The dreariness of pebble-gathering, the hard work of second stockman because no one but herself and Mary could be spared from the dam, all at once began to seem worth while.

With Christmas week came kind Mr. Farquharson to hold a service, this time cosily in the kitchen, where the Bach chorales were certainly heard to better effect than in the windswept spaces of a roofless church. And Gavin and Jamie had their festivity after all. The minister had not forgotten the little boys of Sunay and their passionate interest

199

in God. They and their mother were bidden to the Hog-manay Sunday-school treat at the manse.

"Will Jesus be vere?" inquired Jamie, in whose eyes Mr. Farquharson enjoyed a peculiarly intimate relationship with the Deity.

Och, the other kids will laugh at him, thought Maggie as she anxiously endeavoured to make the distinction between body and spirit clear to the intelligence of five years old. Un-reasonably, she found herself longing to go to the party instead of Hermia, who had after all done nothing for their religious education and would be quite out of place at a Sunday-school treat. Hermia, however, did not appear to think so. She was as excited as the children; one might have supposed she expected to meet the intelligentsia of Gower Street. She debated endlessly what she should wear. "Not, of course, that it matters a damn—they'll all be frumps any-way. Would my black taffetas be overdoing it?"

There was fine feeding on Christmas Day, and a model farm for Gavin and Jamie, built by Ronny and their father and stocked with animals carved by Rory and Kurt. But there was no cessation of work. Maggie found on her bed a cellophane-wrapped casket containing the ingredients of a peerless complexion. She rushed in to Mary in dismay. "We'd agreed there were to be no presents!"

"Lord, you don't call that a present? It's just to keep your freckles down."

"Well, I've naught for you."

"Shut up, idiot!" She found herself thrown on to the bed and pummelled. It didn't do to provoke Mary to displays of skittishness. She had no notion of her own strength.

It was with a wistful heart that Maggie packed the little boys, swathed in rugs and clutching hot-water bottles, into the *Gannet* on New Year's Eve. Then, to escape the horrid stillness of the village, she went resolutely round the sheep-walk with Mary and the dogs. It was after nine, and had been dark for hours, when the boat came back again. The children were bundles of sleep. Rory carried Jamie to bed; Gavin roused sufficiently to follow on his own feet, stopping half-way to announce, in a voice near tears, that they had given him a catapult and it was gone. It was found in his oilskin pocket.

"How did they get on?" Maggie asked.

"Oh, all right, I think. They made as much noise as the other kids, anyway. You seem to have given them some pretty weird religious ideas, but I know you meant well. I needn't have bothered to put on my glad-rags. Lord, how I'd lap up a real party."

This mild taste of social life prompted her to offer herself and Simon as escorts to the stock that were to go to market on the *Loch Coruisk*. As this would mean missing the opening of the dam, it was a job that nobody wanted, and she was able to bargain that they should take a week's holiday and go on south. "We were promised some bright lights and soft music in the second year," she pointed out defiantly, though no one had contradicted her.

"An excellent notion; we'll all take leave in turns," concurred Alexander, who had no intention of stirring off Sunay.

"And the angelic Maggie, I know, won't mind being left in charge of the infants." The irritating part was that Maggie didn't in the least mind. As for Gavin and Jamie, they could scarcely trouble to wave their parents good-bye. All their attention, when the steamer next put in to Sunay, was for Mr. Campbell, his assistant, and the heavy crates which the ship's derrick lowered on to the jetty.

Praise was neither expected nor extracted from Mr. Campbell as he surveyed the completed dam, but beyond recommending a rendering of the lake face with waterproof cement he could find nothing actively to criticize. This finished, Ronny turned the wheel on the top of the dam and closed the sluice.

Maggie and the children watched in great excitement while the burn, baffled in its course, turned back on itself in an eddy which gradually yellowed as the force of the current churned up its bed. They had artlessly expected the lake to fill in a few moments, but half an hour later there were still only widening brown pools up the gorge, and Mr. Campbell's estimate of three days seemed much nearer the mark. They clambered down the stream-bed below the dam, and here the change was sufficiently dramatic. The last trickle of water was drying from the pools, and for the first time in the history of Sunay the waterfall was silent.

A solitary figure stood underneath it; Alexander, curiously subdued. "It seems like murder, doesn't it?" he commented.

"Och, there's thousands of waterfalls in Scotland."

"Anyway, I wish it had occurred to us to colour that concrete. It looks like a livid scar. Rory tells me it shows up now from the Kyle. He seems to think that adds to our credit." He scowled at the fifteen-foot white wall barring the skyline above them. "It's this silence gets me down. I never consciously noticed the sound of the fall, but now it's gone I hear it at the back of my mind. It's like a bad omen."

"Ye're growing a real superstitious Highlander."

"Tut. How unscientific. By all means let us cultivate Lowland common sense." He gave her his ironic grin.

"Zander!" shouted Gavin, charging importantly back up the hill. "You're wanted in the power-house."

It was a scene of immense muscular agitation. Mr. Campbell, Ronny and the assistant were levering the heavy turbine into position. "For God's sake get those kids out of here,' Ronny snapped. "It only needs one of these ten-ton fancy bits to fall on them and the fun will be perfect." He looked exasperated and purple. One nevertheless divined exultation in his heart.

Les and Kurt were erecting the poles to carry the power-line to the village. They too showed a marked lack of enthusiasm for juvenile assistance. Maggie took the children beachcombing.

There were two more days' work before the installations were complete, the pipes jointed, the valves fitted, the wiring taut. Donald brought over as much of the Kyle's youth as the *Annabella* would hold; apparently a disappointed queue had been left behind on the pier. The party streamed up the hill to the lake, which had still not reached the level of the spillway, an excellent sign of its capacity, but was now a sizable sheet of water reaching back into the gorge and engulfing one by one the little rowan trees. It was christened Loch Ronald in honour of its creator, and Mary was already making plans to stock it with brown trout.

It was dusk before Mr. Campbell declared himself satisfied, and set the valve in the power-house to pass the water through the turbine. Then Ronny, up at the dam, opened the valve which sent the flow down the pipe. In the kitchen waited the womenfolk, still slightly sceptical, with all the switches turned down. Faintly the bulbs glowed orange, flickered, glowed again more brightly, and at last flooded the shadowy old room with the ruthless steadiness of electric light. A ragged cheer drifted down from the power-house, and then the procession came charging home, led by Ronny with a small boy on each shoulder, and all three yelling fit to burst.

The ship's company of the *Annabella* grew sheepish at the kitchen door, but Rory, every inch a host, shepherded them in with a flow of Gaelic and a bottle of whisky under each arm. As the good drink circulated, the room filled with bilingual rejoicings, even Mr. Campbell being heard to observe amid the hubbub that it was no' such a bad job after a'. The visitors departed reluctantly, it being plainly impossible to provide them all with beds. From the jetty, where he had seen them off, Rory looked back at Sunay village and saw it a blazing crescent of light.

"*A dhuine*, that will show from the Kyle," he murmured, almost awestruck. "We should be after having a light down here. A big ret one, like a beacon."

"Oh well, if you don't mind carrying the wiring all this way," said Ronny, suddenly bored. "Have your pals mopped up all the booze?" He charged back into the kitchen, where the others were gathered round the electric kettle. "Look, Ronny," cried Mary excitedly, "it works!"

"'Course it works, fathead," Ronny rejoined. His eye sought Alexander's with that old, ominous challenge. "Well, MacSunay, there you are." This jest had seemed mercifully buried, but Ronny was in a resurrecting mood. "That was what you wanted, wasn't it—Soviet power plus electricity? Now then, where do we go from here?"

[II]

Even as power was robbed from the waterfall to light and warm the crofts of Sunay, so did virtue seem to flow out of Ronny Rossiter and into Rory Mor MacLeod.

Everyone was proud of the dam, and thankful for the current and its half-forgotten comforts. But to Rory it was something more. He exulted; it was as though, in this harnessing of Nature, he found revenge for the centuries of brute toil she had imposed on his race. Facets of the island life which had formerly bored him were suddenly of interest. He haunted the kitchen to watch the washing machine at work. He roamed into the dairy whenever Mrs. Rossiter was churning. Step by step he followed the construction of Maggie's electrically-heated frames, he who had held gardening to be fit work for women and slaves. Already, in his handling of the boats and the tractor, he had shown a natural gift for machinery; now he learnt all that Les had to teach of electrical engineering. He even had enough enthusiasm over for the ordinary work of the farm.

Tons of compost had to be dug out of Kurt's pits and spread on the garden and the fields; tons of seaweed dragged up from the beaches to replace it. To Alexander there was a profound satisfaction in this enriching of the patient land. To Ronny it was tedium. He early discovered that there ought to be a machine for doing it. He worked, and with his accustomed muscular fierceness, but he never ceased from grumbling. When one job was finished he would lounge about waiting for orders, although a dozen others lay under his nose.

He continually nagged for Alexander's notice. "How do I know what you want", he would ask, "if you don't say?" "It's not what I want," had answered Alexander on the first half-dozen occasions; after that he gave Ronny orders, and crisply, but the lines of tension deepened on his face. Only when pottering round the dam and the power-house did Ronny ever seem at peace, or when playing with the concrete-mixer. He made the bases for the frames, and a new flooring for the byre. Left to himself, he would have concreted half the island. He was quite without feeling for growing things.

Maggie considered herself still on holiday. It was early yet for digging on this light land, and she had the children in her care. The great gale had washed up more than seaweed, and Gavin and Jamie learned the delights of driftwood-hunting, that are known to every Hebridean child. They scrambled fearlessly down to the beaches, and would have reached the base of the cliff before Maggie had finished telling them not to. In time she desisted, reflecting proudly that so must children have have scrambled on Sunay through the centuries. It was a week from the opening of the dam when they made their longest expedition, over the saddle to the Camas Ban, with Peigi the pony to carry their dinner in her creels and bring back a noble load.

Great spars, bits of packing-cases, sea-bleached logs that could be split for fencing lay about on the white coral strand, and with them pink cowries, lumps of green glass, and the sunset-coloured shells of very dead crabs. Jamie was distracted among such riches; Gavin, who daily grew more sensible and utilitarian, made unerringly for the likeliest timber, and had to be helped to drag up the steep cliff path to the pony pieces twice his own size.

"Rory says there was a keg of rum washed up once on Canna," he informed Maggie; he had suddenly ceased to have trouble with his consonants, and this gave him the sophistication of a schoolboy in spite of his inability to read. "Wouldn't it be super if we found one here?"

"Och, ye wouldn't like drinking that stuff."

"'Course I shouldn't. I should sell it—you know, to that friend of Rory's what took the whisky. Then I could buy us a 'tato plough."

What a remarkable wee bairn he was, reflected Maggie fondly. Surely there couldn't be in all the Isles another lad of his age with such a grasp of economic fact. "Forbye," she said, "we've enough wood for this trip."

"But Maggie! There's mountains of it still on the rocks."

"I ken fine, but we don't want Peigi overloaded. I tell you what, if it's still calm to-morrow we'll see if Alexander will bring the *Carrie* round. I daresay he might when we tell him what a lot of good stuff there is. And we've an hour's walk back from here, and it's a'ready growing dark."

When he saw the track stretching endlessly before him into the brown heart of the moor, Jamie's courage failed. "I'm tired, Maggie," he began to wail. "I want to wide." He was not really tired, but the sight of such a long way to go made him feel weak in his legs.

"Indeed ye canna. The poor wee beastie has enough to carry as it is."

"Well, you tell me Manachar and Munachar, and ven praps I won't fink about it."

Obediently she began: "There once lived a Manachar and

a Munachar, a long time ago, and it is a long time since it was, and if they were alive now they would not be alive then——" This marvellously satisfying jingle, repeated in chorus, lasted them to the top of the pass, from which the white crescent of the village could be seen. The sight of home put new heart into the little boys. They charged ahead triumphantly, Maggie and the pony following at a sedate pace, and soon were abreast of the dam, down the corkscrew bends of the track and into the first field, where Mary was lifting mangolds for the cows' supper.

"Hi, kids," she called to them, "your Ma's back."

"What's that?" said Maggie.

"Hooray," yelled the children, "Mummy's back," and they rushed in to find her, being always glad of new faces and change. Mary straightened herself and looked her friend in the face.

"The Fletchers are clearing out."

"What's that?" said Maggie again.

"Yes. Bit of a dirty do, isn't it? He's got himself a research job with some big electrical firm, Bedford or Luton, or one of those places. Put in for it weeks ago, and the trip was for his interview. They must have had it all worked out. He's not coming back at all. Daren't face Alexander, I suppose.

"Oh, Mary!" Maggie cried. "It canna be true—they couldna do such a thing to him, and they his best friends."

"Don't you believe it, lass. Best friends my foot. I'm not wasting sympathy on Alexander. If he hasn't seen through them long ago, then he's a bigger fool than I take him for. Perhaps he'll realize now who's on his side. Personally, I'll whoop with joy to see the last of Hermia. The one I'm sorry for is you."

"Me?" said Maggie, for a moment blank. For some extraordinary reason, Gavin and Jamie had ceased, in her mind, to belong to Hermia. Then the full meaning of Mary's pity smote her, and she turned sick and white.

In the kitchen Hermia was giving the children their supper. "And you'll be able to go to a proper school and get to know lots of other boys," Maggie heard her say. They looked bewildered rather than dismayed, and Gavin, at any rate, was interested in the school.

"Will Maggie barf us?" Jamie asked.

"No, ducks," said Hermia briskly. "Mummy's putting you to bed to-night. Poor Maggie deserves a rest."

"But I want Maggie to do it."

"Jamie, you heard what I said." She gave Maggie a remote, frigid smile. Of course, she was not jealous; she had always welcomed anyone who would take the hard work of her children off her hands. This was just another act, put on, apparently, to deceive herself. Maggie met her look stonily. She was beyond concealment.

The defection of the Fletchers was felt like a breath of cold air, coming as it did on top of the community's first major achievement. It undermined the general sense of security, exploded the legend—was it, then, only a legend?—that Sunay was a complete success. By dinner time it had been indignantly canvassed in power-house, dairy and byre. Ronny had called it a filthy trick, and Les had remarked on the bloody foolishness of a chap who let his wife wear the pants, and Mary had informed Mrs. Rossiter that she for one wasn't going to sit mum and watch poor old Magsy being torn in pieces. The feeling against Hermia when they sat down to dinner was electric in its intensity.

Mrs. Rossiter, not without dignity, made a little speech expressing her regret and dismay.

"That's decent of you, Mrs. R. I believe you understand Simon's motives. For the children's sake he couldn't turn down such a wonderful chance." Hermia looked round her brightly, ready to answer questions about the chance. No one asked any, and an angry spot of colour appeared in her cheeks.

Only Alexander's manner to her suffered no outward change. Into the wonders of the job he would not enter, but he wanted news of her theatres and concerts, her meeting with the great world. Hermia's ear was acute enough to hear her own voice echoing in an icy void. She replied shortly that they had been very busy. They had had no time for concerts. A horrid silence fell.

When the meal was over, and Alexander had ascertained that there was no business to be brought before Parliament, he and Kurt went off to their cottage with some excuse about seeing to the books. One unforeseen result of electric power had been a gradual breaking up of the evening group in the kitchen. With bar fires and radios possible in every croft, the less sociable were able to retire into the privacy of their own households. And it had already made three female hearts sore to see Alexander so obviously preferring Kurt's company to theirs.

Hermia scrupulously did her part in the washing-up; then she marched next door, entered without formality, switched off the second Brandenburg concerto, to which Kurt had just tuned in, and delivered herself of her pent-up passion.

"Of course, I know that ever since we came I've been considered the resident bitch. It doesn't matter a damn to me now, though God knows there were times when I could have thrown myself into the sea. But anyway, before I go, you're going to hear my side of it. I suppose I've human rights like the rest."

"No one is criticizing you, Hermy," said Alexander with maddening patience. "No one disputes your rights. Won't you sit down?"

"No, thanks, I'm not stopping. I just wanted to draw your attention to the utter, abysmal selfishness of your whole attitude to Simon."

Kurt, whose Viennese gallantry had pulled him from his chair on her entrance, settled back again, put up his feet

O
209

against the wall and prepared with sardonic glee for a session with human nature.

"It's partly his fault, I grant, for being so fond of you. He's always been too ready to fall in with what you want, as though his own gifts didn't matter. But you know as well as I do that he has abilities every bit as brilliant as yours. His line just happens to be less spectacular, that's all. Again and again I've had to watch him sacrifice himself for you, till at last it was more than I could stand. His life here has been a martyrdom. He's highly strung, and sensitive, and not physically strong at all, and yet he's had to work like any peasant on your grubby little fields. He's half killed himself on the dam. You get some sort of a kick out of it, because it's your show. But if you've a spark of conscience left, you'll know in your heart that you ought never to have allowed him to give up his career for your half-baked ideas."

Alexander made her no answer. He was amazed, not at her but at himself, that anything in her behaviour should still be capable of taking him by surprise. For he knew that this was just how she might be relied on to behave; he had watched her often enough with other people. The truth was, he had known her so long, she had become so much a part of the furniture of his life, that he had somehow come to believe she would behave differently to him. Yet it was obvious that their friendship had arisen from their both pulling Simon the same way. On Sunay they had begun to pull him in opposite ways. At this recollection, profound pity for Simon again blotted out every other feeling.

Hermia fetched breath and began on another tack.

"As if it wasn't bad enough to watch Simon being slowly throttled, I also had to see my children turning into little savages. Here's Gavin, seven, and he can't even read. Both of them are quite out of hand. They live an unnatural life, cut off from other kids—I could feel that at the Farquharson party. Maggie Moffat now has far more influence on them than I have, and let me tell you this, I'm not at all satisfied that her influence is a healthy one. She's like so many of these frustrated maternal types, prepared to batten emotionally on any children not her own."

"Hermia, for God's sake! You know damn well that isn't true. If you ever say such a thing in her hearing I'll—heaven help me, I believe I'll strangle you."

"Oh, well, perhaps I do exaggerate there." Hermia had at last drawn blood, and therefore tended to be satisfied. "I've nothing serious against Maggie. She'd be quite a nice little creature if she wasn't so full of Scotch self-righteousness. But at all events, she can't compensate my children for all they're missing here. Now look here, Alexander, I don't want to part enemies. I'll always be fond of you, you know that. You think me a bloody nuisance now, but just try to see the thing with some of your famous detachment, and you'll soon recognize the writing on the wall. You've had your fling here, you've worked whatever it was out of your blood, you've built your dam and had your fun and games. Why not get out while the going's good? You'd get ten thousand for the island, easy, with the publicity it's had, and six habitable cottages. That would give us all a nice little nest-egg to get started again with. I'm advising you as a friend."

"You will get your money back," said Alexander flatly.

"Feel a lot better now, don't you, darling?" Kurt inquired.

"Why, my sweet little refugee, fancy forgetting you! I can well believe this has been a heaven-sent chance for you. You hadn't much else in the way of prospects. No doubt that's why you've been looking so merry the last few weeks?"

If she stung him, Kurt did not give her the satisfaction of knowing it. His quizzical smile widened, and it was Hermia who seemed suddenly to crumple, as though the huge nervous strain of her outburst were too much for her. She looked exhausted; one could see forty waiting for her round the corner.

"Well," she muttered with a little laugh, "I daresay that's enough home truths for one evening. Good night to one and all," and she walked out as unceremoniously as she had come.

Maggie, with a face of stone, still sat with Mrs. Rossiter over the kitchen fire. "Spare me a moment, will you?" said Hermia, putting her head round the door. Maggie got up and followed her like one in a bad dream.

"I'd like you to have my Monet reproduction, pet, as you've always admired it. I shan't forget how marvellous you've been with the offspring—and, as a matter of fact, you've always been decent to me too You're about the only one who has."

Maggie looked up, startled, and her face went pink. Could Hermia really believe that? Did she after all not know who had consistently led the opposition? If so, she must be a simple soul, under all her worldly airs. Maggie's misery was increased by a dawning suspicion that perhaps she had helped to bring it on herself.

"Is there anything else you'd like?" asked Hermia, turning over things in drawers and humming. "Anyway, you can be residuary legatee to all we leave behind. Come on, cheer up now. I know it's a bit of a blow to you, but then, you shouldn't go giving your heart to other people's children."

Her kindness was dreadful. Maggie fought down horrid sobs and muttered something about her being surely right.

"You ought to get a man of your own," Hermia urged. "You aren't going to go on for ever wasting your maternal urge on turnips. This life here isn't fair to you. Don't let Alexander eat up your energy as he did Simon's. Under that gentle manner he's quite ruthless. I don't suppose you've ever noticed, but he has a cruel mouth. I tell you what, why not come away with us? Then you could still have charge of the kids, and I'd get myself a job. We won't be millionaires, of course, but we could pay you some sort of a screw."

So that was it! Not content with betraying Alexander herself, she hoped to deal him a farewell blow by making a renegade of his oldest ally. Maggie said, striving hard to keep the anger out of her voice:

"I'm sure it's verra kind of you, but I've my own job to get on with here."

"Oh, well, just as you like. I only thought that as you'd seemed so fond of Gavin and Jamie, you might be glad of the chance."

"But I am fond of them!" Maggie cried. "Och, Hermia, I love them so well, ye canna think. . . ." It was humiliating, this appealing to the enemy, and besides, it was useless. She checked herself, then added: "Maybe ye could spare them in their school holidays? After a', Sunay's a bonny place for bairns."

"I daresay, but it's also a long way from the Midlands. I don't see us ever affording the fare."

"Maybe", said Maggie piteously, "when the farm starts to pay, I could send you the fare?"

"Lawks, child, how you do take on. Believe me, when I tell you that you'll forget them, and all the quicker if you get some of your own. You think over what I've said."

"Good night," said Maggie shakily, "and thank you for the picture," and she went out into the rainy dark.

All the next day Hermia was packing, and after the children had distracted her for an hour by their constant clamouring to have shells and spars included, she was glad enough to throw them back on to Maggie's hands. Alexander told off Rory, though he could ill be spared from muck-spreading, to take them round in the *Carrie* to the Camas Ban, and they brought her home loaded to the gunwale with driftwood. They seemed to have no notion that a life was ending, and very little interest in the one ahead. One could not be sufficiently thankful that they lived so completely in the present.

Hermia was merry on this, her last evening. She produced the remains of what had evidently been a private Fletcher cellar, and succeeded in getting herself, Mary and Ronny into the first stage of tipsiness. She perched on Alexander's knee and hugged him quite as though they were still bosom friends, and she caused Kurt to accompany her in ribald version of well-known hymns, although it was obvious that Mrs. Rossiter didn't really like it.

Directly after breakfast, Alexander and Rory wheeled her packing cases down to the jetty; the white iron furniture was to follow on the *Loch Coruisk*'s next call. When they saw the cases being stowed into the *Gannet*, the truth seemed at last to dawn on the two little boys.

"I think I'd rather stay here, Mummy," said Gavin briskly. "Can't I?"

"Ducky, of course you must come with Daddy and me."

"But I'd rather stay with Maggie, please."

"So'd I!" shouted Jamie. "So'd I! I want to stay wiv Maggie, please?" And he suddenly flung himself on Maggie, clutching her round the knees. "Loving you," he whispered, his face convulsed with tears. "Loving you."

Gavin was too grown-up to cry, but he planted his feet squarely on the jetty and glared at his mother.

This was frightful. Maggie looked up at her across Jamie's head, expecting to see her furious. But the unpredictable creature was weeping too. The tears were positively blotching the careful journey make-up on her face.

Maggie pulled herself together. "D'ye think there's something wrong again with yon engine?" she suggested. "Rory seems to be having a wee spot of trouble."

"'Spect it's the carburettor," said Gavin. "I say, Rory, let me have a look."

"Let I see too!" clamoured Jamie, and in a trice they were amidships, their fair heads peering over Rory's shoulder. Hermia jumped aboard, Alexander cast off quickly and the

Gannet headed out to sea. Not once did they look back or wave.

[III]

For a long time she sat on the jetty, staring out across the Sound. Then she went up into the garden and started on the spring digging. And some comfort seemed to reach her from the fresh brown earth, the peaceful, rhythmically muscular activity. At lunch she was cheerful, and could eat. But in the afternoon the rain began to fall again. There were all those tons of seed potatoes to be sprouted. She spread the first dozen boxes on the table in the barn, got herself a chair from her cottage, and resolutely began.

Presently she seemed to hear the silence.

Gavin and Jamie had not been noisy children, but their high, clear voices and the patter of their feet had made a continuous throb on Sunay, like the beating of a heart. Now that beat had stopped. Other sounds, the hammer of the sea and the kittiwakes' crying, drifted in on the rainy wind, but the human heart was dead. Gradually, Maggie began to cry.

At first she tried to work on, but it was hopeless. The seed toppled from her hands. The rest of it lay in sacks in a corner. She laid herself down, put her cheek against the rough earth-smelling hessian, and sobbed. She lost all count of time, all power to stop herself. The sobs came up from dreadful depths, from her loneliness, from the hot grasp of Jamie's hands round her knees, from her mother's death, from the agony of her empty womb.

"Maggie, where are you?" called Alexander's voice from a long way off, and then: "Good God, darling, don't. You'll kill yourself. Here, what do I have a shoulder for?" and she felt her face lifted on to something warmer and kinder than potato-sacks. The smell of peaty tweed, the firm grasp of a friend's arm were infinitely comforting. Presently the dread-

ful crying ceased, and she was able to hunt for a handkerchief.

"I didna' mean to be greeting this way. I was for sprout-
ing the seed."

"Right ho. We'll both sprout the seed."

But still she lay with her head on his shoulder, enjoying
that strangely impersonal sense of comfort. "There was a lot
of sense", she remarked, "in what Hermia told me at the
end. She said I was a fool to go giving my heart to other
people's children."

"Lovely for the children, though," said Alexander. "I
believe every child ought to have some adult devoted to it
who's not its parent, and is consequently free from blood-
antagonisms. Well, perhaps they aren't inevitable in every
case, but look at the Rossiters."

"Ye don't think Hermia and Gavin will get like that?"
asked Maggie in dismay.

"No, not to any serious extent. Gavin's too well-balanced
—he already by-passes Hermia quite efficiently. Besides, he
has a good sort of father in Simon."

Mention of Simon recalled Maggie to Alexander's own
loss. Here he was, as bereft as she and much more shamefully
let down, and no one thought of comforting him. And it
struck her that she, too, had in a sense betrayed him. She,
who had supposed herself to love him, was breaking her
heart and not on his account at all. Not but what, if Mary
were to pass the open door at that moment, as she very well
might on her way to the byre, she would get a horrid shock.
At which thought Maggie detached herself with reluctance
from the shoulder and set to work again on the potatoes.

"I'd forgotten, whiles," she nervously began—it always
seemed an impossible liberty to be pitying Alexander—"that
it's just as bad for you."

"For me? Oh no, hardly. Though, mind you, they were
jolly kids."

"I was meaning Simon."

"Simon?" He considered. "Well now, it seems to me, looking back, that I lost touch with Simon months ago. Once that had happened, I daresay we were better apart. I must have been a sort of Hamlet's father's ghost to the poor chap ever since."

"I dinna believe it," cried Maggie stoutly. "He was happy here. He told me so himself. You were his one protection against her. He'll have nothing now. These wee wifies always win in the end." And she glared balefully at a vision of Hermia, not as the weeping creature of the morning but as marital tyranny personified.

"Well, that's fair enough."

"It is not. Why should a selfish body go domineering over a generous one?"

"Wait till you're a wee wifie yourself. Then you won't think the generosity is all on the husband's side."

"I canna imagine——" began Maggie, and stopped. There were certainly a good many things it was better not to imagine out loud to Alexander. Across the potatoes he gave her that shrewd look that always disconcerted her, and she felt that inwardly he was smiling. Perhaps to cover her embarrassment, he said:

"Did I ever tell you how Simon and I met?"

"Why, were ye not both at the university?"

"No, indeed—he's Oxford and I'm Cambridge. It was on holiday in the Lakes. I'd walked up Gable to the Napes, hoping to cadge a climb, and there were two chaps with a rope, having an argument about which one they'd go up. Poor old Simon, even in those days somebody was always pushing him around. . . ."

His quiet voice, the simple monotonous task in hand, and the endless pattering of the rain gradually created an illusion of peace; and little by little she forgot that he most probably, and she for certain, had a lump of lead in place of a heart.

Chapter Nine

[I]

The departure of the Fletchers made a change in the living arrangements at Sunay. Their croft, the roomiest after the kitchen, could not be allowed to moulder in emptiness. After some discussion Ronny and Rory, those old though possibly no longer so firm allies, moved in to it, leaving Kurt and Alexander more space to spread themselves in the end house. Ronny's room in his mother's cottage, thus vacated, was set aside for visitors, and the first to occupy it was Rory's Annag.

The notion of inviting her was Alexander's, when it became known to him that Mrs. Rossiter, though now single-handed for the greater part of the housework, still intended to spring-clean. It was useless to beg her not to. Nothing short of a major illness could set the standards of her generation aside.

"Is there a chance", he asked Rory, "that your Annag would give us a hand? She might like to see how we live on Sunay. It would give her something to talk about at *ceilidhs*."

"Ach, her Ta would nefer let her come," declared Rory. "He iss a terrible selfish one, the *bodeach*. Leets her a treatful life. And she would be shy to come. She would think her clothes wasn't grant enough." Anyone who had heard him would have said there was no hope of Annag. But anyone who watched his gleeful eyes might have guessed that next time the *Gannet* came back from the Kyle, a slender, shrinking black figure would be seated in her stern.

"Chust for two weeks," Rory explained. "Her Ta says she iss not to stay a minute after that. *A Dhia*, we hat a fine scene getting her off as it wass!"

Annag at lunch was so pitifully tongue-tied that Ronny, who sat next to her, decided she couldn't be quite right in the head. But in the afternoon her lover took her into the dairy, and proudly displayed its electrical wonders. Their streams of Gaelic could be heard in the kitchen, interspersed with giggles, but in half an hour Annag had mastered the workings of the churn and separator and was asking to see the washing-machine. Rory departed reluctantly about his duties, and Joyce and Mrs. Rossiter took her over the rest of the village.

Her wonder, her innocent admiration were highly acceptable. "Issn't that pretty!" she murmured every moment, while her large dark eyes noted the marvels that would be retailed at the Kyle. Joyce's house especially appealed to her. When Joyce switched on the new lighting to reveal the beauty of her pink silk lampshades, Annag gasped with sheer pleasure. It was long since Joyce had been envied by anybody, or been anything, in fact, but an object of pity. Patronizing Annag, she forgot for a moment her dread and her weariness and her shameful, top-heavy figure, and became the proud and busy little housewife she could have been in Braintree or Ruislip Gardens.

Annag's lack of suitable equipment for an island life had already perturbed Mrs. Rossiter; for her only clothes were the ones she stood up in, the black coat, a printed rayon dress, evidently her best, and a factory-made woollen cardigan, sad comment on the bankruptcy of Hebridean handicrafts. Mary's dismay when she went along to the byre to help with the milking was more frankly expressed. "Good lord," she said, "that all you've got to work in? We all wear slacks on Sunay. You know—trousers. Tell you what, I'll lend you a pair of mine."

"Ach, no, thank you, miss," said Annag, alarmed.

"Why ever not? You've a nice figure, and nothing much behind."

Annag was not, of course, the utterly untouched child of nature. She enjoyed the travelling cinema when it visited the Kyle, and knew that American and English girls dressed like that, and she had no doubt frequently pictured such garments on herself. It only needed a little more flattery to get her into Mary's green corduroys and cashmere jersey. They transformed her from a downtrodden peasant into a slender Celtic Puck.

"That'll make Rory sit up and take notice," said Mary with a grin.

Annag's face fell. "I could nefer be letting Rory see me like this. He will laugh."

"Well then," counselled Mary, "you think up some nice Gaelic way of telling him to go to hell."

Accordingly Annag appeared at dinner in the trousers. Rory, when he saw her, burst into a loud guffaw, followed by a flow of doubtless insulting language, but Annag, though she turned bright pink, held her ground. By the end of the first week she was using lipstick, and by the end of the second she smoked. With each innovation she gained fresh courage to defy Rory, and was probably helped by a suspicion that for all his sneering he secretly admired her way of assimilating English ideas.

Annag's visit was altogether a success. Once over her shyness, she was gay and game. She had something of Rory's quickness with unfamiliar machinery, and she learned more from Mrs. Rossiter in a fortnight than Joyce had been willing to learn in a year. Mrs. Rossiter had suffered much from Joyce, and might be excused for observing privately to Alexander that it was a pleasure to have to do with somebody intelligent.

But once the fun of emancipating Hebridean womanhood wore off, Mary found herself unhappier on Sunay than she had ever been yet. This sudden wave of black depression puzzled as well as frightening her. She was hardly aware that she had regarded Hermia as her chief enemy with Alexander, and that she had therefore been expecting him to alter once Hermia was gone. But so it was, and when he remained the same, as charming, as friendly, as unencouraging as ever, when, if anything, she found herself seeing even less of him because he deliberately seemed to prefer Kurt's morose company by their own hearthside, then at last she began to fall victim to real despair.

If he had never looked at her, she told herself, she could have thought of something different; but he sometimes did. He never met any of her advances; but it would happen that when she wasn't thinking of him, when she wasn't even aware that he was near, she would catch him watching her with that look that other men had when they knew that she was beautiful. That was the maddening part of it; he did know; he could love her if he would only let himself; he could take what she was so ready to give. Only she was a fool and spoilt it every time she opened her mouth. For it was now dimly dawning on Mary that her manners in some way affronted him, and that if she could just sit mum she would stand a better chance. But you couldn't spend your life sitting mum, and certainly not with someone like Alexander, who was sociable and chatty and fond of argument. It was filthy luck to be born stupid; filthier still always to fall, as she did, for the clever chaps, who would eye her with that covert admiration, and then listen to her with that apologetic smile.

It was a chance remark of Mrs. Rossiter's which gave her fresh and desperate hope. Mrs. Rossiter had been praising Alexander to his face till she drove him, as frequently, from the room.

"If that boy has a weakness, it's his modesty," she commented with a tender smile. "I don't suppose he realizes yet just how much he means to us all."

That she was thinking of herself was obvious, but not to Mary. To her it seemed a plain hint. That, perhaps, was it—that, at any rate, was what the old trout thought—and she had loved, had at some point caught her man, she ought to know. Mary felt herself to be in some sort a favourite with Mrs. Rossiter. The fact had often made her grin, for one would expect the virtuous Maggie to have had the preference, but Mrs. Rossiter had a weakness for a pretty face. And then she was supposed to be a great reader of character, and even someone not very gifted could see that Alexander was the least conceited soul alive. That must be it; he doubted his power; he needed to be shown. Seized with mingled excitement and panic, Mary resolved to throw herself unmistakably at his head. It was only a question of getting him alone.

But on Sunay nobody was ever alone, unless they went for a walk or on the sheep-round, and it was useless inviting Alexander because at present he had too much else to do.

While she was brooding over this tiny, ridiculous obstacle, Alexander removed it himself. The next call of the *Loch Coruisk* came up for discussion. It was he who suggested that Kurt and Ronny should take the remainder of the lambs south, and cheer themselves for a day or two with such frivolities as Oban in the winter might afford. Since the defection of the Fletchers he had been haunted by the notion that everybody ought to have some sort of break.

Alexander alone in the end house—the thought obsessed her. She could hardly endure the wait. It would be a monstrous, an appalling thing to do. If only she were not so bloody ignorant! If only she had let Alan take her, so that at least she knew what it was like! She knew nothing, although she talked so big; nothing, except what she could see of the animals' matings, and the smutty surmises of a girls' public school. She supposed it would hurt, but that wouldn't matter. However bad it was, it couldn't make her as miserable as her virginity did now. The unbearable thing would be that

222

he should refuse. If he did, she would kill herself—or at any rate, she would have to leave Sunay. She had been among the loudest in her denunciation of the Fletchers, yet the thought that it was possible to leave Sunay had been in the back of her mind ever since.

Or perhaps he would prove as ignorant, as stupid as she was. Nice fools they would look then. Surely chaps didn't reach Alexander's age without having had a mistress? The speculation was in itself a torment. She ached to consult someone—Mrs. Rossiter, perhaps. But no, the old rip might give naughty general advice, but she'd be horrified if one asked for details. As for Maggie, she would die of shock. And yet was it so dreadful? Was it so shocking? Unless you showed a spot of guts, how was the world to be carried on at all? Over and over in her mind went the arguments of panic. She had dared herself to do it, and she had never been able to resist a dare. But underneath her parade of crudity and courage lay the agonized embarrassment of the English schoolgirl. She would have to go through with her part, but she thought that she would very likely die.

By the day of the ship's call she was almost hysterical. Even Mrs. Rossiter noticed it, and maddened her by wanting to feel her pulse. She could not bear to look at Alexander, could scarcely bear to be in the same room with him, till it had happened. In the afternoon she announced her intention of doing the sheep-round. The *Loch Coruisk* was to be in at three.

"Shall ye no' stay to see her?" asked Maggie in surprise, for the visits were still an island event.

"Lord, no, what is there to see? I couldn't be bothered to wave to Kurt unless I knew he wasn't ever coming back." Kurt, without her noticing it, was taking Hermia's place as an enemy in her mind. She stuffed some food into her pockets, with a notion of being back late for dinner and so not looking him in the face till the last possible moment; then she called Lady, and set off into the hills.

223

As she climbed she forced herself to rehearse the interview. She knew that whenever she tried to plan imaginary conversations she got them wrong. Yet it would be frightful to stand and say nothing, worse still to blurt out something fatuous. She had a notion that to go straight at it would be the likeliest way to soften him, but there her courage failed. She must have some excuse—pretend to consult him about the cows—a change of bull—anything. Then, when she was leaving—but quickly, before he could open a door for her, or anything final—she would turn to him and say: "Look here, I love you. Please let me stay." Surely that wouldn't sound too silly—not when it was true—not when it came straight from her heart? But at the thought of saying it, and of what Alexander's face would look like as he heard it, her cheeks flamed.

She had reached the top of the Carn Mor before Lady, by signalling to her a sheep on its back, caused her to raise her eyes from the ground. The beauties of nature commonly meant little to Mary when there was no pleasant chap by her side to point them out. But the staggering loveliness of the Isles on that winter morning did get through her unhappy preoccupations and bring her some measure of release. The long days of rain had been succeeded by a mellow, golden clarity, and the purple skeleton of the Outer Isles floated on a sea of moonstone blue, each of its little peaks defined and perfect as they never were in summer time. A longing took her to see out to the other side, over Scotland; perhaps the old Ben would have snow on him? "When we've finished," she told Lady, "damned if we don't go up Torval." It would be an adventure, just the two of them alone and no rope, and in the depths of winter. Also, it would distract her mind from the wait.

They started up the south ridge, girl and dog equally in the perfection of health and training, and quickly made height. After an hour the ridge narrowed, and Scotland appeared on the other side, a fretsaw line of tiny, pale-brown peaks with here and there the glint of snow. The Ben was white, and the great Mamores behind him. "Golly," said Mary aloud, startled in spite of herself by the immensity of sky and sea and a hundred hills. Between Muck and the mainland a steamer left a delicate trail of smoke on the still air. It was the *Loch Coruisk*, heading south.

Lady came gallantly up the loose scree and broken rocks to the point where the ridge steepened to a climb. Then she stopped, disconcerted. The rise was in two sections, with a sloping platform in between, and Mary, by reaching down and hooking her shepherd's crook into the dog's collar, was able to haul her up bodily. Then they raced on together, and shared a crust by the summit cairn.

It suddenly came back to Mary that the descent was considerably steeper on the north or homeward ridge. She broke off her reverie, called Lady after her, and lowered herself on careful hand-holds down the first of the great detached boulders where more timorous parties used a rope. Lady stood poised on the skyline above her, and in response to her encouragement, gave a little whine of dismay.

"Come on, girl," cajoled Mary, reaching up the crook. But Lady was beyond her reach, and had, moreover, decided in her mind that dogs were not intended to go down places like that. Her whine became more positive. Glancing at the yet stiffer pitch below her, Mary gave it up. "All right, you goop," she said, climbing back. "Home the way we came."

But when they reached the descent on the other ridge, Lady dug in her paws again.

Pulling her up had been easy; pulling her down, Mary now realized, would be risky in the extreme. The platform where they had to land was sloping. A large dog, heavy, protesting and off her balance, would very likely roll, and her mistress with her. It was now five in the evening, there was less than an hour of daylight left, and here they were, trapped.

As her predicament dawned on her, Mary could have laughed. Was this to be the end of her brazen scheming, her thoughts of passion and suicide? She could not believe that either of them would survive a January night's exposure, without so much as a blanket, at three thousand feet. To abandon the dog and save herself never entered her head.

She went back to the summit, and peered about. The terrible west face was hopeless; it was precipice far more uncompromising than the ridge. On the east, a narrow scree funnel ran down and lost itself between ominously foreshortened walls of black rock. Had she heard something about a cads' route up Torval, and if so, could that be it? "We'll try it, girl," she said to Lady, who now stood shivering with terror. "It's our only chance."

As they crept slowly down in dust and falling stones, the shimmering landscape paled and faded. Nature was no longer a solace, but a vast unfeeling presence, impersonal and unconcerned. If they were dropping towards their deaths, it would not matter to the insensate hills. The night came up with menacing speed, pulled like a hood over the eastern sky. If only, prayed Mary, desperately encouraging the dog, they could get past the twist in the gully in time to see whether it led them out, or whether, more probably, another drop cut them off from all hope of home.

They did it with hardly a minute to spare, were just able to peer round the corner and see the blessed little ribbon of scree glimmering on down to the brown line of the heather, and darkness fell. The last three hundred feet of descent had to be made by feel alone. As her boots touched the softness of the heather, Mary found that she was trembling. Relief and gratitude flooded into her. Let Alexander do his worst, there would be no suicide. Life suddenly seemed precious on any terms.

It took them two hours more to reach home. This east side of Torval was the part of the island least known to them, and difficult to negotiate even in daylight, a region of peat-hags and featureless, confusing shoulders of moor. Lady, her paws bleeding, her nerve completely broken, clung to her mistress and seemed to have lost all sense of direction; as she crawled through the heather she whined softly. The crescent lights of the village were a blessed beacon at last. The light in Alexander's croft showed that dinner must be over, and he sitting down with his books. For the first time it struck her that he might at least have worried and gone out to look. No one seemed to have given a damn. But when she reached the kitchen door her consequence was soothed by Mrs. Rossiter's anxious face. And it was not so very late, after all. They had her dinner keeping hot on the stove.

When she had finished recounting her adventures, and had been scolded by Mrs. Rossiter and Maggie and rather grumpily congratulated on her nerve by Les, she went off to change and bathe Lady's paws, and summon up her courage for the last ordeal. She felt abominably tired, and had, after all, a first-class excuse for putting it off for another night. But something told her that would be fatal. It was now or never, sink or swim.

In soundless rubber-soled shoes she strode back along the causeway, past the lighted kitchen window—there they still sat, happy creatures, safe and without a care in the world—and stood before Alexander's door. She raised her hand to knock, and lowered it again, and waited for a long moment listening to the thumping of her heart. Then she lifted the latch and marched in, and was half-way across the room before the man in a chair by the hearth had turned his head.

And it was not Alexander. It was Kurt.

[II]

Someone socially acute, a Hermia, might still have carried it off. But Mary, strung up to enormous endeavour, was stunned by this check in her flight and gave herself utterly away.

"Where's Alexander?" she said on a gasp.

"Not here, I'm afraid," answered Kurt, smiling. "But I am delighted to see you, dear Mary. Come, sit down." Still dazed, she sat down, and instantly tried to get up again. Kurt strolled over and shut the door.

There was nothing untoward in his shutting his own door, especially when ill-mannered young women bounced in without knocking. Nevertheless, something in the gesture shook Mary with a cold fear.

"I wanted to see Alexander," she began belligerently. "I have to consult him about the cows."

"Did you now? Well, I'm afraid he's gone to Oban. I cried off at the last minute, and he went instead. Something must have warned me, you know, that it would be terribly worth my while to stay." He leant against the door and continued to smile at her, and she stared back at him, shaken by the smile. "Anyhow, you can consult me. You've always underestimated me. I know much more than you think about cows."

"I'm sorry——" began Mary, getting to her feet.

"Sit down," said Kurt evenly. "You aren't going yet."

"I damn well am! If you think——"

"Yes indeed, I do think. You didn't come to see Alexander about any cows. You thought he'd be alone. My poor girl, it wouldn't have done you the slightest good. You may be thankful I've saved you from that."

"How dare you——" cried Mary, doubling her fists, and then remembered that violence would be useless. She was a big girl, and strong, but she had worked enough beside Kurt in the fields to know that he could worst her easily, for all his pretty looks.

"Yelling wouldn't do you much good, either," continued Kurt, greatly at his ease. "I doubt if it would carry as far as the kitchen, and anyway, if you were rescued, think how undignified! You'd never be able to look any of them in the face again."

"If Alexander were here——"

"He would, of course, save you, being an English gentleman. But I don't believe he'd be at all keen on it. You've had this coming to you for a long time, Mary, and I doubt if there's one of them that wouldn't be glad to know you'd got it in the end."

"You lousy Yid——"

"Quite, yes, that's among the things I complain of. For eleven months, without any provocation, you've insulted me and my race. Yet for all you know I may be proud of it— at least as proud as you are of Widnes or Wigan or whatever happy spot it was that gave you birth."

Even in the midst of her panic, Mary was astounded by the venom in his voice and smile. Never had Alan, at his worst, looked at her so cruelly. It was as though she had unleashed something beyond her powers to understand.

"You were, I believe I am right in assuming, proposing to spend the night with Alexander. You shall spend it with me instead. You will find me an experienced and considerate lover—a great deal more satisfactory, I daresay, than he would have been. To-morrow morning you will be very much happier, and I, for some queer reason which I couldn't, at any rate to you, explain, shall have got even not only with you but with the only woman I seriously happen to want."

"You wouldn't do it, Kurt," said Mary, summoning the powers of sanity which seemed to be slipping from them both.

"Wouldn't I? Why not?"

"People don't do such things. You—hell, your pride wouldn't let you when it came to the point."

"My dear, a dirty foreigner hasn't any pride."

"See here, Kurt——" began Mary passionately. And at that, a black exhaustion swept over her. She lay back in the chair, clutching its arms, and shut her eyes. "All right, go on, do whatever you like. What does it matter? I thought I was going to die on Torval, anyway. Whatever you do can't be much worse than that."

There was a long pause. Then Kurt said in a quite different voice: "Is that where you were?"—and opening her eyes, she saw that he had stopped smiling.

After a moment he added, angrily:

"You can climb well enough. What kept you out?"

"I had the dog with me."

"Oh, I see. The dog."

Again he paused; then he began to laugh.

"Old Ma Ross would have it you were in some sort of a jam. We were going to look for you if you weren't back by nine. Oddly enough, I was organizing the search-party, foreign cad though I am."

And on that thought he left the door and walked over to his chair by the fire.

"All right, Mary. This time we let you off. I fear your estimate of me is only too accurate. I can't do it when it comes to the point. Probably, as you say, my pride."

So she was saved. She only had to get up and go. She thought that he might at least have opened the door for her. She was abominably tired.

"Although, you know, it's your loss," he was continuing reflectively, more to himself than her. "Back you'll go to eat out your heart, never getting any nearer—because you haven't got what he wants, and what you have got he'll never appreciate. Not as I would. For I like you, Mary. Yes, in spite of everything—and not just your shape. I like your vitality. I like your nerve. It was magnificent, the way you came here to-night, and after six hours on a mountain, enough to keep any other girl quiet. Did you think you were going to die on Torval, then? And didn't that teach you how much better it is to live? You've always liked the aloof young men with the high ideals, haven't you, Mary? You've always wanted what you couldn't have, and assumed there must be something wrong with a chap who honestly desired you. When you've given up all hope of Alexander, you'll start again on someone else. Never learning any better. What a criminal waste."

"Shut up," muttered Mary, holding the chair.

"But I'm not being a foreign cad now. I'm telling you all this as a friend."

"I don't know why you are so damned unkind to me. Of course, I say the wrong thing and jump on people's corns. But you know jolly well I never meant to do you any harm."

"All right. We'll call it quits. Hadn't you better go now? My foreign brand of chivalry mayn't hold out for ever."

"Oh, you are *beastly*!" cried Mary, and dissolved into tears.

For a moment more he looked at her, with a sort of comical perplexity. Then he crossed over, gathered the absurd, long-desired, rose and golden creature into his arms, and set his mouth on hers.

[III]

In view of Mary's ordeal on Torval, Maggie decided to let her sleep it out. She got up earlier herself and did the milking, and looking in at breakfast-time, found her friend still sprawled in heavy slumber across the bed. The meal over, she collected food on a tray and after much prodding succeeded in getting her awake.

Mary struggled up, her blue eyes still cloudy, and it was some time before she could gather her wits sufficiently to thank for the tray.

"Ye'd ought to have been in bed earlier last night," said Maggie in amicable reproof. "Ye needed a good sleep.

Where were ye, forbye, when I went to bed? Surely ye'd had enough of the moors?"

Mary bent a surly face over her home-cured bacon.

"Well, as a matter of fact—you'll have to know sooner or later—I spent the night with Kurt. Go on, faint."

Maggie did in truth feel a shock akin to nausea. "Ye canna mean——" she whispered at last.

"Well, it's a longish story. A sort of accident, really. But you can take it from me that it was more my doing than his."

Maggie made a heroic, an almost muscular effort to by-pass the instincts, the training, the beliefs of a lifetime, and not fail a friend in the hour of need. And partially she succeeded.

"Ye ken fine, Mary lass," she faltered at length, "that I'd be glad to see you happy."

"Would you, Mags?" Mary looked up from the bacon, all her surliness gone. "You are a brick. Well, I'm just incredibly happy. It's such a relief, I can't tell you. It's just like being let out of jug. If I could only describe——"

"No, dinna try," Maggie hastily replied. "It's just that—well—you and *Kurt*. You know I always liked Kurt. It was you——"

"Aren't you a pig, reminding me? Though, mind you, it was his fault too. If he was going to be so sweet to me, why couldn't he have been it ages ago, instead of leering at me in that foul way while he was really carrying on with some dreary German female? Naturally I never guessed what—well, what he's really like." And she laid her head back on the pillows and seemed to drift away into a golden dream.

And Alexander? thought Maggie's one-track mind. Not a word of him, not a memory. Could such things be? But she wasn't going to mention Alexander. Impossible for her not to feel that there was everything to be said for Mary's bowing herself out.

It came to her, as she stared at the radiant, satisfied creature on the bed, that she was witnessing a miracle. It was something monstrous, and by all decent standards wrong, but something fiercer and more powerful than her experience had included, or maybe ever would. It had the force of the storm, or of the bursting spring. Sense as well as morality urged that such a back-door entry into love could never be permanent, that the differences of character between Mary and Kurt could never be bridged by this sort of cheating. But were they, after all, so unsuited? With this in her mind, as well as her natural hankering after respectability, she asked:

"Does he—will ye be getting married?"

"Married?" said Mary, and it was all too plain that this was the first time the notion had occurred to her. "Oh, I dunno —marriage is a bit different, isn't it?" But a little smile curved her mouth while she considered the possibility. Maggie felt she had had shocks enough for one morning. She took herself off to unpack the frame-lights brought by the steamer the day before.

At lunch she could not resist covertly examining them both. Kurt entered whistling, and came and sat by her at once. He was the Kurt of the old days restored, loquacious and didactic, comical and charming. He gave her a quite unnecessary lecture on the compost mixture for the frames, and seemed to be bursting with inward glee. Mary sat as far from him as possible and kept her eyes glued to her plate. She only spoke once, at the end of the meal, and that was to announce in a very loud voice that if no one wanted her for anything she was taking her rod up to the top loch. A little pang smote Maggie. That was how it was, and that was how you looked and felt, how you intrigued and covered your shyness. It was impossible that she should ever know.

Loch na Creitheach, a big pool cupped in glaciated red rock in the heart of the corrie under Torval's west wall, was a hidden and lonely spot where no one but Mary ever came. She raced up to it as though the Water-horse himself were after her, and had lain for what seemed to her an unconscionable time on her red rock couch before Kurt's head appeared above the rim of the corrie. He came and stood over her, slowly smiling. "You seem full of beans," he commented. "I believe I let you off too lightly last night."

"Now then," said Mary, "none of your lip." She put up her arms and pulled him down, clutching him with a fierce possessiveness to which his blood instantly responded. "Darling," he murmured between kisses, over and over, as he had in the night, "how beautiful you are. How absolutely beautiful you are."

She was crying again, those comic, little-girl tears, and he found himself shaken not just by desire but by the pity he had never before had occasion to feel in love. No one could need pity less than Ilse, that well-equipped expert, and never had he taken or imagined any creature so ignorant, so scared and pathetic as this great blustering English girl. God only knew what she had expected—some esoteric form of torture —and yet the splendid fire of life in her had driven her just the same. The gratitude, the worship she gave him for his tenderness could have made him laugh, if they had not been so strangely sweet. "My funny little Mary," he murmured, rocking her, "how beautiful you are," and half-forgotten German endearments came caressingly to his lips.

"Kurt," whispered Mary after a long time.

"Yes, darling. What is it?"

"I say—you know—that woman you were talking about."

"What woman?"

"Oh, all right then." Pride and triumph turned her rosy. "What I was getting at was—would you—are you going to marry me?"

Kurt sat up with a jerk and stared at her. "But, darling," he said, his face breaking into a grin, "would you really be willing to marry me?"

"Well, I might. You haven't turned out as badly as I thought."

"A dirty foreigner. A Yid."

"Shut up, you silly ass." She crushed her hands down over his mouth.

"That's all very well," said Kurt, removing them effortlessly, "but I should want a handsome apology first. You take it all back?"

"Right ho, if you insist."

"Indeed I insist. And what about kids? You wouldn't mind them being half-Jewish?"

"I'd like them to be like you," muttered Mary, blushing hotly.

"That seems conclusive. All right, I'll condescend to marry you." He brooded delightedly on this absurd prospect. "Whatever will your father say? But I suppose it doesn't matter what he says. You're independent of him here."

"Yes," whispered Mary, lost in bliss.

A marriage on Sunay—Mary's fine children—sons to carry on the Reclamations—a clan—so Kurt's mind ran, building up from his beloved soil fertility to the most precious fertility of all. Then suddenly, as though the force of his last remark had got through to her, she sat up and looked him in the face.

"But I say, Kurt, you don't mean we'll stay?"

"Why not?"

"Well, I mean to say, if you're serious about getting married and having kids, we wouldn't want to land them here for life. Sunay's been fun, I know, but after all it's just a lark. I'm Pop's only child, and there's lots of brass, and then the mill—it's not what it was in the old days, but it pays its way, and someone with brains like you could brighten it up no end."

"But we—I've my work here."

"Well, you'd have it there, too. Pop was willing to take Alan in, and I'll damned well see he takes you. Anyway, you're much more suitable. He can always do with a trained accountant, and he's for ever complaining he can't find young men to take responsibility. If you could be bothered, you'd be managing that place inside a year. But don't think I'm bullying you. I'll stay here if you really want to. I like it all right—at least, I shall, now I've got you. It's just that it seems a waste."

Kurt looked at her without answering, and beyond her he could see the brown lip of the corrie and a great sweep of sky. Instead, his mind pictured the drab streets of a Lancashire mill-town, the four walls of an office, a villa in some middle-class suburb, with herbaceous borders and a tennis lawn. To that would his confines be narrowed, his windswept freedom changed—in return for power and a place in the world.

Something died in Kurt at that moment. It was the first tender root which he, nomad and alien, had ever thrust into the soil. And its withering left him so arid that for a moment love itself could bring no comfort.

"Anyway," said Mary, "don't look so stricken. I'll write and break the news to Pop, and we'll see if he makes you an offer. It'll be time enough to make up our minds after that."

"No!" said Kurt violently. "We'll have no Fletcher plottings behind his back."

"Behind—oh, you mean Alexander." That it would be a blow to him had never even entered into her calculations.

"If we are even contemplating it, if there is the remotest possibility, then we let him know from the start. You write to your Papa, and I'll have it out with him when he gets back to-morrow night." To himself he added that if he had any influence with father and daughter—and already he knew for certain that he was going to have unbounded influence—not a penny of Mary's money should be withdrawn from Sunay, not a penny of interest charged. Alexander wouldn't like it. To escape from the domination of alien capital had been one of his chief aims. But he would have to lump it, grimly reflected Kurt, who knew exactly how much the dam had cost.

When he broke the first part of his news, the bright

look on Alexander's face smote him hard. How much Alexander had guessed of Mary's feelings, no one now would know. But his abstract approval of all marriages was plainly reinforced with genuine delight at this mating of two Sunay friends. Kurt pursued his explanation with his eyes on the fire. He could not steel himself to watch that bright look fade.

"You sound as though you were apologizing," said Alexander after he had made an end. "You know that there's no earthly reason why you should."

"There's every reason. I loathe myself, I loathe the notion of going. And I do it of my own free will. She'd be perfectly content to stay."

"It would be foolish to miss such a chance."

"You'd miss it. In my place you wouldn't be tempted for one second."

"No—but that doesn't mean that I don't understand."

"Yet I doubt, my friend, if you can understand," said Kurt with profound bitterness. "I doubt if anyone could understand who hadn't lived my sort of life, seen his whole background shattered, believed for years that nobody wanted him, that he'd never have a country, or a circle, or a place. It wasn't just the being abjectly poor and taking charity, though that was bad enough, it was the helplessness. Knowing you couldn't do a thing for a friend—that when you came up against others even worse off, you had to stamp on them so that they shouldn't lessen your share. That's what I've been reduced to, more than once—and you'll be aware that we're a clannish race. If I can step into that old man's shoes I will, and I'll fill his mill with Yid exiles. I'll have power and security and influence, and for those things I'm willing to sell myself into slavery. Fear has bitten into me deep, Zandl, and I can't wash it off. But my son will be born a free man, as you were, and when he's old enough to choose I'll give him the chance of coming back to Sunay, and finishing the job I hardly began."

237

Chapter Ten

[I]

"I've no doubt ye'll be glad to hear", observed Maggie as she looked through the second mail of March, "that I am now an auntie."

Having been congratulated on her nephew, she read on through Jim's letter and discovered that she was expected to go home—what nonsense, home indeed!—and see him.

"I am sure you will not disappoint Jeanie in this," wrote Jim. "She's never been one to complain, as you know, and she would never say anything to you yourself; but she has felt it a wee bit, Maggie, that you seem to be forgetting your own folk. Though we are very glad, of course, that you have settled down so fine——"

Wasn't that just like them, thought Maggie scornfully. They had been delighted to see the last of her, but when they found her getting on nicely without them they were jealous and annoyed.

"Why don't you go home and see the baby, Maggie?" asked Alexander, who retained his general, benevolent interest in any increase of the race.

She was taken aback.

"Why, it would just not be possible. Ye know how short-handed we are, and at a time like this——"

"But this is just the time. Digging and the frames finished, too early for the rest. You could take a week or ten days now and catch up easily at the beginning of next month. After that we'll none of us get a breathing-space till October."

"There'd be no one to give Mrs. Rossiter a hand."

"We will all give her a hand. Now, see here, you're going. It's absurd to maroon yourself, even on Sunay. How often have you got even as far as the Kyle?"

"Och, twice, I think."

"Well, it's disgraceful. We all ought to travel more. We need some fresh ideas." He means, thought Maggie, that I might be the next to start feeling unsettled. There must be some way of showing him that I'm not like the others. She firmly declared her refusal to budge.

For, of course, she had been unsettled, and he was acute enough to know it. But it was not by any longings after Edinburgh and the family circle.

Now that they were gone, she missed Kurt and Mary badly, but their last days on Sunay had not been happy ones for her. She could not help knowing that every night Kurt came to Mary's bed. She told herself they were as good as married, but that was not good enough to suppress her sense of affront—yes, and of something deeper, a hungry, jealous curiosity of which she was horribly ashamed. And if he came stealthily, that was only on Mrs. Rossiter's account. The rest of them knew all about it and laughed, yes, even Alexander. That shook her more than anything. Would he, then, do the same himself? She could not endure the thought of Alexander creeping in the darkness to a lass's door, not even if it were her own.

Alexander, for some reason, seemed set on her going. He harped, he positively nagged. And to her natural repugnance at refusing him anything Maggie now found added the voice of conscience, which told her that Jim was right and Jeanie justified, and that she ought to go. Jeanie was, in truth, her sister and her only close relation. She had promised their mother to look after Jeanie. On Jeanie's marriage it had seemed to her that handing over her share of the teashop and writing a weekly letter were all she could now be asked to do. But was it really so? Had not Jeanie the right to reproach her with a fundamental indifference? She began to feel a wish to see this baby, who was of her blood, and to picture him as another Jamie, brought to Sunay for the summer holidays.

"And if you were in Edinburgh you could call on the Department," said Alexander with cunning, "and perhaps wangle us another reclamation grant. It's important to keep them interested in us. Personal contact is the thing. And there are several other errands I'd get you to run. . . ."

So Maggie went. She crossed the Sound with Rory on a brilliant March morning, and gazing hungrily back from the train, saw Sunay hanging like a silhouette in pale blue velvet between sky and sea. Imposssible not to feel banished, not to resent each cutting in the line that hid it from view. When, on the final eastward curve, it was lost altogether and only Eigg remained, she found herself in tears.

After a while her thoughts were distracted by the strangeness of being once again on the mainland. The great brown hills and desolate swampy glens seemed dark and oppressive after Sunay's perpetual sea-shimmer and wide skies. The miles of slums running into Glasgow were more oppressive still. At the Central Station, where she had to change, the crowd absurdly bewildered her. She had not been in any great concourse of people for a year, and felt herself almost a foreigner as she was pushed and buffeted by so many scurrying, competent folk.

She got into Edinburgh very late, hungry and dispirited, and stood forlornly by the barrier as though she were a stranger to the city, till claimed by Jim, who still ran true to form in the matter of never being quite in time. They met with anxious politeness, each aware that they had never really been friends. Then she was back in the tall, dark Canongate house, and Jeanie was laughing, and looking strongly like their mother—Maggie resembled her in character, but Jeanie in looks—and displaying young Angus,

240

who was just like any baby but really had the most perfect hands and feet. "Och, Maggie," cried Jeanie, "it's grand to have ye home!"

The warmth generated by their meeting lasted quite three days. For her past forgetfulness Maggie inwardly repented. The precious link of a common childhood was like no other, and only with Jeanie could she live those years again. She learned to bath the baby, and fancied that he smiled at her. Jim, on his side, was touchingly anxious to show her how hard he was working at the tea-room. She had to be consulted over the waitresses, the temporary cook, the installation of a new cooker. She had to go through the accounts, which, if not quite up to Kurt's standards, seemed to be thoroughly conscientious. Her going, she conceded, had very nearly made a man of Jim. Jeanie might after all have done a lot worse.

At the end of three days she caught a cold.

No one ever had colds on Sunay; now she came to think of it, no one had ever been ill at all. The comfort of always feeling well had come to be taken for granted. But now she remembered that her life in Edinburgh had been regularly punctuated by colds. She could no longer go near the baby. She grew restive and cross at finding herself choked with the odiously familiar catarrh. The Canongate was gloomy as a gorge, and she seemed to be for ever fighting for breath. And then, it was so cold.

A piercing wind whistled round every corner, and made her shut her eyes. The traffic dazed and worried her, and twice cars avoided her by inches on Princes Street. Jeanie, snug at home with the baby, declared it to be no colder than the usual Edinburgh spring. But presently it began to snow.

"We dinna get snow on Sunay," said Maggie.

The first of the little parties arranged by Jim and Jeanie to show her off to their friends coincided with the heaviest day of her cold. Their friends were mostly hers, too, or rather, the girls were. They all appeared to have acquired husbands in the year she had been away; Jim and Jeanie tending, like other married couples, to lose touch with the unmated in their circle. But now, it seemed to Maggie, she and these former intimates had nothing in common. It was easier to talk to their husbands, who were all interested in Sunay, though they might know nothing of farming.

Such douce, such colourless laddies they were; not compared to Alexander—that did not even arise—but compared to Kurt or knowledgeable Les, or to Rory, or Ronny, whose very naughtiness took on at this distance a romantic charm. They all had safe wee jobs in offices, but in their hearts there lingered a spark of adventure which seemed to have been snuffed in their wives. They eagerly turned over her snapshots, wanting to know all she could tell them about the life, and Maggie, talking herself back into that beloved place, forgot her cold and her disgruntlement. Jeanie suddenly grew jealous.

"I do believe", she remarked with a pinched little smile, "ye're thinking of that wee island all the time. Ye might a'most as well have stayed there."

Bletherer, thought Maggie instantly. But she answered, all conciliation:

"Ach, Jeanie, I'm sorry. But if ye knew what a worriting business farming is, how anything can go wrong, ye'd forgive me. I do try to keep my mind off it, but it willna stay."

At the next night's gathering she was more cautious. The snow had fallen steadily for thirty-six hours, and the Canongate looked exceedingly picturesque. Maggie regarded it sourly. It did occur to her to wonder if they could have had snow in the Isles after all, but it never seemed convenient to listen to the weather report, to which Jim and Jeanie had the townsman's indifference.

All went well until one of the douce young men shyly expressed his longing to spend a holiday on Sunay, and his wife, shuddering, declared that for her part she would choose somewhere warm.

"But it's aye warm there!" cried Maggie, stung. "Ye should see the fuchsia growing outside my wee bit house. I never once was cold on Sunay, and I've been perished ever since I came back here."

"I'm sorry we've no' made you comfortable, Maggie," Jeanie said. "I'm sure we've tried our best."

"Now, *Jeanie*——" The explanations, the apologies followed. But this time the sisters' looks were definitely hostile. You silly wee spoiled creature, said Maggie's. You aye thought the sun went round you, and having Jim and Angus has made you worse. You're a hard piece, Maggie Moffat, said Jeanie's. You've never cared for a soul but yourself. If mother were alive and could see you being so unkind. . . .

Only by absorbing herself in Alexander's commissions could Maggie thereafter keep her temper. She astonished the calm official at the Department—who turned out, however, to be a friend of Mr. Fraser's—by her earnestness. She spent hours looking at farm implements and noting prices in catalogues. After this she felt better and less homesick. Yes, that was the truth of it. In her own sister's house she was homesick. And there were still two days to go.

Next morning on her plate at breakfast there lay one of the Kyle's three postcards—the one of the Highland cattle in a fog. The back was written close in an illiterate hand. It was signed R. MacLeod, which for an instant puzzled her. Then her heart stood still.

"Dear Maggie," Rory had written. "Hope you are having a good holliday but if convenient you better come back. Ronny cleared out, rest going soon except A. and self and he talks of giving up. Yours Truly, R. MacLeod. P.S. Joyce had a boy."

I ought never to have left, thought Maggie incoherently. I didn't want to come, he made me. Why can't Rory say what's happened? Please God make it all right. How soon can I get back?

"Something bad has happened at Sunay," she told Jeanie. "I'll have to go." Jeanie looked at her, disbelieving. Obviously she thought this a repercussion of the quarrel. "Here, read this card I had," muttered Maggie, bitterly unwilling though she was to show any but the triumphs of Sunay to the outsider.

"Well, if ye must," said Jeanie at length. "It looks like the end of yon island to me. I'm sorry, Maggie; I ken fine what it means to ye. But remember, if it comes to the worst, ye've a home with us."

Maggie cursorily thanked her. I have no home but Sunay, she thought. There is my heart and my home.

[II]

So hard-driven was Alexander in the first desperate days of Maggie's holiday that for once he scarcely noticed the change in the wind.

There were now four of them to run the place—for Joyce, of course, did not count. Mrs. Rossiter, indomitable as ever, cooked and washed and kept their rooms clean without seeming to deviate by a jot from the unflurried rhythm of her day. She enjoyed the intimacy of the party round the table; she called it her family, and knew herself, complacently, to be without a rival. The electric current, she would smilingly point out, was worth at least another pair of hands. Alexander did not share her pleasure at their cosiness. He was haunted by the thought of the undermanned weeks ahead.

They were promised reinforcements. Donald was to come, as before, and help with the gathering, and bring with him the pick of the Kyle youth, for Sunay was the fashion since the opening of the dam. And Les had brought forward a friend, one Joe, who might prove a permanent asset. Joe, it seemed, was just such a paragon as Les himself, a farm labourer, a man of all-round skill, who had had his eye on Sunay from the start, and had only been waiting for Les's report and the chance of a house to offer himself. His girl was a farmer's daughter, and had been a Land Army milker for years. Neither could leave their present farms till Michaelmas. But they were plainly worth waiting for. As time went on he caught himself building every project on their arrival. That was a poor sign—when two unknown quantities so outshone those to hand.

With four departures already—impossible to feel over Kurt and Mary's as he had felt over the Fletchers', but the fact remained that Sunay had failed to hold them—he was more than ever sensitive to the moods of those that remained. And yet he could not bring himself to bear patiently with Ronny. Nerves were a luxury he could not afford, yet every day Ronny got on to them. His aimlessness, his utter lack of interest in anything that was not mechanized, were glaring now that he had no partner in naughtiness. He seemed to be perpetually staring at Rory's absorbed back. Between him and Alexander, on whom most of the goading fell, there existed almost a state of feud. "He would do anything for you, dear boy," his mother at intervals continued to urge. What she meant was: in return for flattery, praise and love. Alexander gave praise and flattery, as he felt, till it was an outrage, but the results were yet to see, perhaps because he had not so far been able to season them with love.

The wind, which had been blowing gently from the southeast and bringing them exquisite ploughing weather, shifted due east, and it grew colder. Abstractedly Alexander pulled on another jersey.

Then Ronny put his foot in a rabbit-hole. There was no doubting the damage. A ligament was torn, and a lump the size of a cricket ball swelled up below the ankle. Outwardly concerned and sympathetic, Alexander experienced an inner irritation. It was such a convenient accident for Ronny, so maddeningly inopportune for everyone else.

"Ought we perhaps to have the doctor over?" he asked Ronny's mother. It was the first time anyone on Sunay had ailed, and their isolation and helplessness were suddenly brought home.

"Dear me, no," replied Mrs. Rossiter briskly. "All it needs is rest and soaking in hot sea-water. The swelling will be down in two days. If I may say so, dear, your generation has doctors on the brain." This was an oblique hit at Joyce, who had been gaping unhelpfully at Ronny's foot and now merely scowled. A doubt crossed Alexander's mind as to whether Mrs. Rossiter's calm faith in her own medical powers were really justified. But Ronny was her child, and it was certainly not for him to fuss.

The wind shifted again, into the north-east, and jerseys were not enough to keep it out. Alexander hunted out a battered leather jacket. The forecast for the Hebrides was: "wintry showers, cold." That was a commonplace and no one took much notice. Only Rory, generations of shepherding speaking in his blood, suddenly withdrew his attention from electrical gadgetry and sniffed the icy air. "If it plows like this much lonker", he remarked casually, "we may get a wee pit snow."

"Snow!" said Alexander, startled. "Surely it never lies here?"

"Ach, no, not for long."

"I wish we could gather now," muttered Alexander, the uneasiness under Rory's airy manner communicating itself to him.

"Man, it's too early. You don't want them sheep eating all the grass in the parks by May."

The sky at sunset was ochre, and a few snowflakes fluttered in the lights of the causeway when they went to bed. Next morning they woke to a blizzard.

246

It was unbelievable how much snow had fallen in those few hours. Four inches of it covered the causeway, and the flakes were still coming down so fast that one could scarcely see between them. Nor had it gone warmer, as with an English snowfall. The wind was still relentlessly from the northeast, and outside the harbour a big sea was running.

In the afternoon it stopped snowing, though the wind was as fierce as ever. Les went up to get fodder for the cows; Alexander and Rory collected the dogs and found themselves, despite the snow, almost lifted bodily up on to the moor by that great blast at their backs. Ronny settled down to another detective story by the kitchen fire.

Torval was solidly white, except where the sheer crags of the west face repelled the snow. The moor was bare and brown for wide stretches, where the snow had been blown off into the hollows. The drifts seemed nowhere very deep, and the greater part of the flock, weatherwise, was safe in the tussocky country round Carn Mor. The ewes, heavy in lamb, stood about disconsolately nibbling at any tufts of heather that poked through the snow. They looked the picture of misery, but Rory seemed pleased with them. As long as a Blackface could find any grazing for herself she would be all right, he said. Feeding them was no use. He led the way round to the Camas Ban.

On the ledges of the shaley, broken cliffs that ringed the great sand bay, another score or so of ewes had taken shelter. This, in Rory's experience, was a favourite place with them in a north-east blizzard, and he was expecting trouble, for they were apt to push on along the ledges and become cragfast. Presently his eye picked out three grey lumps huddled together half-way down the cliff-face. How they had got there was obvious; a broad shallow ledge led obliquely downwards. It was plastered with snow, which at one point had piled up and formed a block.

Alexander started down, and found that what would have

been a walk under normal conditions was now a death-trap The ledge sloped out, and the snow, lying over long, slippery grass, shot away under his feet with an evil hiss. He would stand small chance of getting back with the weight of a sheep on his shoulder.

"Why the devil didn't we bring a rope?" he demanded angrily.

"One of us will be having to go pack," responded Rory with that timeless Hebridean smile.

"Oh—all right. I'll meet you here in an hour's time."

But it took him three-quarters of that hour, he found, to beat his way back to the village. The wind was now in his face, and its force and chill were terrifying. He was thankful to get under the shelter of the moorland wall. Ronny was lounging along the dam. "We'll have to open the sluice when the snow melts," he called.

"How did you get up here?"

"Oh, hobbled. My foot's a lot better."

"Glad to hear it," said Alexander shortly. "You'd do better to rest it, all the same." He felt obscurely irritated that Ronny should have the satisfaction of haunting his adored dam while remaining unfit for any useful work. In the kitchen he collected the rope and Les, for it had occurred to him that Rory, with no Alpine technique, might be hardly secure as a second. To Simon he would have entrusted himself and fifty sheep.

The rescue proved very slow and appallingly cold. Rory and Les got the worst of it, up at the belay on the cliff-top, exposed to the blast, and hauling with icy fingers on a rope frozen wire-stiff. Alexander was partly sheltered by the face of the crag, and warmed by the exertion of the climb and the struggle to catch the scared and half-frozen sheep. But even with the protection of the rope, he was acutely aware of the abyss below him, and of the pendulum swing if he were to fall at the lowest point. Climbing for fun on a day like this, one would decide that the fun was over, coil up the rope and go home. By the time he reached the third ewe, it seemed to him that his whole life till then had been easy-going comfort and vain frivolity.

It was night as they hauled him up for the last time. A light flurry of fresh snow blew into their faces as they trudged home. "It will not be much now," said Rory confidently. And at least there was warmth to be gained in the long fight back against the remorseless wind.

They clattered down on to the causeway, and pushed open the kitchen door. Then, above the howl of the wind, another sound brought them to a standstill. It was a girl's high, terrified, suddenly strangled scream.

"Joycie!" gasped Les, his face white in the glare of the electric light, and he turned and ran to his own house.

[III]

After a moment's hesitation, Alexander pushed on into the kitchen. Ronny, comfortable as ever and to his eye quite sound in limb, was back in his old place by the fire.

"What's up, for God's sake?"

"Baby's on the way. She slipped on the causeway—I told you it was a mistake sweeping it. But Ma says it's all right. She has everything under control."

"My God, how can she know? She's not a doctor. It wasn't due for five weeks yet. When did this start?"

"Oh—soon after you left."

"Then why the devil didn't you come after us?"

"How could I, with my foot?" said Ronny sulkily. "Besides, what would be the use? We can't get a doctor. You couldn't take the boat out with this sea running."

"We're bloody well going to. If your foot could get you to the dam it could have got you over the pass." As the door opened behind them to admit Mrs. Rossiter and Les, the ghastly screaming could be heard again.

249

"Now I don't want you boys getting worked up," Mrs. Rossiter was saying in a soothing, self-important voice. "It's very trying for you all, I know, and especially Les, but I've helped in plenty of midwifery cases before, and I can assure you that in a few hours poor Joycie's troubles will be over, and she'll have forgotten everything about them."

"You are not a doctor, Mrs. Rossiter," said Alexander. "You are not even a midwife. You are taking altogether too much on yourself." The ice in his voice struck her like a physical blow, and behind her he could see the white appeal on Les's agonized face. "Go and get your oilskins on," he said, and Les nodded and disappeared.

"But my dearest boy, you can't mean to take the *Gannet* out on a night like this?" wailed Mrs. Rossiter, all her self-confidence gone. Alexander did not answer her; he was rummaging under the dresser for his sea-boots. "You'll none of you come back alive. I give you my word that it isn't necessary——"

"I shan't want Ronny, anyway," said Alexander, straightening. "But I consider that I'm partly responsible for what has happened to Joyce. If she dies you will be partly responsible too." Mrs. Rossiter put out a hand to the table to steady herself. He pushed past her and vanished into the howling darkness.

Lanterns flicked on the jetty. Rory and Les had already got the *Gannet*'s engine started up. He remembered on a sudden that Rory was still a paid servant. "This isn't any affair of yours, Rory Mor," he yelled against the wind. "You bide."

"*Nach ist thu*," yelled back Rory, impudently grinning, and Alexander obediently hushed, with a queer sense of pride in his Highland rascal. There was something after all in Rory besides cheek and charm. His fury against Fate had to fasten on something, and it surged up again at Ronny, when another lantern came bobbing down the jetty and Ronny's voice yelled over the parapet to them to wait.

"I told you we shouldn't want you," Alexander shouted back. "Go home and nurse your foot." He cast off, and Ronny's light dwindled to a pinprick as the launch reached the harbour mouth.

As she emerged from the lee of the Latay cliffs the full fury of the wind smote her, and the inky sea seemed to rise up outraged at her presumption. Short, angry, hissing waves slapped at her sides, and the sound of the engine was drowned in their turmoil. A little further out and she met the real swell. Her stern reared up on the following seas, her bow slithered down into immense troughs of black water. They were in utter darkness. How Rory knew where he was steering it was impossible to conceive. But that Rory had known what peril awaited them, he now clearly realized. He and Les had come because they must, but Rory had come with his eyes open and impudently gay.

Crouched amidships, baling hard and anxiously watching the engine on which their lives depended, Alexander felt the icy wind, the spray, the sickening cockshell tossings of the boat, the stomach-shaking fear of each giddy plunge, resolve themselves into a single point of fear and pain, which seemed to be concentrated on Joyce. He had never known much pain. Looking back, he seemed to have escaped the war and everything else besides. And yet he had condemned that child to a lonely agony, out of reach of help. In his bright, pretty idea of a model community, Joyce and her baby had been picturesque lay figures. The risks they ran had been cursorily foreseen and dismissed. How glib everyone had been in their reassurances to Joyce. They all knew that she was frightened, and yet she had had from them nothing but impatience. They were all to blame—and even that, he told himself, wasn't true. He alone was to blame. He had misled Les into thinking it would be a life fit for her. He had expected the impossible of Mrs. Rossiter. In hitting out at Ronny he had tried to punish what was his own thoughtlessness and folly. Now, perhaps Joyce would die; and as the *Gannet* plunged ever more wildly in and out of the black cauldron, it seemed unlikely that they three could survive.

And would the doctor come? The doubt stabbed him with fresh panic. Would any sane man who valued his life—and a doctor had more excuse for it than most—be prepared to make a crossing like this? He tried to remember what he could of Dr. Macdonald; a big burly type, had seemed interested in Joyce, was always friendly when one met him about the Kyle. He was said, like so many Hebridean doctors, to drink. Well, thought Alexander grimly, if he often makes this sort of trip I daresay he has need of it. Les, who had made the crossing jauntily a dozen times, now quietly slumped into the bottom of the boat and lay there, retching.

Suddenly, as the stern reared on another cliff of water, a light pierced the grey-black, storm-filled night. It was the lighthouse at the Kyle. It looked infinitely distant, yet the sight brought a physical relief to straining eye-balls. They were going somewhere, they were moving, they were not utterly engulfed in heaving chaos. Alexander scrambled aft to Rory, and by signs indicated—for it was impossible to make a voice heard—that he would take the tiller.

The sheer muscular effort required to hold the boat on her course astonished him. And amidships there had at least been some sort of shelter and warmth from the engine. Up here he felt as though he had not a stitch on his body. He braced his feet against the boat's sides and set his teeth. The agonies of the body swallowed up those of the mind. Joyce's pain was his now. They were in it together.

But the light was there, the light that meant help and humanity. Minute by minute it grew larger. And at last it seemed as though the fury of the storm were abating. The huge rollers gave place to choppy waves again; the wind was as cold but its gusts were now more fitful. Alexander was somewhere near the edge of consciousness when Rory relieved him, but now the shape of the lighthouse and the breakwater could clearly be made out. Rory brought the boat into the little harbour, and the sudden calm was startling. Les sat up, ghastly, and hauled himself unsteadily to his feet. They had crossed and had survived.

The streets of the Kyle were silent. They lurched up the quay like drunken men, hunger as well as cold oppressing them. It was Rory who rang at the doctor's door, Rory who, after Alexander had opened his numbed jaws and found no voice, explained to the doctor's wife in a flood of urgent Gaelic why they were there. The good lady stared at them and out into the night, her face expressing understandable reluctance. Then she led them in and went to rouse her man.

There were embers of a fire in the doctor's study, round which they huddled and felt the agony of numbed fingers slowly tingling. I pray to God he comes, thought Alexander, and another, worser, deeper part of his being answered: I can't face the crossing back.

"The doctor will be with ye in a minute," said Mrs. Macdonald, returning, as dour as before, but with a tray in her hands. On it were hot toddy and beef sandwiches. Mrs. Macdonald had not been twenty years a doctor's wife in the Isles for nothing. She might look unwelcoming but she knew how to behave. The food and alcohol seemed to pour into them new life and hope. She watched their ravenous feeding, and a smile broke her habitual composure. "Ye puir laddies," she murmured, and added crisply, "the wind's dropping."

Dr. Macdonald came in wearing oilskins as efficient as their own. His size, his sonsy face, his air of taking a midnight crossing in a gale as routine were immensely reassuring. While he gulped his whisky Les gave him details of the fall. "Yon lassie's had bad luck," was his only comment at the end. "But she's young and there was naught wrong when I examined her. I don't doubt she'll be all right."

And back in the *Gannet* he insisted on taking the tiller. He

253

had been handling boats, he told them, when they were in their cradles. But, indeed, the change in the sea was astonishing. It was choppy and unpleasant, but the ominous swell seemed to have flattened itself out within the hour. And the cruel wind was now at their backs. They were blown to Sunay. "Will there be a bit light on your jetty?" Dr. Macdonald roared down the boat.

God, would there? None of them had thought of it. Ronny thought of nothing. He could never be trusted, he was useless. But half an hour after they had lost the friendly light of the Kyle, pinpricks appeared ahead. Presently they resolved themselves into three storm-lanterns. Rory had used them as flares to mark the line of the jetty. Dimly in his heart Alexander was aware of other injustices done to Ronny. From now on they would be friends. Then he remembered nothing but Joyce. As they reached the causeway a low moaning could be heard from her house. She lived, then, but all these hours she had been in agony. . . .

Rory, who considered that his usefulness to Joyce was now over, departed sensibly enough to bed. But Les and Alexander sat huddled over the electric fire in Joyce's little sitting-room, and presently heard the moaning cease. At least they had brought her that much relief—and with one accord they rose and rifled the larder. An hour later Mrs. Rossiter came out, her little frog-face grey with fatigue. "It's a boy, Les," she whispered. "Congratulations. He says Joycie will do."

Les, looking dazed, was taken in to see the baby, and the doctor joined Alexander. "I'd like to get the lassie away," he observed.

"She's—she'll pull through, won't she?"

"Och, yes, not much doubt, but she's had a bad time, and there's something psychological, some sort of nervous reaction against the place. And the bairn is under five pounds. She's a city lass, isn't she?—not much stamina. She'll do better under observation for a wee while."

254

"You know she was to have gone on the *Loch Coruisk* the day after to-morrow."

"Ay, that's so. I'll telephone to Oban in the morn and have Captain MacLeod put in here for them. It's verra fortunate he's due. He's had experience before in handling such cases, ye'll realize. Yon good lady would see them safe into hospital, I daresay?"

"I'm sure she would. About yourself, Doctor."

"I'll take your hospitality for the rest of the night," said the doctor, smiling. "Two such crossings is enough for one night, even at your age. Maybe ye can make me up a boat-crew in the morning."

Falling like a log into his own bed, Alexander felt the sleep of exhaustion reach out for him. For a minute he fought against it, that he might savour his own triumph, enjoy his heart-warming relief. They had done it, against pitiless odds they had won. Joyce had her baby, Sunay its first-born. It was an achievement that nothing could take from them, a feat of suffering and endurance such as had in ancient days forged the splendid tenacity of the clan. The child belonged to all of them. Everything would be all right.

[IV]

His first thought when he woke was of Joyce, his second, of the hour, for the sun was pouring into his room. He reached for his watch; it was past ten. Ashamed, he pulled on his clothes and made for the kitchen. Mrs. Rossiter had his breakfast hot. She looked an old woman. Her skin might be thick, but it had been punctured at last, and at her age it would be slow to heal.

"What about the doctor?"

"Ronny and Rory have taken him over."

"They ought to have called me——"

"No, dear, I told them not to. Both of them have had a good night's sleep."

"Oh, well—— Look, Mrs. R., I'm sorry about last night. I'm afraid I rather lost my head."

"Nonsense, dear boy; of course I understand." A flush appeared in her cheeks, and he was again uncomfortably aware of her devotion. "But I'm afraid Ronny is a little upset."

"Dash it, yes; he must be. I'll make it all right with him. I suppose they'll be back for lunch. How's Joyce and the baby?"

"They were asleep half an hour ago."

"Would she like to see me, do you think?"

"Well, I hardly think she feels up to visitors yet." He caught the note of evasion in her tone. Evidently Joyce still bore him a grudge for her ordeal. It was perfectly natural; she hated Sunay, and he stood for Sunay. But in his heart he was absurdly disappointed.

It was a sunshiny March morning, full of lark-song. Except that the top two thousand feet of Torval still stood up glittering white and the burn was coming down in force below the power-house, one could scarcely have credited the nightmare of the storm. He resumed the ploughing in the new potato-field; it was a joy to see how the earth turned over, burying the good compost spread with so many hours of labour. They were a month ahead of last year's work, short-handed though they might be. And Ronny's foot was evidently recovered; he could be counted on from now. At midday the return of the *Gannet* could be heard. Alexander went down to make Ronny his amends. But Rory was alone in the boat.

"He wass after taking the train," he said in answer to Alexander's unspoken question. "He gave me this letter for the *cailleach*."

"I'll take it."

Mrs. Rossiter was busy over the stove. She took the note and read it, and he saw her face crumple. "Oh, Alexander ——" she said on a gasp, and then: "You'd better see."

"Dear Ma," Ronny had written. "I'm off. If you like to stay on after the filthy things he said last night, you can. I'll probably go to Aunt Kate's. Anyway you can send my things on there. R."

"He's so fond of you, dear," pleaded Mrs. Rossiter through her tears. "That's why he was hurt. Perhaps if you were to write——"

"I don't think", said Alexander slowly, "that it would be any use." He stood holding the note, seeing Ronny very clearly, feeling for the first time that understanding which would never come when it might have helped.

"I don't know then", faltered Mrs. Rossiter, "what I ought to do."

He pulled himself together. "Why, of course, Mrs. R., Ronny must come first."

"Yes, dear. He's my only child, and no one else quite understands him. But it will be a dreadful wrench, leaving all of you. You yourself, especially. You know what you've been to me. Almost another son."

Her eyes besought him, and for one moment he saw himself landed with Mrs. Rossiter till the end of her days. Then he answered with a hateful, forced brightness:

"We'll miss you terribly, too, Mrs. R. You've been our mainstay. I can't conceive how we'll manage without you. But you couldn't be expected to cut yourself off from Ronny. You'd never know a moment's peace."

"That's just it, dear," agreed Mrs. Rossiter, and not without dignity took her dismissal from the scene of her renewed youth and happiness.

The news was not to be concealed. Rory, of course, had guessed it already, and took without apparent regret the defection of his closest friend. "He wassn't a Hepridean," he remarked with a grin. "Wassn't that what he was always telling us?" That was poor Ronny's epitaph. They returned to the ploughing.

The *Loch Coruisk* crossed over a glassily innocent sea. Joyce, gingerly clasping the bundle of which she still looked scared, was carried down on a stretcher to the jetty. Her face was bloodless and dark marks made her eyes look huge. As Alexander was one of her bearers she could not avoid meeting his eye, and replied to his congratulations with a little, pinched, ladylike smile. Her ethereal looks shocked him and he did not press her, but exchanged a few words with Captain MacLeod (who told him, with rather flattering bluntness, that he and the other laddies had no business to be alive), and then devoted himself to Mrs. Rossiter. Again he blessed the training of the generation that had been taught not to parade its feelings. He knew that she was deeply moved, but that she would not cry with all these folk to see.

Numb and heavy with the sense of failure, he turned his back on the departing ship and made his way into the fields. Les caught him up as he was climbing on to the tractor seat.

"I've something to say."

"Yes?" said Alexander, but he knew what it was.

"She made me promise—before she left." Les stopped as though the words were choking him; his solid red face was strangely expressive in its misery. 'Well, what could I do?"

"Nothing," said Alexander, turning back to the plough; for round them stretched the untended earth, hungry for their toil.

Chapter Eleven

[I]

Maggie left Edinburgh in the very early morning, and watched, unheeding, the cold grey light come up over the Scottish hills. Dimly her mind registered the fact that many of them were now white where a week ago they had been brown. Her thoughts were on Sunay, and the agonizing truth was that Sunay had now receded to the vagueness of a dream. The boring little life in Edinburgh seemed as though it had never been broken by that wonderful year. The sense of banishment was complete. And was it to be banishment for ever? Could it be that Alexander, whom she had loved so well and followed so faithfully, would after all cast her out?

With tears of sheer anger in her eyes she re-read for the twentieth time Rory's postcard. Why couldn't he, while he was about it, have written her a letter, telling what had really happened? How could he be so stupid and unthinking as to leave her in this horrible suspense?

"Rest gone except A. and self and he talks of giving up." But Rory was mistaken. He couldn't think of giving up. No matter if they had all failed him. The island was his; he must find others, and start again. Evidently it was something to do with Joyce's baby—but Joyce would be no loss; no, nor Ronny, anyone could see that he was working up to a smash. She spared an instant of pity for Ronny, who had always been her friend, then impatiently dismissed him. Friend or no, he had proved unsatisfactory, he had got in the way. His mother—maybe that was more serious. There were great good points to Mrs. R. But there must be plenty more like her in the world. None of them really mattered, not one, excepting only Alexander. He was the idea and the impulse; yes, and he was love.

You and I, had said Kurt, are the only ones whose motives in coming were pure. And she had said to herself that it wasn't true. She had come for the sake of a likely laddie. Would the place be anything to her without him? Then, she would have said no. But now—now she had no clear idea of what Sunay was, except that she had known there her moments of greatest happiness, and others of acute jealousy and mortification, that in contact with all of them she had grown a little less narrow and prim, that she had worked hard in rain and sun and wind, and that from the dingy Canongate it looked like a paradise that she would never regain.

She strove to search her own heart, to find out her own desires, and met a blank. Childishly she longed for her mother, to tell her what to do; though almost her clearest recollection was of her mother's voice replying crisply to all such haverings: "Ye're old enough to decide for yourself." Old enough, och yes; and now quite alone in the world, with no one to consider, no one to guide, nothing but that inner voice which had once spoken so clearly and now was muffled. It was easy for the Jeanies. They had their weans and their men. She had nothing but her love for a man who didn't need her, and her work on an island remote as a dream.

As the train plunged down the long descent into Fort William, the sun came out and the snows of Nevis glittered at an immense distance overhead. The run to the Kyle, beside the weed-reddened margins of the sea-loch, was unbelievably beautiful. She stood as before in the corridor, to catch the first glimpse between the cuttings. When it came it startled her. For Torval was white.

But, of course, it was white. Had she not seen the mainland hills snowy all the day? Nevertheless, she only now began to have a notion of what they had gone through. For the hundredth time she told herself: I ought never to have left—and then: I shall never get back. The whole of the island came into view, and she could see that only the peak was snowy; the rest showed the familiar blue-velvet silhouette. Yet she stared at it as a tourist, unable to believe that she had really worked there for a year. She relived all the strangeness of her first crossing, when he and Sunay had seemed equally out of reach.

No Rory or *Gannet* were at the quay to meet her. She had not expected them, yet the emptiness of the dancing blue waters, the cruel, unbridgeable gulf of the Sound, the melancholy wheeling of gulls over the herring-sheds left her unspeakably desolate. She was still a stranger at the Kyle, she who would never cross from Sunay. No one noticed her, or pointed her out as an island girl. Hermia, Mary even, would have found friends and seemed part of the place, but she stood, clutching her suitcase, without a soul to tell her what had happened. "Ye'll have had a storm?" she said to the inevitable lounging fisherman; he gave her an inscrutable Gaelic stare. She turned away, and made her way up the hill to the MacLeods' croft. Donald and the *Annabella* were her only hope.

Mrs. MacLeod, the anaemic and toothless, opened the door and at first did not recognize her; then she was diffidently invited in. The old man was sitting by the fire. Donald was not there.

"I came to know would Donald maybe take me over," began Maggie hurriedly. "Rory sent me this postcard—ye can see it must be verra urgent. I came back fra' Edinburgh the minute I got it——" Mr. MacLeod took the card and turned it slowly over.

"Well now," he said at length, "Tonalt iss out. And this afternoon it will not be fery confenient. Will ye not have a cup of tea?"

"Och, but Mr. MacLeod, I must get across!" She stared

261

in dismay at his politely smiling face, realizing that actual animosity lay behind the smile. Yet what could he have against her? "I'd be glad of tea, thank you," she added, aware that the hospitality which Mr. MacLeod's traditions forced him to extend would at least be an excuse for staying there till Donald came.

"Ye'll have had a pleasant holiday in Edinburgh?"

"Yes, very. See here, Mr. MacLeod, could ye no' spare Donny just this once? I canna tell what's happened there, but if Mrs. Rossiter has gone they'll be sorely in need of me."

"Yess inteet, the olt leddy and the young one and the baby went on the *Loch Coruisk* tay before yestertay. She put in special. But Annag went ofer. She will be looking after them. It wass fery inconfenient for her Tat."

Maggie did not care two hoots for Annag's dad, and nor, she was sure, did Mr. MacLeod. He was just being, for some reason, obstructive. She fought back tears, the honour of Ayrshire could not stoop to scenes in front of a Highlander. "Forbye, ye canna tell me what happened?"

"I am not knowing what happened. We hat a terrible storm, and them latties crost at the worst of it to fetch the toctor, that iss all I know. They haf the Almighty to thank they wass not all trownt. Our Rory did not ought to be risking his life like that."

"Was—was Dr. Sarratt one of them?"

"Ay, I belief so. But it iss my son I am thinking of."

"Why, of course, and I understand ye're being worried. But if it was to get the doctor for the baby——"

"My wife didn't haf no toctor for our three," said Mr. MacLeod with his bland, malignant smile.

Mrs. MacLeod, who had brought in the tea, summoned up all her moral courage and faced her lord. "Ach, Ruaridh, the toctor iss after saying that if he hadn't been in time the poor young letty would haf tiet. She hat a terrible fall."

"Well, that may be. But three to risk trowning for one, iss that sense?"

You wicked, blethering old hypocrite, thought Maggie, who in point of fact was most strongly of the opinion that one Alexander was worth fifty Joyces, with or without babies, but whose Lowland self-righteousness was outraged by Mr. MacLeod's frank assumption that none but his own family counted. She sat drinking her tea, trying to give him smile for smile, and determined to find Donald if she had to comb the Kyle house by house. But it turned out not to be necessary. As she took her second cup he came in.

At once she guessed that he knew why she was there, and held her peace. He wished her good afternoon with his usual shy politeness, and began a long, perfectly respectful Gaelic argument with his father. And presently, without altering his smiling front, old Mr. MacLeod appeared to give in. He observed in English:

"Mint you then, you be back for the milking."

"Och, of course he will," cried Maggie, rightly assuming this hint to be for her benefit, and, jumping up, she thanked the old people for her tea and hurried down with Donald to the boathouse below the herring-sheds where the *Annabella* lay.

Donald was not one to speak unless spoken to, and then he was no waster of words. He offered no explanation of his father's conduct, and Maggie after an inward struggle decided not to ask him anything about Sunay either. Only Alexander could tell her what she really needed to know. But she did get from him, sentence by sentence, the story of the midnight crossing as far as he knew it. Some folks were talking of it at the Kyle, he said, and that was his only comment, but she guessed at the pride in Rory's seamanship that lay behind his words. For herself, all she could think of was that Alexander might be lying now under the treacherous waters of the Sound.

It was cold in the *Annabella*. Compared to the smart *Gannet* she was a dirty, sordid little tub, and maddeningly slow. The crossing took an hour and a half. Maggie sat huddled in her travelling plaid, staring at the island, gradually making out the dam, the church, the beloved, beautifully spaced crescent of the village, and gradually, comfortingly regaining some of her belief that she belonged there. As they swung in to the harbour, she could see two men with the tractor ploughing in the top field, and a third following with Peigi and the harrows. Work, then, was continuing; there was reassurance in the thought. One of them waved to her; it seemed to be Rory, and she waved back, dismissed Donald quickly with thanks to his milking, and went to the kitchen.

"Ach, Maki, I am glat to see you!" exclaimed Annag at the stove. It was the first time she had brought herself to drop the Miss, and Maggie knew that here, at any rate, was welcome. Annag and Rory had been counting on her; she fitted in with some part of Rory's plan. She stared around her with sheer pleasure, drinking in every detail of the familiar arrangements that meant home. It all looked a trifle rumpled, lacking Mrs. Rossiter's guiding hand, but it was plain that poor Annag had been anxiously doing her best.

"It smells to be a grand dinner," she assured Annag in reply to her misgivings. "The lads will fair lap it up. You leave the chickens and the milking to me."

First she had to run round the garden, note how even in a week the lettuces had spread in their frames and the brassica seedlings come through, and look for the first pink buds on the downy bark of the little peach. The dogs trailed after her, frisking and licking her hands, glad to have company after a boring and inactive day. The now sturdy calf butted her with its blunt head. Surely one had some right to a place where the beasts made one welcome? One could not be summarily be turned out of a place where Nature itself showed the traces of one's toil?

The thought of her meeting with Alexander filled her now with mingled defiance and dread. Unbidden, there floated into her mind a phrase of Hermia's: he has a cruel mouth. So it had stuck, as so many of Hermia's unkind and malicious sayings did. Almost there began to seem truth in it. Almost he was the enemy.

The warmth and smell of the byre, the blessed feel of the teats under her fingers, helped her confidence and her slowly returning sense of home. Let him come, let him hurt her, let him do his worst. She still had no clear notion of the answer she would make, but at least she now had something to fight him with, some purpose to oppose to his. The inner voice was at last beginning to make itself heard.

In this shed she had learned to milk, and now, see, she could do it like a professional. Her good friend Mary had taught her that and much besides. They had all had something to teach her, yes, even Hermia. She was no longer the green little Scots girl round whom the clever English, with their high-sounding degrees and education, could spin rings. She would do as she thought fit and none of them should stop her. Let him come.

Yet she did not actually hear him come. Alexander was a quiet mover. "Hello, Maggie," he said, and she looked up and there he was, leaning in his dusty corduroys against the open door.

He was smiling, perfectly self-possessed and friendly, but something in the quality of his smile deprived her of her jaunty response. For it was just like old Mr. MacLeod's, unmeaning and bland. For the first time since she had known him, the light in Alexander was no longer shining.

[II]

Had Mrs. Rossiter been present she might have observed that the famous tension had snapped at last. He was as listless, as flaccid and slack as an overstretched wire. At the moment he was summoning up some last reserve of energy to cope with the irritating human problem represented by Maggie. But he looked as though, when that was behind him, he might lie down on the heather and sleep for a week.

"Hello, Maggie," he said with that flat smile. "Nice to see you. I'd begun to feel like one of those unpopular characters in the mouthwash advertisements."

Facetiousness at such a juncture was more than Maggie could handle. She looked down at her busy fingers.

"Not but what I fear we've got you under false pretences. I was going to write to you to-morrow and tell you of the general exodus. I thought you'd four more days to go. What brought you back so suddenly?"

"I was tired of it at Edinburgh."

"Was it that? Or did somebody send for you? Mrs. R., perhaps? Or Les? They've both been heaping themselves with reproaches, bless their innocent hearts. Anyway, since you're here, I admit it will be a comfort to have your help in winding things up. For I don't see, do you, how we're to carry on?"

He waited, this time, for an answer, and finally she produced it, surlily, into the cow's flank.

"So ye're beat?"

"Yes," agreed Alexander amicably. "Dead beat."

In the silence that fell, the swish of the milk into the pail was musical. Alexander came in, sat himself on the calf's bed of dried bracken, and absently caressed her neck while he continued in the tone of one reviewing an accepted situation:

"Thank heaven you didn't put any money in. You'll have the wee teashop to fall back on. Though, in fact, I don't believe we'll end up much out of pocket. There's no denying we've made it a going concern. The houses and the dam alone are now worth twice what they cost us—and as Hermia used to say, there's the publicity. Some rich man with a

266

taste for experimental farming might easily give us fifteen thousand. Anyway, that's what I thought I'd ask."

"Then see here," said Maggie, facing him squarely. "If it's worth that to sell, it's worth that to stay. A going concern. Ye've said it yourself."

"Yes, sweet, but our fellow-labourers have—er—failed to stay the course."

"Well, we'll get more. Did ye not have many a hundred letters when ye chose that lot?"

"I see. Your notion is, I should go through them again and choose the next best?"

"And why should ye not?"

"Because", said Alexander with gentle finality, "I'm beat."

"I dinna believe it. Alexander, I do not. I will not. Ye've gone through a bit, I can see that. They've let ye down awful bad. But ye'll not pay them that much compliment, to say they've beaten you. They're no' worth it."

Her passion seemed to glance off the cold surface of his indifference. He answered patiently, as to a child:

"I think, my dear, you've got it wrong. I can't console myself with any feeling of being ill-used. They didn't let me down. I let them."

"Now that's absurd."

"It is a fact. Consider. One after another, I failed to give them what they wanted. Not Kurt and Mary, perhaps; they found it for themselves, probably in spite of me; but the rest. I feel bloody awful when I think of Simon—Simon, who can never call on me again. I feel nearly as bad when I think of Joyce and how I nearly killed her—you should have seen the look she gave me as they carried her on board. And I just can't tell you how I feel about the Rossiters. Ronny was my stupidest failure. He'd have been so easy, really; just a minimum of patience and affection. But she was my unkindest. Poor dear soul—she'd have stayed, you know, if I'd asked her. But it would have meant taking Ronny's place. I didn't think she'd forgive me, really—and also I doubted if I could stand it. So I sent her packing too."

"Alexander, you're blethering. If they didna find what they were after here, it's because they were after the wrong things. Next time ye'll pick ones more—more suitable."

"But I think all these were eminently suitable. Not Joyce, I grant—Les, I'm afraid, was so much of a temptation that we overlooked Joyce. But each of the others had qualities that should have made them happy here. Well, look how hard they worked. It wasn't that they failed to stand Sunay, and the hard life, and the isolation. They came through the winter magnificently. What they couldn't stand was me."

"There's no one on the island", said Maggie desperately, "except maybe Joyce, and she's a half-wit—that hasn't loved and looked up to ye."

"Loved? Oh, I wouldn't say. But looked up to me, yes, or tried to. That, don't you see, is the trouble. What these people wanted was leadership. But I had no wish to lead. My whole idea, if you remember, was to set going a community in which there'd be no leading or being led, a community of free people, doing what they collectively thought best. I've let them down, Maggie, not only thoroughly but on principle. All the biggest let-downs happen that way, I believe."

He felt in his pockets for a cigarette and added reminiscently: "Once you yourself gave me a warning. Something about not expecting other folk to have my principles. How right you were. There was I, a dim-witted scientist who had never looked outside the lab and had no idea how human material was constituted; and yet I had the nerve to imagine I could mould it into my notion of how it should behave. Well, now I know better, and I bow myself out. It will be easy enough to found a little Fascist community on Sunay. I daresay that's what our hypothetical millionaire will do. He'll have no trouble in collecting sufficient numbers of romantic enthusiasts, longing to be handed a ready-made purpose in life. We might even make him a present of our five hundred letters. But that's why I shan't be bothered to go through them myself. It would just be the same story over again—and it's not the story I wanted to tell."

Maggie said, in a very small voice:

"I didna want any leading."

"No, Mistress Moffat, I'll hand it to you, I don't believe you did. And you don't want to leave now?"

"No."

"Then I'll have rounded off the job neatly. I'll have let you down with an even bigger bump than the rest. I'm sorry, Maggie, sorry from my heart. But I daresay you'll thank me for it in the long run. You'll be better off at home."

"This", said Maggie, and now it was her inner voice, speaking so clearly that it was as though she had no personal choice, "is my home."

Again the silence fell, and the two looked at each other, but now it seemed as though a faint crack appeared in Alexander's patient and explanatory manner, and the real Alexander looked through it at the real Maggie, suddenly perceiving her as a person and not as a refractory pawn in his game. It was with genuine, and almost respectful, puzzlement that he asked:

"Well—in that case, what do you propose?"

"I'll stay," said Maggie, staring past him to the strip of sea green and gold in the last sunlight, "even if I have to stay alone."

She sought for sensible reasons to add to the statement.

"It's a fact, as ye said, that I put no money in. So I've no right to stop anyone going. Your talk of letting me down is sheer nonsense. You go back to your laboratory—ye'll do fine things there, and that's what matters. But I'm only fitted for this sort of life. I found that out when I was at my sister's. It'd kill me to have to go back. So I'll just stay on

269

under yon millionaire. Maybe ye'll put in a word for me when ye're making the sale. Tell him I was a good market-gardener, that I was beginning to make it pay. He'll be glad of someone that knows the conditions—it's in my mind that I'll be worth quite a bit to him. And I'll no' be alone, at that. I've a pretty good suspicion Rory means to stay."

"Rory?" murmured Alexander. "So it was Rory brought you back."

"It's no' at all surprising that ye feel disappointed. You had your ideas, and yon set of bletherers didna come up to them. But I never had any ideas. It's fine talk, that about communities and freedom, but I never gave any of it a thought. All I want is to see things we've planted grow. I want to see if the peach bears this year, and how Les's pig patch does for potatoes, and if we can get a clean crop of seed. It's the work I've done, Alexander, that's what ties me to this place. Ye canna cut me off from that. It'd be like cutting off my right hand."

Well, there it was. First she had loved Gavin and Jamie better than all the world; now she loved Sunay. She confronted her twice-betrayed Alexander, and found that he was smiling. And it was the old, dear, familiar smile, with the light behind it again. "Thank God for you, Maggie," he said. "If you stay, I stay."

"Now see here, I dinna want to push you into anything. For you it's different. You've your career to think of. Here ye're wasted. Hermia was right in that."

"I stay on one condition," he pursued, as though she had not spoken. "I've had various patronizing plans for you, dear Maggie. I was going to wait till the harvest, and then if the books balanced and we could prove ourselves solvent, I intended to propose to you. It seemed to me a nice, smug, self-respecting way of getting our affairs settled. Now I haven't anything to be smug about. I haven't a thing to offer you. You've proved yourself the better man of the two. Yet

I choose this moment to ask you to marry me. Never let it be said that I lack nerve."

"But—Alexander——" she could not believe that she had heard him right. "Ye dinna surely want to get married. . . ."

"But I do, sweet. Terribly. I have for quite a time—oh, ever since the Fletchers went."

The Fletchers. The day he had found her weeping in the barn. Dimly, painfully, she saw an explanation. "I ken fine ye were sorry for me then—but I'm over it. I'm quite content to live alone, I've shown ye that to-day. If ye stay that's grand, of course, but never imagine ye'll be needing to marry me—to make it respectable, or anything like that."

"Respectable—Maggie, you really are gorgeous. I want to marry you because the waters are closing over me—because I've lost what I set my heart on, and you can get it back. You hold it all in your darling green fingers. Of course, I know that you'll always love the lettuces best. But I love you so much that I'm willing to take second place even to a lettuce. Maggie, I can't go back to that other life any more than you can, and yet unless I have you I can't stay here. I must have you. It would be like a reprieve for someone who had thought to die."

She looked at him in complete disbelief, her face crimson, the ugly tears welling up into her eyes. "I know ye mean it kindly," she faltered. "Ye've aye been verra kind. . . ."

"Look here," said Alexander, suddenly exasperated, "this sort of argument is getting us nowhere." He pulled himself up, laughing and impudent. "It's such an age since I kissed a girl that I can hardly remember how. But I believe it goes like this."

[III]

It was thus that Rory found them; and he stood contemplating the spectacle for some seconds, in high satisfaction, before either noticed him. "And about time too," was his comment then.

Maggie sat up, her face flaming. Awful to be caught—and by a cheeky one like Rory at that—the inhibitions of twenty-four Ayrshire years quite overcame her. Then she saw that Alexander was laughing at her, and that made it worse. "Dearest, what public disgrace to expose you to," he murmured, and through her confusion she did yet perceive that if in fact he loved her, if the long, strong ecstasy of that astonishing kiss were not, as seemed most probable, a dream, then it must be for this very reason—that she made him laugh.

"You are owing me a goot turn for that, you know, Toctor," continued Rory, very much at his ease.

"Any number of good turns, Rory Mor. Whatever you care to suggest."

"Ach, you can bekin by coming in to supper. I mate Annag wait half an hour. I said, we will give them plenty off time. It's a pit hart, at the ent of a day's ploughing, to be having to wait for your foot." And he slapped himself on the stomach and led the way to the kitchen. "They have it fixed up," he told Les and Annag with an air of showmanship.

Maggie found her hands taken, congratulations and smiles poured out on her, as though it were the most natural thing in the world; as though everyone had taken it for granted that she and Alexander would come in from the byre engaged. She remembered with an effort that Les had to be congratulated too, and saw his smile fade. He thanked her in his surly way, and that was all. No word of criticism of Joyce had ever passed Les's lips, but at the moment it was not possible that the new and almost unseen son should compensate him for Sunay lost.

The effort over, Maggie sank back into her dream. She ate without knowing it, she heard nothing anyone said. To her there was nothing likely or natural in what had happened.

Such passionately cherished longings never were fulfilled; that was the whole way of life; it was the first thing you were brought up to know. Reasonable expectation, yes—but there had been nothing reasonable in loving Alexander. He had always been immeasurably out of her reach—he was still. She stole a look at him, wondering what he was thinking, and found he was following some discourse of Rory's. Suddenly she knew that under his apparent attentiveness he, too, was completely bemused. He felt her eyes on him and gave her a comical, rueful grin. Come on, help me out, it besought her. I'm not taking in a word the dear fellow says.

Rory, it seemed, was talking about Sunay. Maggie tried to concentrate. This was important, it meant their future. And now, in some curious way, the initiative had passed from them. It was Rory Mor MacLeod, the pirate, the smuggler, the fey feckless Islesman, who was telling them what to do.

"But Rory," she said when at last the fact got through to her, "are ye really after meaning that you and Annag are staying on like we do, with no pay?"

"Issn't that what I've been saying for ten minutes?" said Rory, justifiably irritated.

"We've a wee bit safed," put in Annag gently. "And we'd have our own house."

"And not have to live with her olt man. That's what been putting me off," explained Rory ingenuously. "With me and her and Tonny, and this Choe frient of Les's and his young letty, we'll not want so many more."

"Donald? Is Donald coming in too?"

Rory sighed over the hopelessness of people in love who didn't listen. But Maggie now understood much that had been obscure. Old Mr. MacLeod's animosity—no wonder he hated Sunay, the place that had stolen both his sons. He and his croft represented the old way of life, Sunay the new, and family loyalty had not stood out against the pull of tractors and dams. Rory and Donald were giving Sunay a vote of confidence beside which her own little gesture hardly counted. Surely Alexander must feel it too? And certainly Rory had his full, bright-eyed attention now. He said, turning to Les:

"But will your pals still want to come, d'you think, now they won't find you?"

"Oh, sure," said Les. "They're coming for the chance, you know—and the house."

"It isn't—it wouldn't be mainly for the house, would it?" Alexander spoke awkwardly. The thought of Joyce was always there. And this time it was so vital to be sure.

Les understood perfectly. "You'll find they're okay," was all he said—a testimonial fully adequate.

"That's sefen of us," continued Rory. "We wass only elefen before. It will be easy enough to find the others. It iss a goot thing now, farm all ready made, not chust chumping in the dark like when we started this time last year. There's plenty now would be glat of the chance. I tell you what I wass thinking, Toctor. You write to wee Mr. Fraser of the Tepartment. He will know all them likely young crofters that have been doing well and perhaps got some nice stock, or even a bit of savings. He could fint us some sensible chaps. It issn't no goot at all going for the silly ones like Ronny, that don't know what they're in for."

"Poor old Ron," said Alexander. "He'll be the awful example to the end of our days. I agree that we don't want to repeat him, but likely young crofters mayn't want to throw up their crofts at a moment's notice. How are we to carry on meanwhile? I know Les has nobly agreed to stay till friend Joe and his young lady come. All the same, we're fantastically undermanned. Here we are at the start of the season, and not a spud yet in the ground. Can we ever do it?"

"We can have a tamn goot try."

"Last year, may I remind you, you confined yourself to

274

shepherding, smuggling and sitting on your behind on the tractor."

"You are treating me like a babby, Toctor!" cried Rory indignantly. "If I am a partner, of course I work like the rest. Anyway, last year we didn't have the electricity in them frames."

"All right, all right," said Alexander, grinning. "I only wanted to make it clear to all that it's going to mean incredibly hard work—harder even than last year, and we felt we were going all out then. And there's another thing. We'll no longer be comfortably cushioned in capital. The Rossiters must be paid back what they put in. My money bought and mainly equipped the place. Mary's about paid our living last year, and the dam. Kurt tells me she's leaving it in, but we'll have to pay her some sort of interest, and keep ourselves, entirely out of earnings. I don't suppose we'll actually go hungry, because we produce most of what we eat, but there'll be nothing over for fun."

"Annag and me issn't used to being millionaires."

"Well, I suppose no one could exactly call me luxury-loving. What about you, Magsy? Come on, pay attention; you're the one that wears the trousers now in our combine. Shall you mind not having a penny to spend?"

"I'll not notice," replied Maggie, pink under his teasing.

"Bless you, I don't believe you will. The most irritating part will be pinching on the farm. We shan't be able to increase the stock as fast as we'd planned, or do any more mechanizing for another year, or get the full advantage from our famous electricity. Of course, we could go further into debt—but I detest having to pay tribute overseas."

"*A dhuine*, we'll have lots of time to do it all," said Rory confidently. "We're all young yet. Now don't you be after worrying, Toctor. We'll start to-morrow on them potatoes. Ant when this Choe comes, and the sowing and the lambing's done, we'll have the minister give us a touble wetting at the

Kyle. Till then it's hart work, hart work, you and me in one croft, Maki and Annag in another. *A dhuine*, what a waste! There now, Maki iss shocked." But poor Maggie was not shocked this time; she had merely choked at the notion of a double wetting, which the climate of the Kyle made only too probable.

"Which croft shall ye choose, Maki?" Annag shyly asked.

Maggie started. "Och, I couldna say. I only got engaged an hour syne, and ye canna expect me to have it all worked out."

"We'll have the Fletchers'," said Alexander instantly. "It's got an extra room." And he gave her an unashamed grin. As ever, his thoughts dwelt longingly on babies, undeterred by the calamity of Joyce.

A child of their own—a Gavin—it would be unbelievable happiness. But we can't afford to have me laid up for at least another year, thought Maggie with a mixture of longing and impatience. Wasn't that just like a laddie, now, all fine ideas and no hard sense?

A silence fell, grave and confident, in which each one saw, like runners looking over a long course, the fields and the labours that lay ahead. And to Alexander it seemed that although they were now but a pitiful four, as against the eleven who had come to Sunay, still they were starting out again with a new factor on their side. For they were four lovers and friends, as against the eleven suspicious strangers who had tried, and failed, to shake down into a population. They would be a core on Sunay; and without short cuts to leadership, they would yet create a sense of security from which the newcomers would draw strength. There I go again, he thought, pulling himself up. An hour ago I was licked, finished; now I'm all set for the earthly paradise. Yes, but now I have Maggie for a talisman. Anything she believes in will turn out right. And he felt for her hand, not coyly, but as a climber feeling the strong pull of the rope.

There was a fifth at the table, who had no part in their silent rejoicing. And in the silence Les's bitter frustration, which had never expressed itself in words, could suddenly be felt.

"Les, man," said Rory, "how about you chanching your mint? You can see now how thinks will work out. Wee Joycie will be liking it all right when she gets back with the bairn."

"No, I couldn't do that," answered Les sullenly. "Her uncle's getting me a job in his garage. It's all fixed up."

"Ach, well, if that iss what you want———"

"It damn well isn't what I want!" Les burst out. "You know that as well as I do. I want to be on my own."

"You will yet, Les," cut in Alexander, "if you're all that keen on it."

"Pardon me, but that's bloody rot. The days are gone by when a working chap could save up enough to start his own show—leastways, not when he's got a wife and a kid. Oh, I'll do all right, but I'll never have the say again."

He stared slowly round the table, his anger subsiding, only the heartache and the longing left. "I bet you don't realize", he said at length, "just how damned lucky you are. You four have got it all in front of you. Nobody and nothing can't get you down."

Chapter Twelve

The idea of a reunion occurred to Mrs. Rossiter because she was the sort of woman who liked reunions. Here she and Ronny were, established in a little flat in Earl's Court, and as she said, sooner or later everyone passed through London. Not through Earl's Court, though, said Ronny gloomily. But if he showed no enthusiasm, his fiancée, one Brenda, showed a compensatory amount. She was the typical English girl, fair and ingenuous and for ever young. Quite the dearest girl in the world, wrote Mrs. Rossiter to Hermia when proffering the invitation. Good old Mrs. R., thought Hermia, her geese were always swans. But as a matter of fact it was true; and in the continuous pleasantness shown to Mrs. Rossiter herself, in the teeth of the example set by Ronny, Brenda might also be said to display definite originality of mind.

She was fascinated by Sunay. Everything Mrs. Rossiter could tell her she had heard ten times over. But it was the one subject, she early discovered, on which Ronny would not talk. More, he turned surly when she pressed him, and treated her to a sample of the rudeness he usually saved for his mother. Because she loved him, she felt as though he had given her a black eye and flinched into silence. But she still burned to know about Sunay those things that only her own generation could tell.

So Mrs. Rossiter wrote to Mary, as the most distant of the erstwhile islanders, requesting to be told when she and Kurt were next in town. Mary named a week-end in September, and Mrs. Rossiter looked up in her admirably kept address book the Turners' address in Lewisham, and the Fletchers' in Bletchley—or perhaps it was Luton, curious that one could never remember—and found them, as she had given six-weeks' notice, all disengaged.

Les and Joyce, with the baby, were on the doorstep at half-past three. That was the worst of entertaining that class; they arrived early and never knew how to leave. Joyce looked stylish and self-satisfied, and immensely proud of her child. Mrs. Rossiter said what a bonny little chap he was, wonderful how he had caught up, but you needed to be very careful with these premature babies, and the winter coming on too; and she recommended a different sort of dried milk. Brenda, who adored babies, took him on her knee. The inevitable question arose; had they found a house?

"Well, no, not exactly," admitted Joyce. "We're at my auntie's for the present. Les has a job in my uncle's garage, you know. He's doing ever so well. My auntie lets us have two rooms to ourselves. But it's a bit awkward sharing the kitchen."

"I'm sure it must be," smiled Mrs. Rossiter. "But I expect your aunt is an experienced housekeeper, so there must be a lot of tips you can pick up from her ready for when you have a kitchen all to yourself."

Lor, thought Joyce, doesn't she say the wrong thing! I'd almost forgotten how she treads on your toes. And the joy of being no longer on that dreadful island almost overcame her, as it had done, off and on, ever since she escaped. They returned to admiration of the baby.

The gentlemen were less well placed for conversation. Ronny had asked Les if he liked his new job, and Les had replied that it was okay, and after that there was a blank. The ring which, accompanied by Mary's well-remembered laugh in the street below, announced the arrival of the Schneiders was a welcome relief.

The Fletchers were there too; they had all met on the

doorstep. One glance showed Hermia that Kurt was no longer the willowy Oberon of Sunay. Already the muscle of the island life had turned to fat; already he had begun to look like a prosperous business man and a Jew. She was consoled for the fact that Simon had likewise tended to put on weight. And suddenly she had a vision of Alexander, eternally lean and brown and boyish, and knew then that her feeling towards him was one of purest hate.

"Well met by moonlight," she said to Kurt, the Oberon theme running in her head; and Kurt, always quick after a literary illusion, replied: "No scratching like your namesake, darling, I trust?"

"Indeed no. All hatchets buried and claws furred. I'm terribly glad to see you both. Doesn't Mary look superb? But then, she always did." Mary was pregnant, and Kurt's eye travelled over her with a glow of fondest pride. In return she flung her arm round his neck, and thus they marched up to Mrs. Rossiter's flat. Hermia put them down as the smuggest couple she had ever known.

Under cover of the greetings, and congratulations to Ronny on his fiancée and to Joyce on her son, there were swift appraisals. "Isn't he a lamb?" smiled Hermia, and thought: astonishing how breeding tells. Even at six months my children never looked like fat white guinea-pigs. But to Mary, self-absorbed as ever, the baby only suggested her own expectations.

"I don't know the first thing about babies," she declared. "I can't think how on earth I'll manage. Kurt says it's rather like rearing calves, but I daresay he's just talking through his hat."

Joyce shrank back, affronted by this talk of calves and the way Mary looked at her precious as though he were one. And fancy shouting out her condition like that—she really was an awful girl. And Brenda, who had heard from Mrs. Rossiter much about her beauty, was disappointed, not having reached that stage of sophistication which sees pregnancy as an enhancement of the female charms.

"So you're chained to the office desk after all, Ron?" said Kurt.

"There's a lot of rot talked about slaving in offices," answered Ronny earnestly. "No wonder it puts a fellow off. Actually, there's a lot to be said for it. We've several decent chaps about my age, and there's a Rugger team, and the great point is, when your work's done, it's done. There's none of that bloody awful feeling that you ought to be always at it or you're letting the party down. It's the freedom I like."

"You know, I'd a notion, after the dam, that you had it in you to become an engineer."

"I don't say I haven't. But I couldn't face years of swot and exams, not at my age. This is my uncle's firm—a lot to be said for uncles, isn't there, Les? I've the chance of a decent screw at the end of the first year. Besides, I've landed myself with this incubus," and he rubbed a lover-like hand through Brenda's curls.

"Kurt's doing marvels," announced Mary without waiting to be asked. "He's really running the show for Pop—not bad after six months, is it? He isn't called manager yet, but Pop loads more and more on to him. You should see the difference he's made to our stuff. We've got three new designers."

"Beginnings of a new Golders Green in the north?" asked Hermia slyly.

"Exactly so," agreed Kurt, impenitently. "The north needs new blood and the Golders Green overflow needs new *lebensraum*. Benefits all round. But I can't agree with Ron that office life is easier. I often think of Sunay, where I had time to breathe." The little fiancée stole him a shyly speculative look.

This conversation came hard on Hermia, who had been

forced to promise her husband that she would say nothing of his present career. "They won't be interested," so he defended his stand. Coming at all had been for him an appalling effort, and she divined why he had made it, and felt her irritation mount.

"How are my old friends Gavin and Jamie?" Mrs. Rossiter was asking. "I do wish you could have brought them too."

"Oh, flourishing—but they make nuisances of themselves at tea-parties, that's why I wouldn't. They've reached the rowdy stage, I'm afraid. It's the influence of school, of course. Not but what it's done them a world of good mixing with other kids," she added quickly. "Gavin learned to read at the end of the first three weeks."

"He could all along, actually," interposed Simon. "It was just that on Sunay he had better things to do."

"H'm, well, that was your version. Maggie has asked them both up there next summer. But I really don't know that we're justified in paying that fantastic fare. Some nice little place like Abergele would probably give them just as much fun."

"I'd like them to go," said Simon softly.

"Ah, Maggie." Kurt introduced the matter which, as he knew, was of the closest interest to Mary, and, as he guessed, to everyone else. "Dear Maggie. So she got him in the end."

"Oh, well," smiled Hermia, "whence all but she had fled——"

Mary sat up suddenly. "I don't believe it was that way at all. You can jolly well take that back." Under Hermia's quizzical look she coloured, but battled her way on. "I believe he'd been wanting her for ages. Anyway, I was a lot closer to both of them than you, so I ought to know."

She stopped, astonished at herself. For indeed, her first reaction to the news, which Kurt had in a letter from Alexander, had been precisely Hermia's. "Does it still hurt, darling?" Kurt had asked, and she had shouted: "No!" with wifely loyalty. But in fact, for a moment, it had hurt like hell. She saw again the dusky-fair face, the penetrating eyes, the crooked smile that had enchanted her. She thought: he was to be had after all, and Maggie was deceiving me, all those months she lived a lie, how could she? I'll never trust another woman again.

Then she saw Kurt's face, so full of wry understanding, and love for him rushed in on her, blotting Alexander out. She put her head on his shoulder and for a moment cried.

"Even if you hadn't been so marvellous to me," she told him presently, "I'd have no regrets. He wasn't a bit my kind when you got down to it. All those noble ideals, and disapproving of deer-stalking—really, he was a bit wet. And d'you know, he and Maggie are rather alike underneath." This discovery amazed her, but the more she considered it the truer it was. "Both fearfully worthy. They'll hit it off like anything."

And when Maggie's own letter came, breathing in every line such humble, astonished thankfulness, the last traces of resentment were banished by generous rejoicing for her friend. "Don't think hardly of me," Maggie wrote. "I couldn't have told you. It would never have done, with us living side by side like that. And yet I would have told you everything, if I'd even suspected I had the ghost of a chance." It was that letter, still in her handbag, which made her now defy Hermia's cynical insinuation that he had only married Maggie because nobody else was left.

"Have it your own way," said Hermia amiably. "But I think I can claim to have known Alexander a goodish while before you came on the scene, and I must say I never pictured him settling down with a stocky little Scots gardener. He was so sensitive to beauty of every kind. Of course, I've nothing against Maggie. In fact, I liked her; one couldn't help it. But she's so fearfully genteel and middle class."

"We were hoping to hear a bit more about the wedding, Les," Simon put in.

"I wonder Alexander didn't insist on being married in that ruin he was so dotty about," said Ronny. "But I suppose the MacLeods wouldn't have thought it suitable. Double event, wasn't it? Did old MacLeod have a bride on each arm?"

"Well, I wasn't actually there," answered Les seriously. "We couldn't all leave Sunay for the day, and naturally Donny wanted to be at his brother's wedding, so I stayed behind and saw to things till they came back."

"Wasn't there any honeymoon, then?"

"Oh yes—Rory and Annag went off to Glasgow for a week. He and Maggie could have gone too—I was willing to stay a bit longer—or they could have put off getting married till my friend Joe and his girl arrived. But they wouldn't. They'd got this idea they'd like to be alone on Sunay. I reckon folks must please themselves. So Donny brought them back in the *Annabella*, and took me off, and they were a week on their own. You can call it a honeymoon if you like."

"Not my idea," said Joyce, giggling, and thinking of her own at Southend.

"And did he—did they—seem happy?" Painfully Simon tried to convey to Les the intensity of his desire to picture Alexander at that moment. And it was as though a part of his longing did get through to Les, who made a further, heroic effort to break down the obstacle words always were to him, and describe something of that return, in the golden light of a July evening, from the Kyle.

"I reckon they were no end happy," he said at last. "They were—well—like a couple of kids. You know how he was always saying Sunay didn't belong to him any more than to any of us—well, he suddenly looked as though he owned the place. Not cocky, you know, but sort of safe. He yelled out to me from the boat: 'It's good to be home,' and then he started chaffing her. 'Mistress Sarratt,' he said—you know how he makes fun of the way she talks—'let that be an end of your gadding to the Kyle. From now on ye'll kindly bide.' "

"Poor Maggie," said Hermia, "that'll just suit her. Her average of trips was two a year."

"I'd got a sort of high tea ready for them, and we had that, and they were making plans for the week—d'you know, she'd never been up Torval, or on Latay? She'd always kept her nose too close to the vegs. Anyway, July, as you know, is the nearest we ever came to a slack time, and we'd all worked like blacks to get as clear as possible beforehand, so after they'd got the stock fed and done the milking they'd have quite a bit of time to themselves. Donny and I saw no point in hanging about, so after we'd finished tea we pushed off. The last we saw of them, they were leaning over the jetty wall, watching us go. It gave me a feeling, I can tell you, them watching us go, when I'd stood there so many times meself and watched other boats, and never somehow thought, you know, that it'd be my turn in the end."

Les had done. There were ecstasies about that day, and agonies, which he could never put into words, but which some might guess at for themselves. It was the little fiancée who broke the silence by commenting in her shy, eager way:

"Gosh, it must be a marvellous place. I wonder, I do really wonder, how any of you could bear to leave."

"Ah well, my child," said Hermia, seeming to give herself a mental shake, "islands are very romantic in theory, but there's another side to it. All you've heard about is the fun."

"I suppose the winter must have been grim."

"It was—but I don't mean that exactly. I think we stood up to the work and the climate pretty creditably. It was the narrowness of the life, all cooped up together—well, that's my impression, anyway. Simon and I, for instance, had a feeling we had rather more to give than Sunay could take,

285

certain—well—abilities, if you like, that were just running to waste."

"I don't remember feeling it," muttered Simon, but she seemed not to hear.

"Oh, I see," said Brenda, not in the least satisfied with this explanation. She tried getting at it another way. "This chap Alexander——" she saw Ronny wince, and knew that the inquiry was as much as her place was worth, but she had to know—"what was he like?"

Neither Mary nor Hermia were prepared to give her a character sketch, though to both of them he seemed so vividly present at that moment that they felt almost haunted. It was Mrs. Rossiter who said, as she had said a dozen times already:

"Alexander is the dearest boy. So gifted and sensitive, and so truly modest. I think he is the most outstanding person I've ever known."

"Oh, God, Ma, you make me sick," burst out Ronny. "We all know you were nuts on him, but how you can still be, after the vile things he said to you that evening, has me beat."

"No, really, Mrs. R.?" exclaimed Hermia in shocked anticipation. Now they were getting somewhere at last. "To such a staunch supporter as you? I can hardly credit it."

"I assure you, Hermia, it was nothing like that," cried Mrs. Rossiter in great distress. "Ronny exaggerates—he was very strung up that evening—so we all were, and Alexander most of all. No one can imagine what we went through. Naturally, things were said that perhaps oughtn't to have been, but in the state of anxiety he was in over Joyce, one couldn't blame him. That is what I could have made you see, Ronny, if you'd only waited another day. Alexander was just his old self to me in the morning."

"Of course, Joyce—you had a bad time, didn't you?" Kurt remembered. He meant it kindly, but to Joyce the very mention of that ghastly night was as talk of torture to the victim of the concentration camp. They had explained it all to her at the hospital; after the doctor's examination, the baby had turned itself wrong way up; such a thing didn't happen once in a hundred times and there was no reason why she should suffer like that with her next. But Joyce, quite simply, didn't believe them. She had been handed enough lines of talk before, and she was taking precautions now to ensure that there should never be a next. Still, she might forget, or something slip, and the ghost of that agony lay over her for ever. She would never be completely free of Sunay, as long as she lived.

"Alexander was grand that night, and so was Rory," said Les almost sternly, making for her the acknowledgement she would never make for herself.

"So that was it," commented Kurt. "Poor old Ron. He took it out on you."

"I'm not discussing it," cried Ronny angrily, and added in the same breath: "as a matter of fact I don't deny that there's a lot of good in old Alexander. In many ways he's quite a decent chap. If he went off his head at the end, he'd got you all to thank for it, and particularly you, Ma. You'd buttered him, and sucked up to him, and made a little tin god of him, till eventually he got to believe it all himself. After that, of course, living with him was impossible. I realized the only thing to do was to clear out and so I did. I only hope he never lets fly like that at Maggie. She's a damn sight too good for him, if you ask me."

"I opine that Maggie will be perfectly safe," said Kurt, smiling, before Mrs. Rossiter could rush in with any more disastrous defences.

"I should think she'd have a marvellous time," said the little fiancée wistfully. "I mean, the two of them like that, on the island—it's all very well for you to say islands aren't romantic, but they *are*—I know I'd give anything——" She faltered under Ronny's glare. "Well, but Ron, aren't you sometimes sorry too?"

"If I am", answered Ronny, "I'll damn well keep the fact to myself."

"It's really taken your imagination, hasn't it?" observed Kurt, looking very kindly at this nice little bourgeois type whose affections Ronny had been lucky enough to engage. "You really can't understand why we failed?" And it struck him, not unpleasantly, that he was the only person present capable of giving her an objective estimate. "Myself, I see it like this. We were none of us quite sufficiently serious. I suppose hardly anybody is dead serious about their jobs, and in most jobs it doesn't matter—Ronald, if he won't mind my saying so, has just demonstrated that with his contentment in the City. But on Sunay it was necessary to be utterly serious, because there were no other outlets. None of us jibbed at the work, but we hadn't that devotion to it which could have kept us from getting on each other's nerves, or brooding over the waste of talents referred to by Hermia, and which I'm prepared to admit in Simon's rather specialized case——"

"No," said Simon.

"—but not in my own, for I could have been, and in fact was, just as talented on Sunay as in Preston."

"I concede", said Hermia, "that it was the human factor got us down."

"You mean, that with a nicer set of people you'd have stayed?"

"Now, Kurt, that's too unfair. I'm not criticizing anyone present. But I think we all see now that Alexander was the wrong type to lead such a group as ours."

"If we'd been as serious as he was himself, we should not have needed leading. And that is what has happened; those who could keep it up on Sunay under their own steam are still there. Of Maggie one could have predicted it; of Rory,

288

no; I admit Rory had me deceived. Yet considered dispassionately, what more natural? Rory's ancestors won against that climate, each generation growing, perhaps, a little wearier and less hopeful; but give him new tools, a tractor and a dam, and he responds instinctively to the old challenge. To Rory, Sunay means a whole way of life. To us it meant an adventure, an escape from whatever we were doing before. There were degrees of seriousness among us, of course. At one end of the scale you had Mary and Hermia, who never intended to stay there at all."

"Hi!" shouted Mary, but Hermia laughed; if she were classed with his own woman she was prepared to let it go.

"And at the other, Les and me. I'd have said I was wedded to the plan, yet when it came to the point I couldn't throw away the chance of poking my fingers into pa-in-law's pie. And Les couldn't bring himself to break poor Joyce's heart. With each of us there was something, you see, that came before the island. Sooner or later—and after all, we built a farm between us, so you can call it later—that something found us out."

Mrs. Rossiter, who had been emotionally troubled ever since Les's description of the wedding, broke the silence with a heavy sigh. "I daresay you're right, Kurt, dear," she said. "But I find myself thinking of Sunay very often, and I don't mind owning that I have many regrets."

"You were told to please yourself, Ma——" Ronny began.

"Yes, Ronny, and so I did. I'm not complaining. I realized it couldn't last. But it was a beautiful place, the most beautiful, I think, that I've ever been in, and it always seemed to me that our life there was a happy one, at any rate till the luck turned against us. Perhaps——" Her voice for a moment trembled—"people of my age don't always notice what's going on. But that is how it seemed to me. And Alexander's continual kindness is something I can never forget."

"Then couldn't we go and visit there?" cried Brenda eagerly. "I mean you and me, Mrs. R., if Ronny really won't?"

Mrs. Rossiter considered it, and for a moment seemed to be tempted; then she shook her head.

"No, dear, I don't think I could. I should love to see Sunay again, and yet I doubt if I could stand it when it came to the point. It's my misfortune to be so sensitive to atmosphere. I am always affected by any place where people have been through tremendous emotions, and Sunay would be the worst of all. I know, of course, that none of us actually died there. But we felt and suffered terribly, and for me it would always be haunted by ghosts."